NEMESIS RISING

By Karen C.P. McDermott

ISBN (paperback): 979-8-9898117-6-2
ISBN (eBook): 979-8-9898117-7-9

Book Cover by Mick Estabrook

1st edition 2025
10 9 8 7 6 5 4 3 2 1

For Karen Pasquale (aka KP1), a great friend and the best alpha reader an author could ask for. I made you work for this one.

Pronunciation Guide

People

Cyra = SEE-ruh
Bressen = BREH-sen
Samhail = SAM-heyl
Talyn = TA-luhn
Surgeon = SUR-jun
Serise = SUR-ees
Aidan = ĀY-den
Jasper = JAS-per
Maziren = MAZ-ur-in
Axenus = AX-en-uhs
Jaylan = JĀY-lin
Brix = BRIKS
Raina = RAY-nuh
Glenora = Gle-NOR-ah
Phaedrus = FAY-druhs
Aramis = AIR-ah-mis
Sandrian = SAN-dree-an
Morland = MOHR-land
Clarice = Cla-REES
Magdalene = MAG-dah-leen
Praya = PRAY-uh
Ariel = EHR-ee-ul

Places

Thasia = THAY-zhuh
Callanus = KAL-an-uhs
Polaris = Puh-LAH-rus
Gendris = JEN-dris
Fernweh = FURN-way
Hiraeth = HĬ-rayth
Solandis = Sō-LAN-dus
Derridan = DAIR-ĭ-den
Seatherny = SEE-thur-nee
Rowe = RŌ, Rown = RŌN
Kern = KURN

Other

Angelus = AN-jell-us
Perimortal = PEHR-ĭ-mohr-tl
Demoni =Deh-MAH-nee

Triumvirate (Trī-UM-ver-et): A group of three people who share power.

In the book, the country of Thasia is ruled by a group of three lords and/or ladies, each of whom also oversees one of the country's three territories. Callanus is the main capital. Bressen rules Hiraeth, whose capital is Solandis. Aidan rules Derridan, whose capital is Seatherny. And Polaris is currently overseen by the High Council in its capital city of Gendris. Cyra is from Fernweh, a small town in the south of Polaris.

Content Advisory

This book includes mature (18+) themes and potentially upsetting situations that include graphic violence; death; suicide, suicide ideation, and mention of assisted suicide; mentions, threats, and brief descriptions of past SA; and multiple explicit depictions of sex, including scenes of aggressive or violent primal play. For full details on trigger and tropes, see https://karencpmcdermott.com/clash-of-stone-and-steel.

Recap of Previous Books in the Series

If you need a reminder of what happened previously, please visit the links below for a brief summary of the major action and plot points.

Recap of *The Last Triumvirate* (Book 1)

https://karencpmcdermott.com/tlt1-summary

Recap of *Of Wrath and Storms* (Book 2)

https://karencpmcdermott.com/tlt2-owas-summary

Recap of *Clash of Stone and Steel* (Book 3)

https://karencpmcdermott.com/tlt3-cosas-summary

Map of Thasia and Surrounding Countries

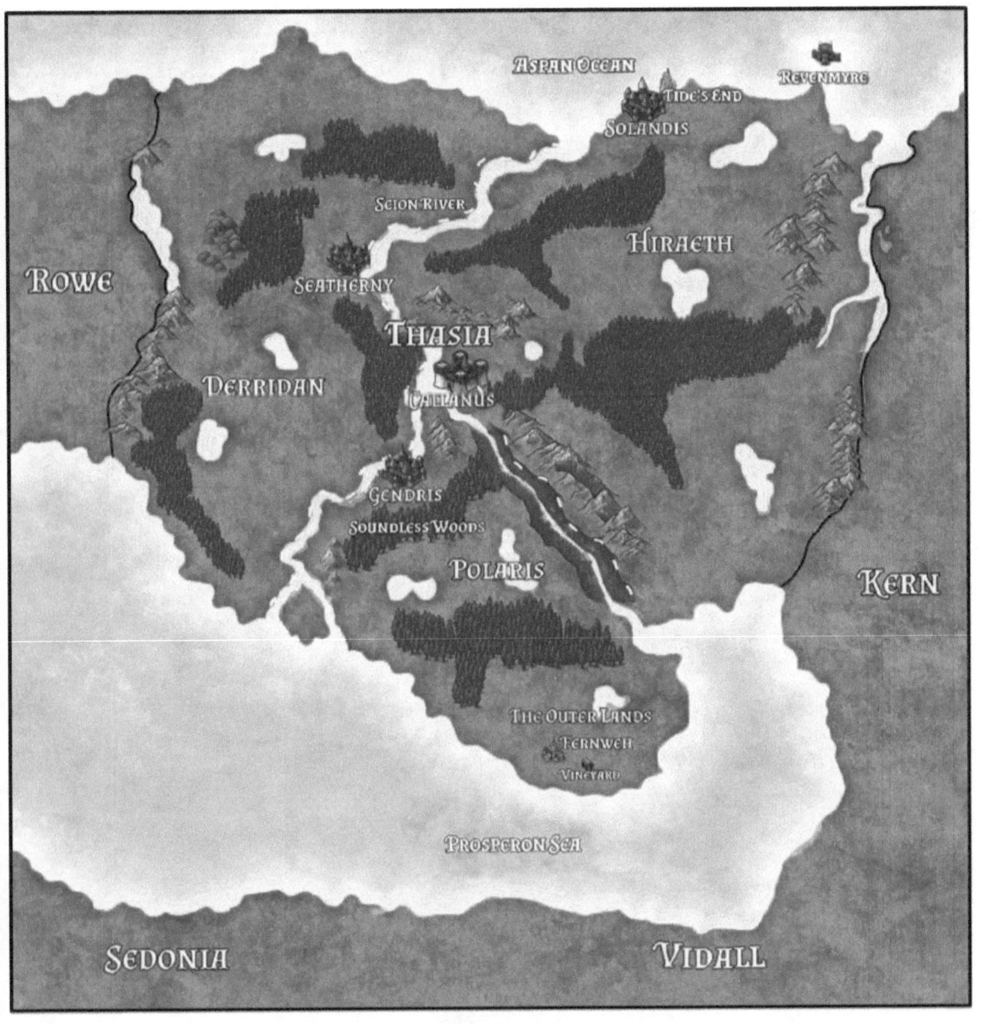

Tandem Reading Guide

The stories in this book (Book 4) and in *Clash of Stone and Steel* (Book 3) overlap, so the two books can be read in tandem. That is, readers can switch back and forth between the two books as the story progresses, depending on what experience the reader wants. Doing the tandem read will let you be a little more 'in the know' if you so desire, but the author does not recommend reading one way over the other. Notations are also included at the ends of chapters of both books to tell readers when to switch.

NOTE: If you choose the tandem read, you will begin with the Prologue of Book 4, *Nemesis Rising*.

Recommended Tandem Reading Order:
Nemesis Rising (Bk 4), Prologue
Clash of Stone and Steel (Bk 3), Prologue-Chapter 14
Nemesis Rising (Bk 4), Chapter 1
Clash of Stone and Steel (Bk 3), Chapter 15
Nemesis Rising (Bk 4), Chapters 2-3
Clash of Stone and Steel (Bk 3), Chapter 16
Nemesis Rising (Bk 4), Chapters 4-7
Clash of Stone and Steel (Bk 3), Chapter 17
Nemesis Rising (Bk 4), Chapters 8-10
Clash of Stone and Steel (Bk 3), Chapters 18-21
Nemesis Rising (Bk 4), Chapters 11-12
Clash of Stone and Steel (Bk 3), Chapters 22-26
Nemesis Rising (Bk 4), Chapters 13-16
Clash of Stone and Steel (Bk 3), Chapters 27-30
Nemesis Rising (Bk 4), Chapter 17
Clash of Stone and Steel (Bk 3), Chapter 31
Nemesis Rising (Bk 4), Chapter 18
Clash of Stone and Steel (Bk 3), Chapters 32-33
Nemesis Rising (Bk 4), Chapters 19-20
Clash of Stone and Steel (Bk 3), Chapters 34-35
Nemesis Rising (Bk 4), Chapters 21-23
Clash of Stone and Steel (Bk 3), Chapter 36

Prologue

Almost twenty-three years ago

Crissail

Crissail steadied the arrow she aimed at the rabbit where it hid – or thought it hid – twenty yards away in the underbrush. She could use any number of her powers to stun or kill the animal, but she liked the challenge of the bow and arrow. It kept her senses sharp, and she took pride that, even at close to eight hundred years old, she could still grip and aim the bow well enough to catch her dinner for the night.

The rabbit stood perfectly still, its nose barely twitching as Crissail prepared to take her shot. She blinked a couple times to sharpen her focus, but it didn't work. One thing that hadn't held up with time was her eyesight, and it took some practice to compensate for the fuzziness in her vision at this distance.

Crissail took note of the way the breeze blew the strands of hair that had come loose from the knot at the back of her head and adjusted her aim. She drew in a breath and held it. She was about to loose her arrow when she sensed a presence she hadn't felt in nearly four centuries.

A presence that made her go cold.

Crissail eased the tension on her bow, and the rabbit, sensing its opportunity, bolted from its hiding place further into the forest.

"How did you find me?" she asked as she lowered the bow and straightened. The weapon was useless against this threat.

"Process of elimination," a dainty female voice said. "You weren't anywhere else, so you could only be here."

Crissail smiled wryly. "You sensed the magic I used a few days ago," she said, finally turning to the blonde woman who stood several feet away.

1

She'd known it was stupid to use *that* magic, but she hadn't had a choice. At least, it hadn't been a choice for her. She'd hoped her use of the power had been minor enough not to draw Magdalene's attention, but no such luck.

The nearest town was half a day's ride from her cottage, and Crissail rarely visited, but when she did, she always stopped at the baker's shop. He was the only one who knew where she lived all the way out here, and she used to talk to him when no one was around. He'd been her only friend for decades now. He tried to gift her a loaf of bread to take home when she stopped by, but she always slipped money into his till for it when he wasn't looking.

The last time she'd seen him, though, she'd known immediately something was wrong.

It had been weeks since she'd visited, and the baker had grown sick while she was away. He'd been in great pain and already beyond her rudimentary healing powers, so she'd done the only thing she was capable of doing. She'd given him a merciful death.

Unfortunately, Magdalene had sensed it.

Crissail let out a deep breath. "What do you want?"

"You know what I want," the woman said. "I want a return to the world we deserve, a world where we rule rather than hide in the shadows." She gestured to the surrounding woods. "Or in tiny little cottages in the middle of nowhere."

"I told you before, I have no interest in ruling anything."

"So then let me do it," Magdalene said stepping forward. "Give me what I want so I can realize my vision, and you can go back to eating bugs and squatting in the bushes."

"And does that vision still involve destroying half of humanity?" Crissail asked.

"Half of mortals," Magdalene corrected. "But why worry about them? They multiply as fast as that rabbit you were about to kill. They'll repopulate in no time."

Crissail shook her head. How this woman had ever been chosen as the Hand of the Protector, she had no idea.

"My answer is the same as it was the last time you asked. No."

Crissail walked around Magdalene, giving her a wide berth, as she headed for her cottage.

"I'm afraid this time I'll have to insist," Magdalene said.

Crissail froze at the cold finality in the woman's voice. "You don't want to do this," she said quietly.

"Yes, I do."

Crissail spun around, but the icy grip of frost seized her chest before she could act. She clutched at her heart as Magdalene strode toward her. She knew the woman wouldn't kill her, not yet, but she couldn't let Magdalene near her either. She wasn't sure what Magdalene had done to acquire the power she now had, but it was moot at this point. She couldn't let Magdalene touch her.

Every move, every breath was painful, but Crissail managed to re-nock her arrow and fire it quicker than anyone might expect of her. Magdalene screamed as the arrow pierced her shoulder, and she stumbled backward as the frost seizing Crissail's heart dissolved.

Crissail pushed to her feet and sent a forcefield at the other syphon. Magdalene had yanked the arrow from her shoulder and was healing the wound, but she went flying backward to slide across the ground when the field hit her.

Crissail stepped toward Magdalene then hesitated. It was forbidden for the Hands of the Gods to kill each other, except under extreme circumstances, and she wondered if this counted. If it didn't, her own life would be forfeit. But what else could possibly count as extreme circumstances if not the extermination of half of all mortals?

Her hesitation was a moment too long. A glowing bubble appeared around Crissail just as she tried to release another forcefield, and the field hit the bubble to rebound back on her. She was thrown into the opposite side of it and fell to the ground.

"Where is Praya?" Magdalene asked as she stalked toward Crissail.

Crissail laughed as she picked herself up. "Dead. You heard the news as I did. Her ship went down in the ocean centuries ago. You can't still be looking for her, can you?"

"If she was dead, another syphon would've been born to replace her, and I would've sensed their power by now," Magdalene said.

That was true enough. If a new syphon had been born at Praya's death, the woman would be around four hundred now, and the chances she'd never used the powers imbued in her by the Creator were remote. The other option was that Praya was indeed still alive and either hadn't used her powers in four centuries, or she was too far away for Magdalene to sense them.

"If she is alive," Crissail said, "you'll never find her."

Magdalene stood next to the containment bubble. "No matter. At least you're not going anywhere. I'll just hold you until I find her."

Crissail gave the woman a wry smile and called on the one magic that could reach outside the bubble. She directed her power under the bubble into the ground, and the earth obeyed. Dirt and stone shot into the air all around the bubble, and Magdalene screamed again as she was tossed into the air before being piled under a mound of earth. The containment bubble fell away, and Crissail began to draw a portal. She had to get as far away from Magdalene as she could.

She'd only drawn half the portal when the earth exploded behind her, and she pitched forward to sprawl across the ground. She cried out as she landed. She had the body of an older woman now, and while she was still fit for her age, she wasn't used to being tossed around. She was slow to rise as she examined her hands and arms, which were scraped and cut.

As if voicing Crissail's own thoughts, Magdalene said, "You're getting old, Crissail. There's only so long you can fight me off. We both know you're coming with me today, so why not give in to the inevitable?"

Magdalene was right. Crissail's power had been fading for a while now as the wear of time and the loss of her mate had taken their toll. She didn't have the power she once had, and – if she was honest with herself – nor did she have much will to keep fighting. She was alone most of the time. Only one other person visited her, one other who knew, or cared, that she was alive. Outside these woods, the world pushed on without her.

Crissail straightened as Magdalene limped toward her. She couldn't fight anymore, and she was tired of running, tired of hiding.

"You won't take me today or any other day," Crissail said, her voice stronger under her resolve.

Magdalene stopped, and something shifted in her face as she took in Crissail's defiance. "What are you doing?" she asked warily.

Crissail smiled. "Going where you can't follow," she said. "Or where you *won't* follow."

She felt strangely light as she put a hand to the center of her chest and let the magic flow into her. *That* magic. She wasn't sure how much time it would buy the world, but she sent a prayer up to the Trinity, to the Nemesis, that what she was about to do wouldn't be in vain. Somehow, someway, she hoped her sacrifice might stop Magdalene.

"No!" Magdalene screamed as she lunged forward, but she yelled out in pain and leapt back again as Crissail's body flared into a ball of fire.

Crissail savored the feel of the flames on her skin. They were more for show than anything, but they sent a comforting warmth through her, an assurance she was doing the right thing.

She took one last moment to savor the look of horror and defeat on Magdalene's face before she called on her god-granted power to take her beyond Magdalene's reach.

Magdalene's scream was the last thing Crissail heard as her body turned to ash and crumbled to the earth, leaving only a lingering gray cloud in the air where she, the now-former Hand of the Nemesis, had once stood.

Tandem Read: Go to *Clash of Stone and Steel* (Bk 3), Prologue-Chapter 14

Chapter 1

Cyra

The face of the first man I'd ever killed floated through my half-waking mind as my eyes fluttered open. The face was long and thin with a slightly large nose and neatly trimmed beard. The man had been young, his eyes dark brown and rich like the soil of the vineyard where I'd grown up, but they'd already been glazed over with the soft sheen of death by the time the symbiont's shell had dripped away from them.

The man was the first of two I'd killed at the gambling den that night before my wedding. He'd appeared to be a monster, but under the symbiont skin, he was so very human.

I blinked away both the dream and the morning sunshine as the face dissolved and I turned over in bed, wanting to wrap myself around Bressen, but his side was empty. Panic rose as I remembered the assassin we'd learned yesterday had been living among us for weeks.

My heart still twinged with betrayal and horror at the thought. The woman had posed as my lady's maid and attended me here in my room, bathing me, dressing me, and listening to me jabber on as I tried to befriend her. Gods above. She'd even walked in on me and Bressen when he'd had his head between my legs. I recalled her reaching toward the daggers I now knew were hidden under her skirt, and I wondered what had stopped her from killing us that day when she'd found us in such a vulnerable position.

I opened my mind to search for Bressen, then relaxed when I sensed him nearby.

Bressen? Are you in your study? I asked into his mind.

Good morning, my love, he answered back immediately. *Yes. Get dressed and come meet us. We have a problem.*

I threw off the covers and rushed toward the closet, tamping down the automatic urge to send for Leeda, my lady's maid. She – or Talyn, as she was actually known – was currently in a holding cell in the basement of the house.

I dressed quickly and hurried out of our bedchamber, through the sitting room next door, and into Bressen's study. He was there with Axenus, but Samhail was absent.

"There's breakfast on the table," Bressen said as I entered, but I walked past it to his desk where he was sitting.

"What's happened?" I asked.

He rose to meet me and pulled me in close for a good morning kiss. His strong arms drew me against his body, and I closed my eyes when his lips met mine, neither of us caring that Axenus was there to witness the way he touched me so tenderly. I opened my eyes again as I sensed something different in his kiss this time. An urgency…a fear.

"Bressen? What's wrong?" I asked as I searched his beautiful turquoise eyes for answers.

"The assassin is gone," Bressen said as he released me.

I stepped back from him. "Gone?"

"Escaped last night. Samhail and the twins are out looking for her."

The twins, Samhail's brother and sister, were gargoyles like him and could manifest giant black leathery wings.

"Escaped?" I said, unable to do more than parrot back Bressen's words. "How?"

A muscle ticked in Bressen's jaw before he answered.

"Apparently she managed to get the key to her cell and let herself out after everyone went to sleep."

I waited for an explanation, and he obliged after a deep sigh.

"When Samhail went down to give her the clothes you found for her, he let her goad him into getting in the cell, and he challenged her to take the keys from him."

I blinked again before my eyes went wide with fear. "And she overpowered him, even without her magic? How? Is he alright?"

"She did take the keys from him, but he stopped her before she could escape," Bressen explained. "However, he didn't realize she'd pulled the key for her cell off the ring before he wrestled it back from her."

I just stared at him, unable to comprehend how the assassin, a woman only a few inches taller than me, had managed to get the keyring away from Samhail, an elite warrior who was nearly seven feet tall and packed with muscle.

"She injured his foot and his nose," Axenus chimed in.

I looked at the merman. Although his expression was grim, there was a hint of unrestrained amusement in his voice.

Samhail and Axenus were friends and allies, but they had a strange, often antagonistic relationship, and I had a feeling this was something Axenus didn't plan to let Samhail live down anytime soon.

"Did she hurt anyone else?" I asked as dread churned in my gut.

"Not egregiously," Bressen said. "She snuck into the stables and stole a horse. One of the stable hands interrupted her, and she knocked him out and tied him up, but he's alive."

I pushed out a deep breath of relief.

"One of the other hands found the young man tied up this morning," Bressen went on, "and we immediately checked the holding cell and found her missing. After we noticed the key to the cell was gone, that's when Samhail admitted what he'd done. I'd have locked him in the cell himself if we didn't need him to help look for her."

His voice was angry, and crimson light flickered in his eyes as he slammed a hand down onto his desk.

"I don't understand why Samhail went into the cell in the first place," Axenus said, shaking his head. "He's not usually that reckless. What was he trying to prove?"

Bressen and I looked at each other.

"Possibly the divine imperative?" Bressen suggested. "He's bound by the Trinity to protect Cyra, so perhaps having an assassin get that close to her stirred something in him."

It wasn't an outright lie, since I didn't see Bressen's skin glow red, but it wasn't the full truth either.

Only Bressen, Samhail, and I knew the assassin had come to Samhail a few days ago looking like me and tried to seduce him. He'd stopped her before anything went too far, but he'd avoided both me and Bressen for days afterwards, and I'd seen the shame in his eyes when he finally sought me out to confront me about what he thought had happened.

Axenus was right. Samhail wasn't usually so reckless as to step into a caronium-lined cell with a trained killer just to prove himself, but what the assassin had done to him was personal, and I wasn't surprised he'd felt the need to confront her.

I'd wanted to confront Talyn myself, but Bressen had pointedly forbidden it. There was nothing he could've done to stop me if I'd insisted, but I'd seen the wild panic in his eyes when I'd told him yesterday I was bringing her down a change of clothes. He'd refused to let me go, and I eventually let Samhail take them down to her instead.

I should've anticipated letting Samhail see her wouldn't have ended well. Bressen had wanted to destroy Talyn after he learned she was here to kill us, so he couldn't have gone either. Axenus probably would've been the best choice, but it hadn't occurred to me at the time to ask him.

"What do we do now?" I asked.

"There's not much we can do," Bressen said. "The gargoyles are out hunting her down, and we just have to hope one of them finds her."

I flinched at his phrasing. *Hunting her down...*

"Did...did you...Are they supposed to bring her back alive?" I asked, half afraid to know the answer.

Despite everything Talyn had done, I couldn't bring myself to wish her dead. She hadn't been a friend to me like Raina, but she'd started to open up to me over the last couple weeks, and I couldn't help feeling we'd made a small connection.

Yes, she'd been sent to kill us, but she ultimately hadn't done it. At least not yet. The wards I'd set up around our bedroom had gone off a few nights ago, the first night I'd put them up, and I was almost certain Talyn had set them off trying to get in, but the fact remained she hadn't tried to kill us again since.

A shiver went up my spine at how close Bressen and I had come to death. The concern I had for Talyn didn't make sense.

If one of the gargoyles did bring her back, Bressen would try to keep me away from her, but I had to talk to her. I had to know what she'd been thinking. I had to know if, maybe, we really had started to become friends.

"I left either option open," Bressen admitted. "Ideally I'd like her alive, only because there's more we can get out of her about Sandrian and Magdalene's plans, but I told Samhail and the twins that if killing her was their only option to keep her from escaping, they should take it."

I inhaled deeply and nodded.

Bressen looked at me in surprise. "You're not going to fight me on that?" he asked.

"I'd prefer to have them bring Lee-…Talyn in alive, but I also don't want Samhail or the twins getting hurt. The assassin's proven to be incredibly dangerous, and if killing her is their only option, I won't take that away from them for their own sakes."

Bressen nodded.

"So we just wait?" Axenus asked.

"She's most likely heading for Rowe," Bressen said, "so, despite my better judgement, I sent Samhail southwest on the most direct route there. I'm hoping his desire to make up for his mistakes gives him some incentive to find her. Surgeon went west along the coast to check the ports, and Serise is trying to cover as much ground to the southeast as she can. We'll just have to wait to see what they turn up."

"There's something we can do in the meantime," I said as an idea occurred to me. "Talyn isn't the only one who's been working with Sandrian. Didn't you say Glenora might have been helping him?"

Bressen's face darkened. "You think I should visit Glenora in

Revenmyer?" he asked.

"I think *we* should visit her," I said, emphasizing the 'we.'

His face darkened even more.

"And if I tell you it's out of the question for you to go-"

"I'll remind you that I'm your wife, not your prisoner, and I'm free to go wherever I want."

Bressen crossed his arms as his chin went up a notch, and I prepared for an argument.

"It's true enough that as your husband I have no right to dictate where you can and can't go," he said, "but as the warden of Revenmyer, I do have authority to regulate who goes in and out of the prison."

I narrowed my eyes. "True, but you might want to think carefully about when you exercise that authority and over whom. I have a bit of authority to regulate who goes in and out of certain places as well."

Our eyes locked, but although I'd intended that last part as a warning, Bressen only smirked at me from under heavy-lidded eyes, and I swore inwardly. He and I both knew trying to deny him sex was an empty threat. Bressen knew my own body better than I did, and he'd have me begging him to take me by evening with nothing more than a few seemingly innocuous touches and caresses throughout the day.

"I'll keep that in mind," he said huskily, and I swallowed, already thinking of abandoning my threat and dragging him to the bedroom.

Axenus cleared his throat, and we broke our stare to look at him.

"Far be it for me to question how you run Revenmyer," Axenus said carefully to Bressen, "but it might be good to bring Cyra with you if you see Glenora. You'll want someone with truth seeing abilities."

Bressen glared at him, but Axenus gave him a 'glare all you want, but you know I'm right' look, and Bressen sighed before running a hand through his night-black hair.

"I really wish you'd reconsider," Bressen said to me. "Revenmyer is a disturbing place, and the idea of subjecting you to it..." He trailed off.

"I can handle it," I said. "I'm a Hand of the Gods, remember?"

Bressen rolled his eyes.

Others might be impressed that I was a powerful perimortal with the ability to syphon different kinds of magic from anyone around me, but none of that phased a man who'd been known as the Nemesis Incarnate most of his life. Granted he'd recently had to cede that title to me when we discovered that, of the three gods in the Trinity, I was bonded to and served the Nemesis.

"Fine," Bressen said, uncrossing his arms. "I'll make arrangements, and we'll go tomorrow, but the deal is that while we're there, you do exactly what I say, when I say it. Revenmyer can be almost as dangerous to visitors as it is to the inmates."

"I promise," I said.

I'd seen only a glimpse of the prison once in a vision I stole from Magdalene, but it was enough that I didn't doubt the truth of Bressen's words. The lack of a red glow on his skin confirmed it as well.

A message leaf suddenly popped into existence in front of Bressen's face, and he snatched it out of the air to read it. His brows pinched together, and I saw the flash of red in his eyes again. He closed them for a moment, and it looked as though he was doing his best to maintain his composure.

"Bad news?" Axenus asked.

Bressen opened his eyes and passed the message leaf to Axenus. The merman read it, and his brows shot up.

"For the gods' sakes, what does it say?" I asked, pulling the leaf out of Axenus's hand.

The message was short and vague, and Bressen took another leaf from his desk to scrawl a longer message on it this time. His handwriting was messier than normal from the anger I felt wafting off him. He held up the leaf when he was done, and it disappeared.

"What does the message mean?" I asked Bressen and Axenus.

"It doesn't matter what it means," Bressen said. "It's unacceptable."

"You don't trust Samhail?" Axenus asked, surprised.

"Normally I do," Bressen said, "but his judgement seems to be compromised where this woman is concerned, and I'll be damned if he's going to keep me in the dark about what he plans to do with her."

We waited in tense silence for about thirty seconds before the message leaf reappeared. Bressen grabbed it and growled angrily as he read it. He slammed it down on the desk where I saw Samhail's two-word answer in all capitals: *TRUST ME*.

I felt Bressen's anger grow hotter as he took two fresh leaves out of his desk and wrote on them. Normally Bressen trusted Samhail implicitly, but this assassin had threatened my life, and Bressen wanted her back here to face his judgement and his wrath. Whatever Samhail was planning, Bressen wasn't willing to entertain it.

Bressen finished writing and held up the two leaves between his fingers to again let them vanish in puffs of smoke.

"What are you doing?" Axenus asked him.

"I'm calling Surgeon and Serise back," Bressen said. "In addition to hunting down the assassin, apparently I need to have them hunt down Samhail now as well."

Tandem Read: Go to *Clash of Stone and Steel* (Bk 3), Chapter 15

Chapter 2

Bressen

I drummed my fingers on the table in the meeting room across the hall from the Great Chamber. A glance at the clock on the wall told me Aidan was almost twenty minutes late for our afternoon meeting here at the Citadel.

The new lord of Derridan and I had enjoyed playing a few power games with each other when we'd first met, but I thought we'd gotten past that when Cyra and I helped him save his husband's life not too long ago. Apparently not.

Under other circumstances I might've given Aidan some leeway, but after finding the assassin missing this morning, then getting Samhail's cryptic message about not bringing her back, my patience was gone.

Cyra had been in danger for weeks, and I hadn't had a clue. Now the assassin sent to kill us was still out there, I was trying to prepare for a war, my general was missing, and my fellow Triumvirate lord hadn't seen fit to be on time to a meeting I'd called to go over preparations.

I was about to send a message to Phaedrus to have him open a portal to Seatherny so I could seek out Aidan myself, when the blue glow of Aidan's own portal flared near the door. Aidan stepped through, followed by Maziren, his Captain of the Guard, and he sauntered over to sit down at the head of the table. I'd taken a seat at the side, even though the seat at the head was mine by right as the most senior Triumvirate member, and I cocked my head at Aidan in question. He only leaned back in his chair, looking bored.

Aidan always looked more serious than his husband Jasper, but lately he seemed more surly than serious. Indeed, when his eyes met mine, I caught a look of irritation on his face.

"What is it, Bressen?" he asked. "Why did you want to see me?"

I effected an expression that said I wasn't amused. Not only had Aidan not shown any gratitude for what Cyra and I had done in getting Jasper back about a week ago, he'd seemed downright hostile to me since.

Granted Cyra had accidentally electrocuted him with her lightning, so it was possible he was still angry about that, but everything I'd learned of Aidan in the admittedly short time I'd known him told me he wasn't the type to hold a grudge. I was starting to wonder if something else was wrong with him.

"I wanted to check in with you about a few things," I said, tamping down my own annoyance at his bad attitude and lack of contrition for being late. "But first, how is Jasper?"

He frowned at the change in subject. His answer was curt. "He's fine."

"And you?" I asked, determined to observe at least a few pleasantries before I launched into business. "Are you feeling better?"

"I'm fine too," he said. "Jasper is fine. Maziren is fine. We're all fine in Derridan. What do you want?"

My eyes narrowed even more, and I glanced quickly at Maziren. The Captain of the Guard's expression was often one of steely determination, but there was something different there now that I couldn't put my finger on as she caught my eye. I held her gaze for a second, but I couldn't glean any meaning from the look she gave me.

"Very well. We can get to business," I said. "I want to know how your preparations are coming." Not a question. If this was how he wanted it...

Aidan frowned. "My preparations? For what?"

I blinked at him. "For war. Have you assembled Derridan's army and begun training them yet? We can't use our normal tactics if we want to-"

"Why would I be preparing for war?" Aidan asked, cutting me off.

I blinked at him again. He was kidding. He had to be.

"Sandrian? Magdalene? Symbionts?" I said, finally giving a little free rein to my temper. "Is any of this ringing any bells?"

Aidan scoffed and waved a hand. "That's your fight. I'm not letting

Derridan get dragged into this. If you want to take on Sandrian and Magdalene and fight those things, go right ahead."

I stared at him, no longer capable of blinking. "What?"

"You heard me," he said. "Derridan isn't getting involved."

My eyes darted to Maziren to see what she made of this, and I thought I saw concern on her face. I was tempted to slip into her mind and check, but Maziren could be prickly, and things were already strained between me and Aidan. Now wasn't the time to piss off his guard if I was wrong.

I turned back to Aidan. "Do you really think you have a choice? Do you think Sandrian and Magdelene are going to let you stay out of this? For the gods' sakes, they'll come through Derridan to get to Hiraeth."

That was assuming they were in Rowe, which I did. In reality, we didn't know where they were. Cyra had tried using her seeker power to find them, but we'd learned the power was mainly used to find objects, not people, so it had been a long shot at best.

Aidan shrugged. He actually fucking shrugged, and I took in a deep breath to keep my blood from boiling. Aidan's flinch a second later said my eyes had likely just flashed red, an indication my dark angelus side was not pleased.

"You intend to let them invade Hiraeth through Derridan?" I asked, still not quite believing what I was hearing.

"I don't intend to get into an unnecessary conflict," he corrected, less self-assured now. "Have you considered diplomacy before you start making plans to kill thousands?"

I clenched my teeth together. It might've been a fair point if Aidan's own husband hadn't recently been kidnapped and almost killed by Sandrian and Magdalene. Perhaps an attempt at diplomacy would've been in order under other circumstances, but he didn't know Sandrian like I did. Sandrian wasn't interested in settling this with words.

"Cyra saw their invading army in a vision," I said. "We'd be fools to rest our hopes on diplomacy while our enemy prepares for war. You're only putting your people at greater risk by pretending this threat isn't real."

Aidan was quiet for a long moment before he sighed heavily and rose. "I'm sorry, Bressen," he said as he pulled a message leaf out of his pocket, "but Derridan isn't going to war."

He didn't look sorry at all. He held the leaf up and it disappeared in a puff of smoke. A few seconds later, a portal reappeared near the door, and Aidan strode through it back into Seatherny, Maziren on his heels.

I stared at the empty space as the portal closed after Aidan. What in the three hells had just happened?

I sat unmoving for several minutes. The one problem with mind powers was they didn't provide much of an outlet when you were upset and alone. I would've traded them at that moment for just one of Samhail's forcefields, because I desperately needed to send someone or something flying across the room.

In the end, I settled for standing up and sending one of the chairs hurtling into the wall. It was sturdy and didn't break, but it at least made a satisfying crash when it hit.

I put my palms on the table and leaned over it, trying to calm myself. Throwing the chair hadn't done anything to dull my fury, and Samhail wasn't here to help me work off my frustration with a sparring match.

I didn't dare go back to Tide's End yet either. Cyra liked our sex rough sometimes, so I'd often fuck her when I was angry or agitated, but what I felt now was beyond rage. I'd hurt her if I went home now and she tried to tempt me into venting myself inside her. No, I needed to find an outlet before I could go back.

Then I had an idea. Something I hadn't done in a while.

I left the meeting room and strode back to my wing of the Citadel. I went straight to my bedroom and into the large closet where I pulled out one of the drawers that lined the wall. I reached in and took out a pair of pants and a shirt that were shoved in back.

I undressed and discarded my fine clothes in favor of the worn pants and simple cotton shirt. Both were black, the color I wore most often for obvious reasons. I found a scuffed older pair of boots in the corner and pulled them on. Then I was ready to go.

I thought about asking Phaedrus for a portal, but a good flight might help right now, so I left the closet and stepped out onto the balcony off the bedroom.

My wings sprang free from my back and stretched across the space. They were black as well, but the feathers held a soft sheen in the golden light from the late afternoon sun.

I flexed then a few times as my body remembered the feel of their weight on my back. It had been a while since I'd flown – really flown – and I already felt better at the thought of taking to the air. It would take me a couple hours to get to Gendris, but hopefully that would be enough time to let some of my anger molt off, and I launched myself into the air.

Bressen

I put up my obfuscation glamour as I approached Gendris a while later. The sun was just setting, but I was still too visible against the dusky sky, and no one could know I was here.

I touched down in a familiar alley and lifted my glamour after I pulled my wings back into my body. It had been good to stretch them, but now they had to go.

The alley was dark and deserted. The only light came from whatever filtered down the narrow space from the lanterns on the busier streets at either end, and I stepped carefully toward the side to feel my way along one of the buildings. I wrinkled my nose at the smell of garbage and the faint tang of urine as I ran my hand along the rough brick until I found the space where a door sat tucked in the shadows. I knocked three times quickly, waited a beat, then knocked once more.

I was just starting to wonder if the place I sought had moved or if they'd changed the knock when the door opened. I didn't recognize the tall, burly man that answered. His hair was almost white-blonde, but his beard was dark brown with a blonde streak down the chin.

"What do you want?" he asked as he looked me up and down.

"I'm here to fight," I said.

He scoffed. "Don't know what you're talking about." He tried to close the door on me, but I threw up a hand to hold it open, and he looked shocked I'd been able to stop him from shutting it in my face.

"Does Xerxes still run this ring?" I asked. "Tell him Lysander is here."

The man furrowed his brow. The name I'd given obviously meant nothing, but if Xerxes was still here, it would mean something to him.

This time I let him close the door on me. I sensed the man was perimortal, but I was sure I could get into his head if he tried to turn me away. I didn't think I'd have to, though.

Indeed, the door flew open a minute later, and a man at least a foot and a half shorter than me appeared there. He was bald with bright blue eyes that traveled up my form as if trying to believe he was really seeing what he thought he saw. A wide smile split his face a second later.

"Lysander!" he said. "I thought you'd forgotten about us." There was utter delight written across his face, but not the delight of seeing an old friend. It was the kind of delight he might've had if I'd shoved a sack of coins into his hand.

I smiled. "Never."

"Come in, come in!" Xerxes said, ushering me inside. "Cuddy says you want to fight."

"That's right," I said as I brushed past the guard and followed Xerxes down the hall. "Do you have any opponents worthy of my time tonight?"

He smirked. "I have at least two I think might give you a challenge."

I looked bored. "We'll see about that. When do I go on?"

"I'll put you in right after the current fight finishes," Xerxes said. He turned to the man named Cuddy, who was still standing by the door looking dumbstruck. "Send word to our elite patrons that Lysander is back," he ordered, and Cuddy sprang into action.

I'd discovered this place almost by accident a few decades ago, and I came occasionally when I needed to blow off steam. Or I had in the past. It had been a while since I'd been back.

While the people of Callanus and Solandis knew me, I was far less recognizable in the cities of Polaris and Derridan. The people in those territories knew the Nemesis Incarnate by reputation, but they had no idea what I looked like. As Cyra could attest, most people pictured me as some sort of monster or an old, gnarled wretch. As long as I wasn't dressed like a lord, Xerxes and his patrons were none the wiser.

That's what I told myself anyway. People may still have suspected I was nobility – it was hard to fully hide – but I doubted they knew it was one of the Lords of the Triumvirate they watched in the fighting pit.

I hadn't even told Samhail about this place, but purely for selfish reasons. I'd quickly become one of Xerxes's top fighters once I got my foot in the door, and that came with a certain amount of prestige here. I knew all that would change the second Xerxes got a look at Samhail. I also knew he'd pit me and Samhail against each other at some point, and while I didn't mind fighting Samhail during our training sessions, fighting him in a secret, underground combat ring where patrons bet huge sums of money on the outcomes of the fights was another story.

It was probably moot anyway. In our younger days, Samhail might've been tempted to fight, but he was less eager to prove himself nowadays. He didn't have to. Anyone who knew him knew not to fuck with him, and those who didn't know him learned quickly, if they were foolish enough to test him.

"Wait here," Xerxes told me as we stopped at the entrance to the surprisingly large arena. There was a round pit sunk into the center of the room with a dirt floor. All around it rose concentric rings of chest-high barriers that the audience leaned over to see into the pit. I couldn't see the fighters currently in the ring, but I wasn't sure I'd recognize them anyway.

Xerxes employed a few regular fighters he could use whenever he needed them, but his bread and butter was actually the fighters like me who came only occasionally when they felt either like doling out some punishment, or – as in my case sometimes – receiving it. I'd come here nightly for weeks after my father had died to let the physical pain dull my mental anguish for at least an hour or two.

A roar went up from the crowd, half cheers and half jeers, as the winner of the current fight was crowned, and Xerxes surged forward to speak to the fight master before she announced the next round.

Fuck. I'd forgotten about Delia.

Xerxes stopped next to a tall woman with long black hair and smooth caramel-colored skin as she bent to listen to hear him over the din of the crowd. A couple seconds later, she jerked up and swung around to look at me in the doorway. I couldn't tell from here if she was furious or happy to see me, but I guessed it was probably the former.

Delia was attractive in a way I'd never been able to put my finger on. The angles of her face seemed too sharp at first, but they only made her more intriguing the longer you looked. Even the scar that ran down part of her forehead, through one eyebrow, and down her cheek gave her a certain strikingness that was difficult to ignore.

She was also the last woman I'd fucked before I met Cyra. Or perhaps more accurately, she'd fucked me.

Delia hadn't hid her interest in me when she began working for Xerxes about five years ago, but sex wasn't usually my priority when I came to the pit, so nothing happened between us for a long time. I didn't discourage her when she flirted with me, but I also didn't do much to encourage her either.

It didn't matter. One night when I'd just barely won my fight, I'd gone into the room where the fighters waited for the healer to tend to them. I was in bad shape and could hardly move, and I'd flopped onto the table to lay on my back. After a few minutes, Delia had entered and locked the door. Without a word, she'd undone my pants, pulled out my cock, and taken me into her mouth.

I doubted I would've stopped her regardless, but I didn't have the energy to try, and my cock was the only thing that felt good at that point.

When I didn't resist after a few minutes, she took off her own pants, climbed onto the table, and rode me until I passed out. I woke up later, mostly healed, with my cock tucked back inside my pants. The healer – a man with just enough power to be called such – admitted Delia had paid him well to give her twenty minutes alone with me.

It was the last time I'd seen her. I'd stopped coming to the fighting pit after that, not because of Delia, but because I'd been tied up with Revenmyer and the Triumvirate. Then Cyra had arrived at the Citadel, and thoughts of any other woman in my bed had become a thing of the past.

It had been nearly two years now since I'd seen the woman.

I walked over to where Delia and Xerxes stood.

"Delia, it's good to see you," I said.

The look she gave me was benign enough, but her fury drifted off her like smoke. Delia was perimortal, although not very powerful, so her mind was open to me if I wanted to read it. I didn't need to, though. Her thoughts were splashed across her face like paint on a canvas. The next time she had access to my cock, she'd do something far less pleasant than put it in her mouth.

Fair enough.

"Lysander," she said, her tone saccharine. "You're not dead after all." Then she added so only I could hear, "How disappointing."

She didn't give me a chance to say anything further before she jumped down into the pit and addressed the crowd.

"Ladies and gentlemen," she said, "we have a special treat for you tonight. Back after a long absence is one of our favorites here in the pit, our own wayward son, Lysander!"

I jumped down into the pit as the crowd roared its welcome. Even as I looked around, more patrons slipped into the arena, the preferred clients Xerxes called when he had something special for them, the ones who had the means to drop everything and get here almost immediately to shell out huge sums of money.

I didn't acknowledge the crowd, but I couldn't help soaking up their excitement, their fervor. Part of me had missed this. And that worried me.

"And his opponent," Delia went on before the crowd dampened their enthusiasm, "is a fighter you know well…Malachi!"

The noise in the arena amplified twofold as the crowd showed their appreciation for Malachi. I didn't know the name, so he must be new, and I looked around to see who would jump into the pit.

I heard feet hit the dirt to my side and turned to see a large man standing several feet away. His head was shaved, and he had a close-cropped golden-brown beard. From what I could tell, he was a couple inches taller than me and more muscled, but I wasn't worried. It was hard to fear most opponents after fighting Samhail.

I sensed the man was mortal, although it didn't really matter since using magic wasn't allowed in the pit. As if on cue, Delia snapped a caronium cuff on my wrist, and my power died.

Xerxes knew I was perimortal, but he didn't know what my power was. The cuff didn't lock, so I could get out of it in an emergency, but fighters were on their honor to keep them on.

All things considered, Xerxes's operation was civilized in comparison to some of the other fighting rings I'd experienced. He kept a healer on hand, albeit not a powerful one, and fighters were forbidden from killing each other. Disposing of bodies was messy, annoying work, and it was the easiest way to attract the notice of people who might be inclined to shut you down. Xerxes stayed in business because he paid the city guard to turn a blind eye and because he didn't give them any reason to come looking for him. He promised blood and violence to his patrons but not death. The venues that dealt in death didn't last long in the city.

Malachi and I stepped to the center of the pit to face each other as one of the guards helped Delia out. This was part of the pre-fight ritual, a chance for the combatants to size each other up or engage in some psychological warfare, some – What had Axenus called it that time? – 'competitive incivility?'

Malachi looked me up and down with an expression like he smelled shit. He huffed a laugh. "Surely this is a joke," he said. "They want me to fight *you*? You're too pretty to hit."

I held back a smile. Samhail had said almost the same thing to me the very first time we'd sparred at the training camp where we'd met. Then he'd punched me.

I remained quiet as Malachi waited for my reaction. I didn't usually exchange barbs at these meetings.

"Or maybe you're pretty because I'm supposed to fuck you instead of fight you," he went on when I didn't speak. "I bet your ass would squeeze nice and tight around my cock." He grabbed his groin and laughed.

My expression didn't waver.

"Get ready!" Delia shouted from above the pit, and Malachi and I retreated to opposite sides of the circle.

A bell clanged, and we rushed toward each other again. He took the first swing, but I dodged it and caught his arm to pull him forward for my answering right hook. He grunted as my punch took him in the temple, and he stepped away, shaking his head.

"Am I twice as pretty when you're seeing two of me?" I asked him.

Fine, maybe I wasn't entirely above a little verbal sparring.

Malachi growled and surged toward me again. I blocked his punch and answered with another to his jaw, then landed a series of jabs into his mid-section. Again he stepped away and tried to circle around me.

The problem with fighters like Malachi was that they automatically assumed they had the advantage because of their size. I was smaller. I was 'prettier,' so clearly I had no chance in his eyes. One of the things I respected most about Samhail was he never underestimated an opponent. He always assumed a fighter was good enough to beat him until they showed him otherwise. Which they always did.

Malachi charged again, and this time I didn't anticipate his combination. I dodged his first punch but stepped right into the second.

Stars burst behind my eyes, and I staggered back a step. My vision cleared just in time to see the look of surprise on Malachi's face. He'd expected me to go down.

That was the other good thing about training with Samhail. I knew how to take a punch.

I swung before Malachi realized I'd moved, and then it was all but over. I hit him again and again with shots to both his head and body so all he could do was keep his hands up to try and protect himself. When he was too slow to get his forearm up in time to block my punch, I connected with his temple again, and he went down.

Malachi crashed to the dirt, and the roar of the crowd swelled to near deafening. I waited a moment to be sure he wouldn't rise again, but he remained still. A second later, Delia jumped into the pit to declare me the winner, although the words looked sour in her mouth.

"Are you up for another opponent?" she asked me. "Or are you too out of shape to go again?"

"I'll let you know when I break a sweat," I said. "Bring on the next."

The smile she gave me could only be described as sinister.

A loud thud sounded behind me as another pair of feet – even bigger feet – hit the dirt of the pit, and I turned to see what fresh hell had entered.

My jaw dropped open at the sight of the huge man standing there. No, not really a man, I corrected myself. The huge *gargoyle*.

Chapter 3

Bressen

"Ajax." I whispered the name.

I stood frozen as I took in the warrior across the pit from me. He and the other two warriors Cyra had freed from Praya's necklace had gone their separate ways the day after Aramis's funeral, and I hadn't expected to see him again so soon. Certainly not here of all places.

Ajax's close-cropped black hair had grown out a little since I'd last seen him. His eyes looked milky from far away, especially against his mahogany skin, but I'd seen them up close, and he actually had white irises that were flecked with gold. Only his pupils were black, but they got lost among the white of his eyes unless you were within a few feet of him.

He was in his human form with no wings, but I knew from seeing him and Samhail next to each other that Ajax was only an inch or two shorter than my friend, which still gave him almost half a foot on me. He was also bulkier than Samhail, with muscles that were on full display across his shirtless torso.

I knew what it felt like to be hit by a gargoyle, and the idea of being hit by Ajax – who had no reason to go easy on me – made me shudder. One good punch would kill me. I was so very, very fucked.

The beating I was about to take was actually secondary to my more immediate concern, though. Ajax knew who I was, and indeed, he looked rather confused as he took a step forward.

"Lor-"

"Lysander," I cut in quickly before he could call me 'Lord Bressen.' "My name is Lysander."

"Lysander, meet Ajax," Delia said, smirking so wide her face could barely contain it. Oh, she was going to enjoy watching Ajax pummel me.

The crowd had yet to curb its roaring, and I saw money changing hands furiously out of my periphery as patrons placed their bets on the fight. Anyone who knew me had likely placed their wagers on me the last round, but I suspected even my most ardent supporters were taking Ajax in this fight. Three hells, my own money would've been on him. Four hundred years ago, he'd been considered one of the greatest mercenaries on the continent. I could only hope he was out-of-practice after centuries of being trapped in a magical necklace.

Ajax and I stepped forward for our pre-fight meet, and I gave him a cold stare I hoped he could see past. He seemed to understand, because he answered mine with one of his own and crossed his arms menacingly over his huge chest. I crossed my arms as well, so we were the picture of two opponents unimpressed with each other.

"You were the last person I expected to see here," Ajax said, just loud enough for me to hear over the din of the crowd. "What's going on?" His casual tone belied the scowl on his face.

"Long story," I said. "The short version is that I had a bad day."

His head ticked to the side the slightest bit. "So how's this going to go?" he asked.

"As a favor to Cyra, just try not to kill me," I said.

He raised a brow. "You don't think you can beat me." An observation, not a question.

I chuckled. "Do *you* think I can?" But I didn't let him answer. "I'm going to try, but I've fought Samhail before, and I'm realistic about how this is probably going to end."

"Have you ever beaten him?"

"Only when he lets me."

His brows arched a bit further. "I could try-"

"Barring a miracle," I said, cutting him off, "no one here is going to believe I can beat you. Do what you have to do. Like I said, just-"

"Don't kill you," he cut in. "Got it. But only because I owe your wife for freeing me from four centuries of imprisonment and the promise of a gruesome death." His eye twitched in a brief wink.

I stretched my neck so it cracked. "Then let's do this."

I turned on my heel and strode back to my side of the pit as the crowd thundered unrelentingly around us, oblivious to the perfectly civilized conversation that had just occurred in the center of the ring.

I looked at Delia, who was still grinning like someone had just made her queen of the continent. She mouthed the words 'Have fun' at me, then sounded the bell, and Ajax and I surged toward each other.

I dodged Ajax's first swing and managed to get in under his arm to land a punch to his stomach before I danced backward. Pain shot through my hand and halfway up my arm from the blow. Ajax might not be in his gargoyle form, but I'd fought Samhail enough to know that gargoyle bodies were denser and heavier than normal human bodies. Even so, Ajax's body might as well have been stone for all the give his muscles had.

I charged again, feinted one way, then moved the other. Ajax seemed to fall for it and swung at empty air while I landed another blow to his side, but I had a feeling he was going easy on me. Still, if he was going to give me the openings, I'd take them. I didn't hold much hope I'd win this fight, but I was going to get in as many hits as I could.

I attacked again immediately, jumping up and swinging with a vicious roundhouse to Ajax's head that was backed by the extra momentum of my leap. He took the blow in the cheek, and it snapped his head to the side, but he recovered quicker than I expected, and a moment later my body left the ground as he picked me up and threw me across the ring.

Pain shot through my shoulder as I landed on it, but somehow I managed to roll and mitigate the rest of the impact. I looked up to find Ajax stalking toward me.

I guessed my grace period was over.

I sprang to my feet and charged him, staying low to plow into his stomach with my good shoulder. The move would have taken any other man to the ground, but it only caused Ajax to grunt and stagger back a couple steps, and I was grateful for that much.

Ajax brought his fists down on my back, and the breath punched out of me, first under his blow, then again as my body hit the hard-packed ground. I coughed into the dirt and tried desperately to draw in a breath.

Panic gripped me as Ajax grabbed me under the arms to pull me to my feet. I brought my knee up hard into his inner thigh, and he flinched but didn't let go. It wasn't against the rules for me to go for his groin per se, but the patrons here tended to see it as a cheap shot, and taking it wouldn't put them on my side. I also couldn't bring myself to do that to another man, especially Ajax.

Not that it mattered. This fight was going to be over soon.

Just not yet.

I came up swinging and caught Ajax with a shot to his jaw that kicked his head back. I got in two more head shots before I concentrated on his mid-section, throwing punch after punch into his stomach and sides. He grunted and jerked as I hit him, but he stayed on his feet, not even swaying. My hands were starting to go numb from the impact.

Ajax finally countered with a blow to my side that made me see stars and likely would've cracked a rib if I wasn't used to taking such shots from Samhail. I tried to recover, but Ajax landed a fist straight into my gut that nearly made me heave up my last meal.

"Go down," he whispered into my ear as I coughed and gasped.

"Take me down," I countered when I had enough breath to speak. "I'm not going to do your job for you."

I was being stupid, but taking a dive wasn't in my nature. Ajax would win this fight, but gods damn me, I'd make him earn it.

"Stubborn bastard," he muttered just before I landed another upper cut to his jaw that made his teeth clack together. He growled and spat blood onto the dirt, which only made me bolder.

I took him in the jaw again with my right hook — he was too tall for me to reach his temple with a good shot — but he answered with a jaw shot of his own that made me wonder if I'd ever chew properly again. He pulled back his fist to swing, and I threw myself back from him. If I hadn't moved when I did, the punch likely would have knocked me cold. As it was, I pulled back enough that he didn't get a solid shot to my head, but not enough that I fully cleared his swing.

I felt the cheek bone near my orbital socket crack as his fist connected, and excruciating pain radiated through my head. The entire world went black – for how long I wasn't sure – but when the arena rematerialized, I was on the ground, and I could only see out of one eye.

I lifted my head enough to see a puddle of my blood soaking into the dirt. I reached up, felt the wetness on my cheek near my eye, and prayed the only reason I couldn't see out of it was that the blood was clouding my vision.

Large hands grabbed me and jerked me backward, and then I couldn't breathe. I clawed at the iron arm wrapped around my neck, but it was no use. There was no way I was getting out of this headlock.

"You fought better than I expected," Ajax said quietly, "but it's time to end this before you get truly hurt and your wife incinerates me."

Logically I knew this was for the best, but a deep-seeded instinct for self-preservation kicked in and made me keep fighting. I thrashed and kicked against Ajax's hold until my body stopped responding to my commands and the world finally dissolved to black.

Bressen

I couldn't see anything as I felt my eyes flutter wildly, struggling to open. They seemed glued shut, and I tried again as muffled conversation around me reached my ears. This time I got a quick, blurry vision of a well-lit room before my eyes snapped shut again.

"My lady! He's waking."

The voice was Ajax's, and terror struck me at the idea Cyra was with us in Xerxes's pit. I opened my mouth to tell her to go, but I couldn't speak either. I tried to move, but my body wouldn't obey just yet.

"Bressen?" Cyra's voice pierced my panic, but all I could do was shake my head weakly. She couldn't be here. Ajax had to get her out.

"Bressen, can you hear me?" Cyra asked, fear in her voice.

"Cyra." I forced the word out as I struggled to pry my eyes open. "You have to leave."

"I'm not going anywhere," she said, her voice turning stubborn. "Not until I've had a few words with you."

My eyes fluttered again, and this time I managed to keep them open as Cyra's beautiful face came into focus. I was about to order her to leave again when I realized how quiet it was.

"Where…?" I started to ask.

"You're home. You're safe," Cyra said, then added, "From everyone but me."

I couldn't help it. I smiled at the threat as I met her silvery eyes.

Cyra put a hand on the side of my cheek. "Are you alright?"

That was a good question. I took stock of how I felt and was hesitantly optimistic when I didn't feel any pain. I reached up to feel my cheek where Ajax had shattered the bone, but everything felt normal, and I realized I could see out of both eyes again.

"I had to call one of the healers from the city to fix that," Cyra said. "I didn't dare attempt to heal it myself."

She glanced to the side, and I followed her gaze to see Ajax looking contrite.

"Sorry about that," the warrior said. "I was trying to knock you out before you got hurt too much, and…well, you moved."

It took me a moment to recall what had happened. Ajax had tried to punch me, but I'd pulled back, and instead of connecting with the side of my head, his fist had struck my cheek.

I looked around. I was in our room at Tide's End.

"How did I get back?" I asked.

"Ajax sent me a message leaf to tell me what happened," Cyra said. "I opened a portal, and we brought you home."

I nodded before something occurred to me. "Wait, does that mean…"

"Xerxes tried to bring you into the back to have his own healer fix you, but I didn't trust him with an injury that bad," Ajax said. "I told Xerxes I was taking you somewhere else to be healed. He tried to stop me…so I had to tell him who you were."

I exhaled deeply. Well, I wouldn't be going there again apparently.

Of course, now that Cyra knew what I'd done, I wouldn't be allowed to go back anyway.

"How did Xerxes take that news?" I asked.

"You mean the news that a Lord of the Triumvirate was lying bleeding and unconscious in his underground fighting pit?" Ajax asked, amused. "When I explained who you were, he couldn't get you out of there fast enough. I doubt the place will still be there by daylight. What did he call you?" He thought a moment. "The Nemesis Incarnate? You apparently have quite a reputation."

I huffed a laugh. "You have no idea."

Cyra growled, bringing my attention back to her. "Do you have any idea what it's like to get a message leaf telling me my husband is in Gendris at a fighting pit and needs a healer?" she asked.

I deflated. I'd hoped she would never learn about my little side adventure, but now that she had, I realized just how much danger I'd put myself in, and I didn't blame her for being angry at me.

"That man – Xerxes was it? – begged me not to let you kill him when you woke up," Cyra said.

"And I told him he should be more worried about what Cyra might do to him," Ajax said. Then he added, "Like I am."

"You redeemed yourself by contacting me," Cyra told him. "If you'd let that other healer try to help him, it might've been a different story."

I reached over and took Cyra's hand in mine. "I'm sorry," I said. "It was a stupid thing to do."

"What in the three hells were you doing there anyway?" she asked. She seemed more hurt than angry, and my heart broke at the pain in her expression. Gods, I was an ass.

"It's a place I used to go to blow off steam, long before I met you," I said. "It's been a frustrating day, and I needed an outlet, but I should've known better."

Cyra gave me a meaningful look. "You have an outlet here at home."

I shook my head. "I was too angry. I didn't want to risk it."

She cocked her head in question. "Why were you so angry?" She paused a second. "You met with Aidan this afternoon. What happened?"

I gave her a brief recap of my conversation with Aidan, and the furrow in her brow deepened with each word.

"Why?" was all she asked when I was done.

I shook my head. "No idea. Aidan hasn't seemed himself lately, and I have this feeling something else must've happened at the temple we don't know about, something serious that's knocked him off-balance."

Cyra nodded. "And you're still upset with Samhail."

"Samhail?" Ajax asked. "What's wrong with Samhail?"

"It's a long story," I said. "The short version is that I sent him after a dangerous prisoner who escaped our holding cell. Based on my last message from him, it sounds as though he found her, but rather than bring her back here to be dealt with, he's decided to enact some kind of plan on his own that he won't tell me about."

Ajax raised a brow. "Her?"

"Yes. We had an assassin, a masque, living under our roof for weeks."

Ajax looked alarmed. "And she didn't kill anyone?"

I waved a dismissive hand. "That's a long story as well."

"Do you need help finding Samhail and this assassin?" Ajax asked.

"I have two other gargoyles on it already," I said. "We'll need to ask a different favor from you in the near future."

"You want help in this war," he said knowingly.

"Would you be willing to fight?" I asked.

He looked at Cyra. "My life belongs to you, my lady. If you wish me to fight, you need only ask. My service is yours."

Cyra looked taken aback at the declaration, but she schooled herself.

"For the first time in four hundred years, your life is your own," she said to him. "I *will* ask you to fight with us when the time comes, but I'll be grateful if you choose to do so."

"Consider it done," Ajax said. Then he smiled. "I assume that means you'll let me leave in one piece now?"

Cyra smiled back. "Of course. Where can I send you?"

"A portal back to Gendris would be appreciated," he said. "You can let me out near the city square. My boarding house isn't far from there."

"You never told me," I said to Ajax as I sat up in bed. "Why were *you* fighting in Xerxes's pit?"

He shrugged. "A few hundred years ago, everyone knew who I was and what I could do. I had enough work that I could turn away any job I didn't want. Now, almost no one knows me, and the few older perimortals who do remember me have no use for my services. Xerxes is well-connected, and his fights give me a chance to show off my skills to a potential new set of clientele."

"I'm happy to serve as a reference if anyone needs proof of how hard you hit," I said.

He chuckled. "And remember to tell them I keep my promises. I did promise not to kill you, after all."

"Indeed," I said.

Cyra looked between us before her eyes landed on me. "I assume you'll explain all that later?" she asked, and I nodded.

She turned and drew a portal in the air, then widened it enough for the big gargoyle to step through.

"Thank you for getting my husband back safely," Cyra said to Ajax as she stepped aside for him to pass.

Ajax gave her a small bow. "My lady," he said, then stepped through the portal. Cyra closed it after him and turned to me.

"How much trouble am I in?" I asked.

"A lot," she said, crossing her arms.

"Are you going to punish me?" I asked huskily. "Maybe you should tie me to the bed and do unspeakable things to me."

"Ha!" she laughed. "We both know our 'punishments' are more like rewards, and I don't intend to reward this kind of behavior. I should make you sleep on the couch out in the sitting room tonight."

She was serious, but I was an expert in breaking down her barriers. I slid off the bed carefully, just in case there was something the healer hadn't fully fixed.

Cyra eyed me as I moved slowly toward her. "If you think you're going to seduce me, think again," she said.

"No, it would be silly of me to try," I said silkily.

She uncrossed her arms and started to back away. I followed, slowly stalking her. She put a hand on my chest to hold me back when I reached her, but I kept moving, and she kept retreating until her back hit the wall. I pressed myself into her, letting her feel my desire.

"You won't leave me in pain like this, will you?" I said, moving my erection against her. "Don't you think I've had enough for one night?"

She looked up at me with determination. "If I give in now, you'll never learn your lesson."

"Hmmm. And what lesson would that be?" I asked as I bent my head to kiss a trail down her throat.

Cyra let out a soft moan, and my fingers threaded through her hair to pull her head to the side so I had better access to her neck. I deepened the intensity of my kisses and began to suck and nip at her neck as well.

When I put my other hand on her breast and began to knead, though, she pushed me back.

"No!" she said.

I didn't go far, but there were a few inches between us, and I let out a long exhale at the loss of friction.

"You went to fight in a secret combat ring without telling me," she said. "What if we didn't know Ajax and he'd killed you? What if he hadn't been able to get you back so we could find a competent healer?"

I closed my eyes against the hurt in her voice. "You're right," I said, opening them again. "It was stupid and risky for me to do what I did, and I promise it will never happen again."

I tried to lean back in, but she pushed on my chest again, stopping me. "And why was that black-haired woman with the scar staring daggers at me when I came to get you?"

Fuck. "I…"

"Is she…Did you…?"

I sighed. "It was years before I met you, and only once, but I'm sure she wanted more. She was angry at me tonight because I hadn't seen her since. I forgot she'd be there."

Cyra considered all this. It was several seconds before she nodded.

"I won't make you sleep on the couch tonight," she said, "but you don't get to touch me. I'm too angry at you right now."

"Cyra, I swear, I only had sex with her onc-"

She waved a hand to stop me. "I don't care about that," she said. "We both have former lovers." She paused. "You have a lot more than me, but I understand that. What I'm mad about is how you almost got yourself killed tonight."

"I promised not to do that again," I offered.

"And maybe you'll keep that promise if you don't get to have me tonight," she said resolutely.

Fucking hells. I wanted nothing more than to bury myself inside Cyra right now and banish the lingering frustrations I hadn't purged during my two fights, but I still felt her anger and hurt. She wasn't going to let me take her tonight, and I wasn't going to push. It was a testament to just how upset she was that she'd brushed off my attempts at seduction.

I stepped away.

"I understand," I said. "If this is the penance I need to pay, so be it."

"I need to come, though," she said. "So you'll have to watch me take care of myself, but you can't touch me."

"What?" I asked incredulously as she pushed past me to head to the bed. "Cyra, that's not penance, that's torture."

"Good," she said, mercilessly. "Then you'll understand what I felt when I thought you were dying. Now sit."

I stared at her as she pointed to a chair next to the bed. I thought about arguing with her but took a resigned seat instead.

Cyra's eyes met mine before she pulled off her sweater and undershirt and tossed them aside. I was already hard, but I went even harder as my mouth began to water.

"Cyra," I said as I gripped the arms of the chair. I wasn't going to be able to just watch her.

She frowned as she looked down at my hands, obviously coming to the same conclusion. Then she turned and headed toward the closet.

"Cyra?" I called after her.

She didn't answer, but she returned a few seconds later, and I watched her breasts bounce as she strode across the room. I ached to close my mouth over her nipples and hear her gasp.

Then I saw the two silk scarves in her hands. Sweet gods above. I didn't like where this was going.

"Cyra," I said, my tone pleading now.

"Hands flat on the arms of the chair," she said.

"Cyra, please." I'd promise her anything as long as she didn't do what she was planning to do.

She only looked at me, and reluctantly, I obeyed.

My cock was painfully hard inside my pants as Cyra tied my hands to the arms of the chair with the scarves, and I was now thoroughly regretting everything I'd done tonight. I'd survived Xerxes's fighting pit only to die watching my wife pleasure herself while tied to a chair.

"Are you repentant yet?" Cyra asked as she toed off her shoes and undid her pants.

I watched in rapture as she shimmied her hips to get the pants down her thighs, then pushed them to her ankles and stepped out of them.

"Gods, yes," I whispered. "I swear to the Trinity, I'll never do anything like that again."

Cyra straightened and ran a hand lightly down her chest so it brushed over one breast. Her nipple peaked, and I strained at the scarves holding me to the chair.

"I don't think you sound sorry enough yet," she said.

"I am," I insisted. "I'm so sorry."

She smiled. "Not yet, but you will be."

I expected her to lay on the bed, but instead she stepped forward and eased down onto my lap, and I nearly exploded right there. She pressed herself back against my chest, and her scent shot up my nose to lodge itself in my brain, making me dizzy. She gyrated her ass against my cock, and I groaned loudly as pain and pleasure mingled together in my pants.

"Fuck, Cyra. Please."

"I don't think you've learned your lesson yet," she said as she trailed a hand from her shoulder, down between her breasts, and over her stomach before she paused at the apex of her thighs.

"I swear I have," I said, and there was a tremor in my voice I couldn't quell. I saw her hand poised between her legs as I looked over her shoulder and down her body, and I was sure I might rip the arms off the chair if it dipped any lower.

"No, I don't think you have," she said, and she let out a soft sigh as she began to swirl two fingers over her clit.

I jerked in the chair and swore as something molten surged through me, but Cyra only pushed back against me and moaned as she continued to massage her clit. I was going to come in my pants any second now, and I didn't care because there was only so much more of this I could take.

Cyra dipped her hand lower to slide her fingers inside herself, and I actually whimpered. I didn't think I'd ever whimpered in my life.

She writhed against me as she tried to find a good position, and I managed to turn one of my hands on the arm of the chair to face inward.

"Lift your leg," I told her.

She did as I asked, and I grabbed her leg under the knee to help hold her open so she could pump her fingers in and out of herself. As she did, I thrust my hips up, desperate to get enough friction for a release.

She tsked. "None of that now, or I can make this worse."

Gods, I didn't know how it could get any worse.

"I'm sorry," I whispered against her ear. "I'll behave."

Cyra lifted her hand up toward my face, and I saw the glistening slickness of her arousal on her fingers.

"Do you want a taste?" she asked.

I groaned. "Yes. Please."

She moved her fingers toward my mouth but then pulled them back when I tried to close my lips over them, and I growled in frustration.

"Promise me and mean it," she said softly.

"Sweet gods, Cyra," I said, my frustration boiling over. "I swear to the Trinity and on my father's soul, I'll never go to the fighting pits again. You have my word. Now just let me taste you."

She moved her fingers back within reach of my mouth, and I sucked them in deep, letting my tongue run over her sweetness. This time my groan was one of pleasure, and I sucked harder as she moved her other hand between her legs to stroke herself some more.

"Should I let you come?" she asked, but I didn't answer. Begging her at this point would only work against me.

Cyra moaned as she moved her hand faster between her legs, and my other hand gripped the arm of the chair with everything I had as I tried to grind myself against her ass without being too obvious. Her chest heaved as her breathing became ragged, and I watched her breasts thrust up and down as she moved against me.

My climax hit seconds later like a fireball, hot and explosive and a little painful as my head kicked back and I roared. My seed spurted against my skin, warm and sticky as it squelched in the fabric between me and Cyra as she continued to chase her own pleasure.

My hand strained at the scarf holding me to the chair, desperate to touch her. I felt the arm of the chair start to give, and I gave it a hard yank.

Wood cracked as the arm broke loose enough for me to free my hand of the binding. My wrist would be bruised and raw later, but I didn't give a fuck. I plunged my fingers between Cyra's legs to work them in and out of her, and her own hand yielded to mine as she pressed back against me.

"Come for me, my love," I rasped against her ear as she undulated her hips in time to my thrusts. "I want you to come all over my fingers."

I'd barely said the words when she cried out and pushed back against me. Her inner walls clamped around my fingers, and she let out a string of soft cries as I curled them inside her, stroking her deeply to coax the last throes of bliss from her body.

Cyra shuddered and went completely slack against me as we sat there breathing hard. I didn't bother to remove my hand from between her thighs. I'd lay like this with her all night if she let me.

She didn't move for a long time, and I started to think she'd fallen asleep when she finally spoke.

"That didn't go quite how it was supposed to," she said.

"It was absolute torture for me if it makes you feel any better," I said, brushing my lips down her cheek. "Consider me well and truly chastised."

She huffed. "I highly doubt that."

She tried to get up, but I wrapped my free arm around her waist to hold her there. "I truly am sorry," I said. "I promise not to do anything to make you worry about me again. Do you forgive me?"

She sighed and nestled back into me. "I suppose."

I chuckled. "That wasn't a very enthusiastic absolution."

She was quiet a moment before she turned her head into my neck. "Do you think Samhail is alright?" she asked.

I understood then that her worry for me had been compounded by her worry for Samhail.

"Samhail can take care of himself," I assured her. "I don't think you need to worry about him." I smiled. "If anything, pray for the assassin."

Tandem Read: Go to *Clash of Stone and Steel* (Bk 3), Chapter 16

Chapter 4

Cyra

The cold nipped at my skin as Bressen and I stepped through the portal before the looming edifice of Revenmyer the next day. I'd only ever seen the prison in a vision I'd stolen from Magdalene's mind, but that vision was nothing compared to the real thing.

The fortress sat at the end of a jetty as the ocean roared at its back, the surf crashing against the stone so that water sprayed into the air, keeping the lower half of the building wet. The entire structure was made of gleaming black obsidian that rose high into the perpetually dark sky.

According to Bressen, the sun rarely shone at Revenmyer. On good days, the sky was a dismal gray canvas as far as the eye could see. On bad days, like today, it rippled with stormy black clouds that flashed with jagged fractures of lightning.

On the worst days, though, when the clouds broke and the sun burst through to reflect off the shining surface of the obsidian, that's when the prisoners cowered the most. Those unfortunate enough to have windows shrank into the corners of their rooms away from the sunlight beaming across their floors. The light blinded them, their eyes so used to the darkness they'd nearly forgotten what color looked like, and any skin exposed to the sun would burn within minutes.

Even those in cells deep within the prison where there were no windows seemed to sense when the sun was out because they were restless and agitated on those days. It was as if they could feel the light through the walls and were reminded that life existed outside of Revenmyer.

Or so Bressen had explained to me earlier in one last futile attempt to convince me to stay behind. It only made me more determined to come.

I wrapped my cloak tighter around me as the wind whipped the hem of it at my ankles, and I took in the façade that in any other place might be considered beautiful. Its black stone walls were intricately carved and rose into arches and spires, the likes of which didn't even adorn the most opulent palace or temple in Callanus. Before I'd seen a vision of the place, I'd expected it to be rough and drab with little ornamentation, but it was the exact opposite. The building drew you in despite itself, as if it were a lovely carnivorous flower that lured its prey only to close around it before the victim could realize it was in danger.

I shuddered and Bressen drew his arms around me.

"It's not too late," he said. "You can go back."

I noticed he didn't say *we* could go back. Now that I'd planted the idea in his head, he was determined to see Glenora. I'd be damned if I let him talk to her without me, though.

I stepped away from him, and he let me go with a beleaguered sigh as I started toward the prison.

"Cyra, stop," he said before I'd gone more than a step or two.

"You're not going to talk me out of this," I told him.

"I'm not trying to," he said, "but you can't go any further until I open the wards. You'll be thrown back if you touch them."

"I can raise and lower wards," I reminded him, turning around.

"You can raise and lower your own wards," he corrected. "The wards around Revenmyer can only be controlled by me and my seneschals."

"And Magdalene."

His eyes flared as he remembered Magdalene had used her control over the wards to help Sandrian escape. "Fuck," he said, running a hand through hair the same color as the prison. "I forgot about that. She can get in anytime she wants."

"Can't you have someone else replace the wards?"

Bressen shook his head. "According to the prison's history, the wards were put in place by the Protector. Magdalene said they were put in place by one of her predecessors, so I assume that means they were put up by a Hand of the Protector. If we're correct that Praya is a Hand of the

Creator, then-”

“Then Magdalene is a Hand of the Protector, and that’s why she can get through the wards,” I finished for him.

He nodded.

“Maybe any Hand of the Gods can get through the wards,” I said.

Bressen canted his head to indicate it was a fair point.

“Let me try,” I suggested.

He paused, and I knew his gut reaction was to refuse me, but we had little choice. Magdalene could get through the wards, so if there was any chance I could take down the current ones and put up ones of my own, we had to take it.

“Wait there,” he said.

He stepped forward and reached out to feel for the wards. A second later his hand touched something and the air became cloudy.

“Here’s the edge,” he said. “See if you can touch them. Go slowly.”

He stepped back, and I moved forward to take his place. I reached up hesitantly, remembering what he’d said about how the wards would react to someone not authorized to go through them.

I felt their presence as my hand got closer, like there was some kind of static electricity in the air that made my hair stand on end. My fingertips tingled, and I saw the space in front of me go opaque as it had for Bressen.

For one exciting moment I thought it had worked. Then I was thrown back violently by a jolt that reminded me of Sandrian’s lightning.

I cried out as the wards repelled me, but Bressen’s strong arms caught me before I hit the ground, and he tipped me back up onto my feet. My legs were like jelly, and I clung to him as I tried to get them to hold my weight again.

“Are you alright?” he asked.

I nodded. “Yes, I…I’m just a little shaky.”

“I guess that answers our question,” Bressen said. “I’ll have to ask Phaedrus if he has any ideas about how to replace the wards.”

I eased my hold on Bressen and tested my footing to see if my legs would hold. He let go of me reluctantly, and I stepped away from him.

"Do you need a minute?" he asked.

"No, I'm fine," I said. "Let's go."

He hesitated, then stepped up to the wards and touched a hand to them. This time an arched doorway opened, its edges rippling.

My body balked instinctively at stepping closer again, but I forced myself to move as I hurried through the doorway. Bressen stepped through after me and closed the passage behind him.

Before us lay a long, narrow stone walkway where ocean water churned on either side. I walked behind Bressen as he led the way up to the prison, and I used my elemental magic to quiet the water so it stayed away from the path. Rocks near the building broke most of the waves before they got this far, but water still rushed into the small bay from an inlet behind the prison, and the water eddied restlessly once inside, lapping up over the path in places. I held it at bay until we'd crossed the walkway and ascended the stairs to the entrance.

"I usually have to fly over the path to avoid getting my shoes wet," Bressen remarked as we climbed the stairs.

We crested the top and saw someone waiting for us at the iron gates of the prison. I stopped walking for a second, and words failed me as I took in the figure standing there.

It was a tall woman with wispy white hair that flew away in all directions, and she wore robes of bright fuchsia that stood out starkly against the dark backdrop of the prison. She was older than any other perimortal I'd met thus far, or at least I assumed she was perimortal. She was slight of frame, and her face was well-wrinkled with age, but she stood straight as she waited for us to approach.

"My lord," the woman said as we stopped in front of her. "Good to see you as usual. I hope you're well."

Her heavy eye makeup made her golden pupils nearly shine like my own silver ones, and up close now I saw her robes had ornate beadwork on them.

"I am," Bressen said. "Hettie, this is my wife, Lady Cyra of Hiraeth. Cyra, this is Hetsibar, my second in command. She prefers Hettie."

I opened my mouth to greet the woman, but the words stopped in my throat as Hettie swept into a deep, almost comically exaggerated bow. I looked at Bressen in alarm, but his face showed only amusement.

"My lady, it's an honor to meet you," Hettie said as she rose and met my eyes. "Please, come in and make yourself at home."

She turned without another word and strode into the prison, leaving me with my mouth hanging open.

Hettie is a little...eccentric, Bressen said into my mind as we followed.

Some advanced warning would've been nice, I told him.

And miss seeing the look on your face when you met her? Not a chance. I'll warn you that she's a mind wraith, though, he said, *so keep your shield up around her.*

"The two of you shouldn't think so loud," Hettie said over her shoulder. "You'll wake the demoni."

My head snapped to Bressen, and I saw he was frowning.

Is she reading our minds? I asked him incredulously.

No, she's just guessing, he answered. *I think.*

We followed Hettie through the front doors and into a small antechamber. It was lit from above by a wrought iron chandelier, but the flames from the candles struggled to light the space as the obsidian walls drank in their glow.

In front of us, a large iron gate barred the way to a spacious atrium lit by more chandeliers as well as lanterns along the walls. Above the gate hung a sign with some kind of ornate, scrolling characters that reminded me of the lettering in the ancient book Phaedrus was translating, and I shuddered as I wondered what dire warning or promise the sign contained. I imagined it foretold the horrors that lay ahead or urged prisoners to abandon any hope of leaving.

Grief hit me as I wondered what my father had thought when he'd first seen the sign upon entering the prison. Aramis had been a special case, one of the few prisoners to leave Revenmyer alive, and the only one Bressen ever knew of to leave it as a free man, absolved of his crimes. I couldn't imagine what he'd felt when he'd entered this room decades ago, knowing he'd spend the rest of his life here in the prison despite being innocent of the crime for which he'd been convicted.

I shuddered, and my body halted of its own accord in front of the sign. "What does it say?" I asked. I both did and didn't want to know, but I couldn't help asking.

"It says, 'Don't feed the demoni,'" Hettie answered.

I blinked at her. Her face was completely serious.

"What…what do demoni eat?" I asked.

"Nightmares," Hettie said, a smile crooking up her lips.

"So the sign is telling prisoners not to have nightmares?" I asked.

"I was told it said, 'Sleep soundly if you can,'" Bressen said. "Or 'if you dare.' It depends who you ask. Everyone seems to have their own theory about what it says. I should have Phaedrus translate it sometime to find out for sure."

"And spoil a good mystery, my lord?" Hettie said, sounding aghast. "Surely we're better off not knowing for certain."

Bressen frowned. "Why would we be better off not knowing?"

"Because right now it can say anything we want it to say," Hettie said. "It can be a warning, a threat, or a promise of eternal pain and suffering. If we don't know for certain, it can be all those things and more. If you translate it, you take away the enigma. Its uncertainty is what makes it frightening." She put her hands on her hips. "What if its real meaning is unbearably disappointing?"

Bressen raised a brow. "Disappointing how?"

Hettie turned a serious gaze on him. "My lord, for all you know, that's a recipe for soup hanging above the door."

I couldn't help the laugh that jumped up my throat, and I clamped a hand over my mouth to stifle any further sound. Hettie didn't take her eyes from Bressen, though, who was trying to suppress his own laughter.

"Now that you mention it," Bressen said, fighting back a smile, "Some of the writing does resemble the word for 'onion' in a text Phaedrus once showed me."

Hettie twirled her hand in a gesture that said, 'Well, there you go.'

I'm sorry I asked, I said into Bressen's mind, and his mouth twitched.

"I suppose we can let it remain a mystery for now," Bressen said. "Lead the way to Glenora please, Hettie."

Hettie turned and touched the iron gate, which swung open to admit her, and we followed. I jumped as the gate swung shut behind us with a resounding clang, but Bressen slipped his hand in mine and gave it a reassuring squeeze as Hettie led us across the huge atrium, then through a doorway and into the depths of the prison.

The stonework on the inside of the prison was just as ornate and impressive as it was on the outside, although the meager torchlight did little to illuminate the intricacies of its carvings. I leaned in to look closer, but I caught movement on the wall in my periphery and pulled up short.

"What is it, Cyra?" Bressen asked, stopping as well.

"I thought I saw something," I said as I examined the wall.

"You likely see the demoni," he said.

Just as the words left his lips, two red eyes blinked at me from within the wall, and a small gray face with sharp teeth emerged from the stone in a swirl of black smoke. I jumped back in surprise, but the creature melted into the wall again almost as quickly as it appeared.

"How…" I started to ask as another face appeared then disappeared into the wall a foot or so from where the first had been. Movement on my other side drew my attention back that way.

"Gods above," I whispered as I realized that the entire wall writhed with monstrous little faces that phased in and out of view before my eyes.

I stepped back quickly. "How do they do that?" I asked.

"The demoni exist in a state somewhere between phantasmal and corporeal," Bressen said. "They can move through shadow or smoke and become solid when they need to be. There are thousands of them hiding in these walls, waiting to be called forth, but it's unusual for them to show themselves so readily. I suspect they're intrigued to have a visitor."

As if in answer, several faces emerged out of the wall, red eyes glowing, only to retreat back into it a moment later.

I jumped as Hettie appeared next to me.

"Shoo! Go on now!" she said, waving her hand at the wall.

The space in front of me quivered as the demoni presumably scattered at her admonishment.

"Pests, the lot of them," Hettie said. "Worse than the rats."

She started walking again, and we followed, but now that I'd seen the demoni, I couldn't help noticing the way the walls rippled ahead. I turned to look behind us, and my stomach lurched to see them undulate as what seemed like a hundred demoni trailed along in our wake, their eyes flashing now and then as they poked their heads out to get a better look.

We came to a staircase, and Hettie began to climb. Again, we followed.

Up and up we climbed, passing landing after landing until my legs burned with the effort. I was just about to request a break when Hettie stepped out of the stairwell and started down a long corridor.

We were about halfway down the hall when I realized the clamor behind us was growing louder, and I shivered as needles pricked up my spine. I glanced behind me, then sucked in a gasp and grabbed Bressen's arm as my eyes widened in horror.

"Bressen!" I cried.

The entire corridor behind us was a mass of thrashing demoni, their eyes flickering like fiery red stars in the darkness. They came at us in a wave, a swell in a storm-tossed surf, and Bressen stepped in front of me ready to take the brunt of their crash. Dark bodies rolled over each other as they fought to get to us, and I braced for their impact, my hands gripping as tightly as I could to the back of Bressen's jacket.

Just as they reached us, the demoni dissipated, the wave that had threatened to break over us dissolving instead into a mist that wafted by.

I let out a soft whimper as cool curls of smoke brushed past on a gentle wind. My hair fluttered around my face and shoulders, and I looked up when the impact I'd been expecting never came.

Bressen turned and gathered me in his arms. I let out a deep breath as I buried my face in his chest and curled my hands in his jacket again.

"Are you alright?" he asked.

I let out another breath and nodded against him.

I couldn't help remembering the way the demoni had engulfed Glenora months ago, how I assumed they'd torn her to pieces until Bressen told me they'd only taken her here to Revenmyer. The demoni were frequent visitors in my nightmares when I had them, and my heart knocked in my chest as if it were asking to be let out.

I lifted my head and met Bressen's eyes. His expression was full of concern, and I tried to smile at him.

"I'm fine," I said. "I…they just brought back memories of Gendris."

The day we'd both almost been killed. The day I'd almost lost Bressen to his darkness.

I stepped away from Bressen, but he kept an arm around my waist as I turned to find Hettie watching me with interest.

"I'm sorry," I said to her. "They're just a little unnerving."

"What's wrong with the demoni today?" Bressen asked Hettie, his arm still holding me. "They're not usually this…rambunctious."

Hettie held my gaze another moment before looking at Bressen. "They know who she is," she said.

Bressen stiffened and drew an arm across my shoulders to pull me protectively against him.

"And who do you think she is?" he asked her. There was a growl of warning in his voice.

Hettie only blinked as if the answer was obvious. "She belongs to the Nemesis," she said, nodding her head at me.

I inhaled sharply. How did she know?

"She belongs to *me*," Bressen corrected her coldly, and I knew his eyes had flashed red like those of the demoni.

My stomach flipped at the dominance and possessiveness in his voice, and I knew he'd claim me when we returned home. He'd accepted his penance last night – sort of – but I knew he ached to remind me that I was his, and the muscles at my core pulsed in anticipation.

Hettie only smiled indulgently at Bressen. "Of course, my lord."

Bressen's arm tightened around me as Hettie turned and continued down the hall. She stopped in front of a door almost at the end and pulled a ring of keys from her pocket. She unlocked the door, opened it, then looked back down the corridor to where Bressen and I still stood, his arm tensed across my shoulders.

Bressen let his arm slip back to his side, and he stepped around me to stride down the corridor to Hettie. I hurried after him but nearly ran into his back as he stopped abruptly before her.

"Take care that you never share that observation with anyone else," Bressen said to her, and there was something ominous in his voice.

His back was to me, so I had no idea what Hettie saw in his expression, but for the first time since we arrived, fear crossed her face as she looked up at him. It was gone a moment later.

"No, my lord," she said, all levity gone. "Of course not."

Bressen turned back to me, and I stepped toward the cell Hettie had opened. He grasped my arm to stop me before I entered.

"The cell is lined with caronium," he reminded me. "I'll lose my powers when we step in."

I nodded my understanding. He'd lose his powers, but I wouldn't lose mine. I was immune to caronium, I assumed, because I was a syphon.

"Are you sure?" Bressen asked me.

"Yes."

He hesitated, then moved aside so I could enter. I stepped past him and got my first glimpse in months of the woman who'd drugged me, kidnapped my family, and nearly killed both me and Bressen.

I wasn't sure what I'd been expecting, but it certainly wasn't this.

Chapter 5

Cyra

The Lady of Polaris I'd met months ago in Callanus had been stately and poised, her hair always neatly coiffed, her clothes ornate and immaculate. She'd been every bit the wife of a Triumvirate lord.

The Glenora before me now sat barefoot and cross-legged on the floor of her prison cell in a high-waisted gown that stretched over her pregnant belly. The skirt bunched around her legs, wrinkled and a bit torn in places, but at least clean. Her hair was still done up in her usual style, but where previously there hadn't been a lock out of place, strands had come loose all over so they formed a wispy halo around her head.

I stood in the doorway and waited for her to acknowledge our presence, but she didn't look up as she pantomimed moving things around on the floor.

"Glenora," I said, willing my voice to remain steady as I stepped in.

She didn't give any indication she'd heard me, and I opened my mouth to try again, but Hettie held up a hand and stepped forward.

"My lady, you have visitors," she said gently to Glenora.

I blinked and looked at Bressen, but he hadn't yet taken his eyes off the former lady.

Glenora's head popped up at Hettie's voice.

"Very good, Hettie," Glenora said. "They're just in time for tea. Please show them in."

She went back to pantomiming what I now realized was preparing a cup of tea. Indeed, she brought the imaginary cup to her lips for a sip.

"Lady Glenora takes tea every day at this time," Hettie explained. "If you want to talk to her, you'll have to sit down and pretend. Otherwise you'll need to wait an hour until she's done, or she won't speak to you."

"What?" I asked. "Can't you make her speak to us? She's a prisoner here, is she not?"

I was annoyed by Hettie's careful treatment of Glenora, but it was Bressen who answered me.

"We've needed to be careful of how we treat Glenora until the baby comes. As you can see, her mental state is a bit precarious right now."

"You're sure she's not feigning it?" I asked.

He nodded. "I checked her mind myself. She has only a tenuous grasp on reality that comes and goes."

"The tea is getting cold," Glenora said from the floor without looking up. She lifted a pretend spoon and stirred her tea before bringing the phantom cup to her lips.

I turned to Bressen, but he gave me a look that asked what I was waiting for. I frowned.

If I have to have tea with Glenora, then so do you, I said into his mind.

He gave me a mournful look, but I flashed one back that promised no reprieve. I read his response in his mind.

You're a cruel woman, he said as we both crouched down to sit cross-legged on the floor in front of Glenora.

As soon as we were seated, Glenora raised her head, and a wide smile split her face. "Cyra, it's good to see you again, my dear. I'm glad you could join me. You prefer the cinnamon tea if I remember correctly."

She looked me straight in the eye, and her sudden rapt attention was unnerving. I leaned back away from her.

"Probably because it smells like your lord," she added, winking.

I glanced at Bressen, but he only frowned and turned his head to give his shoulder a quick sniff.

"And what about you, my lord?" Glenora asked, turning her gaze on Bressen. "How do you take your tea? Light…or dark?"

"No tea for me," Bressen said. "I'm just here for the cakes."

He reached out and pretended to pluck a cake off a plate before popping the nonexistent dessert in his mouth.

Glenora gave him a small smile. "The Nemesis Incarnate has a sweet tooth," she said, then cocked her head at him. "That is still what they call you, isn't it?"

Her eyes returned to me as she held out an invisible cup, and something churned in my stomach. I took it but stopped before sipping.

"The tea isn't drugged this time, is it?" I asked her coolly. I held her stare, but I felt Bressen's attention snap to me.

I'd told him before how Glenora had lured me into drinking tea that had been drugged the day of the coup, but I had a feeling he'd forgotten.

Glenora chuckled, and my hackles rose.

"It's perfectly safe to drink," she said, taking another sip of her own tea. "I'd be more worried about what's not in your tea than what's in it."

I narrowed my eyes. "What does that mean?"

She shrugged and gestured toward Bressen.

"This one looks eager to put a baby in your belly," she said, patting her own rounded stomach. "It's what men do. I'd check your morning tea from now on to be sure the contraceptive berries are still in it."

I looked at Bressen in alarm, but he furrowed his brows and shook his head the barest amount. I saw in his expression he wanted me to read his mind, so I did.

Cyra, don't listen to her. She's trying to throw you off-balance. You know I'd never do anything of the kind. We need to regain control of this conversation, he said.

"Tell me, child," Glenora went on, "how many times a day do you let him fuck that cunt of yours?"

My mouth dropped open, partially at her language and partially at the audacity of the question.

"I used to let Jerram fuck me at least once a day to keep him pliable," she said before sipping delicately from her cup. She sighed. "Then at night I'd have Ursan grunting above me trying to make an heir. It's a wonder I could close my legs properly between the two of them."

Glenora shifted as if trying to find a more comfortable position. She had a chair and table in the cell, so I wasn't sure why she'd chosen the floor for her tea party.

"It's a lady's job to make an heir, you know, so I wasn't allowed a contraceptive," she went on as she patted her belly. "Or so Ursan said. But that means we don't know whose spawn I'm carrying. It's probably Jerram's, since two-hundred childless years of marriage with Ursan would suggest the man was impotent, but there's always a slim chance one of his seeds finally bore fruit." She looked between me and Bressen and smiled. "I hope that hasn't caused any problems for the Triumvirate."

We didn't answer.

Her eyes sought mine again, and I frowned at the gleam in them.

"Does your lord know you fucked the gargoyle as well?" she asked, and I started in surprise at her pivot.

"I realized it as soon as Samhail came out of that portal in Gendris," she said. "That's when I knew Jerram had been right about you taking the beast between your legs as well."

The fiendish look in her eyes intensified as her gaze swung to Bressen. "Did you know, my lord, that your dearest love was fucking your best friend?" she asked as triumph dripped from her words.

Bressen looked bored, but then he gave an exaggerated jolt of indignation and turned to me.

"How dare you," he said to me, and his blasé tone mimicked his bored expression. "You slut. You whore. You…" He rolled a hand in the air to indicate he was too lazy to think of other offensive names.

Glenora looked from Bressen to me, obviously disappointed her attempt to upset him hadn't worked.

"You don't believe me," she concluded.

"I believe you. I just don't care," he assured her. His gaze swung to me as it turned sultry. "I happen to think Cyra looked beautiful taking Samhail's giant cock inside her. I love watching her fall apart with pleasure when she's being fucked well."

Heat pooled between my legs at the look in his eyes, but my attention jumped back to Glenora as she barked a short, mirthless laugh. Her expression turned sour as she looked me over through new eyes.

"You're more of a whore than I gave you credit for," she said. "Just remember that's all you are to them. A broodmare with a soft hole to warm their cocks."

I decided not to point out her hypocrisy of calling me a whore after she'd cheated on Ursan with his fellow Triumvirate lord, but Bressen didn't seem to have any such restraint. I caught the flash in his eyes and heard him inhale as he readied to lay into Glenora.

"Do you know a woman named Magdalene?" I asked, cutting him off.

Bressen froze, and Glenora stopped with her next sip of tea poised in the air.

"I can't say I do," she said as she finished miming the sip.

"You're lying," I said as her skin emitted a soft red glow almost immediately. "When was the last time you saw her?"

Glenora only sipped her tea.

"Answer me, or I'll pry open your mind and find the answer myself," I warned.

"Cyra," Bressen cautioned me.

We'd discussed the possibility of just reading Glenora's mind to find what we wanted to know, but Bressen had warned she was fragile right now. He'd already been in her mind once, but multiple incursions, even without her shield up might be dangerous. Had Glenora not been pregnant, we wouldn't have thought twice about rooting around in her thoughts, but given her condition, we'd agreed that invading her mind would be a last resort if she wouldn't give us what we wanted.

I shifted tactics.

"Answer our questions and we'll grant you a favor," I told Glenora.

Bressen looked at me sharply, and I knew he wanted me to read his mind again. I didn't this time.

Glenora looked up, intrigued. "A favor?"

"Yes."

"Anything I want?"

"So long as it's within my power," I qualified. "Or Bressen's."

I saw out of the corner of my eye Bressen was barely holding in his comment. He was still hoping I'd read his mind, but I knew what he wanted to say, and I didn't care. I'd promise Glenora anything to get to Magdalene.

Glenora paused, not sure whether to believe me, but the fact Bressen was nearly vibrating next to me seemed to convince her.

"I want a Triumvirate seat," she said.

I deflated. There was no way I could promise her that.

"Glenora, I…that's not possible," I said quietly. "You're never leaving Revenmyer."

Glenora shook her head. "Not for me," she clarified as she put a hand on her belly to rub slow circles over it. "For my child. Regardless of who its father is, this baby has a claim to a Triumvirate seat, either that of Polaris or Derridan. Promise me my child will one day rule as part of the Triumvirate, and I'll tell you everything you want to know."

"Not a chance," Bressen said, finally breaking his silence. "For one, if the child is Jerram's-"

"Done," I said, cutting him off. "If you tell us honestly everything you know about Magdalene and Sandrian and what they're up to, I'll make sure your child sits in a Triumvirate seat."

Glenora narrowed her eyes. "You'll make sure my child *holds* a Triumvirate seat as ruler," she specified.

"That's what I said."

"No, it's not," she argued. "You gave yourself a loophole. Sitting in a Triumvirate seat is not the same as ruling from one."

I looked at Bressen pointedly. *Her mind seems just fine to me*, I said into his head.

She has moments of lucidity, he said. *Don't mistake them for sanity.*

"Fine," I said, turning back to Glenora. "I promise your child will one day hold the Triumvirate seat of either Polaris or Derridan. In exchange, you'll answer our questions, truthfully, and in full."

"Cyra!" Bressen said. "You don't have the authority to promise that!"

"But you do, and you will," I said.

"No, I don't," he said getting to his feet. "I have no authority to tell Polaris or Derridan who to appoint as rulers. If I did, Polaris would already-," he cut himself off this time, realizing he'd said too much. Instead he went on, "I can make suggestions or use whatever influence I have to sway them to a course, but I can't dictate something like that. That's the whole point of the Triumvirate."

I thought for a moment before I turned back to Glenora.

"I promise your child will one day hold the Triumvirate seat of either Polaris or Derridan. In exchange, you'll answer our questions, truthfully, and in full," I repeated, ignoring everything Bressen had said. "If you lie to me, the deal is off, and I'll make sure your child never gets near a Triumvirate seat."

I knew Bressen's eyes were glowing like embers right now. I felt the fury pouring off him, but that's what I needed.

"Do you believe I can make this happen for your child?" I pressed.

Glenora considered me. Her eyes flicked to Bressen then came back to mine. "Yes," she said.

"So you'll answer my questions then?"

"Yes."

"The truth, or the deal is off."

Glenora gave me a sad smile. "Everyone always thinks they want the truth until they have it. Then they realize they would've been happier with a pretty lie. I know that better than anyone."

She took a sip of her tea. "You probably still think your ability to always see the truth is a benefit," she went on. "But trust me, after a few decades, you'll wish you couldn't see the lies. It's much nicer to believe him when he tells you he loves you. Much simpler just to take his words at face value than to twist your mind into knots picking apart his carefully phrased explanations of where he's been when he comes to bed late."

Glenora gave me a wistful look. "Sometimes the lie is just kinder."

Despite myself, I felt a pang of sympathy for her. Ursan had cheated on her with her own lady's maid, Raina's mother, and it was clear she'd known about it for longer than she'd let on. Ursan hadn't deserved to die for his indiscretions, nor for his constantly dismissive treatment of Glenora, but I could at least see how his actions had helped warp her. Perhaps Glenora had always had it in her to be the villain she'd become, or perhaps two centuries of dealing with Ursan had gradually eaten away at her until she was raw with resentment.

I steeled myself. "Nevertheless, I'll have the truth from you now."

Glenora nodded.

"Then tell me the last time you saw Magdalene," I said.

Her stare was penetrating as she looked at me for a long time, imaginary teacup poised in the air near her chest. Her eyes flicked to Bressen, and I swore I saw the hint of a smile before she spoke.

"The Harmilan," she said.

My brows furrowed. "The Harmilan?"

"Yes," Glenora said. "I last saw Magdalene on the Harmilan. She's one of the ladies I get…got together with that day each year."

I remembered Glenora telling me she usually spent the day of the Harmilan with a group of lady friends, but I couldn't believe Magdalene had been one of them this whole time.

"How long have you known her?" I asked.

Glenora shrugged before adding a couple cubes of invisible sugar to her cup. "Thirty or so years, I suppose."

I let out a breath. She'd known Magdalene during the time Clarice had held Axenus, and I couldn't help but wonder if she'd used him as well.

"And you helped her break Sandrian out of prison?" I asked.

"No, she'd already broken him out by then."

I thought for a moment. That tracked. I'd overheard Bressen tell Samhail that Sandrian had escaped well before the Harmilan.

"Did you see Magdalene before then?" I asked. "Did you tell her I'd be out riding with Ursan that day we were attacked?"

Glenora poured herself another cup of tea, and I fought to keep from grinding my teeth. I forced myself to wait patiently as she prepared her cup, even going so far as to pass her what I assumed was the cream.

"Yes," Glenora said finally. "Magdalene contacted me shortly after you arrived at the Citadel. She said she needed you for something, and if the occasion ever arose for her to get you away from Callanus, she asked me to contact her. She didn't say why she wanted you, but you were nothing to me, so I didn't ask. When Ursan offered to take you riding that day, I saw my chance to be rid of you both. I contacted Magdalene and told her where you'd be. In exchange, I asked her to be sure Ursan never made it back to Callanus."

Glenora turned a scowl on Bressen. "Unfortunately, this one and the gargoyle somehow learned you were in trouble and arrived in time to save both you and my husband."

It hurt more than I thought to hear Glenora admit I was nothing to her. There'd been a brief time in those first couple weeks at the Citadel that I'd actually liked the lady and felt sorry for the way Ursan treated her.

"What does Magdalene want with me?"

"I told you, I don't know," she said, giving her tea a stir. "I didn't ask, and she didn't offer."

I eyed her closely, but her skin remained pale.

"Did you know Magdalene was a syphon?" I asked.

Glenora's head snapped up, and I now had her full attention.

"Magdalene is a what?" she asked.

I felt a small sense of triumph at having surprised her. "She's a syphon like me. What did you think she was?" I asked.

"I…don't know," Glenora said. "We didn't use our powers much whenever we met. I suppose I thought she was an elemental."

"Why did Magdalene break Sandrian out of prison?" I asked.

Anger flashed across Glenora's face, and she took a sip of her tea to buy herself a moment as I'd once done with a real cup of tea.

"I don't know," she said finally. "Presumably it's nothing I can help with since I'm still here."

I almost laughed. Glenora was bitter her friend hadn't broken her out of Revenmyer as she had Sandrian.

I sobered as I remembered Magdalene could still get into the prison anytime she wanted. Bressen and I really needed to find a way to replace the wards. Perhaps I could add a layer of my own wards on top of the ones currently here.

"Cyra, let's go," Bressen said from behind me. "It's clear she doesn't know anything else useful." There was still an edge to his voice.

"Do you know anything else about Magdalene or Sandrian we'd want to know?" I asked Glenora pointedly.

She considered for a moment.

"Magdalene has always struck me as…ambitious," she said. "But not overtly so. I don't doubt Sandrian hopes to retake Rowe and probably conquer Thasia as well, and I'm sure he thinks Magdalene plans to help him. She's not that magnanimous. If she went through the trouble to break him out of here, she needs him for something."

We already suspected as much, but it was good to get confirmation.

I rose from where I sat, and Glenora looked up at me in alarm.

"You're leaving already?" she asked. "There's still much to discuss."

I stopped. "Like what? Do you have more information about Magdalene and Sandrian?"

Glenora waved a dismissive hand. "No, not them. How is my stepdaughter doing?"

I furrowed my brows. "Stepdaughter?"

She nodded. "Yes, Reena…Your lady's maid," she prompted when I continued to frown at her.

Understanding dawned. Raina. She meant Raina.

"She's none of your concern," I said as I turned toward the door.

"Has she spoken to her mother recently?" Glenora asked, and my insides went cold. I swung back around. "Why? What do you know of

Raina's mother?"

Glenora didn't bother to hide her smile as she shrugged. "I know her mother was fucking my husband behind my back, all while serving me as my lady's maid. I hope you're able to trust your friend more than I was able to trust her mother."

"Did you do something to Raina's mother?" I asked. "Where is she?"

"I never touched the woman," Glenora answered. "How am I supposed to know where she is right now?"

"Those are evasions. Tell me what you know!"

My eyes must have flared red because Glenora's own eyes widened, and she lurched back across the floor.

"You...," she said. "You're...you can't be."

"Tell me what you know," I repeated. "We had a deal."

Slowly the fear left Glenora's face, and her smile returned.

"Our deal was that I'd tell you anything you wanted to know about Magdalene and Sandrian," she said. "Raina's mother wasn't part of it."

I raised a hand toward Glenora – intending to do what, I wasn't sure – but Bressen was at my side a second later, pressing my hand back down.

"Cyra, let's go," he said. "We'll find out what we can about Raina's mother on our own."

Bressen slipped his arm around my waist and turned me back toward the door. I let him steer me until Glenora's voice once again rose from the floor, this time in song.

"Though it waxes and wanes among the stars,
We feel its tug, a tether between our souls.
A beacon in the dark, a promise kept
To find each other and again be whole..."

I jerked around again to look at her. "How do you know that song?" I asked, pulling out of Bressen's hold to stalk toward Glenora.

My heart thudded in my chest as I loomed above her.

"It's just something I picked up," she said. "Do you like it?"

"Cyra?" Bressen said. He was next to me again. He curled his hand around my arm, urging me back toward the door, but I didn't move as I stared down Glenora.

She hummed as she went back to preparing another cup of tea. I started to question her again, but Bressen gave my arm a gentle tug, and I let him lead me away.

Glenora's voice rose again as I crossed the threshold, and her song followed me out the door.

"Though it sets each eve, closing out the day,
We trust its rise again upon the morn..."

Chapter 6

Cyra

"Cyra, what's wrong?" Bressen asked as Hettie closed the door to the cell behind us, cutting off Glenora. "Do you know that song?"

For a moment I couldn't answer. That song had always brought me comfort, but to hear it from Glenora's lips made me cold inside.

"My mother used to sing it to us when I was little," I said quietly, "then Jaylan sang it to me and Brix after she died."

Bressen's face softened, and he pulled me into his arms. I still felt his anger at what I'd done, but he set it aside as he laid his head on mine.

"Is it a common song?" he asked. "Would she have heard it somewhere?"

"I'm not sure," I said. "I've only ever heard my mother and Jaylan sing it, but Fernweh was just a small town. I have no idea if it was well-known elsewhere."

I pulled back away from him again and willed myself not to cry. I couldn't let Glenora ruin that memory for me.

"Cyra," Bressen said sternly as I looked up at him. "You shouldn't-"

"You played your part perfectly," I said before he could scold me.

He frowned at me before understanding dawned on him a moment later. "You baited me on purpose," he said.

"I'm sorry. I had to," I said. "I realized that, more than her child in the Triumvirate, Glenora wanted to sow discord between you and me. She tipped her hand when she tried to upset you by telling you about me and Samhail. You saw how disappointed she was when you didn't react. I figured I could use that, that she'd be more likely to make a deal with me if she thought it would make you angry and drive a wedge between us. But for it to work, she needed to believe you were furious."

"It was a good plan," he admitted, "but the fact remains that neither you nor I have the power to grant Glenora's request."

"I never had any intention of granting it," I said. "The woman drugged me, tried to kill you, and threatened to kill my family. I feel no obligation to honor any promises I made to her."

Bressen stared at me. "You lied to her?"

I shrugged. "Maybe Glenora is right, and a pretty lie is sometimes kinder. We got some information, and she gets to believe her child will one day help rule Thasia."

I couldn't tell if the look on Bressen's face meant he was impressed or horrified. He opened his mouth to speak, but something snagged his attention behind me, and I turned to see what he was looking at.

A middle-aged looking man with blue hair walked toward us. He had a neatly trimmed beard and mustache – also blue – and he was around my height. He wore a long tunic over his pants that came down almost to his knees, but it was a much more subdued shade of dark blue than Hettie's bright arrayment.

"My lord, I heard you were here," the man said brightly as he walked purposely down the hall toward us.

Behind him, the wall writhed with demoni as they rolled behind him in his wake, their red eyes flickering in and out.

"Have you come to show off our most infamous prisoner to…your lady friend?" the man guessed as he looked me up and down. He smiled, apparently liking what he saw.

"Effram, this is Lady Cyra of Hiraeth. My wife," Bressen said, and I heard the possessiveness return to his voice. "Cyra, this is Effram. He's one of our dream walkers."

My gaze snapped to Effram, suddenly more interested in him. He too was more interested in me after hearing Bressen introduce me as his wife.

"You're a dream walker," I said to him.

"I am," he said. "And you are…let me guess."

Effram let his eyes travel up and down me again, and I raised a brow at him. Had he really not heard what I was by now?

Effram doesn't leave Revenmyer much, Bressen said into my head, and I jumped, having forgotten he had his power back now that we were outside Glenora's cell.

"Fire elemental," Effram guessed, stroking his beard contemplatively.

I held out a hand, palm up, and let a flame burst to life in it.

"It looks like you're right," I said.

I closed my palm to snuff out the flame, then reached for one of the torches on the wall. As soon as I touched the handle, it turned to flower petals that fluttered to the floor. The flame of the torch itself remained burning in mid-air, fueled by my magic.

There was a rustle like autumn leaves in the wind as the demoni stirred within the walls. They surfaced like sea creatures above water before they sunk back into the stone.

I ported behind Effram and saw him start in surprise as I disappeared before his eyes. He swung around as I tapped his shoulder, and his mouth hung open in shock.

"Or maybe you're not right," I said.

"How…," Effram started to ask, but Bressen satisfied his curiosity.

"You really should get out of Revenmyer more, Effram," Bressen said. "If you did, you'd know my wife is a syphon."

Effram's jaw fell open even farther. "A syphon," he breathed as his eyes ran up and down me yet again.

"Her mother was a dream walker like you," Bressen added.

Effram continued to stare, and his scrutiny began to unnerve me.

"Effram," Bressen said, bringing the man's attention back to him.

"My lord," the man said, tearing his eyes from me.

"Have you been in Lady Glenora's dreams lately?" Bressen asked.

"No, my lord. I thought we were leaving the lady alone while she's with child."

"Yes, but I'd like you to go into them from now on as often as you dare. That should be a relatively safe way to get into her mind without disturbing her or the child."

"Of course, my lord."

"I'll be by every couple days to check in with you and see if you've discovered anything," Bressen said. "Don't influence her dreams. Just observe and report back to me."

"Yes, my lord." Effram gave a small bow.

"You can influence dreams," I said to Effram, catching Bressen's suggestion. Axenus had told me I could likely do so myself, but we had yet to try practicing it.

Effram turned his attention back to me. "Of course, my lady."

"How do you do it?" I asked. "I'm still learning my powers, and I haven't done much with that one yet."

Effram shrugged. "It's simple enough," he said. "When you're inside someone else's dream, you're in control. You can simply watch, or you can make them experience whatever you will. It works the same way your mind magic does when you're trying to compel someone." He glanced at Bressen. "I assume you have the lord's mind magic if you're a syphon?"

"Yes," I confirmed.

Effram smiled. "Of course you would." He paused. "Has Lord Bressen given you a tour of the prison?"

"Cyra, we should get going," Bressen said, and I heard an edge of urgency in his voice. He wanted to get me away from Effram.

"Leaving so soon?" Effram asked, disappointed.

"We were just here to see Glenora," Bressen said, his voice hardening.

"How was your visit?" Effram asked, his attention still fixed on me.

Bressen stepped closer to me, but if he was trying to get Effram's attention, it didn't work. The man's eyes didn't move from my face.

"She seems to have gone a bit mad since I last saw her," I said.

Effram's head lolled to the side as a wide, slightly unnerving grin spread across his face. "My lady," he said, "we all go a little mad in here."

I didn't doubt that as I looked at him.

Bressen cleared his throat, and Effram finally looked at him.

"My lord, have you shown her some of our other prisoners?" the dream walker asked, and I blinked at the delight in his voice. Revenmyer seemed less a prison to him and more a menagerie of inmates he could show off.

"We don't have time for that now," Bressen said. "We need to get back to Solandis."

I didn't understand the urgency in Bressen's tone until the reason he wanted to leave hit me a second later.

I turned to him. "Clarice is here."

His shoulders dropped as I realized what he'd been hoping I wouldn't.

"Yes," he said, "but we don't have time to see her."

"Of course we do," I said. "There's nothing pressing we need to do back home."

"I assure you, I have plenty of pressing matters," he said, "and you have lots to do at the vineyard."

I paused. There was in fact quite a bit I needed to do at the vineyard, but we were here, and I wasn't going to pass up this chance to see Clarice.

I turned to Effram. "Please lead the way to Clarice's cell," I told him.

He grinned. "A very good choice-," Effram started to say, but Bressen cut him off.

"Cyra, no. We're leaving," he said. His eyes flashed red as he glared at Effram who, for his own part, seemed oblivious.

"This way, my lady," Effram said as he strode past us down the hall the way he'd been going.

Bressen growled behind me as I followed Effram.

"I told you to melt his mind when you had the chance, my lord," Hettie said to Bressen as I passed. "He thinks he's immune to your will."

"Not now, Hettie," Bressen admonished as he caught up to me. His hand wrapped firmly around my upper arm as we walked.

One minute and then we're leaving, he said into my mind. *Promise me you won't do anything. I will stop you if I have to, so please don't make me.*

It was a warning that he'd break into my mind as he had in Fernweh if he felt he needed to. He'd lose his power when he entered Clarice's cell, but he had only to step outside again to get it back, and he could definitely stop me. I'd been practicing my mind powers with him every chance we got, but I had yet to put up a shield he couldn't get past.

I nodded. *I won't do anything to her. I promise. I just need to see her.*

Bressen let out a deep breath.

Effram came to the stairwell at the other end of the hall and began to descend while we followed. The walls continued to ripple with demoni as we went, although the creatures seemed to have settled somewhat.

"I haven't seen the demoni quite this active in a while," Bressen said softly. "They do seem fascinated with you."

I wasn't sure whether to feel flattered or disturbed by that.

I lost count of how many flights of stairs we descended, and I was beginning to get dizzy when Effram finally exited into a hallway. He stopped at the first door on the right and pulled a pair of keys from his pocket to open it.

"My Lady, the former Queen of Sedonia," he said with a flourish as he pushed open the door.

The cell was darker than Glenora's as I stepped inside, and my eyes struggled to adjust. Being on a higher floor, Glenora at least had a window, for better or for worse, and I wondered if we'd descended far enough that we were now below ground. Only a single lantern lit the room, and I searched the shadows for Clarice.

I heard the soft scrape of shoes on stone, and a woman emerged from a corner, stepping forward sensually as if she were prowling toward a lover. The dress she wore clung to her body, and it had been ripped up the sides and down the front to reveal more of her legs and cleavage.

Clarice was tall, as I'd seen her in Axenus's dream, but her long brown hair was gone, cropped roughly so only uneven patches of it remained on her head. She still wore the heavy makeup I'd seen before, but it was muddled at best. Her dark lipstick was smudged down the side of her mouth, and the shadow applied around her eyes had been rubbed into wide circles so it looked like she had two black eyes. The circles were broken in a couple places where tears had run down her face and taken some of the color with them to stripe her cheeks with dark rivulets.

"Lord Bressen," she purred, heading straight for him. "I've been waiting for you. Have you come to take me up on my offer?"

She dropped to her knees in front of him and grabbed for the front of his pants to begin undoing them.

"You won't regret this," she said, her voice eager. "You can use me however you want. I promise I'll make you happy."

Bressen made a noise of disgust and grabbed her hands to stop them from clawing at his pants. He pushed her away and stepped back.

"Have you seen enough?" he asked me.

I couldn't tear my eyes from the woman. "What happened to her hair?" I asked no one in particular.

"She cut it," Hettie answered.

My attention jerked to Hettie. "She did that to herself? With what?"

"With a pair of scissors," Hettie said.

"Where did she get scissors?"

"We gave them to her. The inmates are all under a compulsion not to hurt themselves, so when she said she wanted to cut her hair, we gave her a pair of scissors."

I blinked. "And her makeup? The rips in her dress?"

"Her own doing as well," Hettie said.

"Are you sure about that?" Bressen asked, anger in his voice. "None of the guards have been taking Clarice up on her 'offers?'"

Effram and Hettie looked at each other, suddenly not so certain.

"I...I don't believe so, my lord," Hettie answered after a moment.

"Find out for sure," he told her coldly, "and if you discover anyone who's been abusing their authority, let me know immediately."

"Yes, my lord," both Hettie and Effram said together.

Clarice's shriek brought our attention back to her as she retreated across the room to her corner.

"Keep them away!" she screamed, cowering back. "Keep them away!"

There was a faint red glow on her skin I assumed was an indication of a lie at first, but then I realized the entire room had taken on a gentle red glow from the hundreds of demoni eyes that now peered from the walls. Their faces and heads emerged slowly from the stone as they drifted toward Clarice.

I let out a scream of my own when something closed around my ankle, and I looked down to find demoni emerging from the floor as well. One small creature had grabbed my ankle over my skirt to pull itself from the stone, and it now sat on top of my shoe, holding onto me as if it meant to hitch a ride while I walked.

"Go away!" Clarice screamed. "Make them go away!"

She shrunk back into the corner as far as she could while the demoni closed in, reaching for her. She kicked out at one that got too close, but it grabbed her foot and began to scurry up her leg. She shrieked again, and Bressen stepped forward.

"Enough!" he said, and all the demoni froze in place.

I hadn't realized how loud their shuffling and shifting had grown until they all stopped moving and the cell once again became dead silent.

I also hadn't realized just how eager I'd been to see what the creatures would do to Clarice until Bressen stopped them.

"Out. All of you," Bressen said. "Go play somewhere else."

A noise that almost resembled a collective groan of disappointment sounded as the shuffling resumed, and the demoni melted back into the walls and floor. Their eyes flickered out to leave the room once again in the glow of the sole lantern on the wall.

A persistent pressure on the top of my foot caught my attention, and I looked down to find the little demoni from before, one of the smallest I'd seen, still sitting there. It blinked up at me, and I was surprised to see one of its eyes blink about half a second after the other.

"That one seems to have taken a liking to you, my lady," Effram said.

My answer was replaced by a squeal of surprise as the demoni scrambled up my leg and then up the side of my torso before it perched itself on my shoulder. I shivered from the feel of its little claws catching on my clothes and digging into my skin as it climbed.

"Cyra, are you alright?" Bressen asked me as he stepped forward.

"I...yes, I think so," I said, keeping my body still. I was afraid to startle the thing or accidentally knock it off my shoulder. I wasn't sure if it would try to claw me, either to stay on or in retaliation.

"Leave," Bressen said, glaring at the demoni on my shoulder.

A look of surprise crossed his face as the creature must've blinked its uneven blink at him. The demoni didn't move, though.

"I said go. Now," Bressen told it in a voice he reserved for when he wanted to intimidate someone.

I shivered again as the creature only wrapped its hand in my hair in a show of defiance.

"Fascinating," Hettie breathed as she watched.

Bressen stepped forward, possibly intending to pull the demoni off me, but I held up a hand to stop him.

"It's fine," I said. "It can stay for now."

"No, it can't," Bressen said. "It needs to remember who its master is."

"If you'll forgive me for saying so, my lord," Hettie said carefully, "I'm not sure this one considers you its master anymore."

A moment of stunned silence passed between us before Bressen's eyes flashed red.

"The three hells I'm not!" he said. He took another step, but I stepped back this time.

"Please," I said to him. "Just let it stay." I wasn't sure why I was making an exception for this creature when the demoni as a whole unnerved me so much, but something about its odd asynchronous blink seemed almost...endearing.

Bressen's jaw clenched tightly as he looked at me.

"It's time to go," he said finally, and this time my shiver had nothing to do with the demoni clinging to my hair. Everything about Bressen's tone and the way he looked told me he'd hit the limit of his patience. There was a glint in his eye that said he planned to fuck me hard when we got home, but far from frightening me, I went slick between my legs.

The demoni shifted on my shoulder.

"Yes, let's go," I said, and I turned to leave the cell.

Bressen, Hettie, and Effram followed me out into the hall, and Effram relocked Clarice's cell behind him.

"Are you sure you don't want to show your lady the gargoyle wing before you leave, my lord?" Effram asked.

"Gargoyle wing?" I asked in surprise, and Bressen glared at Effram.

"We're leaving," Bressen said, and even Effram pulled back at the venom in his voice.

We returned to the main hall in silence, the little demoni riding on my shoulder the whole time. When we reached the front atrium, Bressen turned again to Effram and Hettie.

"We need to reinforce the wards on the prison," he told them. "The woman who broke through them last time is a syphon, and she can get through them again. We'll have to put extra protections in place in case she returns. I'll check in with the Priory to see who they have for warders, and then I'll be back tomorrow. I know they have at least one. In the meantime, Cyra will put up an extra layer before we leave."

He looked at me expectantly.

"The wards I put up won't be very powerful," I said to Effram and Hettie. "They'll break down quickly under a powerful attack, but they'll at least give you advanced warning so you'll have a little time to prepare." I turned to Bressen. "Who should have access to get through them?"

"For now, just me and Hettie," he said. He looked at her. "You'll need to let everyone else in and out of Cyra's wards. It's not ideal, but we can't take the chance of anyone or anything else getting out."

"Any*thing*?" I asked.

"Most of Revenmyer's inmates are human or demi-human," Bressen explained, "but there are some exceptions."

"We'll await your return," Hettie said to him. She turned her attention to the little creature on my shoulder. "Shoo. It's time for you to go."

The demoni hesitated a moment, then launched itself off my shoulder toward the wall where it was absorbed into the stone in a swirl of smoke.

Bressen's arm stole around my waist, and he pulled me against him. His breath tickled my ear as he whispered against it. "Put up the wards and draw us a portal home please," he said. "We have some things we need to…discuss."

Chapter 7

Cyra

I closed the portal behind us back in Bressen's study at Tide's End and turned to him.

"I'm not sure we learned anything all that helpful," I said. "Do you think Glenora was bluffing about Raina's mother? We should see if we can find her, just to be sure."

Bressen stood perfectly still as he looked at me, and I was taken aback by the intensity in his eyes.

I furrowed my brow. "Bressen? Are you-," I started to say.

"Run," he said softly.

I blinked at him. "What?"

"Run now, Cyra, because I have the urge to fuck you like I've never fucked you before, and I'm not sure you're going to like it."

My breath caught in my throat, and every muscle in my lower body tightened in anticipation. I started to smile and took a step toward him, but he held up a hand to stop me.

"You need to run," he repeated. "I have no control right now. If I take you, I may hurt you, so go. Run and hide, and maybe – just maybe – I'll have calmed down enough by the time I catch you that you won't hate me when I'm done."

I stood stunned. He was serious. He was actually afraid he'd hurt me.

When Bressen was angry, he needed to work through his rage, to let it blaze hotly and then burn out. Several times in the past, I'd let him use my body to vent his frustrations. I didn't mind my sex on the rougher side, so I liked when Bressen took me hard and fast, pounding into me as he let his anger turn to carnal lust and release itself with his climax. Those times teetered on the brink between pleasure and pain for me, but it made me feel useful to push Bressen through his anger.

I was the opposite. When I was angry, my rage or frustration needed to be smothered and tamed. My anger only fanned itself if I let my passion go. Rather than blazing and flaming out as Bressen did, I only burned more furiously until I nearly exploded. In the days after Aramis's death, Bressen had tried to let me vent my anger in the same way we did for him, but rougher sex had only pushed me hotter and hotter until I'd literally set the covers of our bed afire with my magic one night.

After that, we learned I needed to be calmed, that my inner flames needed to be smothered. It had been that way when I tried to vent my powers of the beach the night after Bressen and I had made love at the Priory. I'd created my own storm to draw off the excess power the gods had bestowed on me, but when I'd started an earthquake, it was Bressen's soft words in my ear that brought me back from the brink.

The next night after I'd set our bedding on fire, Bressen had taken his time with me. He'd held me close and whispered lovingly into my ear before slipping into me and setting a gentle rhythm, even as I'd cried, and thrashed, and tried to provoke him to go harder. When I'd dug my nails into him brutally enough to draw blood, he'd simply taken my hands and pinned them down as he continued to make love to me until my pain and rage broke, and I went limp beneath him. Then he'd pulled me into his arms, and I'd wept quietly against him until my tears went dry.

"Bressen-," I tried again now, but his gaze fixed on me as his eyes blazed red, and I saw it all in his mind. His anger and frustration at Samhail and Aidan, his fear of what had happened with the demoni at Revenmyer, and his annoyance with me over what I'd done with Glenora and Clarice.

He took a step toward me. "I…said…run!"

His tone sent shivers down my spine, and I saw the exact moment his control snapped. Fear sparked somewhere inside me at the look in his eyes. I'd never seen Bressen like this before, and it ignited an instinct deep inside that told me he was right. I needed to flee. Now.

I turned and ran.

Like a predator attracted by its quarry's flight, Bressen launched himself after me, and I felt his hand graze down my back. It sent a sensation between thrill and fear spreading through my body, and I put on a burst of speed. Bressen was right on my heels, so I didn't stop to open the door to his study but instead ported right through it into the hall.

Adrenaline made me lightheaded as I ran, but fear made my legs shake as the door shuddered and groaned when Bressen's solid body slammed into it. He cursed loudly before the door was wrenched open, and he was again in pursuit. He'd fuck me brutally if he caught me, and I didn't know whether to be exhilarated or utterly terrified by that prospect.

I didn't have time to decide which as I flew down the hallway and into the stairwell while Bressen's footsteps pounded behind me, their rhythm at odds with my own thudding heartbeat.

I barely felt my legs as I tore down two flights of stairs before crashing into the door jam on the second floor. I regained my equilibrium by porting into the hallway, then started to run again. It was probably a mistake to exit the stairwell on the second floor since it left me few places to go, but there were too many servants on the first floor who'd see us, and I didn't want to frighten them or, worse, put them in the path of Bressen's wrath. I didn't think he'd hurt them on purpose, but I wasn't sure what he was capable of right now.

You'll find out soon enough, I told myself as I heard Bressen's footfalls gaining on me. The prospect of being caught was like nothing I'd ever felt before, and in the back of my mind, I considered asking Bressen to chase me again sometime when he wasn't furious with me. For reasons I didn't understand, the promise of danger not only had my heart pounding out of my chest, but also the wetness growing between my legs.

Gods help me. I liked this. Liked being chased. Pursued. Hunted.

I didn't need to look behind me to know Bressen was almost on me. I felt him within inches of me. I could port again to put some distance between us, but a tiny part of me wanted him to catch me.

I hesitated for a fraction of a second as I got to the doors of the great room, but I decided against going in. The sane part of me told me to keep running, to not trap myself in a room with Bressen.

The fraction of hesitation cost me, though, and I cried out as Bressen caught hold of my dress and some of my hair and yanked me backward. I slammed back against his body, and then his arm was around my waist like an iron band so I could barely breathe. On instinct I tried to scream, but his hand clamped over my mouth, anchoring my head to his chest.

"Too late," he growled in my ear. "Time for your punishment."

He dragged me into the great room to the large reading table and threw me down on top of it. I immediately ported to the far end of it, my last stubborn instinct of self-preservation telling me to keep fighting.

Bressen was ready for me, though. He pushed the table into me, and I cried out as I was knocked backwards onto my ass. By the time I recovered enough to get my feet under me, he was hauling me up again.

The room spun as Bressen pushed me back down onto the table so I was bent over it, and he kicked my legs open wide. His hand pressed against the back of my neck to hold me down, and I felt him working at the fastenings of his pants with one hand as he leaned over me.

"Say it," he breathed against my ear.

I knew what he wanted to hear.

"I know you love me," I assured him.

"Do you?" he asked. "Are you sure?"

I nodded my head against the table.

"And why do you need to know that?" he asked.

"Because you're about to fuck me like you don't," I answered, reciting the lines we now used whenever Bressen was about to use my body to vent his anger.

Bressen let out a long breath. "Is this what you want, Cyra?" he growled into my ear as he pressed his body down onto me.

He always gave me the choice, one last out to be sure I knew what I was getting into, and that's ultimately what eased my mind despite my fear. If he hadn't asked, that's when I might've fought for real.

I swallowed, knowing this time was going to be even rougher than normal, but I answered honestly. "Yes."

Bressen went still. He was breathing heavily as he fought to bring himself back under control. His hand tightened on the back of my neck, but I only squirmed beneath him so my ass ground into his groin. He'd caught me, and now he needed to make good on his threats.

"Fucking hells, Cyra!" he snarled as he yanked my dress up and tore my undergarment off. The delicate fabric snapped easily in his hand, and he tossed it aside.

He notched his cock at my entrance, and I screamed as he drove inside me to the hilt with one brutal thrust.

"Don't expect gentle," he warned. "I'm not capable of it right now."

I shook my head against the hand holding me down. "No," I agreed.

He began to slam into me then, each thrust digging my hips into the top of the table as my fingers scraped along its smooth surface, trying to find some sort of purchase. As I'd expected, the sensation was somewhere between pleasure and pain. His pounding thrusts vibrated through my body making every nerve come alive, and I made a noise between a whimper and a moan as I gave in to the urge to enjoy the feeling.

I jerked as his cock hit something inside me that sent pain stabbing through my body. Bressen didn't pause as he normally might have, and I wondered if he was too lost in his own rage and pleasure, or if I really had driven him past his endurance this time.

He drove into me relentlessly, and I cried out as my own pleasure started to build. My body hadn't necessarily been ready for him before, but it was now as my own arousal gathered between my legs to ease the way for both him and me.

I screamed again as he thrust in brutally and once more hit something inside that sent pain shooting through me. This time his stroke faltered, but the pain was gone a moment later, and I bit down on my lip as I pushed my hips back to meet his next drive.

"You're taking your punishment so well," Bressen rasped in my ear.

"I think you enjoy it too much when I fuck you like this."

Maybe I did, but I refused to feel guilty for that.

Bressen's fingers moved up to thread through my hair, and I winced at his grip. His other hand wrapped around my hip, and I knew I'd have bruises where his fingers dug in, but the pain tethered me somehow, and I pressed my forehead against the table. Inside the bodice of my dress, I felt my nipples strain against the fabric, and they only grew tighter as my breasts rubbed against the table with each thrust.

Bressen's driving grew faster, his grunting harder, and I knew he must be close. I likely wouldn't climax myself, but he'd take care of me when he was done. I knew that much.

He roared his release only seconds later as he shoved into me with a few last deep thrusts, and I felt his cock pulse as he pushed in as far as he could go to spend himself inside me. The tension in his body eased a moment later as he collapsed over me, and I let out a soft whimper as his body covered mine, his breathing heavy against my ear.

I took stock of my body. My hips would be bruised where they'd been driven into the edge of the table, and I felt a dull ache between my legs where he'd slammed into me. My scalp twinged from his grip on my hair, but I was fine overall. Moreover, the bruises and aches were like badges of triumph for me, proof of how wild I could drive Bressen.

I hadn't climaxed. I'd been close, but Bressen had stopped before I could get all the way there. He'd finish me soon, though. He never left me wanting for more than a few minutes.

As the haze of pain and pleasure cleared, though, I felt something else.

My head snapped up toward the doorway as I sensed the other presence in the room, and my heart dropped into my stomach.

Axenus stood a few steps inside the room, his sword drawn as he looked in horror at us.

There was something frantic in Axenus's gaze as his eyes locked with mine, and I had the terrible feeling he was seeing himself in me. I felt a jumble of emotions rolling off him, but concern was at the forefront, followed by confusion.

He looked like he'd come running into the room, undoubtedly drawn by my screams, only to be drawn up short.

Gods above. How much had he seen?

"Cyra, are you…," Bressen started to say as he rose slowly off me.

Bressen, Axenus is here, I said into his mind, and his body went rigid as his head snapped up.

He immediately pulled out of me and straightened up when he saw the merman. He drew me off the table with him and yanked the skirt of my dress back down as he pushed me behind him to shield me from Axenus's gaze.

"Axenus, this isn't what it looks like," Bressen said quickly.

Axenus's eyes flicked from Bressen to me where I looked out from behind him, and I shook my head. "It's not," I assured him. "I'm fine."

Axenus's grip tightened on the handle of his sword before it eased again, but he didn't resheathe it. He seemed ready to attack Bressen, the man who'd saved him from slavery, if I was actually being forced.

I wondered what he would've done if Bressen really had been attacking me. Would the urge to save me have overridden his loyalty to Bressen? I'm not sure I wanted to know.

Axenus's throat bobbed as he swallowed heavily. "I heard Cyra scream," he said. He turned an accusatory look on Bressen, and Bressen's chin went up.

I put a hand on Bressen's arm. I needed to get him out of here. "You said you had work to do. Why don't you go up to your study, and I'll explain things to Axenus."

What exactly I'd say, I had no idea, but Axenus still looked ready to attack Bressen, and I knew he wouldn't trust anything I had to say with Bressen around.

"Cyra, I don't-" Bressen started to say, but I cut him off.

Go, I said into his mind. *Axenus needs to hear it from me that I'm alright. Your presence won't help anything.*

Bressen sighed heavily, and I felt him warring with himself. He usually held me close after fucking me hard and made sure I found my own pleasure, but that would have to wait for later. He didn't want to leave me alone right now, but he knew I was right.

With a resigned sigh, he nodded. *I love you,* he said into my mind.

I gave him a small smile. *I love you too.*

Bressen pressed a kiss to my forehead and strode to the door. He slowed as he reached Axenus, who hadn't yielded the grip on his sword.

"I'm sorry you saw that, Axe," he said. Then he was gone.

Axenus seemed to freeze at the words, and he waited several seconds – presumably for Bressen to make his way down the hall – before he resheathed his sword and turned to me.

"Come sit down," I said as I headed for the armchairs by the fireplace.

Axenus followed silently and sat across from me in one of the chairs.

I opened my mouth to speak, but Axenus beat me to it.

"Did he hurt you?" he asked, and I realized he was angry. I'd only ever seen him angry one other time, and that was after I'd accidentally dream walked into his nightmare with Clarice and Magdalene.

I clamped my mouth shut. The honest answer was, yes, Bressen had hurt me, but I savored that dull ache between my legs as I sat there now. I wasn't sure how to explain that to myself, let alone Axenus.

"Everything you saw was consensual," I said after a moment. It wasn't an answer to what he'd asked, but it was the only answer that mattered.

Axenus looked at me in disbelief. "How?"

"He would've stopped if I'd asked him to," I said. Despite what Bressen had claimed when we returned, I knew that for certain.

Axenus considered this. "Why didn't you ask him to? It looked as though he was hurting you."

I felt my face flush. Gods, he was going to make me admit it.

"Because…I enjoyed it," I said. I held his gaze only long enough to see his look of shock before I turned away.

Seconds of silence hung between us before Axenus spoke again.

"Is this...always how you...?"

"No," I assured him. "Only sometimes. It helps Bressen when he's angry or frustrated."

Axenus looked horrified again. "He takes his anger out on you?"

"I let him use me to release some of his pent-up energy," I corrected. "He doesn't take anything I don't willingly give, and when he feels better, he gives me pleasure back."

Axenus continued to stare at me. "But he enjoys hurting-"

"I know you probably don't understand what we do given your own experiences," I interrupted, "and I can't explain why I like it, or why Bressen does, but we need you to accept that this works for us."

The words came out sharper than I would've liked. I'd seen Axenus's trauma firsthand and wanted to be sensitive to it, but I also didn't want to be judged, to be made to feel as though there was something wrong with me or Bressen because we liked our sex this way.

Axenus continued to stare at me, and I felt bad for snapping at him.

"Have you ever known Bressen to be the type of man who loses control?" I asked Axenus, trying a different tactic.

He blinked at me, and his mouth worked a little before he answered. "No," he said finally. "Bressen is usually very in control. That's why-"

"Exactly," I interrupted. "He's one of the most feared rulers on the continent, and one of the most powerful perimortals to ever live. There can be dire consequences if he loses control, so he doesn't get the luxury of letting himself slip."

Axenus's shoulders sagged as he saw where I was going with this. "Except with you," he said.

"Except with me," I confirmed. "Everyone needs an outlet, and I'm Bressen's. I take his pain and his frustration and his anger for him, and I enjoy doing so. Whether Bressen likes hurting me or not, it doesn't matter because I give him permission to do it." I shrugged. "For what it's worth, I'm not sure he does like it, but it does help him."

Several more seconds wandered away before Axenus nodded slowly.

"I'm sorry you had to witness that," I went on more gently. "And I'm sorry I made you think I was in trouble. You shouldn't have been in a position where you felt like you needed to help. We shouldn't have done that out in the open where anyone could see. It won't happen again."

Axenus looked away. "But I *didn't* help," he said. "I came through the door and saw what was happening, and I couldn't move. I just…stood there and watched what he was doing to you. If it had been real…"

He trailed off, and I heard the shame in his voice.

My own shame rose. The thought of Axenus watching Bressen and I aroused me more than I cared to admit.

"If it had been real, you would've stopped it," I said, pushing the other thought down. I reached across and took Axenus's hand in mine to give it a bracing squeeze before pulling back.

He smiled weakly. "You're more certain about that than I am. All I could think of was how I owed Bressen for saving me." He shook his head. "Was I really willing to let him hurt you because of that?"

It was a rhetorical question, but I answered anyway.

"Maybe on some level you knew it wasn't real because you knew Bressen wasn't the type of man to hurt me like that."

He nodded. The thought seemed to put him at ease. "Maybe," he said.

I stood, and he did as well.

"Just do me a favor," I said. "Well, two actually."

"Anything," he said.

"Don't hold this against Bressen. He didn't do anything wrong, and neither did you."

Axenus paused, then gave a quick nod. "And the other favor?"

"Forget everything you saw and let's never speak of this again."

He forced out a deep breath, followed by a small laugh. "Gladly."

I put a hand on his arm. "Thank you. Now, if you'll excuse me, I need to get back to Bressen." I turned to head for the door.

I'd only taken a few steps when something on the floor caught my eye. A black piece of lacy fabric.

My face flooded with color again as I realized it was the undergarment Bressen had ripped off me and discarded earlier. I detoured toward it and bent quickly to snatch it up as I hurried out of the room, knowing without having to look that Axenus was still watching me.

I'd asked Axenus to forget what he saw, but whether I could ever forget it myself and look him in the eye again remained to be seen.

Tandem Read: Go to *Clash of Stone and Steel* (Bk 3), Chapter 17

Chapter 8

Cyra

Dinner that evening was quiet. Bressen had tried to make an excuse to eat in his study, but I'd nixed the idea and insisted he come down to the dining room. I chided him for trying to hide from Axenus and told him that if I had to face the merman, so did he. When he remembered that eating in his study would leave me alone with Axenus, he relented.

Part of me wondered if Axenus himself would find some reason to avoid eating with us, but I'd underestimated him. He entered the dining room shortly after we did and gave us a polite, if brief, greeting.

Thankfully it was just the three of us, since Surgeon and Serise were still out looking for Samhail and the assassin.

Bressen and I had clearly both forgotten Axenus was in the house earlier. Bressen had been sending him on occasional trips to speak to other lords and rulers, so the merman was often gone nowadays. When Bressen had told me to run, I'd remembered that the three gargoyles were gone, and I'd just assumed Axenus was away as well.

I considered trying to make small talk while we ate, but in the end, I just didn't have the energy. It was a victory for now that me, Bressen, and Axenus could at least sit in the same room with each other after this afternoon. Tomorrow we'd work on looking each other in the eye again.

Or perhaps in a few days, since I learned the next day that Bressen had sent Axenus on another trip to Kern after all. He'd been waiting to hear from Kern about getting an audience with their Primus – the Kernish name for the king – and the country had conveniently responded late last night to invite Axenus to the palace.

I felt Bressen's relief when he told me. Maybe a few days away from each other would help ease the awkwardness between us and Axenus.

Bressen had a trip of his own planned to Callanus. As the most senior member of the Triumvirate, there were certain duties at the Citadel that fell to him, especially given that Aidan was new, and the High Council of Polaris had no standing in the Triumvirate. He was the only one who could handle some of the mundane business that was necessary to keep the capital city and the country running.

I decided to forego my daily trip to the new vineyard and go with him. I'd hired some staff at the vineyard to help me out, including a manager, and she was quickly proving herself extremely capable, so I felt confident leaving things in her hands for a day or two.

In truth, Bressen and I both needed to be near each other after the incident in the great room. We always gravitated toward each other after sessions of especially rough sex anyway, but we'd been denied our chance to reconnect emotionally when Axenus had accidentally interrupted us.

I knew Bressen felt guilty for how he treated me when he took me hard, and he tried to make up for it by being extra attentive and affectionate afterwards. For my own part, I needed to be near him to assure myself he really did care for me. It was as if we stretched ourselves so far in one direction that we needed to spring to the other extreme before we could return to normal.

Unfortunately, while we were at least in Callanus together, Bressen was currently locked in a meeting with his advisors and the Citadel's steward, so I wouldn't see him for a couple hours. Instead, I was in his library trying to be useful.

Bressen had asked Axenus to research the religious wars that had ultimately led to the breakup of the continent into separate countries centuries ago. He hoped we might learn more about syphons and the continental triumvirates. The merman hadn't had much chance to look with his travel schedule, though, so I'd decided to start on it for him.

Bressen's librarian had managed to get the library back in order since I'd destroyed it several months ago. Well, not destroyed it per se, but every book had come flying off the shelves the last time I was here when

Samhail had tested me to see if I could use his summoning power. That I had been able to use it was some of our first evidence I was a syphon.

The librarian, an older-looking man with gray hair and a long gray beard remembered me well enough. His cool demeanor when I asked for books on the history of the religious wars told me he likely hadn't forgiven me yet for what I'd done to the library.

Still, he brought me about two dozen books he thought might contain relevant information, and they now sat stacked on the table in front of me. I was only halfway through the first one, and my eyes were already starting to glaze over.

I blew out a long breath and flipped another page. I liked to read, but Protector save me, this was going to take forever. There had to be an easier way to find the information I needed.

As soon as the thought entered my mind, I felt a twisting tug in my chest, and my eyes flared at the feeling. I realized a moment later I'd felt that tug before. Weeks ago, I'd syphoned the ability to find something I was looking for from a priestess at the Priory – seeker power – and that tug was the power trying to lead me to what I sought.

Gods above, could it really be that easy?

I closed the book I was reading and stood. The tug pulled me toward the door, and I left the library. I turned left down the hall, following the tug's urging, and it led me toward the stairs. I descended, letting my mind go blank as I gave myself over fully and trusted the magic to guide me to what I needed. I didn't bother to question it when it led me out the front door of the Citadel, down the stairs, and straight toward the main gate.

"My lady?" one of the guards at the gate questioned as I approached.

I didn't answer. I didn't want to risk breaking the connection or losing my direction. My mind and body were focused on following the magic.

"My lady, where are you going?" another guard asked me, trying to step into my path, but I put a hand out and sent a gentle forcefield to push him back out of my way as I stepped through the gate and out onto the street in Callanus.

Straight, the magic told me. *Go straight.*

Instinctively, I knew where it was taking me. A little ways across the city stood the radiant white walls and minarets of the Priory, and I walked toward them, barely aware I'd stepped out into the street into traffic.

A strong hand yanked me back just before I stepped in front of a team of horses drawing a wagon of goods toward the market.

"My lady!" the guard who'd grabbed me yelled, panic lacing his voice. "What are you doing?"

"I need to go to the Priory," I told him.

"Now?" he asked.

"Now," I confirmed, and I stepped into the street again, this time checking for any vehicles coming my way.

"You four, go with her!" the guard ordered, addressing several of the men at the gate. "If something happens to her, Lord Bressen will have our heads on spikes lining the wall."

I heard the sounds of rustling and clanking behind me as a number of guards surrounded me. They stopped traffic in the street to shepherd me across as my feet carried me forward of their own accord, the tug in my chest pulling me along as if I were a fish on a line.

My steps were brisk as the guards hustled to keep up with me. Two pushed ahead of our group to part the crowd in front of me while the other two flanked me and brought up the rear to guard my back.

I had no concern anyone might actually hurt me. Indeed, most people bowed low or dropped to a knee before me as I passed, and the din of the street quieted into a curious murmur as people watched.

I felt a spike of hostility in my mind as someone in the crowd objected either to my presence or to how the guards were shunting people aside, and I heard a shout and a scuffle behind me as the guards reacted to a potential threat, but I never broke stride. Each step toward the Priory felt more urgent than the last, and soon I was climbing the wide marble stairs to the entrance of the city's main temple.

I stopped suddenly in the middle of the stairs, and there was a string of whispered swears and clanking behind me as the guards who followed me tried to pull up short to keep from running into me.

Something else had pulled at me all of a sudden, but I wasn't sure what until I looked up and saw…them.

Stone-carved gargoyles – not real ones like Samhail – lined the parapets around the roof of the Priory and perched at the tops of its three minarets. I'd always known they were there, but I'd never taken the time to look at them until now.

The gargoyles were made of light gray granite, so they stood out against the gleaming white marble of the Priory's façade, but they looked nothing like Samhail. At least not from what I could see down here. Most sat on their haunches as they surveyed the city almost lazily, many looking like hairless dogs or ape-faced demons. None of them captured the sense of latent danger Samhail exuded even in his human form, the promise that one wrong move might unleash the violence barely contained below the surface. The statues were grotesque, designed to be frightening or disturbing as a warning to enemies of the Trinity, but they were a mockery of the majestic menace Samhail wore like a crown. Their postures and expressions didn't remotely harness his lethal grace, which still sometimes sent a shiver through my body, despite how well I knew him.

I knew Samhail hated these gargoyles, but I didn't know why. I didn't need to know, though, and one of these days, I'd make sure the gargoyles were taken down and smashed to rubble, just for him.

The tug in my chest brought me back to myself, and I hurried up the remainder of the stairs and straight through the front doors of the Priory. Once in the foyer, my magic tugged me to the right, and I followed it without hesitation, the heavy steps of my guards echoing through the halls as they followed along in my wake.

Further and further into the heart of the Priory I strode as I obeyed each twist and tug in my chest. I never once questioned the magic as it led me into a stairwell, and I circled down and down the winding stairs to levels I never knew existed.

I'd gone on a scavenger hunt once recently in the Priory to test this very power, and I'd learned just how big the temple was, but it seemed as though I'd only scratched the surface of the place.

Finally, I came to the bottom of the stairs, my guards still hustling along behind me. There was a door there, the only way to go without ascending back up, but it was locked when I tried the handle. I tested my seeker magic by moving back, but the magic's pull assured me what I sought was through the door.

I held a hand over the lock and loosed a small forcefield into the mechanism to break it open, but I was shocked when – instead of the door opening – something pushed me backward. I furrowed my brows and held out both of my hands toward the door. I loosed another forcefield, intending to blow the door off its hinges, but I cried out when the same force blew back, sending me sprawling into the guards behind me. Two of them caught me and set me back on my feet as I snarled at the door and lurched forward to slam my palms against it.

"Let me in!" I yelled at it, but the door remained immovable.

"My lady…" One of the guards laid a gentle hand on my shoulder, but I shook him off.

I ran my hands along the door, trying to sense what I needed to do to open it. It had a keyhole, but instinctively I knew there was more to it than that. Still, having the key would be a good start.

I turned and held my hand out, palm up, as I concentrated on summoning the key to me. I had no idea how far away it was, nor had I ever tested just how far my summoning power reached. I'd never tried to use it on anything that wasn't in the same room as me, but I tried now, letting my power snake through the Priory to find the key and bring it to me. Very faintly, I felt my power seize on something, and I concentrated on drawing it to me.

I waited for close to a minute while nothing happened, and I was about to give up when something metal finally slammed into my palm. I looked down in wonder at the set of keys now clutched in my hands. The guards around me only stared as if they had no idea what I might do next despite the set of keys in my hand.

I turned toward the door and tried the keys on the ring until one of them finally fit. The tug in my chest grew more urgent, like a second heartbeat as it pushed against my ribs.

The door didn't move as I turned the key in the lock, though. I threw my shoulder into it, but it didn't budge, and I screamed my frustration.

"Let me in!" I yelled again.

"My lady, would you like us to get one of the priests or priestesses?" the closest guard asked.

"Yes, find Phaedrus!" I ordered, then winced as my body felt strange.

The guards around me all recoiled back, and I frowned at them.

"My lady, you're…," one guard said.

I frowned deeper. "What is it?"

The guard unsheathed his shortsword and held it up so I could see my distorted reflection in the polished blade. I gasped as I took in the brown skin and male face looking back at me. I lifted my hands to see that they too were dark-skinned and manly.

I understood a second later what had happened.

The assassin, Talyn, was a masque, and I'd syphoned her power to shift into other people. When I'd ordered the guard to find Phaedrus, I'd unconsciously shifted into the priest.

Wondering if it might make a difference, I turned back to the door and tried the key in the lock again. This time the door clicked open, and I smiled. I pushed it wide and strode through, the seeker's tug once again in control.

I strode forward down another hall until it branched left and right, and I waited for the tug to direct me which way to go, but it seemed to pull me straight toward the wall. I frowned and tried to go left, but the tug pulled me back. I turned right, but again the tug pulled me straight ahead toward the wall. I stepped closer and ran my hands over the stone, looking and feeling for a seam. The wall must open somehow.

"What's going on?" Phaedrus's voice came from behind me sounding angry. "Why has the Citadel invaded the Priory? What are you all doing down here? How did you get through that door?"

I turned to face the priest, and he stopped dead as he caught sight of me, then recoiled back the way the guards had. I'd almost forgotten I was still wearing his face, and I shifted back into myself.

"Cyra?" Phaedrus asked incredulously. "What are you doing here?"

I blinked as I looked at him. I thought I saw a white glow flare around his body, but it was gone a second later. It must've been a trick of the lights, a halo created when he walked through a particularly bright area.

I tossed the keys I'd summoned back to Phaedrus. "What's behind this wall?" I asked, ignoring his questions.

Phaedrus looked at me for a long moment before speaking. "Send your guards back upstairs. They can't enter."

The lead guard started to protest, but I held a hand up to cut him off. "I'm safe with Phaedrus," I told him. "Go back up and wait for me."

None of the guards moved for a few long seconds, and I didn't need to read their minds to know they were weighing if they were more afraid of what I might do if they defied me, or of what Bressen would do if they let anything happen to me.

"Go," I said, "or I'll make you go."

The lead guard swallowed and ordered the rest back upstairs. He started to leave as well, but then thought better of it and turned back to me. He unsheathed a dagger from his waist and handed it to me.

"Just in case," he said.

I took the dagger and smiled at him. "Thank you." I didn't bother to tell him I already had a dagger sheathed to my thigh under my dress. It seemed to make him feel better that I accepted his, and I didn't want the fact that I wore one of my own to make him rethink leaving me alone with Phaedrus.

When the guards were finally tromping back upstairs to the main level of the Priory, I turned to examine the wall.

"What's behind it?" I asked Phaedrus again as I continued my exploration of the stone. My hand skimmed over one spot that seemed smoother, and I frowned. It didn't look smoother, but it felt so, as if the touch of thousands of hands over the centuries had worn it down. Behind me I heard Phaedrus hold his breath as I pushed on the stone.

To my surprise – and apparently Phaedrus's as well – the stone glowed green for just a moment, then the seam in the wall I'd been looking for earlier appeared.

"How did you do that?" Phaedrus asked from behind me. "Only Priory workers are allowed…" He trailed off, then answered his own question. "You're a Hand of the Gods."

I didn't acknowledge Phaedrus but only pushed open the hidden door that was now visible. I stepped into the cavernous room it revealed and gaped at what I beheld.

Phaedrus appeared at my side and gestured for me to enter further. "Lady Cyra, welcome to the Priory's library."

Chapter 9

Cyra

The library was unexpectedly bright considering we had to be underground. I looked straight up and saw paneled windows in the ceiling far, far above us, but the windows couldn't be letting in nearly this much light. It was probably some kind of magical illumination like I sometimes encountered in the Citadel.

All around us, the floors of the library rose in circles around the center area, and I tried to imagine where on the Priory grounds we were in relationship to the main entrance and worship hall. Even if most of this space was underground, there were only so many ways to keep it hidden, which seemed to be a priority.

"Are you looking for something in particular, my lady?" Phaedrus asked, breaking me out of my stupor.

"Yes," I said, "but I'm not sure what. I was following my seeker power since it seems to know what I need."

Phaedrus frowned. "I've never known seeker power to work like that, but you're the exception to most of the rules, so I suppose anything is possible. Lead the way and I'll do what I can to help."

I nodded to Phaedrus and started walking again as my seeker power renewed its tugging.

Despite the insistent pull of the magic, I had trouble keeping my focus as Phaedrus followed me through the hallways. I'd never in my life been in a library anywhere close to this large. The stacks of books seemed never-ending, with floors reaching up far above us, containing what I imagined must be millions of books.

I'd just turned down a new corridor when the smell of old paper and leather binding gave way to the sweet scent of hot cinnamon and musk that I knew so well. I jerked to a stop and swung around, expecting to see Bressen, but my search came up empty.

"Lady Cyra? Are you alright?" Phaedrus asked next to me.

"I thought I smelled…" I trailed off, still looking around for Bressen.

Phaedrus sniffed the air, and a knowing look stole over his face. "You smell something…or *someone* you desire," he said. He walked toward an area enclosed by glass walls. The glass door to get in stood slightly ajar.

"Someone must've left this open by accident," Phaedrus said, reaching for the door.

"What's in there?" I asked.

Phaedrus paused with his hand on the doorknob and smiled. "This is the room that holds the Priory's collection of erotic literature."

I felt myself blush, but Phaedrus didn't seem at all embarrassed by the subject, and my interest piqued. I stepped closer to look into the room. Like everywhere else, the space was stacked floor-to-ceiling with books, the only difference being that it was enclosed.

"You keep it restricted?" I asked, nodding to the door.

"Not at all," Phaedrus answered. "This door is never locked. Anyone with access to the library itself can get in here. We just had to wall off the area, and we keep the door closed because some of the books can be rather…potent, and it's easy to get distracted if you're around them for too long. That's where the smell comes from. Several of the more powerful magical texts can stimulate a person's desires just by being around them."

"What do you…," I started to ask, but then rethought my question. "Does everyone smell something different in there?"

Phaedrus smiled. "Yes. I, for instance, smell citrus and lavender."

I opened my mouth then closed it again. I wanted to ask Phaedrus why he smelled those things, but I didn't want to pry. He read the question in my face.

"It's how my current lover often smells," he offered.

His words struck me, and I looked at Phaedrus for the first time as a woman might. He appeared older than me, somewhere around middle age, perhaps a bit older than Jasper. In perimortal years, that meant he was likely several hundred years old, but I noticed now that he was a fairly striking man. His robes hid the finer contours of his body, but I could tell he was broad-shouldered and fit. His jawline was sharp, and it narrowed into a pointed chin with a tuft of short, just-graying hair. His crystal-clear blue eyes were almost as haunting as my own silver ones were, and they stood out brightly against dark skin the color of cacao.

It was only now I realized how attractive he was.

"Do you want to go in?" Phaedrus asked, drawing me back from my perusal of his features.

I shouldn't. There was a reason I was here, and it wasn't for this. The seeker magic was a persistent tug in my chest, urging me on toward what I'd come here to discover, but this room pulled me toward it as well, just in a different way.

I found myself nodding, and Phaedrus opened the door to let me in. Bressen's scent was faint out in the hall, but it flooded my nose when I stepped into the room, and I sucked in a breath as I felt an instant tightening between my thighs. Potent indeed.

I let my eyes scan the books on the shelves as I walked slowly down the first aisle. Some were in the common tongue while others were in unfamiliar languages.

"Those are all novels and stories of a sensual nature," Phaedrus explained. "The books on this side are instructional." He pulled a book off the shelf from the other side and handed it to me. The title read, *Teachings on Desire*.

I opened the book, and my eyes flared. "It's…illustrated," I observed as I flipped through the pages. My gaze snagged on one image, and my eyebrows shot up. I was probably not flexible enough to try that position.

"We have several copies of that book if you'd like to keep it for a while," Phaedrus suggested seriously. There was no sly tone to his words. It was simply a keeper of knowledge offering that knowledge to another, and it was perhaps that alone that made me accept.

I closed the book. "I think I will," I said. "Some of this may be relevant to…my healing magic."

Phaedrus raised a gentle brow at my attempt to justify taking the book, but he didn't say anything. I was about to turn to go when a cry sounded from somewhere deeper in the stacks, and instinct had me running toward it with Phaedrus on my heels.

"Lady Cyra! Wait!" he called after me, but I didn't stop as I followed the sound of the cries, turning down another row where the stacks broke. Ahead of me the space opened up, and I tore into the clearing to find…

I pulled up short as I took in the man and woman before me. The woman, who appeared to be in her forties or early fifties, was just slipping her priestess robes back on over her head, while a much younger man retied the sash that held his own robes together. The man was tall and built like a soldier while the woman was almost as petite as Maziren. They couldn't have been more opposite, yet it was obvious what they'd been doing, and I was well aware I'd just done exactly what Axenus had done yesterday, followed sounds of seeming distress that turned out to be a couple fucking.

Phaedrus came up next to me as my eyes drifted to a wooden crate at one end of a table next to the couple. The crate sat by a large book while a number of smaller objects lay scattered around it. My eyes widened as my brain finally recognized what the objects were.

"Are those…stone cocks?" I asked.

"Ah yes, they are," Phaedrus said, as if the sight of a dozen or so stone genitals sitting on a table made perfect sense to him.

"What?…Why?" I asked incredulously.

Phaedrus didn't answer but instead addressed the man and woman who'd just noticed us. "Velania, Marcus, I don't believe you've met Lady Cyra yet?"

The priest and priestess froze in the fixing of their garments as their eyes landed on me, and a second later, both sunk quickly to one knee.

"My lady," Marcus said. "Please forgive us. We didn't recognize you. We were just…um…" He trailed off, at a loss to explain what they'd just been doing.

"Please, stand," I told them. I still wasn't used to people bowing before me. "It's quite alright. I'm no stranger to…giving in to one's passions."

They rose, and Velania bobbed a small curtsy. "Thank you for understanding, my lady."

"We found the dick for the statue of Rubin the Bold that's in the Great Chamber at the Citadel," Marcus said in what he seemed to think was an explanation. "And we, uh, decided to celebrate."

I looked at Phaedrus, hoping he'd fill in the details, and he obliged.

"As near as we can tell from the records," Phaedrus said, "several thousand years ago, one of the High Priests of the Priory decided all the naked statues around the city were indecent. He ordered the genitalia of the male statues chiseled off, and they were replaced by stone or bronze grape leaves. About fifty years ago, an acolyte who'd been tasked with cleaning out one of the Priory's many storage rooms came across half a dozen crates containing all the missing cocks."

I just stared at Phaedrus, and he gestured to the priest and priestess. "Velania and Marcus have been working on trying to match the missing cocks with their original statues so they can be restored."

My brows shot up. "So you were working?" I asked the couple.

"It's a hazard of working in this area," Marcus said sheepishly. "Those of us who are in here a lot tend to end up having sex with each other periodically."

"And you can't take the box somewhere else?" I asked. "Surely it doesn't need to stay here."

Velania glanced at Marcus, then smiled at me. "Those of us who work in here usually *want* to work in here."

I gave her a quick nod of acknowledgement. I couldn't really fault her or Marcus for having a healthy love of sex.

"In any case, we finally found a source that had a drawing of the original statue," Velania explained as she pushed a text toward me and pointed at a drawing in it. "As you can see, Rubin's member curves a little to the left in the image. From there it was easy to find the correct appendage in the crate."

I pursed my lips to hide the smile that threatened. "Congratulations. It's good to know Rubin the Bold will soon be reunited with his cock."

"Just doing our part to help restore the city's historic works of art to their original states," Marcus said seriously, and I nodded again.

"Indeed," I said. "Please keep up the good work and let me know if I can help in any way."

Their task had originally seemed comical, but hearing it described as a restoration effort changed my mind, and I was sincere about helping.

My seeker magic tugged on my chest then as if to remind me why I was here even as Phaedrus spoke up again.

"Lady Cyra, we should go. It will become harder to resist the magic of this room the longer we're here."

Whether Phaedrus's warning was more for my own sake or for his, I wasn't sure, but he was right. I felt my arousal rising, and we turned to leave after bidding Velania and Marcus goodbye and good luck with their genitalia-matching efforts.

I walked swiftly back toward the door. Between the magic of the room, the stone cocks, and imagining what Velania and Marcus had been doing, I was starting to feel the urgency to leave before I did something I'd regret. Now that I'd noticed Phaedrus was a man, and an attractive, albeit older one, I was all-too-aware of him hurrying behind me.

We reached the exit, and I yanked the door open to throw myself through it before I inhaled a deep, cleansing breath as the lighter air of the main library hit me. I hadn't realized just how thick the air in the erotica room had been, how it had seemed to swirl over and caress my skin like a lover's touch. The tension between my thighs was already easing, and I turned to Phaedrus when the door clicked shut behind him. One look at his face told me he was just as relieved as I was to be out of there.

"That was certainly…intense," I said, giving Phaedrus a weak smile.

He returned my smile, his own equally weak, and I noticed he was trying to take calming breaths.

"I'm sorry," I said. "I didn't mean to get us into an uncomfortable situation."

He shook his head. "Not at all. I should have warned you about some of the things that go on in there and about the effects of staying inside too long."

I held up the copy of *Teachings on Desire* still in my hand. "Is this safe to read? It isn't infused with any of that magic, is it?" I asked.

Phaedrus gave a soft chuckle. "No, it's just a normal book. You should be fine. There are copies of it all over Callanus."

I looked at him in surprise. "Really? It's not…controlled?"

Phaedrus shook his head again. "No, of course not. The Priory isn't in the habit of keeping people from reading about such things, and neither is the Triumvirate. Sales of the book actually increase in the weeks leading up to the Harmilan."

I started walking again as the tug in my chest urged me to get moving, and Phaedrus followed.

"I'm not sure I understand," I said. "You have to be from the Priory to get into the library, don't you? This place is well-hidden."

"Yes, but that's mainly to protect the books from outside threats. There are various ways for anyone to access them," he said as he fell into step beside me. "The Priory holds the originals of many old books, and our primary focus is to help preserve them. When books are of general interest to the public – as many of the books in that room are – we have scribes work to translate or copy them. Book merchants then pay for the right to print their own and sell them."

"What about the authors of the books?" I asked. I turned left automatically as my magic pulled me in that direction.

"The authors of any books we sell to merchants are long-dead,"

Phaedrus said. "Allowing merchants to print and distribute such books is our way of ensuring that the knowledge and those stories live on."

"And what about the magical books?"

"If someone wants to read something we can't reproduce, they submit a request with the Priory, and then they're given an appointment to come read the book here. The only time we might deny a request is if there's a real threat that reading it might cause physical harm to either the reader or someone else, but there are very few books in the library that are restricted in that way."

"What about the book you're translating?" I asked him.

I sensed Phaedrus's unease at the question, and indeed, it was several seconds before he answered.

"Lord Bressen believes the information in that book puts you in danger," he said carefully. "As such, there's an argument for restricting access to it...for now."

"For now?" I prompted.

He hesitated before going on. "There's also an argument to be made that the information in that book is of importance to people all over the continent. It's part of our history, and it contains information that's particularly relevant to the Trinity and its doctrine. That isn't information the Priory can ethically withhold forever. Eventually, we'll need to make a translation of the book available to the public."

I was quiet a moment as we walked. "And if Bressen objects?"

Phaedrus sighed. "As much as I respect Lord Bressen, and – admittedly, fear him when your safety is concerned – he won't be able to stop the Priory from releasing the book. But as much as I know he wants to protect you, your husband is a reasonable man...usually. I don't believe he'll stand in the way of us releasing the book when it's time. To be clear, though, that won't be anytime soon. We still need to do more research into the book's origin and its authors. I also still have a lot of translating to do, and even when I'm finished, my translation will need to be reviewed and corroborated by the few others around the continent who can read this particular dialect of ancient Arystrian. It will be a long while before there needs to be discussion of making it generally available."

I considered this before nodding. "When it's time, I'll help you convince Bressen to release the book," I said. "You're right. We have no right to restrict the information."

Phaedrus relaxed a bit next to me. "Thank you," he said.

I stopped suddenly as the tug in my chest jerked me toward a huge iron door we were just about to pass.

"Here," I said, turning to the door. "My magic says what I'm looking for is in here." I looked over the door, then turned to Phaedrus.

"That's the vault," he said.

"I need to get into it," I said when he didn't move.

Phaedrus opened his mouth, then closed it again and nodded. He held his hand up to place it on the door but paused and lowered it again. "You try," he said. "I'm curious to see if you have access to the vault as a Hand of the Gods. Put your palm against that center panel."

I did as Phaedrus asked, and the spot around my hand glowed green as it had before. The door clicked, and I pushed it open. Phaedrus nodded for me to enter, then followed me into a small room with several tables and chairs where people could sit and read. Across the room was another glass wall and door. Behind it were several rows of bookshelves, but there were also locked boxes sitting on tables and locked cabinet doors built into the far wall.

"There's only minimal air in the vault room for preservation purposes and to inhibit fire," Phaedrus said. "Normally I'd need to call one of our air elementals to come and refill the space so we can open the door, but since we have you…"

I stepped toward the door and sent my magic into the vault room. Indeed, I felt how little air was inside and began to refill it.

"It should be filled enough," I said, and Phaedrus opened the door.

A puff of air rushed out and fluttered the hair at my temples as he opened it, and I stepped through, letting my seeker magic lead me. I went straight toward the back of the vault until a tug pulled me to the right and all the way to a part of the wall with small doors built into it. I raised my hand and hovered it over the doors until I felt the sensation that told me I'd found what I was looking for.

"This one," I said, turning to face Phaedrus. "What's in this one?"

Phaedrus didn't speak for a moment, and I frowned at the wary expression on his face.

"My lady," he said, "that's the lockbox that contains the text I'm translating. The one that told us you were a Hand of the Gods."

Chapter 10

Cyra

Phaedrus pulled a ring of keys from the pocket of his robes, a different set from the one I'd summoned, and unlocked the wall box. Inside was something wrapped in cloth. He pulled it out, set it on a table in the middle of the room, and carefully pulled back the fabric to reveal the book he'd shown me and Bressen weeks ago.

"Your seeker powers are telling you the answers you want are in here?" he asked.

I held my hand over the book and felt the tingle that confirmed it.

"Yes," I said. "Open it, please."

Phaedrus pulled out a drawer under the table and removed a pair of cloth gloves like I'd seen him wear the last time he handled the text.

"Anywhere in particular?" he asked as he put the gloves on.

"In the middle," I said.

Phaedrus did as I asked, and I hovered my hand over the first half of the book on the left. I didn't feel anything, but when I hovered over the second part of the book on the right, my hand prickled again.

"It's in the second part," I said. "Open those pages in half again."

Phaedrus saw what I was trying to do. He reached back into the drawer and took out a ribbon that he laid between the two halves. Then he again split the pages of the second part.

I hovered my hand over the two parts of the book again, and this time the section on the left made my hand prickle. We now knew the information I sought was somewhere between the pages we'd marked with the ribbon and the new split. Phaedrus pulled another ribbon from the drawer, marked our split and opened the section in half again. We continued this process until we'd narrowed it down to a single page. I held my hand on both sides of the page, and my magic told me what we needed was on the right-facing side.

"Have you translated this part yet?" I asked Phaedrus.

"I don't think so, but let me check," he said.

He went back into the lockbox where the book had been and pulled out some papers. His notes. He flipped through them and shook his head.

"No, I haven't gotten there yet," he said.

"How long will it take you to translate that page?" I asked.

He eyed the page. "Maybe a couple hours."

"Can you do it now?"

Phaedrus looked hesitant. "I can try," he said.

"Please. This could be very important."

He nodded. "Of course, my lady. Do you want me to send you a message leaf when I'm done?"

"I'll wait here for you to finish," I said.

He raised a brow. "You plan to…sit and watch me translate?"

I held up the copy of *Teachings on Desire* I'd taken from the library's erotic section. "I'll just do some research of my own," I said.

He gave me a small smile. "Very well, my lady. But I need to insist you find somewhere else to sit while you wait. We try to limit occupancy of the vault to one person at a time."

I nodded. "Fair enough. I think we passed an alcove with some chairs down the hall. I'll be there when you're done."

I left the vault and headed back down the hall to where I thought I'd seen a sitting nook. Sure enough, an alcove had been built into the wall just large enough to fit two cushy chairs and a small table.

I sat down with my book and began to read.

Cyra

An hour later, I was getting restless in more ways than one. I was anxious to see what Phaedrus had discovered, but I'd also realized that reading an illustrated book on the myriad ways couples could bring each other pleasure while I was alone in public was a mistake. I desperately wanted to find Bressen and show him some of the things I'd learned, but I couldn't go until I knew what Phaedrus had found.

I was actually surprised I hadn't heard from Bressen yet. When we left our minds open to each other, which we did often, we could each feel the strong emotions of the other, and what I was feeling now should've had him swearing into my head. I assumed the Priory's wards were keeping him from sensing me, and that was probably for the best.

I closed the book and decided to check on Phaedrus. I walked back down the hall, entered the vault, and found him leaning over the text in concentration. He held a pen in one hand and scratched something on a piece of paper before turning back to the book. He looked up when I approached the table.

"I'm sorry to bother you, but I was curious to see what you've found so far," I said.

Phaedrus stood up straight and let out a shallow sigh. "Not much yet, I'm afraid," he said. "As far as I can tell, it's a poem, but I haven't translated enough to make any sense of it. Supposedly it came to one of the ancient seers in a vision, and it was recorded here."

"The poem is from a vision?" I asked, and Phaedrus nodded.

I frowned. "Raina once told me visions usually come true within a month or two of when someone has them. If so, why would I need to know about a vision someone recorded thousands of years ago?"

"Most visions do usually come to fruition within a couple months, if at all," Phaedrus said, "but that's not universally true. A uniquely gifted seer can sometimes see things that won't happen for hundreds or even thousands of years into the future. This may be one of those cases."

"What have you got so far?" I asked.

Phaedrus picked up the paper he'd been writing on. He looked at what he'd written, sighed, then read.

"Though it waxes and wanes among the stars,
We feel its tug, a tether to our soul.
A beacon in the dark, a promise kept
To find each other and again be whole."

My mouth had gone utterly dry by the end of the second line as my eyes widened. It couldn't be.

"That's the first stanza," Phaedrus said. "It's likely about the moon, but I can't begin to guess at its significance. I'm almost done with the second stanza." He bent his head to the paper once more and read.

"Though it sets each eve, closing out the day-"

"We trust its rise again upon the morn," I said, picking up the verse. "A sacrifice for love, a bargain's made, To grant a gift and help a bond reform."

Phaedrus's head snapped up, shock written across his normally placid face. "How...how did you know that?" he asked.

"It's a song my mother sang to me and my brothers as children," I said. "It always calmed me when I was upset or helped me sleep when I was restless. Jaylan and I just thought it was a convoluted love story."

Phaedrus seemed unable to do anything but blink at me. "Your mother used to sing this to you as a lullaby?" he asked incredulously.

I nodded.

"Where did she hear it?" he asked.

"I have no idea. But when Bressen and I went to Revenmyer yesterday to question Glenora, she knew it too. She started singing it to taunt me. I don't know how she could've known I knew the song."

"You know the rest of it?" Phaedrus asked, and I nodded again. He handed me the pen. "Please, write it down."

I took the paper from him and bent over it, then paused. "Shouldn't this be 'souls,' plural, in the second line?" I asked. "A tether to our souls?"

Phaedrus looked at his translation then back at the book. He picked up another book that lay open on the table, flipped through it to check something, then shook his head.

"No, the word is definitely singular, although I can see why you think it would be plural," he said. "A tether to our souls makes more sense than soul." He paused. "Unless…"

I knew immediately what he was thinking. "Unless it's a reference to the Souls of the Moon," I said, "men and women who share a soul. If that's what it means, then a singular soul would make sense."

Phaedrus nodded. "Yes, and look at the next stanza. Something that sets at eve to close out the day. It must be the sun, so perhaps that next part is about the Souls of the Sun."

"Yes!" I said excitedly. "The third stanza is about the earth, if I remember correctly."

I bent over the paper again and began writing. It was possible parts of the song had evolved over the years and the version my mother knew wasn't the same as the version in the book, but Phaedrus could check my work against his own translation. If nothing else, having a starting point should make his work easier.

I finished writing and handed the paper to Phaedrus.

"Though it sets each eve, closing out the day,
We trust its rise again upon the morn.
A sacrifice for love, a bargain's made
To grant a gift and help a bond reform.

Though battered hard by tide and wind and flame,
It stands the tests of time, remaining strong.
An old wound healed, and forgiveness granted
To act as one and right a grievous wrong.

When moon and sun and earth align once more,
When hand to hand to hand are joined as past,
Then will the separate once more unite,
And live in peace again until our last."

Phaedrus looked up at me again. "You and your brother thought it was a love song?" he asked.

I shrugged. "We had no idea what it was. Love song sounded as reasonable an explanation as any."

"Well, theoretically, if it's about the Souls of the Moon, Sun, and Earth, then I suppose it is at least partially a love song," Phaedrus said. He pointed to the third to last line. "And look at this reference to hands. It specifies three, 'hand to hand to hand.'"

He furrowed his brow and looked back into the book. He stood up a second later, nodding. "Yes, the word 'hand' is capitalized in the book. It likely refers to the Hands of the Gods."

I bit my lip as I considered this. "It sounds like the Hands of the Gods are supposed to come together, but I don't see that happening. For one, I want to kill Magdalene, not work with her. As for the other Hand, Praya could be anywhere. No one has seen her in four hundred years, so she's well-hidden, if she's even still alive."

The warriors I'd released from the collar insisted Praya had to be alive, or they would've died at the bottom of the ocean, but there was no way to be sure. Bressen must've told Phaedrus about this discovery because the priest didn't question my suggestion that Praya was alive.

"Let's not get too far ahead of ourselves," Phaedrus said. "Before we start interpreting the text, I should verify it against what's in the book."

"Of course," I said.

"You should go back to the Citadel," Phaedrus suggested. "After I verify the text is correct, I want to check some other sources to see if I can give the poem…uh, the song, some context. I'll report to you and Bressen as soon as I have something."

I hesitated, not wanting to leave now that we'd made these discoveries, but I also realized Phaedrus likely couldn't do his work as effectively with me hovering over him.

"Very well," I said. "I'll go back, but let us know the minute you have something solid."

It took every ounce of my willpower not to bother Bressen with what Phaedrus and I had learned until later that night. He'd spent all day either in meetings with his advisors or in his study working, and I reminded myself how grateful I was that I had very few responsibilities as his consort. I attended public and political functions with him, and I gave him advice when he asked for it, but I was happy to leave the paperwork and decision-making to him. I wasn't cut out to be a ruler.

I practically attacked Bressen when he finally returned later that evening, though, as I excitedly explained my trip to the Priory's library and what Phaedrus and I had learned. I knew he was tired, but I'd been holding the news in all day, and I followed him into the closet to relay my story while he undressed for his bath.

I was just getting to our interpretation of the last stanza when Bressen grabbed me to his now-naked body and kissed me deeply.

"I'm eager to hear the rest of this," he said when he lifted his mouth from mine, "but first I need to fuck you."

All I could do was nod before he swept me up and laid me down on the large cushioned bench in the middle of the closet. I didn't protest as he pulled my undergarment off, settled himself between my legs, and pushed inside me with a deep groan. Any thoughts of the song flew out of my head for the next several minutes as Bressen moved inside me.

I climaxed quickly, apparently still wound up from my excursion into the erotic literature room, and Bressen came a minute or so later with a shuddering growl as he wrapped himself tightly around me.

We lay entangled in each other's arms for several minutes until Bressen pulled out of me and got up.

"You were saying?" he prompted as he held out a hand and pulled me up from the bench when I took it. "Tell me the rest while I bathe."

It took me a few fits and starts to remember where I'd left off before Bressen had interrupted me with closet sex, but I eventually found my place and told him the rest of the story while I helped him with his bath.

"Did Phaedrus say when he expected to have more news?" Bressen asked as he stepped out of the bathtub to towel himself off minutes later.

My mouth opened, but I was struck mute at the sight of his body glistening with water. It trailed down his skin in rivulets, and I watched the muscles in his arms flex as he moved the towel over himself. My eyes lingered on the small, dark trail of hair that ran down under his navel to his groin before they fixed on the hard muscles of his thighs. I'd never considered how beautiful a set of legs could be on a man until I'd seen Bressen's, Samhail's, and Axenus's legs, and now I couldn't seem to get enough of them.

I was so fixated, I didn't even realize Bressen had walked over to me until he hooked a finger under my chin and tipped my head back to meet his eyes. I blinked his face into focus to see he wore the hint of a smile.

"I'm sorry, what did you say?" I asked.

"Is something wrong?" he asked, amused. "You seem distracted."

"I…" My mouth was suddenly dry. "I was just wondering what was wrong with your legs. They're so lumpy."

Bressen nearly choked. "Lumpy?"

I closed my hand on the top of his thigh above his knee and ran my hand slowly up his leg, letting my fingers roll over the swells of muscle. His skin was warm and still slightly damp from his bath.

I moved my hand up until I got to where his leg met his hip, then let my fingers graze over the muscle that made part of the V near his groin.

Bressen released a long, low groan as my fingers followed that ridge of muscle down toward the patch of night black hair between his legs.

"Is bumpy a more accurate word?" I asked as I let my fingers tease the curls of the coarse hair.

"You're playing with fire, woman," he said in a voice thick with gravel.

I hadn't looked down yet, but I already knew what I'd find, and I wrapped my hand around his swollen cock. He closed his eyes and leaned into me as I gave his shaft a long, hard stroke.

"Gods, Cyra," he ground out, "you have no idea what I'm about to do to you."

I remembered my other find at the library then, and I let go of him to head into the bedroom. He grunted in protest as I released his cock.

"Cyra?" he asked in confusion.

"Actually, I have some ideas about what you can do to me," I called back over my shoulder as I left the bathing chamber and strode across the room to retrieve the book Phaedrus had given me.

I grabbed *Teachings on Desire* off the table near the fireplace and turned to go back into the bathing chamber. Bressen had already come out and was standing naked in the middle of the room. I walked over and handed him the book.

He read the title and raised a brow.

"Just look," I said. "Phaedrus let me borrow it."

He opened the book, and his brow shot higher.

"It's illustrated," he observed.

"That was my first thought too. Look at chapter 55."

He flipped forward in the book and looked where I indicated. His brows pinched together, and he angled his head. Then he turned the book sideways as his furrow deepened.

"Oh, I see," he said finally. "Well, that's certainly an interesting position. I'm not sure I'm that flexible, though."

I pressed up next to him to look at the illustration and frowned. "That would be my leg, not yours," I said, pointing at the drawing.

He looked again. "Ah, of course." A pause. "Are *you* that flexible?"

I looked up at him and smiled wickedly. "Do you want to find out?"

Heat filled his gaze as he pulled me over to the bed, the book still open in his hand. "Gods yes."

Tandem Read: Go to *Clash of Stone and Steel* (Bk 3), Chapters 18-21

Chapter 11

I pulled my cloak tighter around me the next day as I waited for Jaylan to finish his examination of the last row of barrels in the cellar of my new vineyard. Twenty-two years I'd lived and worked with Jaylan, and I still misjudged his thoroughness. I'd estimated it would take us forty-five minutes, maybe an hour, to tour the cellar, but we'd been down here an hour and a half already.

My brothers had been out at the market when I'd arrived at the Citadel yesterday with Bressen, so I hadn't seen them that morning, but I'd gotten a chance to catch up with them in the afternoon. I probably should've told them I was coming to Callanus, but I'd wanted to surprise them. As such, I'd missed out on seeing them for a few hours, but the tradeoff was that I'd ended up at the Priory and discovered the song with Phaedrus.

Jaylan and Brix had been living at the Citadel since our vineyard in Fernweh was destroyed, and I hadn't seen nearly as much of them as I would've liked. We'd had time in the afternoon and evening to visit yesterday, though, and I'd peppered Jaylan with questions about the song and anything he could remember about our mother when I finally saw him. Unfortunately, he didn't remember much more than I did.

In any case, Jaylan and Brix had agreed to come see the new vineyard in Solandis today. It was a visit that was long overdue.

I'd wanted to get a few things in order before I brought my brothers over because I knew Jaylan would spend a ridiculous amount of time scrutinizing every stave and bunghole in the place. Brix, on the other hand, had already sampled wine from half the barrels and was now waiting impatiently – and slightly drunkenly – for Jaylan to finish up so we could go outside and walk through the vines.

"It looks like the previous owner did a decent job of keeping his barrels in good condition," Jaylan said finally as he straightened up from where he'd been crouching.

He opened the stopper of a barrel, dipped a small ladle inside, then pulled it out and poured the sample of wine into his glass. He took a sniff, swirled the contents, then sniffed them again before taking a swig of the liquid. He swished it around his mouth before swallowing.

"Not bad at all," he said. "It looks like you'll have a good first vintage."

"I'm not considering it my first vintage," I said. "The previous owner did all the work, so it's still his. He actually ages his wine in the barrels for two years instead of one before he bottles."

Jaylan and Brix both looked at me in surprise.

"Two years?" Brix said. "Why so long?"

I shrugged. "He swears the extra aging does wonders for it."

We'd only ever aged our wine for about a year back in Fernweh, but that was because there was a high demand for it in the area. We never had time to let it sit for much longer.

There were quite a few vineyards up here along the Hiraethian coast, though, so competition was stiffer. The man who'd owned the vineyard before me had been able to let some of his wine sit longer because there was less demand for it, and the extra time had proven to be a boon. He'd since made it standard practice to age his wine for two years, and people were starting to notice the difference. Demand had gone up, and I was determined to see if I could continue his way of doing things.

"How many bottles can we take back with us?" Brix asked as he slid off the barrel he'd been sitting on. He swayed before catching his balance.

"You can take what you can carry in one trip," I told him.

Jaylan let out a deep sigh. "Don't tell him that or he'll load himself down with cases, and then you'll have broken bottles all over your floor."

I smiled. "Don't worry," I assured Brix. "I'll send you back with a good supply. Let's go up and look at the vines before it gets dark."

It was an exaggeration. It was still mid-afternoon and wouldn't be dark for several hours, but it was a playful jab at Jaylan for how long he'd taken, and he rolled his eyes.

"I'm really happy for you, Cyra," Jaylan said as we headed for the door. "This looks like a great place."

"It is," I said, "and I'm excited to try some new things. I'll need a lot of help, though."

I let the thought hang in the air, but neither Jaylan nor Brix jumped in to offer any assistance. I was hoping this tour might convince them to move up here and work the vineyard with me like we'd done together in Fernweh, but they hadn't taken the hint.

I missed my brothers and wanted them closer than Callanus. More than that, I wanted to work with them again. For all we'd fought and gotten on each other's nerves over the years, we'd also had a lot of fun and produced wine that had made its way into the Citadel's cellars.

"There's something we've been meaning to talk to you about, Cyra," Jaylan said as we finished ascending the stairs from the cellar and emerged again into the tasting room.

Unlike our vineyard back in Fernweh, where we made the wine then sent it elsewhere to be consumed, this vineyard had a social space where people could come and drink. It was almost like a vineyard and tavern in one. It was on the outskirts of Solandis, but it was located close to another town, so it provided a convenient halfway point between the two places for travelers to stop and have a drink. The previous owner had always planned to build up this part of the business but had never quite gotten around to it. Once we took care of the threat from Magdalene and Sandrian, I hoped to pick up where he left off.

"What did you want to talk about?" I asked as I led Jaylan and Brix through the tasting room and out back into the rows of vines.

My heart fluttered faster in anticipation that maybe they were ready to take me up on my offer to have them work here after all.

Jaylan fell into step beside me as we headed down one of the rows. It was almost Spring, and some of the vines had started their bud break after the last week of milder weather.

"Brix and I have given this a lot of thought over the last couple weeks," Jaylan said, "and we came to a decision."

"Oh? A decision about what?" I asked pretending ignorance.

"We can't stay at the Citadel forever," Jaylan said. "We're grateful to Bressen and Aidan for letting us stay there while we decided what to do, but we're starting to overstay our welcome."

"I'm sure that's not true," I said.

"You wouldn't say that if you saw the relief on the faces of the kitchen staff after every meal when Brix finally leaves the dining room."

I smiled. Brix had always had a prodigious appetite, and he'd been given access to a limitless amount of food while staying at the Citadel. When he'd worked on the vineyard, he'd burned off whatever he ate quickly, but I'd noticed recently that between his lack of activity and the abundance of food at meals, he'd gotten softer in the middle.

"So what did you decide?" I asked.

Jaylan was quiet as we walked a ways. "It's time for us to go back to Fernweh," he said finally.

I jerked to a stop, and Brix swore as he had to sidestep to keep from crashing into me.

"Fernweh?" I asked incredulously. "Why?"

Jaylan stopped as well and turned to look at me. "Cyra, Fernweh is our home."

"People can move," I pointed out. "And the last time you were there your so-called neighbors burned our vineyard to the ground and beat you bloody. It's not safe for you to go back."

"We don't expect you to understand-"

"What's that supposed to mean?" I cut him off.

Jaylan sighed. "I'm not trying to dismiss what you went through when the Triumvirate took you away from us," he said, "and I know it wasn't easy for you to leave Fernweh and move up here, but you had a reason to move. You have Bressen."

"And you don't have a reason?" I argued. "The townspeople almost killing you isn't enough reason? *I'm* not enough reason?"

My voice had grown a bit hysterical, but I couldn't help it.

"Cyra, you'll always be our family, and you'll always be important to us," Jaylan said, "but Brix and I can't build our lives around you. We need to find our own way. We need to build our own families."

Understanding struck me. "You want to go back to Maeve," I said.

Jaylan had been seeing Maeve for almost two years before the incident at the vineyard. He'd planned to marry her, but she'd cut ties with him when people had learned I was perimortal and turned on my brothers.

Jaylan inhaled deeply. "That's one of the reasons," he said. "I have to at least try to see if she'll give me another chance. Then there's the house and the vineyard. We can't just leave them to rot."

"The vineyard is gone," I said, more brutally than necessary.

"Much of it is," Jaylan said, "but not all, and it can be replanted. The land is still there. It will be a lot of work, but it's a chance to start over and maybe do something new. Plant different grapes."

"The vines need to mature for a few years before you'll be able to make decent wine," I said. "What do you plan to do until then?"

"Whatever we can," Jaylan said. "We haven't figured everything out yet, but we need to go back and see if we can start over."

"And what if the people in town decide to burn the vineyard again?" I asked, desperate to talk him out of this. "What if they come after you, try to hurt you?"

"You think they'd dare after what you did last time?" Brix asked, chiming in for the first time. "They're all afraid-"

"Brix!" Jaylan interrupted him. "Nemesis take you!"

"What?" Brix asked, oblivious to the look of horror I wore. I'd nearly killed three men by trying to make them walk into a burning building the last time I was in Fernweh.

"Between Bressen and Cyra, they'll be too..." Brix trailed off as he finally noticed how pale I'd gone. "Cyra, are you alright?"

I held up a hand. "I…I'm fine," I said. "You just…You can't expect me to come down there every time there's trouble. For one, Polaris isn't our territory. Both Bressen and I got into big trouble with the High Council that last time. I was under house arrest for what I did."

Truth be told, I should've been in jail, but I'd gotten off easily, and it made me angry that Brix seemed to be counting on me to rush in and vanquish his enemies, or whatever he was imagining.

"If you go back to Fernweh, you'll be on your own," I warned. "I won't be able to help you again."

Brix was quiet a moment before he shrugged. "Maybe not, but the townsfolk don't know that."

I made a sound of frustration. "Why do you even want to go back?" I asked him. "The vineyard is Jaylan's, and you don't have anyone wai-"

I cut myself off when I realized the cruelty of what I'd been about to say. No, Brix didn't have someone he cared for as Jaylan did, but it made me an ass to point it out. He had both women and men in Fernweh and the next town over he flirted with, but to my knowledge he'd never shown an inclination to make his dalliances with any of them more serious.

"Never mind," I said. "I just don't understand what you're so eager to get back to in Fernweh."

"The vineyard may not go to me," Brix said, "but neither will yours. Does it matter if I work for him or for you?"

My heart sank. He had a point.

"I…maybe we could share the vineyard," I offered hesitantly. Part of me loved the idea of working with Brix again, but another part already thought of the place as mine and was reluctant to give up any control. I wanted to create my own vision for it without being answerable to anyone else, and making Brix my partner would mean compromising that.

Brix seemed to realize as much because he just smiled. "And how long do you think it will take before you and I aren't speaking to each other?"

"I'm sure we could make it work," I said stubbornly.

"Cyra, I appreciate the offer, but Bressen gave this vineyard to you,"

Brix said. "I want you to be able to make it what you want it to be. Right now, though, Jaylan needs my help more than you do." He reached out and ran his hand along the cordon of a just-budding grape vine, a reminder of what I had that Jaylan didn't.

I sighed, sensing defeat. "When do you plan to return?" I asked.

"By the end of the week," Jaylan said. "We'd appreciate a portal when we're ready."

A small, bitter part of me wanted to make them go back to Fernweh on foot – or at least by horse – but I couldn't be that petty. For one, it wasn't safe to travel nowadays, and I'd never forgive myself if something happened to them. For another, I did understand on some level why they wanted to return. The vineyard had belonged to our parents. To just let it go and leave it to lie fallow wasn't something any of us could live with.

Still, I wasn't sure the residents of Fernweh would accept Jaylan and Brix back. Even if they were too afraid of my wrath to harm them or the vineyard in any way, there were other more subtle ways the people there could make my brothers' lives miserable, and I wasn't sure a fear of me or Bressen would stave off those attempts.

I wanted to go down with them and issue a warning to the people of Fernweh about treating my brothers kindly and fairly, but I knew Jaylan and Brix would balk at the idea, and both Bressen and the High Council would forbid it.

Warding, I realized suddenly. I could at least put up warding to keep them safe. It wouldn't stop the townspeople from treating them badly when they went into town, but at least I'd rest easier knowing no one could sneak up on them at the vineyard.

"Whatever you need from me is yours," I told Jaylan. "If I have a good harvest this year, maybe I can even give you some of my grapes to get you started."

Jaylan's face eased, although he stopped just short of smiling. "We'll see," he said. "You're just starting out. We don't want to do anything that's going to put you at a disadvantage." He paused. "But…we were thinking of asking Bressen for a loan."

I felt the pain in every word of that request. Jaylan could be proud, and I knew the idea of asking Bressen for a loan was killing him. It was a testament to just what an uphill battle my brothers faced that he'd even brought himself to voice the idea.

"It's yours," I said. "I know Bressen will be more than happy-"

"We'd pay back every coin," Jaylan assured me. "We're not asking for a donation, just a loan."

I gave him an indulgent smile. "Of course. If you really want to make it official, we can even have Samhail break Brix's legs if you're late with your repayments."

"What?" Brix said in alarm.

"She's joking," Jaylan said.

"He'd be happy to do it," I went on mercilessly. "Samhail likes breaking bones. I told you he broke Eddin's arm, didn't I?"

Brix paled. Occasionally his naiveté ran away with him, and I couldn't help taking advantage.

"Cyra," Jaylan warned me.

I sighed. "Fine. No one is going to break your legs, Brix, least of all Samhail. And you both have me and Bressen's full support. We'll do what we can to help."

I looked to the west where the sky had begun to darken early with an approaching storm.

"We should head back to the tasting room," I said. "The storms in this area roll in fast, and I could really use a drink after this news."

I turned to head back, but Jaylan caught my hand, and I stopped.

"I know this wasn't what you wanted to hear," he said to me, "so Brix and I appreciate you supporting us in this decision."

"It comes with stipulations," I said. "First, I'll be putting up warding around the vineyard, and that's non-negotiable."

Jaylan opened his mouth to object, but he closed it again at the resolute look I gave him.

"You'll also check in once a day for at least the first few weeks until I'm certain things are safe," I went on, "and you'll be honest and tell me if people are making things difficult for you."

"What would you do if they were?" Jaylan asked warily.

"I'm not sure yet," I said, "but I promise I won't overreact and try to burn the village down."

"Again," Brix added, and I glared at him. He only winked.

"Do we have a deal?" I asked Jaylan.

"Fine," he said. "We can agree to those terms."

"Good," I said. "Then let's go drink a few bottles of wine. You can celebrate, and I'll drown my sorrows. Either way, we'll drink to the rebirth of your vineyard in Fernweh."

"*Our* vineyard," Jaylan corrected, nodding his head toward me. "It will always be partially yours, Cyra. You worked just as hard to make it what it was as Brix and I did, and we won't forget that just because we're starting over."

Tears gathered in my eyes, but I willed them back. It was a generous and beautiful sentiment, but it only made me sad. I was excited about my new vineyard, but Jaylan's words reminded me how little connection I had to this place compared to the vineyard in Fernweh.

I'd worked our old vineyard from sunup until sundown almost every day for nearly two decades. I'd used my meager – at the time – magic to help our vines grow. I'd sweated and bled into that dirt. A part of me would always belong to that place, and it would always belong to me.

I smiled at Jaylan. "Thank you. That means a lot." I paused. "Does that mean I still get part of the profits once you're up and running again?"

He smiled back. "Well, maybe we'll forget it sometimes."

Chapter 12

Bressen

"I trust you were well-received?" I asked Axenus as he settled into the chair across from my desk.

I'd taken a moment to glance through the portal he'd just stepped through from Kern before it closed behind him, but aside from seeing the royal portal master and some views of the intricate palace architecture, nothing stood out to me. The Primus of Kern apparently hadn't decided to see Axenus off.

"Well enough," Axenus said. "The Primus wasn't exactly warm in his welcome when I met with him, but I was offered every hospitality while I was there." He looked at me significantly. "*Every* hospitality."

I raised a brow. I'd never been to Kern, but I'd heard stories of the delights the Kernish palace offered its visitors. The revels and 'hospitalities' – as Axenus called them – were the stuff of legend, and as a result, the Primus received hundreds of requests a year from rulers and nobles around the continent who wanted to visit. Many had only flimsy excuses for why they needed an invitation, so I'd had my work cut out for me convincing the Primus's steward that my business with his sovereign was legitimate and time-sensitive.

In the end, that I planned on sending an emissary rather than coming myself convinced him my business was real, and my promise that I had an offer the Primus might find intriguing moved me to the top of the invite list. Or rather, it had moved Axenus to the top.

"I hope you partook of those hospitalities to the fullest," I told him, although if I knew Axenus, he hadn't. His response surprised me, though.

He shrugged. "I might've accepted a few…amenities."

I grinned at him. "Good for you."

A measure of awkward silence stretched between us, and I knew we were both thinking back to the day he'd caught me fucking Cyra as I bent her over the table in the great room. I'd had the table replaced with something in a very different style since then so Axenus wouldn't have to remember what he'd seen every time he looked at it.

He and I hadn't had a chance to talk about the incident before I'd asked him to go to Kern, and while I was sure we were both grateful for the respite, we needed to address it sooner or later. As much as I might prefer to let things be, I needed to give Axenus the opportunity to express himself if he chose.

"Axe, I need to apologize again about what you saw in the great room before you left for Kern," I said, deciding now was as good a time as any. "It was inappropriate and irresponsible of us…of me to do that with Cyra out in the open where anyone could see, especially you, and I hope you'll forgive me for putting you through that. If there's anything you'd like to say, please feel free to do so."

I shut up then and waited for Axenus to speak. He sat for a long time just looking at me, and I resisted the urge to squirm under his gaze. I wasn't sure if his silence meant he was gathering his thoughts or if he had no desire to say anything. I was about to say something else when he finally broke his silence.

"I don't understand it," he said. "I spent eight years being used against my will, sometimes violently by the people Clarice lent me to. Cyra explained things to me, but I'll still never fully understand why you take pleasure in hurting her, or why she seems to take pleasure in letting you. It will never make sense to me why you both seem to enjoy…reenacting the kinds of horrors I endured."

I lowered my head and looked away, unable to meet his eyes. I opened my mouth to say something, but I had no idea what I *could* say to that. Axenus saved me from having to try.

"But I don't need to understand it, or even accept it," he said, and my eyes snapped to his. "It's not for me to judge what you and Cyra do in the privacy of your own bedchamber…So long as it remains in the privacy of your own bedchamber," he added.

I nodded in understanding. "Of course. You're absolutely-"

"I had a long time to consider this in Kern," he said, cutting me off, "and the biggest difference between what happened to me and what you do with Cyra is consent."

I found myself nodding as if in assurance.

"Cyra swore to me you had her full consent for everything that happened, and she trusted you to stop if she asked you to," he went on. "And so long as that remains the case, then I won't feel like I have to castrate the man who saved me from eight years of hell."

I blinked at Axenus as my mouth fell open, ready to voice a response that never manifested. I was shocked he'd dared to threaten me, but I was also proud of him. There'd always been a kind of barrier between me and Axenus. Not a huge one, but one that kept him from seeing me as more than just a lord and the man who'd rescued him, a barrier high enough to keep him from being a real friend in the way Samhail was to me.

In a strange way, the antagonistic friendship Axenus had with Samhail almost seemed closer, more authentic, than what I had with Axenus, and I hoped perhaps this might be a turning point for us, despite what had prompted it. If Axenus felt comfortable enough to threaten me, then he no longer had me on a pedestal. In an odd sort of way, my mistake had probably brought us closer together than anything else in the last twenty-some years of our friendship.

"Understood," I said, smiling. "My balls and I will take that to heart."

Axenus nodded, and a moment of acceptance passed between us.

"Shall we get back to your visit to Kern then?" I suggested.

"Of course, my-," he started to say, formality back in his tone, but I held up a hand to stop him.

"You just threatened to castrate me," I said. "You don't get to call me 'my lord' anymore. We're well past that now."

A smile crooked his lips. "Of course. Bressen."

Saying my name clearly felt awkward to him, but he'd get used to it.

"Back to Kern then," I said. "What I really want to know is if the stories about the Primus are true. Does he actually…?" I trailed off, inviting Axenus to fill in the blank. Rumor had it the Primus had gotten eccentric in his old age, and I was curious to know just how much.

Axenus's eyes rolled back in his head as if he was remembering all too well what I was talking about. "Yes," he said. "It's true. I'm more used to it than most people, but having a conversation like that does get a bit interesting."

"I hope I get to meet him someday," I said, chuckling. "Speaking of conversations, how did yours go?"

"He balked at the idea at first, but after I laid things out for him more fully, he was at least receptive," Axenus said. "He spoke to his advisors, and they came back with some questions we'll need to answer before they agree to anything, but I was optimistic when I left. I suppose your next step is to run this by the High Council and then Aidan?"

"Yes, I scheduled a meeting with them together tomorrow, but…" I trailed off as my mind tried to wrap itself around the nagging feeling that something was wrong.

"But what?" Axenus prompted.

"I thought convincing the High Council might be the hard part, but I'm starting to worry about Aidan's reaction as well."

Axenus's brow furrowed. "Why?"

"I met with him a little while ago, and he was different. More hostile. More…combative." I looked Axenus in the eye. "He's refusing to assemble his army, and he hasn't made any preparations for war."

Axenus's brows shot up. "What? Why not? You'd think after Jasper was taken that would be his priority."

"That was my thought too, but apparently not," I said.

"Hiraeth can't take on Sandrian and Magdalene alone," Axenus said. "You need Polaris and Derridan on board."

"Believe me, I'm aware. We're already at a disadvantage because

Polaris lost part of its army during the coup, and its people haven't forgotten that loss. I'm not sure what we'll do if I can't get Aidan to change his mind."

Axenus looked at me meaningfully. "You could always…change it for him," he suggested.

I let out a frustrated growl. I could do that. My mind magic was easily strong enough to compel Aidan to see things my way, but if I was willing to do such a thing, I might as well not have even bothered to reform the Triumvirate. I was as good as a dictator if I wasn't going to let my fellow rulers make their own decisions.

Even if those decisions were stupid and dangerous and likely to get us all killed.

"I can't," I said. My frustration boiled over, and I slammed my fist down on the desk.

"Is…Samhail back yet?" Axenus asked tentatively.

"No. The twins are out looking for him when they should be guarding Cyra. I have half a mind to throw him in Revenmyer when I find him."

"Have you tried sending him a message leaf?" he asked.

"Yes, a couple. He won't answer."

"That's unlike him. Are you sure he's alright?"

I was about to respond when the meaning of Axenus's question hit me like a battering ram. I'd never considered even once that Samhail might be injured or even dead. It had always been a given that he was just ignoring me, that he had some plan he didn't want to tell me, but the gravity of the situation hit me then. He was alone with a highly dangerous assassin. I had every confidence in Samhail's ability to take care of himself, but it wasn't out of the realm of possibility the assassin had somehow overpowered him or tricked him or…

I shook my head to banish the thought. No, I wouldn't even entertain the notion. Samhail was fine. He was just being a pain in my ass.

A wave of relief passed through me that I thought at first was about Samhail, but I realized a second later I was sensing Cyra's return from the vineyard. I could always breathe easier when I knew she was home, but relief was quickly replaced by concern when I felt something different about her. I let my mind reach out to hers and found it not only wide open…but drunk.

A smile tugged at my lips until I sensed Cyra's turmoil below the surface. She was upset about something.

I guessed the turmoil explained her drunken state, but I couldn't see what was causing it through the jumble of her thoughts.

"Axe, do you mind if we pick this up later?" I asked. "Cyra just returned from the vineyard, and she seems upset."

Axenus looked concerned. "Of course," he said. "Is there anything I can help with?"

A jolt of arousal from Cyra hit me, and I managed to hold back my grunt. "I don't think so," I said, "but I'll send for you if that changes."

Axenus nodded and left my study via the door to the hall. I got up from my desk and headed for the interior door that led through our sitting room and into the bedroom.

I found Cyra standing next to an armchair by the bed. She held onto the back as she swayed on one foot while trying unsuccessfully to pull her boot off. I stood for a moment and watched in amusement as she struggled to keep her balance while tugging at the boot with one hand. Her foot on the floor wobbled precariously, and I decided it was time for me to intervene.

"Did you have fun at the vineyard with your brothers?" I asked as I strolled toward her.

She gave a yelp of surprise and let go of the boot she'd been trying to pry off. Even on two feet she stumbled and grabbed the back of the armchair with both hands to keep from falling over.

"Nemesis take you, Bressen," she said with a breath of relief. "Don't sneak up on a person like that. You're lucky I didn't send you flying across the room with a forcefield."

I heard the slur in her voice and decided it was concerning, but also adorable. I closed the distance between us and guided her down into the chair to sit. Then I knelt in front of her and started to pull off her boots.

"Not to be a mother hen," I said, "but just how much did you and your brothers have to drink?"

Cyra looked down at her fingers and flexed them one at a time as if trying to count.

"I…don't remember," she said finally. "Could've been four, maybe five…" She trailed off, her fingers still flexing lightly.

"Glasses?" I offered.

"Bottles."

I raised a brow. "What was the occasion?"

One boot slipped free, and Cyra lifted her head to meet my eyes.

"Jaylan and Brix are moving back to Fernweh at the end of the week," she said. "There was nothing I could do to talk them out of it."

My hands stilled on the second boot. "Oh. Not a celebration then."

She scoffed. "Maybe for them it was."

I tugged off the second boot and tossed it aside. I knew Cyra wanted her brothers to move up here and help her with her new vineyard, but I always suspected they'd decide to go back to Fernweh. Or at least I suspected Jaylan would. Brix might've gone either way, but Jaylan was too independent, and he had a woman back in Fernweh. She'd rejected him, but if Jaylan was anything like me – and it appeared he was – he wasn't taking that as a final answer. Had it been me and Cyra, I wouldn't have left her alone until I was certain there was no way she'd take me back.

I reached up and cupped Cyra's cheek. "I'm so sorry, my love. You'll still see them. Just not as much as you were hoping."

"I'm putting up warding around the house and vineyard," she said as she shot out of the chair and began to pace.

I had to lurch backward out of her way to avoid being knocked over, and I knelt there a moment as I watched her. I pursed my lips to hold back the smile at the slightly serpentine path she took. I'd never seen her this inebriated before, and for some reason I found it highly amusing.

I stood and put myself in her way so she had to stop and look up.

"Warding sounds like a good idea," I said.

She shook her head, her eyes never leaving mine. "Gods help those people if I find out they tried to hurt my brothers or treat them like shit."

I raised a brow. Cyra rarely swore unless I was fucking her.

"I'm sure Jaylan and Brix will be fine," I assured her. "We'll both make sure they're safe."

The anger in her face eased a bit and she nodded.

"You're upset they decided to go back," I said, "but deep down I think you knew they would."

Her expression darkened into one of stubborn denial.

"What can I do to help?" I asked, trying a different tactic.

Cyra crossed her arms. "Let me lock them in a holding cell under the house until they come to their senses."

I chuckled. "Let's make that Plan B. Why don't you let me brush your hair instead."

Cyra loved having her hair brushed. There were apparently more nerve endings in the scalp than I was aware of, because I'd been dumbstruck at the pleasure I'd felt from her the first time I'd done it.

Cyra's gaze heated, though, and her expression turned sultry.

"How about you fuck me instead," she said. "Better yet, how about you get on the bed and let *me* fuck *you*."

My brows shot up as half the blood in my body rushed to my groin.

Cyra reached down and unbuckled my belt. When she got it undone, she whipped it through the loops and tossed it aside.

"Your clothes need to go," she said, her voice taking on a husky purr.

"Yes, ma'am," I said as I unbuttoned my jacket and shrugged it off. I tossed it onto the chair Cyra had been sitting in and began to step slowly backward toward the bed.

Cyra caught the waist of my pants, stopping me. "I said your clothesss…need to go," she slurred.

She laid her hand on my chest, and I jerked back as my shirt exploded into a kaleidoscope of blue butterflies that scattered in all directions.

Gods above, the feeling of dozens of velvety wings grazing my chest, back, and arms was certainly a new experience.

The butterflies fluttered madly around us for a few seconds before they began almost as one to lose life and pirouette to the floor. They were a trick she'd learned from Aidan when she'd syphoned his transfiguration power, made only of paper, but a way to give life to something inanimate for a short time.

When the last of the butterflies had settled to the floor, Cyra reached for my pants, but I grabbed her wrist.

"I'll just take them off," I said with a half-smile.

"Better hurry," she said, and I did.

I toed off my shoes, yanked the pants down my legs, and kicked them to the side after I stepped out of them.

"Now get on the bed," Cyra said.

She didn't give me time to comply, though. Instead, she put her hand on my chest again, and I was thrown back onto the mattress as she loosed a small forcefield at me.

I grunted as the blow knocked the wind out of me, and I looked up in surprise from the middle of the bed. I wasn't sure whether to be concerned or aroused, but my cock decided for me as it went rock hard.

"Cyra," I breathed. "What are you doing?"

She stood at the end of the bed and stripped her own pants off along with her undergarment. She stumbled sideways a little as she stood up straight again.

"Claiming what's mine," she said as she climbed onto the bed and prowled toward me, and gods damn me if I didn't get even harder.

She crawled over me to straddle my hips, and she settled herself down so her sweet heat rested on top of my cock. I let out a low groan and grabbed her hips to rock her back and forth over me.

"Take your sweater off," I ordered.

Cyra smiled and pulled both her sweater and undershirt off over her head with a little difficulty. Her hair spilled back down over her shoulders and chest, and I pushed it aside so I could cover her breasts with my hands. They were barely a handful – although admittedly my hands were large – but they were perfectly shaped, and her nipples were soft pink buds that stiffened into pert peaks when I rolled them in my fingers.

Cyra let out a moan of pleasure as I kneaded her breasts. I tried to sit up, eager to have one of those tight little nipples in my mouth, but she sent another small forcefield into my chest to push me back down.

I considered myself an aggressive man – in the bedroom at least – and I loved to dominate Cyra, to hold her down and wring pleasure from her until she couldn't stand it anymore, but gods, there was something to be said for the occasional times she took charge and dominated me instead.

I could easily flip her over right now, pin her down, and fuck her until she screamed into the mattress, and I was sure she'd let me, but that's not what I wanted. I wanted her to explore this little power trip of hers, and if she wanted to hold me down instead, then so be it.

"What are you planning to do to me, my love?" I asked her.

She swayed as she sat up straight, and I put my hands back on her hips to steady her. Her only answer was to lift herself up, line my cock up with her entrance, and impale herself down on top of me.

"Fuck!" I yelled as I threw my head back against the bed.

It never failed. Every single time I entered Cyra, I felt a euphoria I couldn't get from anything else. Warmth spread out to every part of my body like that first sip of a hot beverage on a cold day, and my eyes rolled back in my head.

We'd learned recently the legend of the Souls of the Moon, Sun, and Earth, beings that had once been stuck together but had later been split in two by the anger of the gods. Those beings now existed as separate entities that each held half of the original soul, and they spent their days trying to find each other and put themselves back together.

And damn me, but that's what fucking Cyra felt like. As insane as it sounded, sheathing myself between her legs was like making my soul whole again.

Cyra began to move, and I clamped my hands on her hips as she slid herself all the way up my length before plunging back down.

Fucking hells. I wasn't going to last.

Cyra moaned as she rocked her core against me, and she let her head fall back to expose the column of her throat.

I couldn't help it. I bolted upright and wrapped my arms around her before I fastened my mouth to her neck. She cried out in surprise, but the cry turned into a whimper as I teased her neck with my tongue, lips, and teeth. She ground herself harder against me, and I put one hand back on the bed to give myself enough leverage to thrust up into her.

Her head lolled on her neck, and I remembered she was still drunk.

"Cyra, are you alright?" I asked.

Her eyes flew open, and I swore I caught a flash of red in them before she pushed me down on my back again and began to ride me like she was being pursued by bandits. I cursed again and grabbed her waist as I tried to hold on for dear life while she drove herself down onto my cock. She had one hand braced against my chest while her other gripped my shoulder, and her nails dug deep into my skin.

"Gods, you're beautiful," I told her through gritted teeth as she continued to fuck me wildly. My eyes drifted lower to watch her breasts bounce with each thrust. I wanted to touch them, but I didn't dare let go of her waist for fear she'd fly off the bed.

I couldn't hold back my own urgency at this point. I bucked my hips up into her, meeting her thrusts so we were driven together almost viciously. The sound of our bodies slapping together echoed in the room.

"Bressen! Gods, Bressen!" Cyra cried out.

I felt her inner walls clamp around me as she screamed out her climax, and what little self-control I'd had left broke.

I flipped her quickly so she was beneath me, then drove myself into her as far as I could, once, twice, then a final time as I exploded. My seed spilled into her, hot and thick as she squeezed around my throbbing cock, and my legs trembled with the power of my release. I struggled to hold myself up as my limbs turned to jelly, and my breathing came in shuddering gasps.

It was a few seconds before I could move again, and I bent to kiss Cyra, but a red flash in my periphery caught my attention as I pulled back. I jolted as a pair of red eyes blinked out of the shadows, one eye blinking half a second after the other.

"Fucking hells!" I shouted as I launched myself up off Cyra and put my body between her and the creature crouched on the corner of the bed next to the pillows.

"Bressen, what is it?" Cyra asked from behind me. I felt her hand on my shoulder, and I put my arms out to hold her back.

I narrowed my gaze as the red eyes blinked again in that staggered pattern. Gods above, was it…?

"Come here," I ordered, and a moment later the little demoni that had taken a liking to Cyra at Revenmyer crept out of the shadows.

The tension in my body eased. I had no idea why the thing was here, but at least I knew…or thought it wasn't a threat.

"Bressen?" Cyra asked again, and I felt her peek over my shoulder. "What…is that doing here?"

"Good question," I said, then addressed the demoni itself. "What are you doing here?"

The thing blinked again but didn't answer. I hadn't necessarily expected it to. The demoni obeyed my orders, but I never communicated with them beyond that. They understood and followed my commands whether I voiced them aloud or in my mind, but I never received any messages back from them. Truth be told, I had no idea what level of sentience they had.

The ridiculousness of the situation hit me then. Here I was, kneeling naked on the bed, my cock still half-hard and dripping with my seed, as I faced off against a wayward demoni that had somehow wandered into our bedroom and watched my wife fuck me.

"Go back to Revenmyer," I ordered it, "and don't leave again until you're summoned."

The thing looked over my shoulder at Cyra, and I wondered if it had sensed something off with her and come to investigate. It wasn't normal for demoni to act on their own, but it was clear there was something different about this one and that it felt connected to Cyra.

The creature blinked a final time and dissolved into smoke.

I turned to Cyra. "I'm sorry about that. They don't usually leave Revenmyer unless called. I'm not sure what's wrong with that one."

Cyra sank down off her knees to sit on the bed. Her eyes fluttered, and she swayed a bit.

Gods, she was still very drunk, and I was an ass for fucking her when she was like this.

"I…I don't feel well," she said as she pressed a hand to her forehead.

All the excitement had made her blood pump faster, which had sent the alcohol screaming through her veins.

I rolled off the bed quickly and leaned over to lift Cyra off it as she wrapped her arms around my neck. If I could get her to throw up, maybe that would help.

I carried her into the bathing chamber, threw a towel onto the floor in front of the toilet, and set her down on it. She immediately lurched her head over the bowl and vomited into it without me having to do anything. I made a mad grab for her hair to pull it back from her face as she continued to cough and retch.

"Get it all out," I said as I ran my hand in circles over her back. She shivered, and I kicked myself for not bringing a blanket or my jacket. "Wait here. I'll be right back," I told her.

I started to get up, but her small hand landed on my forearm.

"Bressen, don't leave me," she said, her voice small and still slurred.

"I'm going to get you a blanket," I said and tried to rise again, but she tightened her grip on my arm.

"Don't leave me," she whispered. "Please don't ever leave me."

I went deathly still at the desperation in her voice. She didn't mean now. She meant ever, and I felt a stab of undeserved anger toward her brothers. I knew they had to do what was best for them, but coming on the heels of Aramis's death, their departure felt like abandonment to Cyra.

I eased down onto the floor and tried not to flinch as my ass hit the cold marble. Cyra seemed to be done throwing up, so I pulled her against me and wrapped my arms around her to keep her warm. I wasn't planning to sit here long, but Cyra needed a minute, just one minute, where she was assured that I was here and that I wasn't going anywhere.

I squeezed her even tighter and felt the slackness in her body. A quick peek into her mind told me she was asleep, so she wouldn't hear my next words, but I said them anyway.

"I'm not going anywhere, my love. I'm afraid you're stuck with me, now and until the Nemesis parts us."

Tandem Read: Go to *Clash of Stone and Steel* (Bk 3), Chapter 22-26

Chapter 13

Bressen

The thoughts of the High Council members bombarded me as soon as Cyra and I walked through the portal into Gendris the next morning. I wanted to block them out of my mind, but I forced myself to listen for a moment before shutting them out. Cyra could only read minds when she tried to, but my mind powers were stronger, and I could often read those around me unless they or I put up a mind shield. Especially mortals. Perimortal minds were harder, but mortal minds were open to me.

As a rule, I tried not to read minds indiscriminately. I generally only allowed myself into someone's head if they gave me reason to believe I should know what they were thinking, but there were exceptions, and this was one of them. I liked to know what I was dealing with whenever I stepped into a situation that required diplomacy, and I could often glean important bits of information at first meeting before people were prepared to govern their thoughts against me.

If I'd hoped to hear anything useful, however, I was disappointed.

Don't think. Don't think. Don't think…

Is someone baking? I smell cinnamon.

She's not that pretty. If I were younger, I could steal him from her.

Is my brain melting? I feel like it's melting…

Lord Bressen, if you're reading my mind, your pants are unfastened.

My hand twitched toward the fly of my pants, but I stopped just in time and searched the group for the face of the man whose voice I'd recognized. My eyes met those of Lord Varun of Turlan. I half expected him to be smiling at almost making me reach for my groin in front of the whole council, but he was as stone-faced as ever. I wasn't sure I'd seen the man smile in the three decades I'd known him.

A good effort, Lord Varun, I said into his mind and was pleased to see him wince.

No matter how much you were expecting it, hearing a mind wraith speak into your head could be disconcerting if you weren't used to it. Even Cyra had jumped the first time, although she'd adjusted quickly to having me in her head. At least part of that was likely due to our soul bond. The other part was probably because she was a syphon. Once she'd started accumulating powers, she'd done so quickly, and she'd had to adapt to them just as fast.

My eyes went to Cyra now as if drawn of their own accord. She was so gods damned beautiful. She'd felt better this morning after her overindulgence last night, thanks to her healer magic, and I'd fucked her again just before we came here. I was almost certain I'd redone my pants after I'd let her up from where I'd bent her over the table in our bedroom.

I glanced quickly at the back of her dress to be sure her own clothes were in order. There was the hint of a wrinkle where I'd pulled the fabric up over her hips, but nothing obvious.

I stepped in front of Cyra and pressed my lips to hers tenderly. She blinked at me in confusion when I pulled back, but I only smiled at her. The kiss was partially compelled by the sudden wave of love that washed over me, but it was also for the benefit of Lady Yadwyn, who seemed to think there was a chance in the three hells I would've ever chosen her over Cyra. She knew better now.

Cyra smiled back, and my eyes widened as I felt her hands work gently at the front of my pants. Gods above, was she…?

Your pants really are unfastened, she said into my mind as she redid them for me.

I grunted, both because I now owed Lord Varun an apology and because I was getting hard again with her hands brushing my groin.

"For the gods' sakes, you should've gotten all that out of your system before you got here," a teasing voice said from the back of the group.

Cyra and I both turned, and Cyra let go of me to hurry toward Raina, who'd just pushed her way in front of everyone. The women threw their arms around each other in a fierce hug, and I sighed indulgently. Raina was the only person who could compete with me for Cyra's attention, and – given that the two hadn't seen each other in a few weeks – Raina currently took precedence.

In truth, I was grateful Cyra had Raina. The need for Cyra to hide her powers growing up meant she hadn't had the luxury of friends outside of her brothers, so she was overdue in that area.

I also liked Raina as a person, although I'd never admit it to her. While Raina had originally been terrified of me, as most people who didn't know me were, she'd learned quickly I was harmless to those who weren't a threat to me or anyone I cared for. Unfortunately, that sometimes led her to speak her mind a little too freely around me, but I grudgingly respected her for that.

I surveyed the council members. Varun was the only one who didn't fear me, as evinced by his earlier boldness. All the others looked as though they were waiting for me to make Raina drop dead.

They didn't look at me directly, but that's because I had my halo glamour up. The glamour was a kind of undulating aura that surrounded me and kept people from being able to look at me for too long. Perhaps I was a giant ass for wearing it, since it often made people dizzy or queasy, but I was a statesman above all else, and I'd use every trick in my political playbook to get what I wanted when necessary. I'd let the glamour fade gradually once we were seated and discussions were underway, but until then, I wanted the Council off-balance.

I surveyed the six members of Polaris's current ruling body. I hadn't heard anything in the mind of Lord Marcus of Karch, but he was one of two perimortals in the group and could put up a mind shield. He still held the slim hope the council might choose him to ascend to Polaris's Triumvirate seat, but the other members were too petty to let one of their own take the seat.

All but Varun anyway. The man was shrewd, and – if not for Raina - he would've been my own choice to ascend to the Triumvirate. To be sure, he would've been a huge pain in my ass, but I welcomed the challenge. Despite what people thought, I believed in the diffusion of power. I could easily have disbanded the Triumvirate after Ursan and Jerram's deaths and made Thasia a monarchy, but I'd never considered it.

There was still time for me to regret that decision, but for now…

"Lord Bressen, Lady Cyra, welcome back to Gendris," Lord Wendel said as he gave us a small bow. He'd been the one trying not to think, and he was usually the unofficial spokesperson for the council.

"Thank you for granting my request to meet," I said as Cyra and Raina only now pulled themselves apart. "Lord Aidan hasn't arrived yet?"

"No," Wendel said. "We expect him at any moment, though."

I turned to Cyra. "I assume you and Raina have some catching up?"

This would be a meeting of Triumvirate business, so while I often involved Cyra in matters pertaining to Hiraeth, and the council let Raina sit in on matters related to Polaris, neither of the women could be here for this meeting. Officially, Cyra was only my consort, and Raina had no standing in the Triumvirate – yet – so they'd have to find somewhere else to be while I spoke with Aidan and the council.

Technically the council wasn't actually part of the Triumvirate either, but they were currently the authority in Polaris, so I needed to loop them in on what was going on with Sandrian and Magdalene.

I was also prepared to put my foot down with regard to their selection of a new ruler. It was long-past time for them to either appoint Raina or choose someone else. Luckily, I had something up my sleeve that might finally tip the scale on that count.

"Of course," Cyra answered. "We'll just do the things young women like us usually do when left to our own devices."

"Drink, gamble, and fight?" I asked.

"Not necessarily in that order," Cyra said with a wink.

I winked back at her. The last time she'd joked about doing those three things, I'd found her and Raina doing exactly that a few days later. I hoped this time it really was a joke.

"Let me know when you're done," Cyra said as she looped her arm through Raina's and the two headed off to do the-gods-only-knew-what.

I felt a stab of guilt as I watched them go. Cyra knew my main reason for calling this meeting with Aidan and the council, but she didn't know what else I planned to discuss with them. I hated keeping secrets from her, but if I told her, she'd feel obligated to tell Raina, and I couldn't have her doing that. Not yet. Not until I had a full plan.

I just hoped she'd eventually understand that this was the best possible outcome.

Cyra and Raina had just disappeared around the corner when another portal flared open and Aidan stepped through it from Seatherny, followed by Maziren. Aidan looked as happy to be here as he'd been the last time I'd seen him, and I prayed this meeting would go better than our last.

"Ah, Lord Aidan," Wendel said. "Welcome to Gendris. Now that we're all here, shall we move into the meeting chamber?"

"Lead the way, Lord Wendel," I said, and the man turned to head out of the foyer and toward the palace's meeting rooms.

I fell into step beside Aidan as we walked. "Good to see you again Aidan. How are you?"

He grunted. "As I told you before, I'm fine."

"I just wanted to be sure," I said. "You haven't seemed yourself lately. Have you recovered from your brush with Cyra's lightning?"

I watched his brow pinch out of the corner of my eye.

"It takes more than a little lightning to do me in," he scoffed. "But I'll take an apology from your wife when she's ready to beg my forgiveness."

It was my turn to furrow my brow. I knew Cyra got along with Jasper better than Aidan, but I didn't think she was on bad terms with the lord. If he wanted an apology, Cyra would be happy to give it – she did feel guilty about the lightning – but it surprised me Aidan wanted one enough to demand it, let alone use the words 'beg my forgiveness.'

"I'll let her know you're ready to hear it," I said, more coldly than I intended.

I glanced behind us at Maziren and was surprised again when she met my eyes. Maziren was normally a pillar of aloofness who only gave anyone any attention if it looked like they meant her lord harm, but there was something in her face this time that struck me as odd. Moreso even than the last time I'd seen her. Was I mad in thinking she wanted to tell me something?

I nearly tried to read her mind, but if I was wrong, I didn't want to set her off. Maziren and I had our own past tensions. I'd once attacked her mind when she'd dared to touch Cyra, so I wouldn't do anything just yet.

I was starting to get the distinct impression something was off in Derridan, though.

Chapter 14

Cyra

I followed Raina to the solarium of the palace as she complained to me about the latest squabbles she'd had with the High Council over one issue or another. Nothing had changed since the last time I'd spoken to her. The council still treated her like a figurehead, parading her around at state functions but giving her little power or say in anything that happened in Polaris. She was getting tired of it, and I didn't blame her.

I'd been meaning to talk to Bressen about pushing the council to make Raina's claim to Polaris's Triumvirate seat official, and I'd have to be sure I did that when we got home.

The solarium was bright and warm when we entered. With the direct sunlight it got and the weather just starting to get warmer during the day, the room was rather toasty.

There was a tea and coffee service laid out for us on a table between two chaises, and I sat down as I reached for the coffee. I paused as movement outside the solarium caught my attention, though.

Several large black birds, likely crows, had landed on one of the bare trees outside, and a few more joined them as I looked on.

"So is there something you want to tell me?" Raina asked.

I finished pouring my coffee and glanced up. "Tell you?" I asked dumbly, trying to gauge how much trouble I was in. I hadn't yet told her about Aramis, and I surmised she must've heard it from someone on the council. I didn't doubt she was hurt that I hadn't told her myself.

"Yes," she said. "You know, important information that maybe I would've appreciated hearing from my best friend rather than through the gossip circles?"

I let out a deep breath and set down the cream I'd just picked up. "I'm sorry. There's been a lot going on. I was planning to tell you shortly."

"You didn't think this was something I'd want to know sooner rather than later?" she asked.

"I…I didn't think it was all that urgent," I said. "I didn't think you knew him that well."

Outside the windows, more crows had gathered in the tree.

"You didn't think I knew him that well?" Raina said incredulously. "Did you forget that I fucking slept with the man, Cyra?"

My brows shot together as I stared at her incredulously. "You what? When did that happen?"

Raina looked at me as if I'd gone mad.

"You know when it happened," she said. "On the Harmilan."

I blinked at her. "You slept with my father on the-," I started to say, but I cut myself off as it finally occurred to me we were talking about two separate things. "Wait, what are you talking about?"

"What are *you* talking about?" Raina countered. "Your father?…" Her eyes flew open wide. "You think I slept with Aramis?" Her voice had gone so high-pitched I imagined dogs in the next town perking their ears. "Why in the name of the Trinity would you think I slept with Aramis?"

"I…No, I thought you wanted to know why I didn't tell you my father died," I said.

Raina's face fell. "What? Aramis is dead?"

I nodded.

"Oh gods! When did this happen? How?" Raina asked as she leaned forward to grasp my hands.

I gave her the brief version of how Jasper had been taken, the vision I'd had of Bressen's death, and how I'd lost control when we fought Sandrian and Magdalene at the temple. I told her how I thought we'd circumvented the vision when it turned out Bressen was alive, at least until we found Aramis and realized Magdalene had killed him. I told her Magdalene was a syphon, but I left out how both Axenus and I had recognized her, as that wasn't my secret to tell.

Raina sat unmoving in her chair as I finished the story.

"Cyra, why didn't you tell me?" she asked, hurt in her voice.

I sighed. "At first it was because Bressen didn't want the High Council to know what happened," I said. "I think it's some kind of information game. He's trying to make the point they aren't in the Triumvirate, as much as they might want to think they are."

Raina nodded. "At first?" she prompted, catching my word choice.

I gave a half shrug. "After a while, I just couldn't talk about it."

"Of course not. You're grieving," Raina said. She got up, sat down next to me on the chaise, and pulled me into a hug.

I swallowed against the lump in my throat that always formed when I thought of Aramis. "But more than that, I'm…ashamed," I said.

I hadn't realized how true it was until just now.

Raina pulled away. "Ashamed of what?" she asked as she took my hands in hers again.

Tears sprang to my eyes.

"It's my fault he's dead," I told her as my voice broke. "Aramis was a healer, not a fighter. I should've protected him, but I was too worried about making sure Bressen didn't die, and I was too angry at Magdalene for-" I cut myself off. "For taking Jasper," I finished.

If Raina noticed my hesitation, she didn't say anything.

"Cyra, no one is going to blame you for being distracted by the potential loss of your husband," Raina said. "You couldn't have known."

"I nearly killed everyone!" I cried. Tears streamed down my face as the pain and guilt I'd been trying to suppress for days broke free. "If Samhail hadn't shielded Aidan, Jasper, and Maziren, they'd all be dead. As it is, I may have done lasting damage to Aidan. He hasn't seemed himself since we got back."

Raina gathered me in her arms again, and I buried my face in her shoulder as the tears poured out. I hated crying, but it seemed like it was all I did lately.

"Cyra, please stop crying," Raina said as she began to sniffle. "Other people crying makes me cry too."

I only cried harder, and I felt Raina start to shake against me as she caught the contagion of my sobbing. It was several minutes before both of us wound down enough to pull away and look at each other.

"I'm sorry," I said as I used my thumb to wipe at the wetness on Raina's cheeks. "I didn't mean to make you cry."

Raina pulled a handkerchief from the pocket of her dress and dabbed at her eyes. "It's fine," she said. "It seems like you needed it." She wiped at my own face with a dry part of her handkerchief.

"Thank you," I said as she stood and went back to her chaise again.

"You should've sent me a message," she said. "I could've come with you. I could've helped."

I shook my head. "Absolutely not. I can't lose any more people I love. Three hells, I almost succeeded in keeping Bressen from going, and he's a lot more-"

I stopped, realizing I was about to say something potentially offensive, but Raina knew what I'd been about to say.

"He's a lot more powerful than me," she finished. "You're right. He is, and so are you, but that doesn't mean I can't fight."

"I know, but just because you can fight doesn't mean I want you to."

"Just promise me," Raina said, "no more keeping me out of the loop. I don't have to tell the High Council what's going on, but I shouldn't have to learn big things like this days after they happen."

"Fair enough. I'll be sure you know about major events," I said, then frowned as something occurred to me. "Wait. I thought you were upset because I didn't tell you about Aramis. If you didn't know about his death, then what did you think I knew that I wasn't telling you?"

Raina blushed and waved a dismissive hand. "Never mind. It's not important."

"It was important enough to upset you. Tell me."

Raina sucked in a deep breath, then exhaled it before she went on. "Damian is leaving Callanus. He's moving to Gendris, and he's going to be a guard in the palace. In *this* palace," she said. "I gave one of my old friends at the Citadel some message leaves so she could keep in touch, and she told me."

I took a moment to digest this news. Damian was a guard at the Citadel that Raina had hoped to get into a relationship with at one time. They'd slept together once, but then Raina had left for Gendris, and their involvement had ended.

"And you thought I knew about this and didn't tell you?" I asked.

Raina shrugged. "In hindsight I may have jumped to unreasonable conclusions, but in my defense, Damian usually works in Bressen's wing. I thought maybe you'd heard about it."

"No, this is definitely the first I'm hearing of it. But…congratulations? That's a good thing, isn't it?"

Raina looked horrified. "No! It's not a good thing."

I frowned. "Why not? I thought you two…"

"We had sex together once on the Harmilan, and then he avoided me until they came to take me to Gendris."

My frown deepened. "He avoided you?"

Raina sighed. "I didn't realize it at the time, but yes. He was acting a bit strange after the Harmilan. Distant. But I thought he'd just reverted to his shy ways. I didn't realize until later he was actively avoiding me."

"So you don't want him back, and you're…afraid he's coming to Gendris to try and get you back?"

"I don't know why he's coming, but either way, I can't have him here. I've moved on. I have someone else."

"Another guard," I said, remembering what she'd told me a while ago.

"Yes, Lucas. It's nothing serious for either of us. He has other women, and I have other men, but he comes to my room occasionally, or we find quiet corners of the palace, and I don't want to risk Damian finding out about us. Is there anything you can do?"

"Me?" I asked in surprise. "What do you want me to do?"

"I don't know. Keep the palace from hiring him?"

I huffed a laugh. "I don't think that's an option. Bressen and I are both on thin ice with the High Council after Fernweh. We have to be very careful where and when we call in political favors. I know Damian being here will make things awkward for you, but I don't think we can risk asking a favor for something like this. I'm really sorry."

I waited for Raina to be angry at me, but she only leaned back on her chaise in defeat.

"I had a feeling," she said, "but I had to ask."

"Just be careful about where you and Lucas have sex. Maybe limit it to your room instead of..."

I trailed off, not sure I wanted to imagine where Raina and this guard had been fucking each other. She satisfied my curiosity anyway.

"The pantry, the armory, the garden, the-"

I held up a hand to stop her. "Three hells, Raina! It's a miracle the two of you haven't been caught already."

Raina's expression turned into a smirk. "That's part of the appeal."

I sighed. I wasn't one to judge how Raina liked her sex. As long as everyone involved was willing, then people were free to do whatever they liked in bed. Or in Raina's case, in the pantry, the armory, the garden, the...wherever.

"What if someone from the High Council catches you?" I asked.

Raina shrugged. "Who I take to my bed has nothing to do with either my claim to the Triumvirate seat or my ability to rule the territory."

"They may not see it that way," I argued.

"Then they'll have a fight on their hands," Raina said. "I haven't exactly been twiddling my thumbs this whole time. I've been making allies of my own."

I was about to ask her who, when I became aware of the noise outside. I startled as I looked out the window to see that the large tree just outside the solarium and several small trees nearby were all covered in hundreds of cawing crows. It was as if the trees had suddenly sprouted black leaves that now hid their branches. The collective ruckus the crows made pierced through the windows and echoed in the solarium.

"Sweet gods," I said. "Where did all those crows come from?"

"Oh, don't mind them," Raina said. "That's just my murder."

I blinked at her. "Excuse me?"

Raina cocked her head. "My murder. A flock of crows is called a murder, and they're my friends."

I stared at her.

"That's the other news I wanted to tell you," she went on. "It looks like I inherited some of Ursan's ability to communicate with animals after all. It only appears to work on birds, but it's something."

"You can communicate with them?" I asked, shocked. "All of them?"

"Well, more collectively," she said. "It's not like I have one-on-one conversations with each of them. They seem to be able to sense my thoughts, and they do things for me."

"I…That's wonderful, Raina," I said, smiling. "I'm really happy for you. A little disconcerted, but really happy."

"They just like to be near me when they can," Raina said. "I can send them away."

She turned to look at the crows, and a few seconds later, the entire mass of them took to the sky, momentarily blocking out the sun.

"That's incredible," I said to her.

I'd managed to communicate with an eel once when Axenus and I had gone down to the shipwreck for *The Stalwart*, but commanding an entire murder of crows was something else.

I was about to ask her more when a message leaf poofed into existence in front of me and floated to the table. I picked it up and read it.

"It's from Jasper," I said. "He wants to talk. He says it's urgent."

"Invite him here," Raina said.

I stood and opened a portal to Seatherny. Jasper had said in his note he'd be in his sitting room if I was free, so that's where I opened the portal. He rose from his chair and looked through it at us.

"Come join us," I said. "We're having a meeting for consorts and not-yet-Triumvirate ladies.”

Jasper hesitated. “Is Aidan nearby?”

My brows pinched. “He’s on the other side of the palace meeting with Bressen and the council.”

Jasper nodded. “Can you obfuscate me so no one can see I’m there?”

My frown deepened. “If you want. Jasper, what’s wrong? You’re worrying me.”

Jasper stepped through, and I immediately put up a glamour over him before closing the portal. He hugged me and Raina in greeting and kissed our cheeks.

Jasper was mortal and older than me and Raina by almost two decades, but both of us had taken an instant liking to the Lord Consort of Derridan. Jasper was smart, good-natured, and generous with his time, as he’d demonstrated when he’d spent several days leading up to my wedding teaching me how to dance. Once we finally got rid of the threat from Sandrian and Magdalene, I hoped me, Raina, and Jasper would be able to spend more time together.

“Come. Sit,” I said as I sat down again on my chaise, moving over to make room for Jasper. “Tea or coffee?”

Jasper waved a hand to decline the offer. “No, thank you. I can’t stay long. I just needed to talk to you when I knew Aidan was otherwise occupied.”

Both Raina and I frowned deeply at him.

“What happened?” I asked.

“There’s something very wrong with Aidan,” he said. “He’s been different since the temple. At first, I just assumed he was recovering from the lightning, but it’s more than that.”

“Different how?” I asked.

“Well, to start, he’s been very distant with me,” he said. “He’s not one to show affection in public, but when we’re alone together, he’s always been warm, even effusive. Now he’s…cold. Sometimes even cruel.”

I nodded, urging him to go on.

"He was also very…uh, aggressive in bed the other day," Jasper said with a slight blush. "I'm normally the more dominant one, but we're flexible depending on our mood, and the other day…"

He trailed off as if unsure how to explain.

"He hurt you," I guessed.

Jasper met my eyes. "Yes. It wasn't just rough, it was almost violent. I've made excuses since then to avoid having sex."

I laid my hand over Jasper's. "I'm so sorry."

"There's more," he said. "I went into the library the other day, and Aidan had one of the female servants pinned against the shelves."

"What?" both Raina and I said together.

"He let her go when I came in and told me he was scolding her for not cleaning well enough, but there was definitely more to it," he said. "The woman looked frightened when she ran by me out of the library, and what he was doing definitely didn't look like scolding."

"What do you think happened to him?" Raina asked. "Why would he act this way?"

Jasper shook his head. "There's one other thing. We were talking about something the other day, I don't even recall what, but when I asked him a question, he brought up one of the other contestants from when they had the trials to select the new lord. I was confused because I didn't see what the man had to do with anything, but then I pretended to know what he was talking about."

"And this man was significant why?" I asked.

"He was disqualified from the trials because they learned he lied about who he was," Jasper said. "He claimed to be a lord, but he wasn't."

Raina and I looked at each other.

"I'm not sure I understand," I said.

"To be honest, I'm not sure I understand either," Jasper said. "It just made me wonder. After that, I started making little mistakes on purpose in what I said to Aidan. Whenever I spoke to him about things he should know, I'd be sure to get subtle details wrong to see if he'd correct me. In the past couple days, I've made at least a dozen mistakes, and he hasn't challenged me on any of them. What's more, every now and then Aidan himself will say something that's a little off. The other day I asked if he remembered how many years we've been married, and he was off by one. That's not a number Aidan would ever forget."

"What does that mean?" Raina asked.

Jasper looked between us, pain and terror written across every line of his face. "This is going to sound insane," he said slowly, "but I think it means the man I've been living with since the temple isn't Aidan."

Chapter 15

Bressen

I fought back a yawn as Lord Marcus continued his long-winded history of the ruling houses in Polaris. Thank the gods the council had no appetite to appoint him to a Triumvirate seat, because I really would've considered melting his brain – or maybe my own – if I had to listen to him drone on regularly. The man could take a question that needed only a yes-or-no answer and give an hour-long speech on the topic without ever answering the question.

My eyes actually started to flutter when Cyra's voice filled my head.

Bressen, wake up.

I fought down the smile that threatened. *Eavesdropping again, my love? Will you never learn?*

We may have a problem, she said, and I couldn't help the twitch of my brow at hearing the concern in her voice.

What is it?

Jasper is here with me and Raina. He wanted to talk, so I portaled him over. I can give you the details later, but the crux is that he doesn't think the man with you now is actually Aidan.

I was ready for bad news, but I still just barely managed to keep my features neutral at this information.

What do you mean he doesn't think this is Aidan? I asked.

It's a long story, but Jasper said Aidan has been acting very strange, very unlike himself. He hurt Jasper in bed the other day, for one.

Once again I only barely managed to keep myself from reacting. I glanced briefly at Aidan, who looked like he was seconds away from getting up and physically silencing Lord Marcus.

I agree Aidan's been acting strangely, I said. *Are you thinking it's another masque?*

I don't know, but we need to find out. A pause. *I know you're worried about crossing boundaries and setting political fires, but I think you need to read Aidan's mind.*

I considered this a long moment. *Alright*, I said. *Let me get back to you. I need to make sure he's distracted before I try.*

I could easily break into Aidan's mind, but doing it so he didn't notice was somewhat trickier. I was practiced and powerful enough that it shouldn't be a problem, but I wanted to take every precaution I could to ensure Aidan didn't sense anything.

I turned my attention back to Marcus. He seemed to be winding down his lecture. We'd started out discussing Sandrian and Magdalene, but the imminent threat from them had naturally segued into the topic I really wanted to address, which was making the Triumvirate whole again.

We needed the government at full strength in order to handle the coming war, so I'd told the council it was time for them to step aside in favor of a new ruler. I'd even thrown caution to the wind and put my support behind Raina.

It was the discussion of a new ruler that had prompted Marcus's lecture on the history of Polaris's nobility. He favored letting someone from one of the prominent houses ascend, but the problem was that if a person from one house was chosen, all the other houses would object. There was no fair way to choose a successor without planning something like the lord trials in Derridan, and it was far too late to do that now. The council had delayed too long. Half-mortal and illegitimate though she was, Raina had the strongest claim to the seat as Ursan's daughter.

To my surprise, Aidan hadn't backed me. In fact, he'd balked at the idea of letting a half-mortal ascend to the Triumvirate, which I'd thought strange given that he was married to a mortal, but that made more sense now in light of Cyra's news that this might not be Aidan. An imposter would welcome a chance to sow discord.

Suddenly Aidan's refusal to assemble his army also now made sense.

Nemesis take me.

I realized too late that everyone was looking at me, apparently waiting for me to speak. Marcus had finally stopped talking, and they were waiting for my response.

Fine. If they wanted a response, I'd give them one. It was time to stop playing it safe and put on a show.

"Thank you for that history lesson, Lord Marcus," I drawled. "But it's all irrelevant. Raina has the best claim to the Triumvirate seat. It's time to put her in it."

The council members all exchanged glances. They knew I favored Raina, but this was the first time I'd been so bold as to actually tell them – not ask them – to ascend her.

Lord Varun huffed a laugh. "Yes, ascending Raina would be convenient for you, Lord Bressen, wouldn't it," he said. "She's your wife's best friend, so that would give you control over both her and Polaris."

I scoffed loudly. "First of all," I said, "you've interacted with Lady Raina enough to know she doesn't take kindly to control of any kind, which – for the record – is one more reason she's an excellent candidate. For that matter, you've seen firsthand how little deference she pays me. I would've thought that might put her at the top of your list."

Varun opened his mouth to respond, but I cut him off.

"Moreover, had I wanted control of Polaris, and even Thasia," I went on, "make no mistake. Neither you nor Aidan would be here to argue with me about it."

I sat back in my chair, fingers tented in front of me, and I let my eyes glow red. Not just a flare, but a sustained burn that reminded everyone in the room I was in fact a threat they had no answer to.

The truth was that I did have the power to take all of Thasia, especially with Cyra by my side, and they all knew it. They'd always counted on my own restraint, my own indifference to ruling the whole country, but it was time to remind them that I could and would take matters into my own hands if necessary.

Three long seconds of silence balanced on the edge of my threat before everyone began talking at once.

I paid no attention to any of it. Instead, I took advantage of the chaos to reach my mind out toward Aidan. My power was a shadow slipping under the crack of the door in his mind. His mental shield was strong, heavy and solid like the gates of a fortress, but ultimately not impenetrable. I stole inside as a thief would, using the commotion for cover before disappearing into the crowd of Aidan's thoughts.

I sensed immediately something was wrong. To start, the thoughts and memories that swirled around me couldn't have belonged to Aidan. I hadn't known him long, but I knew enough about him to know this wasn't him. In particular, the intense hatred of mortals I sensed was wholly incompatible with a man who'd taken a mortal as his partner, a man who, only a week or so ago, had gotten onto his knees in front of Cyra and begged her to help him save that partner. No, this couldn't be Aidan.

But then…I sensed the second consciousness.

There was another presence, another mind pushed so far back into the darkest recesses that I thought at first it was merely an echo I was hearing. But no, that was a separate voice, a separate set of thoughts.

Aidan.

Yes, it was Aidan, but he was merely a passenger now, a stowaway in his own body, and the consciousness in charge belonged to…

Morland.

The realization was so jarring I nearly gave myself away. As it was, I felt Morland's mind pause for a moment, like he'd just hiccupped and was waiting to see if there would be another. I remained perfectly still, not daring to do anything that might alert him to my presence, but then his attention turned back to the flurry of comments and questions that the council was still throwing my way. I casually ignored them all as I slipped back out of Aidan's…no, Morland's mind. I should've stayed inside and tried to figure out his plan, but I was too shaken to try.

It was inconceivable that Morland had, for a second time, eluded death by jumping into the body of another.

I sat frozen for several long minutes as I tried to let my mind wrap itself around the situation. Morland had been with us when we'd returned from the temple because he'd been in Aidan's body. He knew about the three warriors Cyra had freed, and he knew Praya was probably alive.

And now he was sitting here in the middle of a meeting between a Triumvirate lord and the High Council of Polaris as they discussed what to do about the threat Sandrian and Magdalene posed. He'd undoubtedly been in contact with Sandrian already, and likely would be again later.

I stood up suddenly. We couldn't have this conversation. Morland couldn't be privy to our plans.

"Lord Bressen?" Wendel asked, alarmed by my abrupt movement.

"Gentlemen and ladies," I said, forcing myself to re-adopt an air of arrogant indifference, "Cyra informs me something important has come up in Hiraeth I need to attend to. I have to cut this meeting short."

I'm breaking up the meeting, I told Cyra. *Get Jasper back home now.*

What's wrong? What is it? she asked.

"But, Lord Bressen," Wendel said, confused. "You're the one who called this meeting. There's still much to-"

"And now I'm canceling it," I practically snarled at him. "Something's come up that needs my attention, and I must return to Hiraeth. I'm sure you understand."

Morland, I said. *Morland has taken over Aidan's body. Aidan is still inside, still alive, but he's not in control.*

A pause on the other end before a dread not my own filled my mind.

Sweet gods, came Cyra's disbelieving voice.

"Besides," I went on to the people in front of me, "I think we all need a moment to come to terms with what needs to happen, what *will* happen. It's time to ascend Raina."

I was met with silence on all sides. Aidan…Morland scowled at me, as did Lord Varun, but the rest of the council members looked only shellshocked. I'd told Cyra recently I didn't have the power to tell Polaris who they could appoint as a ruler, but – gods damn it – I'd do it now.

"I'll be in touch to schedule another meeting," I said. "In the meantime, decide what questions and concerns you have, and we'll work to address them. But make no mistake, our discussions moving forward will be with an eye toward finalizing Raina's ascent. I've been very patient with this council. I've given you ample time to solve this issue on your own, but the Triumvirate can no longer await your leisure. War is coming, and the Triumvirate must be whole."

Under other circumstances, I might've let the council have a little more time to come around to my way of thinking, but the news that Morland was alive and in possession of Aidan had changed all that. Their time was up.

Cyra, come get me. We need to return to Solandis.

I'm outside the door, she answered back. *The guards won't let me in.*

They will now, I said as I took over their minds.

A moment later the door to the meeting room opened, and Cyra hurried inside with Raina on her heels. Cyra immediately drew a portal as I came up next to her.

"Keep me posted," Raina told Cyra as they hugged.

Cyra nodded. "I will."

My eyes met Raina's as Cyra stepped through the portal, and I gave her the barest nod. Raina's chin dipped in the hint of a nod back.

I doubted the council would tell her anything of what I'd told them just now. They were likely still in denial, but Raina would learn soon enough that I'd just made her the new ruler of Polaris and a Lady of the Triumvirate.

Whether she'd accept the terms and conditions that would come with that appointment remained to be seen.

Chapter 16

Bressen

Jasper sat across from me at the meeting table in my study that evening, looking the way Aidan had looked not so long ago when Jasper himself had been taken by Sandrian. The Lord Consort was dazed, his skin off-colored and clammy as he sat staring vacantly past me. I checked his chest to be sure he was still breathing and saw it rise shallowly.

Cyra sat beside him with her hand wrapped in his while Maziren stood behind him, also looking much like she had that night weeks ago when she'd come here with Aidan.

Cyra had filled me in on the details of their conversation this morning when Jasper had told Cyra and Raina of his concerns over Aidan. Jasper had probably suspected a masque or even compulsion magic from another mind wraith, but I was certain he hadn't suspected there was another person entirely – and a sadistic sociopath at that – inside his husband. He'd been living and sleeping with another man for weeks, and one that had apparently been treating him and the servants at Seatherny like shit.

Gods damn fucking Morland.

"How did this happen?" Jasper asked.

He seemed to be speaking to himself. I wasn't entirely sure he knew there was anyone else in the room with him.

He'd gotten away from the palace by telling Aidan – or Morland, gods this was confusing – that he was going into the city market. He'd taken Maziren with him for protection, and the two had sent me a message leaf as soon as they were in a place Cyra could draw them a portal.

Morland hadn't questioned them going at all. He'd seemed eager for them to go, in fact, and they'd come straight here.

Of course, this left Morland alone in Seatherny unsupervised to do the-gods-only-knew-what.

"I'm so sorry, Jasper," Cyra said as she squeezed his hand tighter. She looked at me, and I saw the guilt in her face. "This is my fault. I thought my lightning killed Morland, but I must've moved him into Aidan."

Jasper didn't seem to hear her, but Maziren did, and the captain scowled. I shot her a warning look not to say anything to Cyra.

"What do we do?" Maziren asked instead.

Cyra and I looked at each other.

"Well, to start, you and Jasper need to watch Ai-…Morland as closely as possible," I said. "Between attacking the servants, trying to sabotage our preparations for war, and just creating havoc in general, he can't be left alone for long. But we also can't let on that we're watching him."

"Can't we just imprison him?" Maziren asked.

Jasper flinched at the suggestion but didn't say anything.

"Your only proof that he's not really Aidan is me," I said. "Think how that would look. One Triumvirate lord calling for the imprisonment of another without any clear indication of wrongdoing."

"Lady Cyra could corroborate the claim," Maziren suggested.

"My wife?" I said, giving her a dubious look.

Maziren waved a hand. "Fine. Forget I mentioned it."

"We can get Morland out of Aidan's body, right?" Jasper said, speaking up finally. He looked hopefully between the three of us. "If Cyra put him in there, she can get him out again, can't she?"

We all looked at Cyra. It was a valid question.

"I…I'm not sure," she said. "In theory I could, but where would we put Morland? I'd have to transfer his mind into something, and I don't think we'll get any volunteers to let Morland share space in their head."

"Does it matter?" Jasper said urgently. "Just get him out of Aidan."

"It does matter," I said. "Morland is extremely dangerous, and as much of an issue as it is to have him inside Aidan, at least we know where he is and can keep an eye on him. If Cyra tries to pull him out without any clear place to put him, we risk losing track of him. Or worse, he could get into Cyra's mind, and then we'd have a psychotic bastard with access to syphon powers on our hands."

I'd also die before I put Cyra in a position where I might lose her to Morland the way we'd lost Aidan. I wouldn't survive without her.

My eyes met Jasper's, and I was sure he saw what I was thinking because he looked away.

"We don't have an immediate solution," I said, "but I promise we're not going to give up looking for one. We'll do everything we possibly can to get Aidan back."

Jasper nodded absently. He looked down at the hand Cyra held and pulled it away from her. I felt the hurt and guilt spike through Cyra at the gesture. I wanted to yell at Jasper for making her feel that way, but I held my tongue. Jasper was in pain, and he needed someone to blame. Like it or not, Cyra was the easiest target, and I would've done the same thing if the situation were reversed.

Don't let it upset you, I said into Cyra's mind. *It was an accident, and we'll find a way to fix it.*

She didn't answer back.

"What do we do if things get…bad?" Maziren asked.

"In some ways that's almost better for us," I said. "If Morland does anything overt to endanger Derridan or the Triumvirate, the High Council and I can step in. Thasia isn't a monarchy where the king or queen can act with impunity. The Triumvirate is designed to provide these kinds of checks and balances."

"You'd remove him from power?" Jasper asked.

I nodded. "At least temporarily. I'm not sure how far Morland will push things, though. He's already done enough to cast suspicion on himself, but whether he'll be bold enough to cross a line into something actionable is another story."

We were interrupted by a loud, urgent knock on the door, and I let my mind reach out to find Surgeon and Serise on the other side.

"Come in," I said, confused as to why they were back. I'd sent them out to look for Samhail, but as far as I could tell, he wasn't with them.

The two gargoyles entered the room and came to stand before me.

"Did you fulfill your mission?" I asked, pointedly looking at the empty space behind them.

The twins looked at Jasper and Maziren, then back at me in question.

"Speak freely," I told them. At this point, there was no reason to hide what was going on.

"We found Samhail and the assassin," Serise said.

"But there were complications bringing them back," Surgeon added.

He held up his left hand while Serise held up her right. They each had a bloody bandage wrapped around the palm.

"Assassin?" Maziren and Jasper asked together.

"What happened?" Cyra asked, standing and coming over to them. She took Serise's hand and examined it with her healer magic.

"We found ourselves on the wrong side of the assassin's blades," Surgeon said wryly.

"She stabbed you?" Cyra asked incredulously.

"Lord Bressen, exactly what assassin are they talking about?" Maziren asked, stepping forward. Her hand rested on the hilt of her sword as it did when even the idea of danger was mentioned.

I leaned back in my chair and entwined my fingers. "Sandrian hired The Raptor of Avril to spy on me and Cyra, and a few days ago he gave her the go-ahead to kill us. Luckily Cyra picked up warding just in time."

"What?" Jasper asked, shooting forward in his chair. He looked at Cyra in concern. She gave him a weak smile and went back to working on Serise's hand.

"And what does Samhail have to do with this?" Maziren asked.

"The assassin escaped, and I sent Samhail and the twins after her," I said. "Samhail found her, but he apparently decided he had a better plan than bringing her back here to face judgement, so I sent Surgeon and Serise after them both."

I looked at the twins. "Did you at least find out what he's planning?"

"The assassin offered to turn Sandrian over to Samhail," Serise said. "Sandrian has a bounty on my dear brother's head, so they plan to contact him, and the assassin will pretend to turn Samhail over."

"What? No!" Cyra cried. She'd just finished healing Serise's hand, and she let go of it. "You need to go back and stop him!"

"My lady," Serise said, "we did try, and we got daggers in our hands for the effort. We're good fighters, but Samhail is…" She sighed, looking as if the next words tasted bitter. "Admittedly he's better than us, and with the assassin by his side, there wasn't much we could do."

I exhaled deeply. "Where did you find them?"

"In the village of Hallendale," Surgeon said. "Samhail took the rest of my message leaves and told us we'd have to fly to the Priory in Callanus to get back here. He directed us to a priest named Phaedrus who let us out in front of the manor a few minutes ago."

I groaned inwardly. This was why I'd let Phaedrus keep his secret about being able to portal for so long, because once it became known he could do it, he was called upon continuously to move people about. It was bad enough I'd used him as often as I did before Cyra learned to portal.

I added 'misuse of Phaedrus' to the list of things I needed to discuss with Samhail when I finally caught up to him.

"Is he at least planning to send me a message if he took all your leaves?" I asked.

The twins hesitated.

"That was his claim," Surgeon said as Cyra began to work on his hand.

I rubbed my temple. I really didn't need this aggravation on top of the Aidan-Morland situation. What good was being the Nemesis Incarnate if my own best friend defied me? Maybe I needed to start living up to my reputation.

"Is there anything else I should know?" I asked, looking at the twins.

They glanced at each other.

"Speak," I said, my patience long gone.

"There seems to be something between Samhail and the assassin," Serise said.

"What kind of 'something?'" I asked, although I could guess.

"Currently, only tension," Serise said. "Of the carnal variety. But I have a feeling our dear brother will end up between her legs soon."

I raised a brow. "You don't think he already has?" I glanced at Cyra to see what she made of this news, but her expression was unreadable, and I didn't sense anything in her mind. She seemed to be concentrating on healing Surgeon's hand.

"Serise has an uncanny sense about these things," Surgeon offered, "and she believes the little assassin is still keeping Samhail…unsatisfied."

"I see," I said.

"But I also sense her resistance wearing down," Serise added.

"Thank you for letting me know," I said. "If that's all, you can go for now. Rest tonight. Tomorrow you resume your normal duties with Cyra."

"They really don't-" Cyra started to argue as she let go of Surgeon's newly healed hand, but I cut her off.

Still not up for debate, I said into her mind.

She gave me a frustrated look and crossed her arms.

The twins, sensing I'd won the almost-argument, bowed to me and hurried out the door.

"What are you planning to do about the assassin?" Jasper asked me when they'd gone. "Gods above, what in the three hells is going on here?"

He stood and began to pace.

"What's going on," I said, "is that twenty-five years ago I let one dangerous enemy live, and another escaped death all on his own. Then the two of them reunited and found an even more powerful enemy with her own agenda."

I hit my fist on the table. And to top it off, we also had one Triumvirate lord who'd been taken over by the enemy, and one territory that hadn't even replaced theirs yet.

"As for the assassin," I went on, "let me worry about her. For now, you and Maziren need to keep an eye on Morland while Cyra and I look into options for getting him out of Aidan. Do what you can to undermine him. We can't let him sabotage Derridan's defenses, or Magdalene's army will march right into Thasia unopposed."

Jasper nodded. "I'll see what I can do." He met my eyes. "You're sure Aidan is still in there?"

I nodded. "He was as of this morning," I said gently. "Aidan is strong and resourceful. He'll fight Morland."

"I think he has been," Jasper said. "I told you Morland kept saying things that were just a little bit wrong. I think Aidan's been feeding him information, but he's been getting the details wrong on purpose to try and signal me. Maybe I can communicate back in the same way."

"Why would Aidan agree to feed Morland information anyway?" Cyra asked. "Wouldn't it help his cause to let Morland flounder?"

"Not if Morland is threatening to hurt Jasper," Maziren offered. "Aidan will do anything to protect Jasper, so if Morland threatened Jasper with harm if Aidan didn't help, then maybe this is Aidan's solution."

"I haven't known Aidan long," I said, "but that wouldn't surprise me."

"We should get back, Lord Consort," Maziren said as she checked the clock on the wall. "As Lord Bressen said, we shouldn't leave Morland alone for long."

Jasper nodded, and Cyra stepped up to take his hands in hers.

"I promise we'll do everything we can to get Aidan back," she said.

He gave her a sad smile and hugged her. I felt Cyra's relief at the gesture, proof that he didn't hate her for what had happened to Aidan.

Cyra drew a portal for Jasper and Maziren back into the market in Seatherny, and the two slipped through quickly before Cyra closed it behind them.

"Are you alright?" I asked her.

Her head snapped to me as if I'd just caught her lost in thought.

"Yes. Why wouldn't I be?" she asked.

I debated whether or not to bring it up but then decided to be blunt.

"Are you upset about Samhail and the assassin?" I asked.

She blinked at me. "What? No. Why would you think so?"

I shrugged. "You're close to Samhail. I just wonder how you feel about his possible interest in another woman." I stepped close so I was right in front of her. "It's okay to be upset."

She frowned at me. "I'm not upset."

She glanced down at her hand, and I knew she was looking to see if her own skin glowed with a lie. I resisted the urge to look into her mind and learn what she saw.

"It's strange to consider," she said, "but I wouldn't say I'm 'upset.'"

She seemed to be arguing with herself.

"Alright. But you know you never have to hide how you feel from me, right?" I said as I pulled her into my arms. "It's fine if you're still sorting through your feelings for Samhail."

Cyra had always been close to Samhail, and coming to terms with her complicated emotions toward him had been my burden to bear. In truth, I was just grateful it was him and not some other man she'd connected with. I could live with her loving Samhail.

Cyra just nodded.

"Would you like a distraction?" I asked huskily.

Fine, the distraction was as much for me as it was for her.

She smiled. "What did you have in mind?"

I lifted her onto the meeting table and slid her dress up over her thighs. My fingers skirted over the bare skin of her hips searching for the waistline of her undergarment, but they found nothing but smooth skin. I frowned and looked down.

Then all the blood rushed to my cock.

"You're not wearing anything under your dress," I whispered.

She let out a breathy laugh. "I was going to tell you about it while you were meeting with Aidan and the High Council to tease you, but the whole day went sideways before I had a chance."

I groaned. "Fucking hells, Cyra. You planned to tell me about this during my meeting?"

She nodded, and I threaded my fingers through her hair to grip near the nape of her neck. My mouth closed over hers to kiss her deeply as I held her in place. She whimpered, which only made me harden even more.

I pressed her back against the desk and pushed two fingers inside her. She was wet already, and I moved them slowly in and out as her hips undulated against my hand.

"We really need to have a conversation about appropriate times for you to arouse me," I rasped against her ear. I curled my fingers inside her, and she gasped in pleasure. "But first I'm going to make you forget all about Samhail."

"Sam who?" she asked with a laugh as I sunk to my knees and dipped my head between her legs to feast.

Tandem Read: Go to *Clash of Stone and Steel* (Bk 3), Chapters 27-30

Chapter 17

Cyra

I was at the vineyard the next morning when I felt the surge of Bressen's overwhelming relief tinged with anger reach me all the way from Tide's End. It made me lightheaded for a second, but I caught myself before I spilled the wine I'd been tasting down the front of my shirt.

Bressen? Is everything alright? I asked into his mind.

Can you come home? he responded a second later. *I finally heard from Samhail, and he has a bit of a situation.*

I portaled home immediately with Surgeon and Serise, and we found Bressen in his study. He pulled me into a long embrace as soon as I stepped through and buried his face in my hair. I hadn't realized just how worried he'd been about Samhail, and I hugged him back hard, letting him release his worry silently in my arms.

"What's going on?" I asked when he pulled back. "Where's Samhail?"

"Samhail sent a message leaf," he said, his voice lighter than I'd heard in days. "He and the assassin found a Rown encampment in the middle of Derridan. They followed a band of soldiers back from a village the men raided, and he and the assassin attacked the encampment."

"Gods above," I said. "Are they alright?"

"I assume they're both fine," he said, "but thankfully Samhail realized the situation warranted bringing me into the loop finally. Can you open a portal there?"

He handed me the message leaf Samhail sent that included directions on where to find them.

"You won't overreact when we get there?" I asked.

He raised a brow. "Overreact?"

"You won't attack Talyn or Samhail?"

He gave me a look that said I was being ridiculous. "Of course I'm not going to attack Samhail."

"Or Talyn?" I pressed.

He pursed his lips together.

"Promise me, or I won't open this portal," I said. Then I added into his mind, *And I won't open other things tonight.*

His lips curled into a wicked grin. *Do you really think that's a promise you can keep?*

It probably wasn't, but I wouldn't admit that.

"Promise me you won't attack the assassin," I said instead.

He sighed. "Fine. I promise."

I waited a few seconds to double-check the color of his skin, but there was no red glow.

"I sent a message to Aidan as well," Bressen said.

"What? You know he's not actually Aidan. We can't-"

"We have to proceed as if we don't know Aidan isn't Aidan," he interrupted. "It's not ideal to bring him in, but at least we can control the situation this way. We can't give him any reason to suspect we know something isn't right, and if he finds out we went into Derridan without telling him, it will only complicate things. For now, we play along." He paused. "And not a word to Samhail or the assassin just yet."

"You'd keep this from Samhail?" I asked.

"Just for a little while," he said. "I'm not looking forward to breaking it to him that Morland survived death yet again."

That was fair enough. Samhail had a special hatred for Morland after the man had almost used him to kill Bressen decades ago, and Samhail hadn't taken it well when he'd learned Morland was still alive the first time. I didn't envy Bressen the job of telling him it had happened again. Or that it was my fault. I only hoped Samhail would forgive me for that part.

I nodded, then turned and opened the portal to Derridan.

The first thing I saw was Samhail's huge form standing next to a table spread with papers. I caught only a glimpse before he stepped back quickly away from Talyn, but it had looked like he'd had his body pressed against hers as he leaned over her. I didn't have time to react before Bressen stepped in front of me to block my view.

"Samhail," he drawled, his own mask of cool collectedness back in place now that he knew Samhail was safe. "I was starting to think you forgot about us. It was a pleasant surprise to get your message."

He was trying to keep his anger in check by dampening it behind his swagger, but I felt his rage grow as his eyes landed on the assassin, and I suddenly wasn't so sure he'd be able to keep the promise he'd just made. Now that he knew Samhail was safe and his relief had passed, his dark angelus side was clamoring to be set free.

The two of us stepped through the portal, followed by Surgeon and Serise, and I closed it before coming to stand next to Bressen.

Samhail eyed us both warily. "I understand you don't agree with how I handled things," he said to Bressen, "but I had my reasons for doing things this way."

"I suspect I know your reasons," Bressen said, his attention landing on Talyn again, "but what makes you think I don't agree?"

"You sent *them* after us," Samhail said, eyeing Surgeon and Serise.

Bressen smiled and inclined his head toward the gargoyles. "And you sent them back with holes in their hands. Or rather, the assassin did."

"They deserved it," Talyn and Samhail said at the exact same time, and my brows arched.

Behind us, the two gargoyles growled softly.

Serise was right. Something had clearly changed between Samhail and Talyn. A few days ago, he'd been ready to kill her, as Bressen had. Now the two of them seemed…close.

Talyn was a beautiful woman, and Samhail had once told me gargoyles rarely passed up the chance to have sex, especially if it was with a beautiful woman. It made me think Serise had been right in her assessment.

"At least the verdict is unanimous," Bressen said, chuckling.

We need to handle this carefully, I said into Bressen's mind. *Something is definitely going on between the two of them.*

He's fucked her, Bressen responded.

Something lurched in the pit of my stomach. I'd known the day would come that I'd have to confront the idea of Samhail taking other women to bed, but to have Bressen confirm it so bluntly…I just wasn't prepared for that. Serise's theory was one thing, but Bressen knew Samhail better than her.

You know that for sure? I asked. *Did you read it in his mind?*

I don't need to read it in his mind. I can read it in his face and in the bulge in his pants he's trying to hide.

I tried not to look, but my eyes flicked quickly to Samhail's groin. I couldn't see anything since Talyn was in front of him, but Bressen had a better angle.

All the more reason to tread carefully, I said. *You may recall, unbridled lust can make men do strange things.*

Bressen scoffed into my mind.

"What I think Bressen means to say," I said finally, "is that we were worried about you, Samhail."

"I understand," he said, "and I apologize for worrying you, but I needed to do it this way to give you deniability." He looked at Bressen. "As you're aware, I can get away with things you can't in your role as a Lord of the Triumvirate."

"So you were protecting me?" Bressen said, crossing his arms.

"In a way," Samhail said.

"Or were you protecting someone else?" Bressen asked, looking pointedly at Talyn.

"That's not what I was doing," Samhail insisted, then looked at me.

I wasn't surprised to see a slight rosy hue bloom on his skin, as if he'd spent too long in the sun today, but I forced myself to keep my face neutral. I suspected Samhail didn't even realize it was a lie. He'd looked at me, seeking confirmation he was telling the truth, but I couldn't give it.

"Regardless of your motivations," Bressen went on, "now would be a good time to tell us what in the three hells is going on."

"I need a favor first," Samhail said.

"Oh?" Bressen said.

"Talyn was injured in the fight against the soldiers." Samhail turned to me. "Can you heal her?"

I opened my mouth to speak but stopped short when the resounding *No* from Bressen boomed in my mind.

We've been over this already, I replied. *I won't refuse to heal someone who's injured.*

Bressen had already tried to keep me from healing Talyn's broken ribs the day we found her, and he'd lost that battle, as he'd lose this one.

"I'm happy to do what I can. We just need to have Lord Aidan join us first," I said.

I turned and opened another portal behind me so Aidan could step through, followed by Maziren.

"Someone needs to start explaining now," Aidan said as I closed the portal behind him and his captain. "What's going on? Why are you all in Derridan?"

"I'll explain in a minute," Samhail said. "First, Cyra needs to-"

"Why don't you go talk to Bressen and Aidan outside," I suggested. "I'll stay here and take care of Talyn."

"No!" Samhail and Bressen both said together, and I raised a brow.

"Talyn and I will be perfectly fine here on our own. Won't we?" I said, turning to her. "I assume you're not planning to assassinate anyone?"

The woman frowned but nodded. "No assassinations today, my lady. I don't mean you any harm."

"She speaks the truth," I told Bressen, and his mouth thinned.

Cyra-

I'll be fine, I said, cutting off his protest. *Maybe she'll talk to me if it's just the two of us. We were starting to become friends before all this.*

I wasn't as certain about that as I sounded, but I liked to think I'd been breaking through Talyn's shell. She'd still tried to get into our room one night to kill me and Bressen, but maybe she wouldn't have gone through with it. Maybe.

"Fine," Samhail said as he turned back to Bressen. "This way."

Bressen, Samhail, Aidan, and Maziren all left the tent, but Surgeon and Serise didn't budge.

"Please go outside and guard the entrance," I said to them.

The twins exchanged glances.

"My lady, I don't think-" Serise started to say, but I cut her off.

"Talyn and I will be fine alone," I said. "Please go guard the entrance."

They exchanged another look but turned reluctantly and went outside.

I looked at Talyn when the flap of the tent closed behind the gargoyles, but she avoided my gaze.

"So Talyn, is it?" I asked lightly. "It's nice to meet the real you."

She met my eyes finally, and there was a strange mix of regret and defiance in her look.

"You have an injury I should heal?" I asked, determined not to let the awkwardness keep me from doing what Samhail had asked me to do, or what Aramis would've expected me to do.

"It's barely a scratch," Talyn said as her hand went to her stomach.

"Let me see anyway," I said. "Maybe you can lie down on the table."

"Not the table," she said quickly, and I blinked.

"Very well," I said. "You can stand I suppose."

I stepped closer to her, noticing the way her muscles tensed as if she meant to run, but she stayed where she was. I lifted my hands and let my magic search for injuries. She had a gash on her arm and two deeper cuts across her abdomen.

"Let me see your arm," I said, and she pulled up the sleeve and held it out. It looked like she'd tried to bandage the cut, and I removed the bindings so I could see it.

"This wasn't made by a blade," I noted. "It's jagged instead of clean."

"There were a few symbionts among the soldiers," she said. "I let a couple of them get too close."

I nodded and hovered my hand over the wound to heal it.

"At least I understand now why you resisted my attempts to be friends so strongly," I said. "I suppose it's hard to make friends with someone you plan to kill."

If I'd expected an apology, I was disappointed. Talyn only clenched her jaw and remained silent.

"Let me see your stomach," I said.

She lifted her shirt and unwrapped the binding from around her waist.

"You put the bandages on?" I asked.

There was a long pause before she answered. "Samhail did."

Something twinged in my chest. Samhail had bound her wounds. He'd insisted I heal her, and he'd been standing close to her when I'd first opened the portal.

I clamped my jaw shut to keep from asking the question I wanted to ask right now, especially given how creased and matted the bandages looked. Instead, I focused my energy on healing Talyn's stomach wounds.

We didn't speak as I healed her, and I stepped away when I was done.

"Thank you," she said.

Then her eyes lit on something behind me, and she blanched. I spun around to see what had caught her attention, but there was no one there and nothing out of the ordinary.

Then I saw it.

I walked toward the side of the tent where a rumpled bedroll lay on the ground, the blankets streaked with blood.

"Gods above," I breathed. "What happened here?"

I looked at Talyn. She watched me with wide eyes, her jaw working to speak although no sound came out.

"It looks like someone used these blankets to clean blood off them," I observed.

"Yes," Talyn said unsteadily. "That's certainly what it looks like."

Her carefully worded answer didn't fool me, nor did the false look of calm she was trying to effect.

I looked back at the blankets on the ground. Someone's bedroll...

The pieces all fell into place as I took in the streaks of blood still smeared on Talyn in places. Samhail's clothes had been clean, but I'd seen blood on his skin. He would've removed his clothes to shift...

"Did...did you and Samhail have sex here?" I asked Talyn.

I wasn't going to tiptoe around this with her. I suddenly needed to know what they'd done. She could tell me to go to the three hells if she wanted, but I had to ask.

Talyn opened and closed her mouth again. "Yes," she said finally.

My stomach felt like something was trying to claw its way out. I knew I had no claim on Samhail, that he was free to be with whomever he wanted, but being faced with the evidence he'd moved on was an entirely different thing. That he'd chosen to fuck a woman who'd been sent to kill me was even harder to accept.

Exactly what had happened between Samhail and Talyn on their journey to cause such a turn?

"You had sex here? While you were both still covered in blood?" I asked incredulously, still not quite willing to let myself believe it.

"It was...battle lust," Talyn said, her voice a bit hoarse. "We were both wound up from the fight. It was nothing more."

My chest tightened as the rosy glow bloomed on her skin. Like Samhail earlier, though, I suspected she didn't realize it for the lie it was.

"This was the first time?" I asked.

"Yes."

"You won't be with him again?" I had no right to ask such questions, but they jumped from my mouth before I could stop them.

Talyn seemed to wrestle with herself before she said, "No, I won't."

I waited to see the glow again, but her skin remained its normal hue.

The tightness eased in my chest, but I chastised myself inwardly at the relief I felt. Raina had recently told me my problem wasn't that I still wanted Samhail. It was that I'd chosen Bressen, but I didn't want Samhail to have anyone else, and that wasn't fair.

She'd been right, of course, but it appeared I still had a ways to go before I could accept the idea of seeing Samhail with someone new. I wanted him to be happy, and I had to acknowledge that his happiness might involve someone other than me.

"Why not?" I asked, then forced myself to add, "I can see the two of you being compatible in a strange sort of way."

It was true. There was something about Talyn that reminded me of Samhail, and now that I let myself consider the possibility of them being together, I couldn't shake the thought.

Talyn only huffed an incredulous laugh. "We've tried to kill each other a few times now," she said. "I'm not sure compatible is the word I'd use."

I opened my mouth to ask her when she'd tried to kill Samhail, then shut it again. I'd choose to believe she was just exaggerating.

"We should burn those blankets before anyone else sees them," I said.

Talyn looked relieved by the suggestion, and we gathered them up. I followed her to the entrance of the tent, but she jerked to a stop.

"The gargoyles. We can't-"

"Surgeon and Serise will be asleep for a few minutes," I told her. I'd already slipped into their minds and put them to sleep standing up.

We both looked out to see the coast was clear. Sure enough, the two gargoyles still stood at the entrance to the tent, but they didn't move when we walked out, and I heard Surgeon snoring softly.

We couldn't see the others from here, so we stepped out to the fire pit in front of the tent, and Talyn started to feed the blankets into the fire.

"Just toss them on top," I told her. "I'll make sure they burn."

She nodded and dropped the blankets onto the fire. It began to smoke as they smothered the flames, but I held out a hand, and my fire magic engulfed them. We stepped back as the flames roared up in the pit and the blankets burned in earnest.

I looked at Talyn, but she was staring into the fire with a strangely vacant expression.

"Are you alright?" I asked.

She started at my voice, then shook her head. "I'm fine."

We went back inside the tent, but now that she was healed and we didn't have anything to do, an awkward silence fell. Until Talyn broke it.

"You've fucked Samhail as well," she said.

I choked. On what, I had no idea. Air apparently, but I coughed for several seconds before I could talk. Fair enough. I'd been blunt with her.

"He…he told you?" I asked.

"He admitted it, yes," she said. "But I've suspected for a while there was something between the two of you. It's why I came to him looking like you that time. I took it further than I should've, but he all-but admitted he'd fucked you then. Something about having Lord Bressen's permission to touch you."

My jaw hung open as I listened. I knew Talyn had been watching us closely, but it unnerved me to think my involvement with Samhail was obvious enough to see.

"How many times?" Talyn asked, snapping me back from my daze. "Do you take him to your bed regularly?"

"No," I answered quickly. There was something in her tone, and for reasons I didn't understand, I felt the need to reassure her. "Only twice, and it's over now. Samhail and I became very close due to…certain circumstances. We're still close, but our last time together was the end."

Talyn cocked her head in interest. "Why?"

Gods above. I had no idea how to answer that without giving her the whole sordid tale, and I had no intention of doing that. I thought for a moment before I finally said, "From what I understand, gargoyles can have sexual relationships without getting emotionally attached. I can't."

A complex cocktail of emotions passed across Talyn's face that made me wish I'd been reading her mind.

"You don't believe Samhail has an emotional attachment to you," she concluded, and I wondered if I imagined the relief in her voice.

"Samhail cares for me and always will," I said, "but he's not in love with me. According to him, gargoyles don't fall in love in general."

I knew I should've stopped a sentence earlier as Talyn flinched. She quickly masked her reaction, and I wondered if she knew she was falling in love with Samhail. The emotions I saw on her face were barely there, and she had her mind shield up, but I was certain of her feelings for him.

I hadn't observed Samhail as closely, but I now suspected I'd see something similar in him. He'd tried to shield this woman from Bressen's wrath, and that spoke volumes.

I was surprised to realize that the idea of Samhail and Talyn in love with each other didn't upset me as much as I expected. Strangely, I found it easier to accept that Samhail might spend the rest of his life with one woman than to think he'd continue to fuck whoever struck his fancy. Three hells, perhaps I'd even take credit for making him realize he could care for a woman beyond the bedroom.

"Would you really have killed me and Bressen that night you tried to get into our bedroom?" I asked suddenly.

Talyn was as surprised to hear the question as I was to speak it.

She smiled. "Him, easily." She paused. "You would've been harder."

I wasn't sure if she was kidding about Bressen. Her skin didn't show any sign of a rosy hue, but I couldn't believe she would've killed him.

I started to ask a follow-up question, but the flap of the tent opened then as Bressen, Aidan, Samhail, and Maziren reentered.

"Everything alright?" Bressen asked as he strode straight for us, and I saw the relief on his face. I'd closed my mind off to him during my conversation with Talyn so he couldn't hear what we'd said.

"Perfectly fine," I said. "Talyn and I were just catching up while I took care of her wounds. Neither were anything serious."

"That's good," Samhail said, eyeing us as if he was terrified by what we might've said to each other while he was gone.

I supposed he should be a little scared.

"And what about you?" I asked him as I looked for visible injuries.

"What about me?" he asked.

"Were you injured? Any wounds I can heal?"

"I'm fine," he answered quickly. Too quickly. "No injuries."

I started to nod, then paused as a slight rosy glow tinted his skin. I looked him over again but didn't see anything obvious.

"Are you sure?" I asked.

"I wasn't injured in the battle," he corrected himself. "I let the beast out to play for a while, and you know he doesn't bruise easily."

I noted his careful wording and decided I probably didn't want to know. At least I was getting more adept at discerning when people were attempting to skirt my truth seer powers.

Glenora's words came back to me then, and my stomach dropped. I dreaded the first time I might catch Bressen trying to carefully word an answer to my questions.

"Is there anyone else that needs to be treated?" I asked, turning to Bressen and Aidan. "Dare I even ask what it looks like out there?"

"It's probably best you don't," Bressen said. "I haven't checked to see if anyone is still alive, but I can do that now."

"I meant to leave one or two alive for questioning," Samhail said, "but things didn't go as planned."

Bressen paused to let his mind powers search the camp for survivors, and I did the same. I did sense a few people alive beyond the tent, but only just barely, and none were conscious.

Near the tent I sensed nine consciousnesses, but something cold trickled down my spine when I counted only eight of us, including Surgeon and Serise just outside. Both Bressen and I looked in unison toward a cabinet in the corner when our powers zeroed in on the ninth consciousness.

"We're in luck," Bressen said. "One person survived the slaughter, and he's been here in the tent with us this whole time."

Tandem Read: Go to *Clash of Stone and Steel* (Bk 3), Chapter 31

Chapter 18

Bressen

Back at Tide's End half an hour later, I sat across from the man I considered a brother and suppressed a smile at the defiance in his face. Part of me was furious with him. The other part was…amused.

We'd returned from the camp in Derridan, and I'd immediately called Samhail into my study to speak. The tension in his body and every line of his face told me he was ready for a fight.

One of the reasons he and I were friends was because he was the only person in the world who'd never been afraid of me and likely never would be. I'd always respected him for that. I appreciated it.

I'd already had a reputation as a dangerously powerful perimortal when I'd first arrived at the training camp for my father's army just over a century ago. Even my father's generals had stepped aside when I passed, and every soldier in the place had given me a wide berth.

Every soldier but one. Samhail had stepped right in front of me on the first day and simply stood there.

Truth be told, I'd gotten used to everyone moving out of my way, and I hadn't known what to do when the seven-foot giant with long white hair suddenly blocked my path.

Despite the strength of my powers – or perhaps because of it – I didn't use them often. Back then, they frightened me sometimes. I was hesitant to use them unless needed, and making the mountain of muscle in front of me move didn't qualify as 'needed.' Not yet anyway.

So we'd both stood there staring at each other as the minutes ticked by, neither me nor Samhail willing to be the first to step aside. We'd drawn quite a crowd by the end of the second minute, everyone waiting for the fight they were sure was coming. We both knew what happened next would determine our standing in the camp moving forward.

I'd heard about Samhail before coming to the camp, and I spent the entire time we stood there hoping the meeting didn't turn physical because I was sure he'd beat me to a pulp. I knew he was a gargoyle, and I'd heard they had hot tempers and quick fists. It took me a while to learn that only the latter applied to Samhail.

Ten minutes later, my father came to see why his entire camp had ground to a halt, and he'd broken up the standoff.

Being feared might seem desirable, but I'd found it a lonely existence. When Samhail had refused to move that day, I'd gotten my first taste of what it was like to be on the other side of that fear, and something in me was jarred loose. Samhail and I hadn't become friends immediately after that, or even weeks after, but it had nevertheless been our first step.

Now he sat across from me looking just as resolute as he had that day a century ago in the training camp, and I needed to understand why.

"I'll admit she's pretty," I said, "but is she worth a cell in Revenmyer?"

Samhail rolled his eyes. "We both know you're not sending me to Revenmyer, so why don't you tell me what's really bothering you."

I'd had bigger chairs made for my study since Samhail was often the one who sat there, but the chair he occupied now still looked small beneath his massive frame. He sat with his knees apart and his arms crossed, looking not the least bit intimidated by my threats of prison.

I raised a brow. "What's bothering me is that the person I trusted most to find and bring back the woman who was hired to kill me and my wife, instead went on the run and has been hiding from me for days."

His expression faltered briefly before his mask of defiance returned.

"I told you," he said, "I saw an opportunity and I took it."

"Right. You and the assassin were going to hunt down Sandrian, and you didn't tell me because you wanted me to have deniability."

"Yes."

"Bullshit."

Samhail scowled at me.

"Did you fuck her?" I asked, and the way his lips pursed together gave me my answer. I'd already known, but it was confirmation.

"What does it matter?" he asked.

I raised a brow. "It matters because I think you need to examine the real reason you went on the run with this woman."

He shook his head. "It's not what you think," he said. "I only fucked her for the first time just before I sent you that message about where we were. It was battle lust. Neither of us could help it."

I frowned. "Let me get this straight. You were alone with the woman for several days, and the two of you did nothing until this afternoon?"

He opened his mouth, closed it, then opened it again. "I didn't fuck her until this afternoon," he repeated, and I saw what he wouldn't admit.

"But the two of you did other things before today," I confirmed.

"It's complicated," he said. "She tried to kill me at least twice while we were traveling, but then she also saved my life. I honestly don't understand it all myself."

"So then help me understand why you agreed to this deal with her, because this makes no sense right now."

He sighed heavily. "It seemed like a viable option at the time. I caught up to her early the morning she escaped. She tried to fight me, but I managed to get a caronium cuff on her. She was terrified of going to Revenmyer, so she offered to give up Sandrian in exchange for me not hauling her back here to you. You didn't know where Sandrian was, and she had a reasonable plan for drawing him out. You just wanted her head, and I didn't think you'd give her a chance if we pitched the plan to you, so I made a judgement call."

"So you didn't tell me the plan for the sake of deniability, or because you were protecting her?" I pressed.

He sighed again. "Both."

I leaned back. "I see." I wasn't sure what to do with that admission.

"What happens to Talyn after tomorrow?" he asked.

I'd grudgingly agreed to let the assassin draw Sandrian and Magdalene out as she and Samhail had originally planned, but there were some complications.

I shrugged. "I haven't decided yet whether to send her to Revenmyer or just kill her outright."

Samhail sat forward in his chair. "You're still thinking of sending her to Revenmyer?" he asked incredulously.

"Or killing her," I reminded him.

He waved a hand and sat back again. "You're not a murderer."

"But she is. Or have you forgotten that?" I asked. "She's an assassin. She was sent to kill me and Cyra. That's easily punishable by death."

Samhail slammed his fist down on the arm of his chair, and I heard the wood splinter under the blow.

"Gods damn it, Bressen!" he said. "She's a powerful perimortal with a valuable set of skills, and she's on our side now. You'd be a fool to pass that up, and I've never known you to be a fool."

"I'd be a fool to trust her as easily as you seem to," I countered, my ire rising. "Is your cock so desperate to be between her legs that you're willing to risk my life and Cyra's for this woman?"

To my shock, Samhail surged out of his chair and slammed his hands on my desk. It groaned ominously under his weight. His eyes were nearly black as he stared me down, and I had a sudden flashback to the day we'd first met a century ago when he'd planted himself in front of me, stubborn and immovable.

"There are some things about me you can question," Samhail said, his voice deadly cold, "but never question my commitment to protecting you and Cyra. If I had any doubts about Talyn, I'd have broken her neck myself already. She's not what you think she is, and I don't appreciate you accusing me of thinking with my cock. My desire to fuck her – and yes, I do want to fuck her again – doesn't supersede my pledge to you and Cyra."

Our eyes locked, and I was sure we were both right back there in the training camp in that moment, staring each other down as the seconds bounced between us, wondering which of us would step aside first.

"I've never had cause to question your judgement before now," I said. "I hope that remains true after all this."

"It's not Talyn you should worry about," Samhail said as he sat back down. "It's Aidan. Doesn't he seem like he's been acting strange to you? I swear he killed that man on purpose today."

We'd found only one conscious survivor from the slaughter Samhail and Talyn had wreaked on the camp, the captain of the regiment who'd chosen to hide inside a cabinet in his tent rather than fight. It was a smart, if cowardly choice on his part.

I'd tried to question the man to ascertain the location of Sandrian and Magdalene's base, but as I'd expected, Aidan – really Morland – had tried to silence him before I could get anything out of him. Morland had instigated an altercation that allowed him to grab a dagger from Talyn and plunge it into the man's chest before he could reveal anything.

Luckily, I'd already slipped into the captain's mind and determined he didn't know where Sandrian and Magdalene were. I'd pretended to interrogate him only to see what Morland would do, how far he'd go. It hadn't been my plan to actually get the man killed, but Morland had acted before we could stop him.

I sighed. "He *did* kill the man on purpose," I told Samhail. "He wanted to stop him from revealing Sandrian's location to us."

Samhail's brows shot up. "What? Why?"

"Because he's not Aidan. Or, at least, he's not *only* Aidan," I said.

This was the part of the discussion I'd dreaded most.

"Morland is still alive, and he's in Aidan's body," I said deciding bluntness was the best approach.

Samhail stared at me.

"While you were away," I went on, "Jasper came to us with concerns about Aidan's behavior. I happened to be meeting with Aidan and the High Council at the time, and I broke into his mind."

I paused, remembering the horror of what I'd discovered.

"I found Morland there," I said. "Aidan was still inside, but he'd been pushed into a dark corner, and Morland had taken over. Morland wasn't able to destroy Aidan's consciousness, but he'd suppressed it somehow."

Samhail closed his eyes. "Fuck. We'll never be rid of that piece of shit, will we. How the fuck did he get into Aidan?"

"We believe it happened at the temple when Cyra was using the lightning she'd taken from Sandrian. You hadn't been able to fully shield Aidan from it. His foot was exposed, and we think the lightning connected Morland's mortal body and Aidan's."

Samhail frowned. "But how did that transfer his mind?"

"Cyra was wearing the two rings we found on *The Stalwart* at the time. Sandrian had wanted her to use the rings to transfer Morland's mind into me. As it turned out, the plan was a sound one, but Cyra ended up moving Morland into Aidan by accident instead."

Samhail let out a string of curses under his breath.

"So what do we do?" he asked. "Sandrian must know by now our meeting tomorrow is a trap. Do you expect him to cancel?"

"No, I expect him to set his own trap. We need to be prepared for Aidan to turn on us. I've assigned Serise to stay close to him."

"Does Maziren know?"

"Yes. She'll stay close to him as well, but she's too loyal to Aidan. I can't trust her to do what needs to be done in a worst-case scenario."

Samhail was quiet a moment. "You'd kill Aidan?" he asked.

I gave him a serious look. "I'll do absolutely everything in my power to keep Aidan alive so we can find a way to get Morland out of him, but we also have to prepare for the likelihood that it's not possible to remove him. I can still send him to Revenmyer if necessary, but we need to be ready to kill him if things go irrevocably sideways."

"Why haven't you put him in Revenmyer already?" he asked. "If you know Morland is in there, just do it. Why keep him free to make trouble?"

"Two reasons. First, we were hoping for just such an opportunity as tomorrow. We wanted a way to lure Sandrian and Magdalene out, and I have to imagine Morland has contacted them to let them know he's still in play. They're thus more likely to come if they think they can use him to get the upper hand."

Samhail considered this and nodded. "And the second reason?"

"Thasia has only my word that Aidan isn't really Aidan. I can't just lock up a Triumvirate lord without any clear indication of a crime or punishable offense. Derridan would revolt at what they saw as a power grab on my part, and the High Counsel of Polaris would support them."

He canted his head to acknowledge the point. "So then we show up for this meeting tomorrow, pretend we don't know Aidan is really Morland, and hope to the gods we can take down Morland, Sandrian, and Magdalene before they double cross and kill us all?"

I gave a resigned nod. "That sounds about right."

He let out a deep breath. "What do you need me to do?"

"You get to be the bait, so we have to find a way to make you look weak and helpless by tomorrow."

He gave me a knowing look. "Should I plan to meet you in the training yard so you can get some hits in?"

I shrugged and gave him a half grin. "A few bruises wouldn't hurt."

He stood. "I'll meet you there in twenty minutes."

"Make it forty-five. There's something else I have to do first."

He nodded and stood but then stopped before turning to leave. "Did you hear what the captain said about being immune to the symbionts?"

I nodded slowly. "I forgot about it in all the excitement, but yes. I wish we'd been able to keep him alive if only to learn more about that."

"I don't think he knew why he was immune," Samhail said.

"Maybe not, but if we'd been able to question him further, we might've figured it out. I'll have to sift through what little I was able to read in his mind before Morland killed him."

"You'd searched his mind already," Samhail observed. "Trying to get him to talk was just for show."

I gave him a look that said I was disappointed in him for not knowing that sooner, and one corner of his mouth quirked up in a smile.

"Right," he said. "I always forget how easy it is for you. So what are we going to do about this potential immunity thing?"

"I'll put Phaedrus and Axenus on it," I said. "Now that we know it's possible, we can look for a solution. We'll start by going back to all the villages that were attacked and talking to the people. Maybe we'll get lucky and find someone the symbionts tried to turn but couldn't."

He nodded and started to leave.

"Don't tell the assassin about Morland," I called after him.

He stopped and frowned at me. "Why not?"

"Just a precaution. I don't want her to be able to warn Sandrian."

His frown deepened. "She won't. I trust her."

"And while I'm almost convinced she can be trusted, I'm not taking any chances," I said. "If everything goes as planned tomorrow and she's still on our side by the end of the day, we can tell her everything."

He nodded and strode to the door.

"What are the chances you'll stay away from her tonight?" I asked.

He paused with his hand on the knob and grinned at me. "None at all. If there's a possibility I might die tomorrow, then I plan to spend tonight with my cock buried balls-deep in a fiery little red-haired assassin."

I rolled my eyes. "I suspected as much. Do I need to warn you to keep any sharp objects away from her?"

"That's a given," he said as he opened the door. "I'll be counting the knives at dinner."

I chuckled as he closed the door behind him. I knew Samhail well enough to guess what appealed to him about the assassin. I'd admit she was beautiful – I'd understated her at pretty – but she could've been half as attractive, and Samhail still would've wanted her. She was a challenge, and he could never resist a challenge. Gargoyles were drawn to strength and power, and the assassin had that in spades.

I suspected that tendency was part of the reason he'd initially been drawn to Cyra. Some part of him had sensed her power. He'd also seen my connection with her right away, which had made her forbidden, and it was a law of nature that men inevitably wanted what they couldn't have.

I sent a mental message to Ferris, my steward, and asked him to find the assassin and bring her here. Talking to Samhail had eased my mind about her a bit, but I needed to speak with her myself.

I wasn't sure I'd ever fully forgive her for the danger she'd posed to Cyra, but Samhail was right about one thing. The woman had a damned useful set of skills, and I was loath to simply dismiss that over my personal issues with her. If I could find a way to trust her and get her to trust me – I didn't think she'd forgiven me yet for clawing into her mind and nearly killing her – we might be beneficial to each other.

I didn't have to wait long before there was a knock on my door, and the assassin entered when I called for her to come in.

"I'm told you wanted to speak with me, Lord Bressen?" she said. She took only a step or two into the room, and she looked ready to bolt for the balcony again if she felt me in her mind. She wore a dagger at each thigh, and her hands rested on the hilts.

That should've been concerning, but it was telling that Samhail had let her carry weapons while they were together, and she hadn't killed him.

"I do," I said, motioning for her to take a seat. "And I promise not to kill you, if you promise not to kill me."

She looked as though she was seriously considering the pros and cons of this agreement. Finally, she strode the rest of the way across the room and took a seat in front of my desk.

"So then tell me, Lord Bressen," she said as she crossed one leg over the other. "Who *do* you want me to kill for you?"

Tandem Read: Go to *Clash of Stone and Steel* (Bk 3), Chapters 32-33

Chapter 19

Cyra

I stood next to Bressen in the woods by the clearing the next day where we waited for Sandrian and Magdalene, my ears attuned to any sign of danger. Surgeon stood behind me while Serise was several feet away as close to Aidan – or Aidan's body – as she could get without looking suspicious.

Maziren was close to him as well, but I was more confident in Serise's willingness to act when Morland made his move. Maziren knew the man standing there wasn't really her lord, but knowing that and being able to act accordingly were two different things.

Samhail knelt out in the clearing with Talyn standing next to him. The plan was to convince Sandrian and Magdalene that Talyn had drugged him and was handing him over. He appeared subdued but, of course, wasn't.

Samhail said something to Talyn, and they started a hushed exchange I was eager to hear. It was obvious the two of them were attracted to each other, but it was equally obvious they were fighting it.

Well, Talyn was fighting it. Samhail was…being Samhail.

They broke off their conversation as a portal flared to life across the clearing. Sandrian appeared on the other side, but he made no move to step through.

"I hear there's a reward for this one," Talyn called to him.

I let my mind reach through the portal to see if I could sense anyone else. I thought I felt Magdalene, but she was the only one. Of course, Magdalene might be masking the presence of others the way Bressen was hiding us. Bressen was also trying to steal past Sandrian's mind shield, but we had to tread carefully. If they sensed us and closed the portal before they came through, we'd lose our opportunity.

Morland had undoubtedly warned them this was a trap, but as long as they still believed we thought Morland was Aidan, this could work.

I kept half an ear on Talyn's exchange with Sandrian. She was trying to explain why she hadn't contacted him and how she'd subdued Samhail, but it didn't seem like Sandrian was keen to believe her story. Talyn tried to coax him through the portal to help her with Samhail, but he resisted.

It's not working, I said to Bressen. *He doesn't want to come through.*

We both jumped as Samhail suddenly fell forward and planted face-first onto the ground.

Gods, is he-, I started to ask.

He's fine, Bressen assured me. A pause, then, *Here he comes.*

I was confused for a moment until I realized the second 'he' Bressen meant was Sandrian. Our quarry had finally stepped through the portal, a cruel grin turning up his face.

My attention immediately narrowed to Magdalene as she stepped through after Sandrian. The hair rose on the back of my neck, and my skin flushed with anger as I pulled my power to me. I'd vowed to exercise restraint, but I couldn't control how quickly my power swelled inside me, begging to be released at the sight of the woman who'd killed my father.

The ground shook as I channeled everything I had into the earth behind Sandrian and Magdalene. A giant fissure ripped the field in two and separated them from their portal. I called on my aunt's plant magic next, and vines sprung up from the ground to wrap themselves around the two of them.

"Magdalene, you and I have unfinished business," I snarled at her as I stepped forward out of the woods, the obfuscation glamour lifting.

The other syphon only smiled as the vines holding her and Sandrian loosened and fell away. "Did you get that power from your auntie?" she scoffed. "I've had that one for a while. You'll have to do better than that."

One of Serise's containment fields appeared around Sandrian and Magdalene next, but the syphon only raised a brow and sent her power into the ground. I heard a shriek to my side and turned to see Serise fall through a hole Magdalene had created in the earth beneath her.

Thankfully, Maziren reacted quickly enough to grab Serise's hand and haul the gargoyle back up, but Magdalene's move had the desired effect as the containment field around her and Sandrian fell away.

Sandrian laughed. "You traitorous bitch," he said to Talyn. "I knew I couldn't trust you. I knew they'd get to you. Luckily, I planned for just such an eventuality."

I instantly turned to Aidan, sure this was when Morland would make his move, but he still pointed the crossbow at Sandrian. Samhail's urgent voice snapped my attention back to the clearing, though.

"Bressen!" he yelled. "There's something behind them on the grass."

I frowned, not seeing anything at first. Then I noticed it. The air on either side of Sandrian and Magdalene seemed to quiver ever so slightly, just enough that one would only notice it if they were looking for it. I remembered the effect from the first time Bressen had showed me his obfuscation glamour at the Citadel, when he'd caught me eavesdropping on his conversation with Jerram and Ursan. This time, though, the waver in the air stretched out widely on either side.

I looked down and noticed what Samhail had been talking about with the grass. It was matted down in the same area as if dozens, maybe even a hundred pairs of feet were standing on it.

"Symbionts," I whispered to Bressen. We couldn't sense the creatures' minds, but we'd at least expected to be able to see them.

"You're not the only one who can cast obfuscation glamours, Lord Bressen," Magdalene purred to him.

"And you may have taken one of ours, but we've taken one of yours," Sandrian said, grinning nastily.

The meaning of his words hit me, and I swung around to see Aidan already pointing his crossbow straight at Bressen. My scream was cut off as Serise slammed her arm down on the crossbow just in time that the bolt lodged itself in the ground at Bressen's feet rather than in his head. The gargoyle hit Aidan with a brutal punch next that knocked him to the ground, but my relief was fleeting as another crossbow thwacked from somewhere across the field.

Bressen's shoulder kicked back as the bolt hit him this time. He swore loudly but didn't go down.

"No!" I yelled as I lunged for him.

Several crossbows came flying toward us from across the field and landed at Surgeon's feet. He'd apparently summoned them, and I gave him a grateful nod.

"They're coming!" Talyn shouted, and I looked to see that the matted grass was now moving our way as the sound of stomping feet grew closer.

Dread pooled in my stomach. Magdalene hadn't lifted her glamour, so we couldn't see the symbionts. I had to do something or our people would be ripped apart by the unseen creatures. Or at least me, Bressen, Maziren, and Talyn would be. Surgeon and Serise were already shifting into their gargoyle forms and moving toward the symbionts.

There was only one thing I could think of, and I prayed it would work.

I called on my elemental water power, but instead of creating a deluge, I let the water form into mist. Infinitesimally small droplets materialized to shroud the clearing in fog, and what it revealed was horrifying. I couldn't see much more than fifteen feet in front of me, but there were dozens upon dozens of figures moving toward us.

"I need to find Magdalene," I said.

"Cyra-," Bressen tried to argue with me, but I cut him off.

"I'm going to find her and put a stop to this," I insisted.

I started toward the fog, but Bressen grabbed my wrist. I realized the crossbow bolt was still stuck in his shoulder, and I was torn between staying to heal him and going to find Magdalene. Worry for him made me pause, but there wasn't time to heal him, and finding Magdalene seemed more urgent. We'd be torn apart by the symbionts if I couldn't find her and make her drop the glamour.

"Bres-"

"Be careful," he said, his beautiful turquoise eyes capturing mine.

"Don't do anything reckless."

In other words, don't try to kill Magdalene. I couldn't promise that.

"I love you," I said instead and leaned up to kiss him.

It sounded like a goodbye, but I hadn't meant it to be. I'd just learned with Aramis that I could never tell someone I loved them too many times and that I should never wait to say it. After my father's death, I'd vowed to never let Bressen out of my sight without first telling him I loved him.

He seemed to understand. "I love you too," he said. "Be safe, and call if you need me."

I nodded and rushed into the fog to where I'd last seen Magdalene.

Bressen

I swore loudly as I pulled the crossbow bolt out of my shoulder and threw it to the ground. We'd known Morland would turn on us, but there was no way we could've known what else Sandrian had planned. It never occurred to me they'd put the symbionts under an obfuscation glamour.

I tried to let my power reach out to find Sandrian, but something still seemed to be blocking it. Maybe the tip of the bolt had been coated in some sort of poison?

I drew my sword, but pain from the crossbow wound shot through my shoulder, and I switched the sword to my right hand. There was still some pain, but it wasn't as bad, so I'd have to fight right-handed for now. I wasn't as good with my right, but I was competent enough. Samhail had made sure I learned, and now I was grateful for his insistence.

A void in the mist barreled toward me, and I swung the sword at it. My blade scraped across something firm, but the void only pivoted and came back at me. This time I stabbed instead of swiped, and I drove the blade forward with both hands as hard as I could, gritting my teeth against the pain. I felt the resistance as it pushed through something solid.

A high-pitched shriek rent the air as the blade disappeared about four inches, presumably into a symbiont, and I shoved harder so it pushed through more. Seconds later, a human form became visible as the dark blue substance of the symbiont slid off the body to puddle on the ground. Killing the symbiont had lifted the glamour, and I took a moment to acknowledge the vacant human face before I pulled my sword from its body and it slumped to the ground.

The face was that of a middle-aged man with light brown hair just graying at the temples and a couple days' worth of beard stubble. The man likely had a wife, perhaps children. He was someone's son. Someone's brother. Someone's friend.

In war, he was just another casualty, and one of many to come. I never took death lightly, but I also couldn't dwell on it. If I stopped to mourn everyone I killed, I'd end up dead myself.

As if to emphasize that, I had to throw myself out of the way as another void in the mist shot toward me. Thank the gods Cyra had gotten the idea for this fog. I couldn't see what was going on elsewhere, but at least I could tell when something was coming at me.

I turned to face the invisible symbiont as it circled around for another pass. I readied my sword and braced to shove it through the hard exoskeleton of the creature.

Just as the thing was on me, a massive form hurtled out of the mist and caught the symbiont by the throat, or what was likely its throat. A twist and crack of its neck, and the blue matter slid off yet another body.

I looked up at the giant stone form of Samhail and nodded my thanks. I'd know his gargoyle form anywhere. His glowing blue eyes met mine, and he nodded before disappearing back into the fog.

My body went cold as Cyra's scream pierced the air. It was a long keening sound full of pain, and every nerve in my body went raw as terror rampaged through me. What in the three hells had caused her to make that sound? I couldn't tell from which direction her cry came because the fog made the sound bounce around, and my frantic call to her was drowned out by the roars of three gargoyles who undoubtedly felt the tug of the divine imperative that willed them to help her.

"Cyra!" I yelled again, but either she didn't answer, or I couldn't hear her above the fighting.

I tried to access my power and reach out to her, but I still couldn't feel anything, and my skin prickled in fear. I had to get to Cyra.

I took off in the direction I'd last seen her run, but I didn't get far before a familiar figure emerged from the fog in front of me.

"Where are you off to in such a hurry?" Sandrian asked as he stepped in front of me. "Going to help your lady?"

I didn't bother answering. I just attacked. I swung my sword at Sandrian's head, but to my surprise he blocked the blow. I immediately swung again, but he parried that swing and my next two as well.

Sandrian had always been a competent fighter if not a great one, but he'd apparently improved.

I waited for him to attack, but he seemed content to stay on the defensive. He wasn't trying to kill me, I realized, just keep me from getting to Cyra. He couldn't beat me, but he could keep me at bay.

Dread flooded my veins as my mind went wild imagining what was happening to Cyra across the field.

"Cyra!" I yelled. "Answer me!"

"Have no fear," Sandrian said. "Your lady is fine. Magdalene just wanted some time alone with her, so you get to play with me instead."

Adrenaline coursed through me, and I attacked Sandrian in a frenzy. His eyes widened as I rained down blow after blow on him while he did his best to deflect them.

I half expected a bolt of lightning to hit me at any moment, but I supposed that was another benefit of Cyra's fog. With all the droplets of moisture permeating the air, Sandrian seemed afraid to use his lightning. I didn't know for sure what would happen, but it was possible it would diffuse enough to shock everyone, including him.

It was a small blessing, but a fleeting one. On my next wild swing, Sandrian dodged the blow and then lunged forward to press his hand to my chest. I cried out as his lightning jolted through my body, but, luckily, I was thrown back quickly enough that I only got a small piece of it.

My vision blurred for a moment, and I shook my head. I was on the ground as Sandrian loomed over me, and I rolled out of the way just in time as the point of his sword came flying down at me. The blade sunk into the earth where I'd just been a moment earlier, and I kicked out at his legs. They buckled under him, and he went crashing to the ground with a cry of surprise.

I was on him a second later. I didn't have the leverage or angle to use my sword, so I dropped it and punched him as hard as I could across the jaw. My shoulder screamed in pain as I forgot about my wound, and Sandrian took advantage of the second I took to collect myself. He pressed his hand to my chest again, and I was barely able to throw myself off him as his lightning jolted me again.

I groaned as I lay on the ground. I was starting to feel like my insides were being cooked. Thankfully, Sandrian was just as slow to get up.

We staggered to our feet, ready to fight again, when we both felt something change.

A pulse of power reverberated over the field and echoed in my chest. The air was already cool, but the temperature dropped several more degrees, and the sky darkened as if night had started to fall early. A strange clamor rose across the field from nowhere in particular, like the sound of hundreds of bodies moving and grunting.

The effect felt familiar, but it couldn't possibly be…

No one had that power but me.

Chapter 20

Minutes Earlier

Cyra

Spaces of seemingly empty air rushed toward me, but I pushed them back with a forcefield. I had my sword out, but I wanted to avoid killing any symbionts if I could, knowing now they could be people of Thasia.

"Magdalene!" I shouted. "Show yourself!"

There was no answer, and I pushed further into the fog. I tried to reach out with my seeker power to find her, but it was no use. The power was for finding objects, not people.

I reached out with my mind power next. I could be overwhelmed if I tried to use it in a crowd, but Magdalene, Sandrian, and our own people were the only ones I was able to sense. The symbionts were invisible to Bressen and I in more ways than one right now.

I sensed something to my right and followed it. I'd only gone a few steps before Magdalene materialized in the fog. She seemed to be waiting for me to find her.

"You're going to pay for what you did to Aramis," I told her. There was no venom in my voice, only matter-of-factness.

I drew a ball of sunfire to me and sent it roaring toward Magdalene, but a shield of blue light formed in the air in front of her and dissipated the sunfire before it hit her.

"I don't want to fight you, Cyra," Magdalene said. "I was hoping we could help each other."

I let out a bitter laugh. "You're mad if you think I'd ever help you."

"You want to kill me because you think I killed your father," she said.

"You *did* kill my father," I snarled.

She shook her head. "No, I didn't."

I stared blankly at her. "You expect me to believe that?"

"You have truth seer powers," she said. "Is my skin red?"

I froze. No, her skin was as golden as ever.

I shook my head. "I know you killed him. Your frost-"

"I froze his body after he was already dead," Magdalene cut in. "If you thought I killed your father, I knew you'd come looking for me." She smiled. "Rather than try to get to you, I figured I'd let you come to me."

My legs felt like stone as her words sunk in. If she hadn't killed him…

"If you didn't kill my father, who did?" I asked, but there was already a chill creeping up my spine. I prayed one of the symbionts had killed him, because the only other answer was too horrifying to consider. Please, gods, let it have been one of the symbionts.

But I could tell by Magdalene's pitying smile what the real answer was.

"You did, my dear," she said. "You killed him with that lightning you let loose when you thought your mate was dead."

The ground dropped out from under me, and I tried to blink Magdalene back into focus as my vision spun.

"You're lying," I croaked, the sound barely making it up my throat in any form resembling words.

She didn't smile, but her look still showed how much my willful blindness amused her. "You can see I'm not," she said.

I could. Her skin wasn't the faintest bit red.

Bile forced its way up my throat, and I began to choke. I dropped to my knees just in time to heave the entire contents of my stomach onto the grass. I gasped and retched as the horrifying truth of what Magdalene said settled on my chest like stones. Months ago, I'd felt the weight of a huge pile of earth pushing me down, but this was far worse. It was a weight that threatened to crush me.

A low wail pushed itself up my throat. It began as a murmur but built quickly until it turned into a full-blown scream of agony that vibrated my entire upper body.

Somewhere across the field, the roar of three gargoyles responded, but all I could do was clutch at my heart as tears streamed down my face. I heard Bressen call for me as well, but I had no breath to answer.

I'd killed Aramis. It had been me. I'd killed my own father.

If I'd thought I'd become accustomed to the feel of bone-deep pain by now, I was wrong. That same feeling of being torn apart from the inside that I'd felt when the vineyard had burned, when I thought I'd lost Bressen, and when I'd first found Aramis dead returned threefold now. My body caved in as I crumpled to the ground, wondering just how much more anguish my heart could take before it stopped beating altogether.

I felt a presence and lifted my head enough to look up. Through a blur of tears, I saw Magdalene standing over me.

"It's unfortunate," Magdalene said. "Your father was powerful. I don't like to see perimortals lost when it's the mortals that need to go."

I blinked back more tears as I stared at her. "What?" The question was barely a breath.

"Mortals are a scourge, and you're going to help me thin the herd."

My brows furrowed deeply. "I don't understand," I said as I tried to push myself up to my knees.

"I'm sure you've been wondering about my plan," Magdalene said. "It's to get rid of as many mortals as I can. Not all of them of course, but it's long past time to control their population before they overrun us more than they have."

I blinked again, not believing what I was hearing. "You serve the Protector. How can you justify that?" I asked.

"Protection is…subjective," Magdalene said. "Anything in excess can be dangerous. We use plants and herbs as medicine, but most, if taken in excess, can kill instead of heal. Fire can keep a person warm or be used for cooking, but when it rages out of control, fire will destroy everything in its path. Mortals are much the same way. A few of them are fine, but they become dangerous and uncontrollable when there are too many."

She knelt down on one knee next to me. "People pray to the Protector to cure them from disease, or for their loved ones to make it home safe from war, but if the Protector answered all those prayers, do you know how large the population would be? Disease and war are necessary to keep us all from starving to death or living in squalor from lack of resources. You're going to help me prevent that. Mortals reproduce far too often and too quickly, so it's time to do a little weeding."

"No," I said. My legs were still wobbly beneath me, and I couldn't stand yet. "No, the Trinity won't let that happen."

"They already have," she said. "Do you remember the Great Flu? That was my doing. I created that pandemic to clear out the weak, and it worked for a time. Unfortunately, the human body is frustratingly resilient, and mortals built up an immunity faster than I'd hoped."

I stared at her, hatred coursing through my veins. "The Great Flu killed my parents," I spat at her.

"Those people weren't your parents," she said. "They were mortal and thus expendable."

I surged to my feet and put everything I had into a ball of sunfire. Magdalene screamed as it hit her squarely in the chest. She must've seen me negate her frost with sunfire at the temple, though, because she did the reverse now, quenching the sunfire.

I didn't wait for her to recover.

Magdalene's eyes widened as she felt me fill her lungs with earth, but she reacted immediately with her own magic to pull it back out. For several seconds, our powers engaged in a kind of tug of war as I tried to pull dirt into her lungs while she tried to keep it out, much like she and Axenus had done at the temple with water.

She sent a blast of her frost at me that sent me sprawling back onto the ground again, and I clutched at my chest until I was able to melt its icy grip with my sunfire.

"War is the next step," Magdalene went on mercilessly. "So I created the symbionts."

"How?" I asked, getting to my knees. "You don't serve the Creator."

"There are ways around that," Magdalene said, "but I seem to be experiencing some side effects. That's where you and the other syphon come in. I need access to your powers so I can do what I need to do to thin the mortal population and put the world back in balance. Then we'll dissolve the borders between countries and the three of us will rule the continent again as we were meant to."

"You're mad," I whispered.

"I'm practical," she countered.

Magdalene's frost seized my chest again, and she reached toward me where I knelt on the ground. I tried to draw my sunfire, but I couldn't move. Pain radiated out from my chest as the frost seized me, and I tried to cringe away from Magdalene. Somehow I knew letting her touch me would be disastrous, but she was using all her strength to hold me.

Her fingers were only inches from me when Talyn appeared next to Magdalene and slammed into her, knocking her to the side.

Magdalene and the assassin rolled on the ground, and Talyn tried to raise a sword to strike, but Magdalene put a hand to her chest. Talyn grunted as a strong forcefield sent her flying backward. She landed hard, and her head kicked against the ground as she tumbled back toward the rift I'd opened in the earth.

I screamed as Talyn's body rolled again and fell over the chasm. I tried to rise, to get to her, but I sensed Magdalene bearing down on me, and I called on my magic. What erupted from my hands was part sunfire, part fire, part forcefield, and part something else I couldn't name. Magdalene met my attack with a wall of her own magic, and the force of the power meeting between us pinned me back against the ground.

For what seemed like minutes but was likely only seconds, Magdalene and I remained locked in battle. I looked quickly toward the fissure, and relief broke over me as I saw Samhail pull Talyn up over the edge. I turned back to Magdalene and rallied my power to push against her as I struggled to my feet.

We both seemed to break off our powers at the same time as we faced each other, panting with exertion.

"I know you saw part of the vision I had," Magdalene said through heavy breaths as she straightened. "I let you see it at the temple, but you only saw part of it. You weren't ready to see the rest of it then. You have no idea the death and destruction you've been prophesied to cause. It will be incredible. Let me show you."

I felt her press at my mind, but I didn't let her in.

"I'll kill you," I said, biting out every word as I gathered my strength.

"No, you'll kill tens of thousands before this is over," she said. "But you won't kill me."

My gaze roamed over her body, searching madly for any hint of red on her skin, but there was none. "No," I whispered.

She prodded my mind again, and a small part of me wanted to see what she was trying to show me. I needed to see it, to find the loophole that would show me how she was wrong. I'd learned by now that visions didn't turn out the way we anticipated, so I needed to see this for myself.

I opened my mind shield a crack, and images of the vision I'd seen the day in the temple flooded my head, but this time, I saw things I hadn't before. A ball of fire rose into the air before bursting into a shape I couldn't make out. As I'd seen before, the army of symbionts stretched out over acres of battlefield, but this time I saw them charge. They crashed into our own troops and chaos reigned as soldiers fought desperately against the creatures, trying not to be injured, trying not to be turned.

Then I saw myself as I rose above them over the battlefield, darkness at my back. My eyes glowed red as shadows loomed behind me, and I felt myself draw on a terrible power that stirred inside me. It awoke, stretched, then unleashed itself on the symbionts until each crumpled where it stood. The oozing substance of the creatures leaked from the men and women, citizens of Thasia and Rowe alike, as their bodies lay in puddles of blue as far as I could see. Unmoving. Dead.

"No!" I screamed. "I wouldn't…" But the words lacked conviction.

"You would if it was the only way to defeat my army," Magdalene said, and there was an almost manic glee in her tone. "You, Cyra. You're my ultimate tool to rid the world of excess mortals."

"No!" I screamed again as my power pulsed, sending a shockwave across the field.

A weight dropped onto my shoulder, and I turned to see the little demoni with the odd blink crouched there. It hissed at Magdalene, and she recoiled away from it.

That's when I knew what I had to do.

I felt the power of the Nemesis gather around me as the temperature dropped and the sky darkened, much like it had so many months ago in Gendris when Bressen had called the demoni to aid him during the coup.

At least I assumed it was the power of the Nemesis. It was like nothing I'd felt before, and Magdalene's eyes widened in fear.

"What are you doing?" she asked, her voice slightly hysterical.

I didn't answer but continued to let the power fill me. The little demoni shifted on my shoulder, and I sensed the creature's excitement as black smoke swirled around my feet and a commotion rose within it.

I was calling the wrath, and they were obeying.

I felt the icy chill of the smoke as it curled around me, but it didn't burn me as it had in Gendris when I'd tried to get to Bressen. The power coursing through me was like a beast awakening, like death stretching its wings, and I wondered if this was what Bressen experienced when he called the wrath. I caught Magdalene's gaze as I readied to send the demoni straight at her, and I reveled in her terror as she stumbled backward, nearly tripping and falling.

I took a step toward her.

Bressen had spared Glenora. He'd sent her to Revenmyer rather than letting the demoni tear her apart, but Magdalene wouldn't be so lucky. I wouldn't be so merciful. I saw that the way to keep from killing thousands in the future was to kill one person now.

The creature on my shoulder tensed as it prepared to launch itself at Magdalene as soon as its brethren emerged from the smoke. They were almost here, and a thrill surged up my body as I sensed my victory.

That's when Magdalene turned and ran.

Bressen

"Get back through the portal!" Magdalene's voice echoed around the field as I tried to stand, and I heard true terror in it.

Next to me, Sandrian was already on his feet. He hesitated only a second before he turned and ran back toward the portal. I lunged forward on my knees to grab his ankle, but I missed and ended up on my stomach. Fighting through pain and dizziness, I pushed myself up again.

The fog had started to clear so I could see partially across the field now. The bodies of symbionts littered the ground, and the gargoyles were scattered across the area as they fought the last remaining creatures. I made out Maziren's small form still fighting as well, and I scanned the field desperately for Cyra. My heart lurched in relief when I found her off to the side. The vestiges of some kind of black smoke curled at her feet as they mingled with the dissipating white mist.

Ahead, Sandrian raced for a new portal Magdalene had drawn on this side of the rift in the earth. She'd somehow closed the other one.

I pushed myself to my feet and scanned the field. Aidan was running for the portal as well, and one desperate thought filled my mind. We couldn't let Morland escape with Aidan's body.

I picked up my sword and was about to run for the portal when Talyn appeared next to me. I felt something snap onto my wrist, and I looked down in confusion.

She'd put a caronium cuff on me. "What the-"

I grunted as her fist slammed into my gut and the sword was pulled from my hand.

"I'm so sorry, Lord Bressen," she said a second before the world turned upside down.

Tandem Read: *Clash of Stone and Steel* (Bk 3), Chapters 34-35

Chapter 21

Bressen

I blinked as the world came back into focus, and it took me a moment to realize we were no longer on the field. The air was dry and warm, and I now stood on stone instead of grass.

Something hit the back of my legs, and my knees crashed onto that same stone. I grunted in pain but went still again as the cold steel of a blade pressed against my neck.

My stomach dropped as I looked up to see Sandrian, Magdalene, and Morland looking down at me in shock. I couldn't see behind me, but I knew it was Talyn there with my life in her hands.

Rage coursed through me as her betrayal sunk in. For Samhail's sake I'd given her a second chance, and she'd stabbed us in the back.

"Raptor?" Sandrian said, furrowing his brow as he looked from Talyn to me. "I wasn't expecting you to return with us, nor was I expecting you to…bring a guest?"

"A prisoner," Talyn clarified. "As a show of good faith to prove this is where I want to be."

Sandrian raised a brow at her declaration. "I was under the impression you'd abandoned your contract with me and switched sides," he said.

"So were they," Talyn said coolly. "But believe me when I tell you they'll kill me on sight if I try to go back now."

Oh no. She wouldn't get off that easily. The second I got my powers back, I'd teach this woman a new definition of pain.

Sandrian looked at me. "Indeed. But why should we believe you? How do I know you're not still helping him, and this is all an elaborate ruse?"

"This man tried to kill me," Talyn bit out as she reangled her sword at my neck. "When he found out who I was, he peeled my mind open like an orange and almost willed me to die. Cyra is the only reason I'm alive.

Look at him. He wants to tear me apart."

I punctuated her words with a growl of fury, although it was mostly at myself for believing the assassin could be on the side of anyone but herself. I'd thought we'd gotten past me clawing into her mind and attempting to kill her, but apparently not.

In fairness, I didn't blame her for holding a grudge about that. Part of me, perhaps the bigger part, was more angry at her for betraying Samhail. He'd been so certain she could be trusted. Worse, he liked her. A lot. I'd never seen Samhail this attached to a woman before, and he'd gone up against me to protect her and let her prove herself.

I felt no satisfaction in being right about her. In fact, I'd never wanted to be wrong about someone more in my life, and I felt nothing but disappointment on Samhail's behalf now.

I knelt quietly, silently fuming as I listened to Talyn admit to using Samhail for sex. It was no secret gargoyles were lusty and could let what was between their legs have too much sway in their decision-making, but I'd never known Samhail to be foolhardy in this respect. I had trouble reconciling the man I knew with the one who'd let this woman wrap him around her finger.

I frowned as I listened to Talyn try to convince Sandrian, Magdalene, and Morland that she was on their side. Clearly she hadn't been working with them this whole time, because they were having just as much trouble understanding her change of heart as I was.

Why *had* she switched back to Sandrian's side?

Suddenly it didn't make any sense. Based on what I was hearing, Sandrian had assumed she was with us now. If she really had been working with him, it made more sense to stay with us and continue spying. Why would she come back here – wherever here was – and try to convince them she hadn't betrayed them?

Talyn wanted to be here for some reason, although I couldn't conceive of why. Everything I knew about the assassin told me she was a smart woman, and this move seemed anything but.

"I work for you because I'm being paid to," Talyn said to Sandrian as I focused back in on their conversation. "If you want loyalty, get a dog. Otherwise, the only thing you can expect from me is my best effort to do what I can to fulfill my end of the contract. I may have failed to kill Lord Bressen and Lady Cyra as you asked, but I bring you Lord Bressen now."

Magdalene's head snapped to Sandrian. "What? You ordered her to kill Cyra?"

Sandrian looked surprised at the anger in her tone. "Yes. A week ago," he confirmed, disgruntled.

"You idiot!" Magdalene thundered at him. "I told you I need Cyra alive. How dare you try to have her killed?"

I watched carefully as Sandrian and Magdalene began to argue. Apparently, it wasn't completely understood who was in charge.

My body twitched as Magdalene attacked Sandrian with her frost. He countered with a charge of lightning that made her stagger backward, and she responded with a forcefield.

I readied to take advantage of the chaos, but Talyn pressed her sword tighter to my throat.

"Don't do anything stupid," she hissed at me, "and I'll make sure you get out of this alive."

I huffed in disbelief, but I was now even more curious what she was up to. Apparently my death wasn't part of her plan, although I wasn't sure I trusted her to keep me alive. Even if she convinced these people she was on their side, Sandrian and Morland would enjoy taking me apart, piece by piece. It would be a miracle if I survived the night.

As if reading my mind, Morland said, "If we can kill everyone else, then I'm starting with him."

The fight had wound down, and Magdalene appeared to have the upper hand for now, but I tensed as I prepared for Morland's attack.

"No!" Talyn shouted, surprising me. She moved her sword from my neck to hold it out toward Morland.

Morland raised a brow. "Protecting your new lord?" he asked with a cruel smirk. "I thought you didn't care about Bressen. If you don't care about him, prove it. Slit his throat."

"Are they always this stupid?" Talyn asked Magdalene. "Aidan would have me kill your only leverage. If you want Cyra, you just need to dangle Lord Bressen as bait. She'll come to you to get him back."

Ice ran through my veins as I realized she was right. I had to find a way to get out of here before Cyra walked right into their trap.

"Under other circumstances, I'd hold your botched attempt to kill the lord and lady against you," Magdalene said to Talyn, "but your failure was fortunate, given that I need Cyra alive. And since you seem to have more sense than these two put together," she indicated Sandrian and Morland, "I'm inclined to give you a second chance. After you let me read your mind."

Talyn went rigid behind me.

Magdalene stepped forward, but she turned her attention to me instead, and a weight like stones settled over my chest. She put a hand on my head, and I yelled in pain as she tore into my mind. With the caronium cuff on, I was powerless to stop her. I still tried, but my effort was futile. Without my magic to strengthen my mind shield, she could read my thoughts easily enough, and I knew instinctively she was making it hurt on purpose, as I had for Talyn.

I must've been screaming. I heard my voice as if it was far off and felt the vibration in my throat. My mind was being rattled loose, like there was an earthquake in my head and everything was falling off the shelves. I didn't know how much more I could take before my mind fractured.

I found myself on the floor at Talyn's feet, eyes wide. Whether it had been seconds or minutes, I didn't know. Disbelief overwhelmed me as I lay there panting, partially from the pain, but also from the enormity of what had just happened. Just as Magdalene had broken off her connection with my mind, I'd felt something pop, like the door of a cabinet bursting open, and an entire day's worth of memories had come spilling out.

"I remember," I whispered. The words were involuntary. Uncertain.

It wasn't just that I'd forgotten an entire day. I'd forgotten events that didn't seem possible.

We'd found that island after *The Maidenhead* had gotten caught in a storm out on the ocean. Whereas I'd previously believed we'd left without exploring it, though, I now had a flood of memories that said we had in fact made it onto that island…and met two women.

Two women who'd somehow been powerful enough to get into *my* mind and suppress my memory of ever having seen them.

Chapter 22

The Memory

Bressen

Cyra, Axenus, and I climbed into the rowboat along with the first mate and three other sailors from *The Maidenhead*. The boat was lowered, and the sailors pulled at the oars to send us cutting through the water toward the island. The tide seemed to be with us, or perhaps Axenus was quietly using his water magic as he had with the ship itself, because it didn't take us long to reach it.

We piled out when the boat hit the beach and hauled it ashore before making our way up the sand to look around.

"Bressen, look," Cyra said, pointing, and everyone turned to where two figures walked toward us. Behind them was a small house set far back from the beach that looked to be well-kept.

"Perimortals," I said in astonishment. "They have mind shields up."

"Should we go meet them?" Cyra asked.

"Stay behind me," I said as I began walking.

Both figures were female and older, about the age mortals in their early fifties might look, but given perimortal standards of aging, that probably meant they were several hundred years old. The first woman was of average height with soft chestnut skin and long black hair that gleamed in the sunlight. Only the streaks of gray near her temples hinted at her age. Her companion was taller and oddly pale-skinned for someone living on an island in the middle of the ocean. Her hair was white-blonde, cut short just above her shoulders, and her body was leanly muscled like a warrior's. Her age showed mainly in the crinkles near her eyes and mouth that suggested she spent a lot of time smiling.

Indeed, the women smiled at us as they approached now, although I sensed a wariness about them. We all stopped about ten feet from each other, and the black-haired woman spoke first.

"Welcome," she said warmly. "I'm Miranda, and this is my wife Ariel. We don't get many visitors to our island, but you're most welcome."

She's lying about something, Cyra said into my mind, and I ticked my head toward her the slightest bit to acknowledge I'd heard.

"I'm Lord Bressen of Hiraeth, a Triumvirate Lord of Thasia on the Arystrian continent," I said, and the woman called Miranda raised a brow at my titles. "This is my wife, Lady Cyra, and one of my counselors, Axenus of the Aspan Ocean. This is First Mate Bellamy of *The Maidenhead*." I gestured to one of the sailors who'd come with us. "Please accept our apologies for dropping in on you like this, but our ship was sent off course after a storm last night, and we need to make repairs before we're on our way."

"The storms in this area can be brutal," Miranda said. "You're fortunate your ship made it through at all. You're more than welcome to rest here while it's repaired. We're happy to help if we can."

I nodded. "Can I ask how you came to be here on this island? Or perhaps more to the point…do you need help getting off it?"

Miranda and Ariel looked at each other and smiled again.

"Lord Bressen, we came to be on this island quite a while ago, much like you did after a storm," Miranda said. "It's since become our home, and we have no plans to leave it."

Truth, Cyra said into my mind.

"We'd be interested to know what's changed in our time away, though," Ariel said, speaking for the first time. Her voice was lower than her wife's, but still friendly. "You should join us for some refreshments while your ship is being repaired. You'll have to forgive us for our limited offerings, though. As you can imagine, we don't entertain often."

"We're grateful for any comforts you can provide," I said.

"This way," Miranda said.

The two women turned, and we followed them back up to the house.

It turned out to be a larger home than it looked like from the beach, and I marveled at how well-constructed it appeared to be, given that it had been built by only two people with limited resources. It made me wonder what powers Miranda and Ariel had, but I couldn't ask without revealing my own power.

Ariel gestured for us to sit as we entered the house, and Cyra and I took seats on a couch of sorts while the first mate and a couple of the sailors found chairs or stools around the room. Axenus stood, as did the last sailor, since they'd run out of chairs. Cyra and I could've made room for Axenus on the couch, but I had a feeling he preferred to stand.

The furniture was simple and wooden, but well-made, and the couch was covered with cushions that at least made it comfortable, if not plush.

"How long have you been on this island?" Cyra asked the women as we looked around the living area.

Miranda paused just as she was about to slice some kind of fruit I'd never seen before. "I feel like I've lost track by now. Let's just say it's been a long time."

I studied her closely. I had a feeling she'd worded her answer just carefully enough that it told us nothing while also avoiding an outright lie.

"What brings you out all this way?" Ariel asked as she leaned against a door frame. Her posture seemed at ease, but there was something about the way she held herself that made me suspect she wasn't as relaxed as she appeared.

I'd seen Samhail stand much the same way countless times before, his body feigning repose. Meanwhile every muscle was half-coiled and ready to move. Ariel didn't trust us, and she'd attack if she sensed a threat.

I conveyed all this to Cyra in her mind, and she barely nodded.

"Treasure hunting," I answered Ariel. "We were looking for *The Stalwart*. Have you heard of it?"

We all turned as the knife Miranda was using to cut fruit clattered loudly on the counter, and she swore under her breath. "Sorry about that," she said with a short laugh. "The fruit is juicy. I lost my grip."

She picked the knife up and resumed slicing.

It was just the reaction I'd been looking for. I'd considered making up a more mundane reason why we were here, but I'd wondered what the women would do with the truth.

Ariel was only slightly better at hiding her surprise than Miranda. She tried to school her features quickly, but I caught the moment of unguarded shock on her face just as I turned back.

"Is that a name we should recognize?" Ariel asked, trying to recover.

I shrugged. "I suppose that depends how long you've been on this island. It's a fairly well-known shipwreck where we come from."

I glanced at Axenus and saw the slight roll of his eyes. I hadn't in fact known the name of the ship when we'd first discussed Cyra's vision. Only he and Phaedrus had.

Miranda piled the fruit she'd cut into a bowl carved of wood, and Ariel pushed off her spot to take the bowl and set it on a small table before us. A bandage on the inside of her forearm caught my eye as she set it down.

"Are you hurt?" Cyra asked her, noting the same thing. "I have healing powers if you'd like me to look at that."

My head snapped to Cyra, and she flinched as I yelled her name into her mind. Miranda and Ariel had likely guessed I was perimortal, given that I was a Triumvirate lord, but I'd wanted to avoid giving them any more information than necessary. Cyra's healing power was now the only power she could use in front of the women without drawing suspicion that she might be more than a simple healer.

Ariel looked surprised for only a moment before she smiled again. "It's nothing of concern. There's no need to trouble yourself."

"Are you sure?" Cyra asked. She'd already given herself away, so she was now committed to helping if she could.

I went still waiting for Ariel's answer. If Cyra touched her, even to heal her, she'd syphon whatever power the woman had.

"It's fine. Really," Ariel said, stepping back to emphasize her refusal.

The woman resumed her post, and Miranda joined her. Ariel wrapped an arm around her wife's shoulders.

"What's so special about this shipwreck that it's so well-known where you come from?" Miranda asked.

"There were supposedly some powerful magical items on board," I offered as I took a piece of fruit from the bowl. "A spyglass that can see across continents, a dagger that always hits its mark, a necklace that can trap people inside it, gold rings that can transfer items between them…"

I listed off the items and watched the two women for a reaction as I took a bite of the fruit. Neither so much as blinked at the first two items – I'd made up the dagger entirely – but Miranda flinched noticeably at the mention of the necklace. Yes, she was definitely aware of it.

"And did you have any success?" Ariel asked. She turned toward Axenus. "I assume you were the designated treasure hunter?"

It was no surprise she knew Axenus was a merman. His lightly iridescent skin gave him away.

Axenus shifted, unsure if he was supposed to answer.

"Alas, we came up empty-handed," I said, and here again I watched the women closely. Miranda's chin ticked up ever-so-slightly at my lie, and a moment later, Ariel leaned her head closer to her wife.

Gods damn me. Maybe I was reading too much into their body language, but those were the exact tells I'd expect to see from a woman who just saw I was lying and mentally told her partner about it.

Did you see that? Cyra asked into my mind. I wasn't the only one who'd noticed it.

I did, I answered.

My eyes met Miranda's, and I had the distinct impression she'd figured out just as much as I had.

"Perhaps we should be on our way," I said, starting to rise. "We've imposed on you enough."

Miranda stepped forward and held out her hand in a halting gesture.

"Please, Lord Bressen," she said. "Stay a while longer. It's been so long since we've seen other people. I dare say we could use the company if you have time to spare."

I eased back down onto the couch. "I suppose we can stay a little longer," I said.

She doesn't want us to leave for some reason, I said into both Axenus and Cyra's heads. *Be on your guard.*

"Perhaps Cyra can come help me get some more food," Miranda said. "We want to be good hosts, but I'm afraid I don't have much here in the house at the moment." She turned to Cyra. "Would you mind coming to help me get some things from the storehouses?"

I didn't hide my look of alarm well because Miranda added quickly, "She'll be perfectly safe. I promise she'll come to no harm."

I looked at Cyra.

She speaks the truth, she said into my mind.

Alright. Go, I said. *But keep your mind fully open to me at all times. I want to be able to see what you're seeing, and if anything seems off, don't hesitate to attack.*

I don't think that will be necessary, she said as she stood, *but fine.*

"I'm happy to help," Cyra said to Miranda.

"Wonderful," Miranda said. "Perhaps the rest of you can fill Ariel in on what we've missed on the continent for the last few years or so."

I cocked a brow at her. "The last few years, decades…or centuries?"

Miranda smiled resignedly and nodded. "Very well, Lord Bressen. I suppose there's no hiding that Ariel and I are perimortal, and yes, it's been a few centuries since we've been on the continent. And perhaps we should get it out in the open now that, as long as you have no intention of harming us, we have no intention of harming you."

Truth, Cyra confirmed.

I nodded. "Then let me assure you we have no ill intentions toward you. We'll accept your hospitality a little longer, then we'll be on our way, and – if you're serious about remaining here – we'll leave you be."

The tension in the woman's shoulders eased.

"That sounds perfect," she said. She turned to Cyra. "Shall we?"

"Lead the way," Cyra said.

Keep your mind open, I reminded her. *I don't care how much she assures me she means us no harm, I want to be able to see you.*

Cyra didn't answer, but I sensed her mind widen to me fully, and I let my consciousness drift along with her, almost as if I was on her shoulder.

"I imagine much as happened back on the continent," Ariel ventured when Cyra and Miranda were gone.

"I'll defer to Axenus on that," I told her. "He's the resident historian of the group."

Axenus looked surprised to have all the attention suddenly on him, but I sent a message into his mind asking him to carry the conversation so I could focus on Cyra, and he gave a small nod of understanding.

Axenus began speaking, and I tuned my mind back into Cyra's. Miranda had led her out to a series of storehouses and was explaining the climate on the island and the crops they grew.

"Do you have plant or elemental powers?" Cyra asked her. "I realize you've been here a long time, but what you've been able to do is still impressive."

Good girl, I thought. *See what information you can get out of her.*

"I've always had a bit of a green thumb," Miranda said, which didn't answer the question either way. "Come look at this."

Cyra followed her to a greenhouse next to the storehouses. They went inside, and I was surprised to realize I could smell the place through Cyra. The humid, earthy air mixed with heady floral aromas and stuffed itself up my nostrils as if I was there with them. Bright green plants and vines covered the place, and rows of planting boxes were laid out in grids in the center. I recognized several kinds of fruits, vegetables, and herbs.

I felt Cyra's awe at the place mingle with my own. It really was incredible what Miranda and Ariel had built here.

A bright white flower that looked a bit like a rose caught Cyra's eye, and she went over to look at it. She leaned down to smell it, and the sweet scent reached me back at the house.

I felt, or rather, Cyra felt Miranda's hand on her arm.

"Beautiful, isn't it," Miranda said. "It's a gardenia."

Miranda reached down and picked one of the white flowers off the bush. She pushed Cyra's dark hair behind her ear and stuck the flower into the strands. She let her fingers trail gently down Cyra's face, and I realized I'd let my brows shoot up at the gesture. I quickly schooled my features before Ariel noticed.

Back in the greenhouse, Miranda's hand lingered on Cyra's shoulder as her fingers caressed the strands of her hair.

I felt Cyra's confusion. She opened her mouth to speak, but before she could make a sound, Miranda took her face gently in her hands and brought her lips close to Cyra's. She hovered above them for a second as if to give Cyra a chance to object, and Cyra and I both realized at the same time what she intended.

We both also realized that, whatever Miranda's power or powers were, Cyra had likely just syphoned them.

Unless what I strongly suspected about Miranda was true, and she was actually…a syphon? Could syphons take the powers of other syphons?

Miranda's lips closed over Cyra's, and an odd sensation fluttered through Cyra's body. One of Miranda's hands dropped to Cyra's waist, and Miranda's tongue slipped inside her mouth to tease Cyra's own.

Back in the house, I swore inwardly as my cock started to harden.

Cyra's mind hazed over as her focus narrowed to the feel of Miranda's lips on hers, and I felt my own mind blur for a moment as well.

Cyra didn't move as Miranda kissed her for several seconds before pulling back. She ran her thumb over Cyra's bottom lip and then stepped back, taking her hands off my wife's face and waist.

"My lord? Are you alright?"

Ariel's question jolted me out of my daze, and I realized my mouth had been hanging open.

I clamped it shut. "I'm fine," I said too quickly. "I just…It's been a long few days, and I'm afraid I let my mind wander. My apologies."

I shook myself mentally. Something felt off all of a sudden, but I couldn't put my finger on what. I checked my mental shield, but it seemed intact except for the part that was open to Cyra.

I slipped back into Cyra's mind just as Miranda spoke.

"I'm sorry. Please excuse me for being so forward," Miranda said. "Your lips just looked so inviting all of a sudden. As you can imagine, it's been a while since we've seen anyone else on this island, let alone a woman as beautiful as you. I'm afraid I forgot myself."

Cyra's mouth opened and closed a few times, but words eluded her.

"I don't suppose that lord of yours would let Ariel and I borrow you for the night?" Miranda asked wistfully.

Back in the house, I actually choked – on what, I had no idea – and Axenus broke off what he was saying as everyone turned to me.

"Bressen?" Axenus asked. "Are you alright?"

Ariel was in front of me the next moment, pouring me a glass of water from a pitcher.

"Something to drink, Lord Bressen?" she asked, holding out the glass. Maybe I was seeing things, but she seemed to be suppressing a smile.

I took the glass of water and gulped down half of it.

"Thank you," I said. Gods above, it had been a long time since anything had thrown me this off-balance.

"Are you…are you inviting me to your bed?" Cyra asked Miranda as I once again tuned in to their conversation.

"I am," the woman said.

"And you think Ariel would approve of that invitation?" Cyra asked.

Miranda's expression seemed more certain all of a sudden, and I felt Cyra realize she was giving Miranda the impression she was considering her offer, when really she was just curious.

"Ariel and I used to invite others to join us occasionally when we lived on the continent," Miranda said. "After a few hundred years of being here by ourselves, I think she'd jump at the chance to have you join us."

Cyra smiled warmly at her. "I'm truly flattered by your invitation, and in truth, I'm sure Bressen would support me if I chose to join you-"

Only if I can watch, I said into her mind.

"…especially if he could watch," Cyra added without missing a beat, "but I have to decline."

Miranda sighed and nodded as if she'd expected as much. "You can't blame a woman for trying, can you?" she said.

"Not at all," Cyra said to soften the blow of her rejection. "To be honest, I'd consider it under different circumstances, but we've had a very trying few days, and I suspect I won't want to do anything but sleep tonight. Kind as your offer is, it comes at a bad time."

"I understand," Miranda said. "Think nothing of it." A pause. "We should finish getting some food and get back to the house before your lord comes looking for you. I get the feeling he doesn't like to let you out of his sight for long."

Miranda's smile seemed shrewd. "After all," she said, "I can tell you're an exceptional woman."

Chapter 23

Present

Bressen

My mind reeled as the memory of what had happened on the island settled in my head. Magdalene must have jarred something loose when she invaded my thoughts, but how or why I'd lost the memory to begin with still bewildered me.

I quickly replayed the events on the island until it hit me.

When Miranda had kissed Cyra, we'd both been taken by surprise, and admittedly, my dick had taken control of my conscious thought for a few seconds. If either Miranda or Ariel was a powerful mind wraith, they could've gotten into my head while I was distracted. One of them had to have mind powers. It was the only way they could've suppressed the memory in not only me, but in Cyra, Axenus, and the entire crew of *The Maidenhead*.

Nemesis take me. That was powerful fucking mind magic.

I didn't have time to fully consider the enormity of this when I was jerked to my feet by two guards.

"Let's make one thing clear," Talyn was saying to Magdalene as I remembered where I was. "I brought him here, so he's *my* prisoner. Nothing happens to him without my say-so."

"Fair enough," Magdalene said after a pause, and then I was being dragged out of the room.

I was still groggy, but I forced myself to focus on my surroundings. I needed to figure out where I was and start working on an escape plan.

I was in a castle or fortress of some sort, one that appeared to be at least partially in a state of abandonment or disrepair. There were empty spaces on the walls where paintings or tapestries had been removed, and those that still hung were damaged or dusty. Scraps of fabric, crumbles of stone, and other pieces of litter lay here and there in the hallways, which told me there weren't enough servants in the place to spare for cleaning.

I glanced surreptitiously at the guards dragging me down the hall as I tried to give the illusion I was still out of it. There were four of them, too many for me to take with no weapon and no powers.

We started down a set of stairs, heading – I assumed – for the dungeon. I tried to stumble to see if I could get the guards holding me off-balance, but they stayed steady and simply put my arms over their shoulders so I was being carried along instead.

We went down at least two flights of stairs before the guards exited into a dark corridor. One of the guards not carrying me lit a lantern and pushed ahead to lead the way as the fourth guard lit torches along the wall behind us.

We got to a row of cells, and the guard with the lantern used a set of keys to open one.

I had a decision to make. I could let them put me in the cell and hope I had an opportunity to escape later, I could trust the assassin – who was the reason I was here to begin with – to keep her word and find a way to help me, or I could fight now despite the odds.

When the guards tried to pull me forward into the cell, I shoved sideways so one of them was crushed against the bars. He grunted in pain, and his hold loosened on me. I shoved to the other side next, hoping to catch the second guard the same way, but he moved so my own shoulder hit the bars instead.

Pain radiated through the shoulder I'd been shot in, but I couldn't let myself feel it yet. The guard who'd moved still had a hold of me, and I yanked him forward so his chest and face hit the bar instead. His head cracked against the metal and blood gushed down his face before I shoved him aside.

The other guard I'd shunted into the bars had recovered and came at me, but I grabbed his shirt and redirected his momentum into the cell. He stumbled inside, and I shut the door, trapping him. It would've been better to get two of the guards locked in the cell, but one would have to do for now.

By this time the other two guards had caught on, and both came at me swinging. The corridor was too narrow for them to draw their swords, but they rushed me together, and I did my best to swing for their heads in the close quarters. I connected with the temple of one guard, but the other guard sunk his fist into my stomach, and my breath whooshed out as nausea took its place.

I tried to swing again, ignoring the searing pain in my shoulder from the crossbow wound, but I hadn't yet drawn in another breath, so there was no power behind my punch.

The guard I'd hit in the temple came back with a blow of his own that caught me in the jaw, and I grunted as pain shot through my head. Another punch took me in the side, then another, and soon the blows from the guards rained down on me.

"Stop!" a voice boomed through the corridor, and the blows ceased.

I was on my knees, and I looked up to see a man coming toward us.

"What's going on?" the man asked, and I recognized it as Aidan.

Fuck. There was no way Morland was here to rescue me.

"He was trying to escape," one of the guards explained quickly. "He attacked us."

"Get him up, and get that cell open," Morland ordered.

I was hauled to my feet again by two of the guards as the third unlocked the cell to let the fourth out.

"Put him in," Morland said, "and hold him."

I tried to struggle, but the guards wrestled me into the cell, then turned me around to hold me between them as Morland entered.

"Ah, Bressen," he said. "I'm not sure exactly what that bitch has planned or why she brought you here, but I'll be sure to thank her when I'm shoving my cock down her throat later tonight."

I didn't say anything. I wasn't sure if Morland's comment was a threat against Talyn or an admission she was working with him. I thought I'd sensed tension between them, maybe even hatred, but I could've been mistaken. I didn't yet understand what was going on.

Cyra and I had both believed we could trust Talyn. Samhail had certainly believed it. I couldn't conceive of why she'd betrayed us, especially since her welcome back with Sandrian and Magdalene had been less than warm. There was something else going on. There must be.

"What is she up to?" Morland asked as he stepped toward me.

Again I didn't answer.

Morland's fist sunk into my gut, and I grunted in pain as I tried to double over. The guards held me up, though, and I coughed as I struggled to draw in breath again.

Talyn had told Magdalene no one was supposed to touch me, so clearly no one knew Morland was down here right now.

"What is she up to?" Morland asked again.

"Fuck you," I got out as I spit blood onto his boot.

Morland's next punch was to the side of my head, but, thankfully, he didn't hit nearly as hard as Samhail.

That was a major benefit of training with Samhail. He might not hit as hard as he was able to when we sparred, but he still hit harder than any man I'd ever fought, and my body had gradually gotten use to taking punches from him. Or about as used to it as a body could get when those punches were like getting knocked in the head by stones.

"I'm not supposed to kill you because we need you as leverage," Morland said, "but I don't think Sandrian cares much what condition you're in. As long as you're still breathing, that should be sufficient."

"The assassin said you weren't to touch me, and Magdalene agreed," I pointed out, although it was obvious he didn't give a shit.

"I don't take orders from useless cunts," he said, "and I'll make sure the red-headed bitch learns that tonight."

So not working together. That much was clear. I hoped Talyn was smart enough to keep an eye out for Morland. She wasn't my favorite person right now, but – my own recent desire to kill her aside – she didn't deserve whatever Morland obviously had planned for her.

"One last chance to tell me what the assassin is up to," Morland said.

I huffed a laugh. "As you said, she's the one who brought me here to get beaten. Why would I know what she has planned?"

Morland landed another punch to my stomach, and I tried to take it as best I could. He wasn't Samhail, but that didn't mean it didn't hurt.

"One final question, then, and I'll let you settle in," Morland said. He leaned in close to me. "I have to know. What's it like to fuck that wife of yours? Do you think she'd cry for me if I shoved my cock up her little pink ass? Would she beg me to stop? I like it when they do that."

My teeth were clenched together so tight I was afraid they might crack. I shook with rage at the thought of Morland coming anywhere near Cyra. My only consolation was that if he got near her, she'd likely incinerate him. He couldn't suppress her power with caronium, so he had no way to subdue her.

Unless he drugged her. Jerram had done just that shortly after Cyra had arrived at the Citadel. I'd nearly killed him when I'd found him trying to drag her, half-conscious, from the ballroom that night. I'd always hated Jerram, but only a supreme effort of will had held me back from ripping into his mind and ordering him to drop dead.

Morland was waiting for my answer with the hint of a grin crooking his mouth.

"That's three questions," I managed to grit out. I wouldn't give him the satisfaction of exploding in a fit of rage and showing him just how much the thought of him touching Cyra affected me.

He paused before laughing. "Fine, I'll just have to find out for myself if you're not going to be helpful," he said before turning on his heel and striding out of the cell. Then to the guards he said, "Take a few more hits, then lock him in. He just needs to be alive when you leave."

I was in no condition to resist when the guards obeyed Morland's order. They took turns holding me up while their companions beat and kicked me, and I lost track of how long it went on.

I passed out at some point, and when I came to, I was lying face down on the cold stone floor of the cell with a puddle of blood and saliva pooled beneath my head. I tried to get up, and my entire body screamed in pain. After a good minute I managed to get myself onto the cot and take stock of my injuries.

One of my teeth felt loose, and I was covered in bruises and cuts from my waist up, but by some miracle, the only thing broken was my nose. I yelled out in pain as I reset it and fought down the wave of nausea and dizziness that welled up.

I lay down on the cot and tried to stay as still as possible. There might be internal damage I wasn't aware of. I closed my eyes but didn't try to sleep yet. For one, I almost certainly had a concussion, so staying awake was better right now. For another, I wanted to be alert in case anyone else decided to pay me a visit.

That turned out to be a good idea when I heard Magdalene's voice in the corridor a few hours later.

"Give me the key and leave us," the woman told the guard.

"I can't do that, my lady."

"You can and you will."

"My lady, I-"

"Do you want to know what it feels like to have your heart freeze in your chest?" Magdalene's cold voice asked. "However unpleasant you imagine it might be, I promise it's worse."

I heard the jingle of keys but didn't try to look beyond the fleeting glance I'd already taken when I first heard the voices.

"Now leave," Magdalene said.

My next interrogator had arrived, it seemed, and I steeled myself to feel more pain because she'd get as much out of me as Morland had.

The sound of the guard's boots faded down the hall.

"Lord Bressen. I need to speak with you," Magdalene called out softly.

The softness surprised me, but I didn't move. If she wanted to talk, let her come in here and face me.

"Lord Bressen," she called a little louder, but I remained still.

I heard a sigh before the key clicked in the lock and the door creaked open on its hinges. There was the soft scuffing of shoes before the door shut again with a clang that echoed in the emptiness of the cell.

I wondered if the caronium had taken Magdalene's powers. She was a syphon, and caronium didn't affect Cyra, so in theory Magdalene still had all her powers.

But something nagged at me. Sandrian had made us all put caronium cuffs on at the temple when he'd taken Jasper, and they'd known Cyra was a syphon. If caronium didn't affect syphons, Magdalene would've known that and planned for it. Wouldn't she?

"Lord Bressen, we don't have time for you to play possum. I only have a few minutes, and I need to speak with you. It's in your best interest to hear me out."

It took every ounce of my remaining self-control not to bolt upright off the cot. The voice wasn't Magdalene's. It was the assassin's.

Well, wasn't this convenient.

Morland had beaten the three hells out of me to find out what Talyn had planned, and I couldn't tell him because I didn't know.

But it was time to find out.

Tandem Read: Go to *Clash of Stone and Steel* (Bk 3), Chapter 36

Chapter 24

Cyra

Aramis's face was the first thing I saw when my eyes fluttered open. I blinked, excited to see him for reasons I couldn't grasp in my half-waking state, but when I tried to focus, his face faded away.

I blinked again and lifted my head. The faint whiff of smoke caught my nose, and I frowned.

"Cyra?"

I tried to place the voice calling my name. It wasn't Bressen's, and something strained in the back of my mind as I tried to recall why that realization sent cold dread seeping through me.

Axenus. The voice belonged to Axenus.

I turned my head and found his face as he came to stand over me. I was in my bed at Tide's End. But why was Axenus here?

I looked to the other side of the bed expecting to see Bressen, but it was empty. I frowned and was about to ask Axenus where Bressen was, when the memory of Talyn slapping a caronium cuff on him and escaping through Magdalene's portal came back to me.

I tried to jolt up to a sitting position, but my body didn't seem capable of that movement, and I managed only a slow lurch.

"Where's Bressen?" I asked, panicked.

Surgeon and Serise were in the room as well, one of them at the entrance to our antechamber and one near the doors to the balcony.

My attention swung back to the merman. "Axenus, where is he?"

His answer was a pained, apologetic look.

"Axenus!" I said, and the authority I infused in my voice wasn't for show. It was the Hand of the Nemesis that spoke now. I needed answers.

"I…we don't know," he said. "Samhail explained what happened, but we haven't yet been able to find out where the assassin took Bressen. We suspect Sandrian and Magdalene are in Rowe somewhere, but we haven't been able to determine where."

I sat silently in bed letting that news sink in. Axenus seemed to be prepared for an outburst from me, but I didn't move. I remembered everything now from our failed attempt to capture Sandrian. I remembered every horrible thing Magdalene had told me, and I remembered Talyn betraying us and taking Bressen.

Then I remembered the heat of the fire I'd created to manifest my own rage and hate. And I remembered the destruction I'd wrought.

Something squeezed the breath from my lungs. Bressen was now in the hands of our enemies, and the only thing that was holding me on a hairs breadth of sanity was the certainty that if he was dead, I would've felt it in my soul. Somehow, I knew he was still alive, and that knowledge was the only thing that kept me from burning the world to the ground.

That didn't mean someone wouldn't suffer for this. If I ever saw Talyn again, I'd kill her.

I didn't have access to her right now, though, so someone else would have to serve as my outlet.

I swung my legs out of bed and stood up. They felt shaky, but I stayed upright. My whole body was numb, and it seemed to move as if by rote.

"Cyra?" Axenus asked. He sounded wary, which was wise of him.

I didn't answer. I looked from Surgeon to Serise, and both seemed watchful as well, not for threats against me, but watchful of me myself. They both twitched the barest amount as I raised a hand in the air and began to draw a portal.

"Cyra?" Axenus asked again, confused now. "Where are you going?"

I didn't answer but finished my circle and then widened the portal as it flared open.

"Cyra!" Axenus's voice turned to alarm as the dark edifice of Revenmyer appeared on the other side. "What are you doing?"

I again ignored him. I liked and respected Axenus, but I wasn't answerable to him. I wasn't answerable to anyone but the Trinity, and right now the Nemesis was guiding me.

I stepped through the portal as Axenus called my name again. I turned to close it behind me, but Axenus quickly stepped through.

"Cyra, please…," he said, but I shifted my attention over his shoulder to the two gargoyles who'd just stepped through the portal as well.

Axenus turned to them. "Help me stop her," he said to them.

Surgeon and Serise looked at each other before the latter answered.

"It's not our job to stop anything the lady wishes to do," she said, "nor even to question it. We're here only to protect her."

She looked uncertain as she said this, but neither she nor Surgeon moved to stop me as I closed the portal behind them. Perhaps it was only Revenmyer that unnerved them…Or perhaps it was something else.

I turned and walked toward the prison. I only vaguely remembered where the wards began, but I could feel those I'd put up after our last visit to help bolster the prison's usual ones. Bressen was doubtful about how much help they'd be in keeping Magdalene out if she came calling, given that warding was one of her strengths, but we hoped my wards would at least slow her down enough for the prison's seneschals to call for help.

I lowered my wards, then reached out to see if I could detect where the prison's ancient protections began. I couldn't pinpoint them exactly, but I felt they were close enough.

I raised a hand out in front of me and sent a forcefield blasting into them. I cried out as I was immediately thrown back.

I expected to hit the ground, but I fell into a pair of waiting arms that caught me. A moment later, Surgeon set me back on my feet.

"My lady," he said, "I certainly don't question your actions, but may I suggest that trying to blast through the wards like that won't work?"

Under other circumstances I might've smiled at the way he'd framed his advice as a question, but I didn't need him to tell me my approach wouldn't work.

"I'm not trying to get through them," I said. "I'm trying to get someone's attention."

"Of course, my lady," he said, stepping back.

I turned back to the prison to see I had indeed gotten someone's attention. A figure emerged from the front doors and hurried toward us across the narrow path over the water. I could tell it was Hettie from the shape of the figure and the fly-away hair, even if the robes of orange and lime green didn't suggest who it was.

Hettie reached us and took a moment to survey our small party before she spoke.

"My lady?" she asked. "Is there something I can help you with? Where is Lord Bressen?"

"Lord Bressen has been taken by our enemies," I informed her. "I need to speak with some of your prisoners to find out what I can about where he might've been taken. Lower the wards."

It was an order, not a request, but Hettie didn't move at first.

"And they are?" she asked, eyeing the three people behind me.

"My bodyguards and Lord Bressen's emissary," I said, not taking my eyes from the older woman's.

"Please, don't let her in," Axenus said to Hettie, and I glared at him.

"Mind yourself, or I'll send you back to Tide's End," I told Axenus. To his credit, he returned my glare with a look of defiance.

"I'm not just Bressen's emissary," he said to me. "I'm your friend and your mentor, or so you've told me. And I'm asking you not to do whatever it is you're planning to do."

Something twinged inside me. Whether it was his confirmation of our friendship or the pleading in his voice that spurred it, I wasn't sure, but it made me pause.

I shook the doubt away and turned back to Hettie.

"Lower the wards and let me in," I said to her, "or we'll see how long they can stand up to a Hand of the Nemesis."

Hettie considered this a moment before she nodded. She reached out, and the wards quivered where she touched them until a passage opened to admit us.

I strode forward, and I felt Surgeon and Serise on my heels. I also felt their shock and remembered belatedly that Bressen had never told them what I was. They didn't ask any questions as they followed, though.

I assumed Axenus followed as well, but I didn't know for sure until we ascended the stairs toward the prison, and he stepped up next to me.

"Cyra, please," he said. "Bressen wouldn't want you to do this."

"Do what?" I asked. "You don't know what I'm planning to do."

"What are you planning to do then?" he countered.

"Visit some old friends."

"Cyra, don't."

"Stay outside if you want," I said, "but I'm going in."

We followed Hettie into the foyer and through the door that led to the main part of the prison.

"I assume you'd like to see Lady Glenora again," Hettie said.

"Not yet. First I need to visit Clarice of Sedonia."

"Cyra, no!" Axenus said. He put himself in front of me, forcing me to pull up short. "I can't let you-"

His words were cut off with a grunt as I sidestepped him and loosed a small forcefield that pushed him out of my way.

I strode forward again, half remembering the way to Clarice's cell. All around us, the walls began to pulse, and a commotion rose as the demoni stirred. Surgeon and Serise stepped in closer to me, and I felt their anticipation of a fight like a vibration.

"The demoni won't hurt me," I told them.

As if on cue, a weight settled on my shoulder, and I turned my head to see my little demoni sitting there. It dug its claws lightly into my shoulder to hold on as I walked.

"My lady!" Serise exclaimed as she noticed the creature.

I held up a hand to stay her before she could swat it away.

"It's fine," I told her. "This is Blink."

I hadn't really meant to name the creature, but it came to me as I remembered its asynchronous blink pattern.

"Blink?" Serise asked.

She let out a sound of surprise a second later as the demoni demonstrated how it had gotten the moniker.

"Why…why does it ride on your shoulder like that?" she asked.

I turned my head slightly to glance at the little creature out of the side of my eye. "I don't know. Convenience?"

Hettie barked a laugh. "There's nothing convenient about demoni."

Indeed, she kicked out as she said this at a small horde of them that had materialized in the corridor before her. They dissolved in a swirl of smoke and reformed to the side out of her way.

Surgeon cried out in pain behind me, and I turned quickly to him.

"They're freezing cold," he said as he rubbed his fingers. "One of them grabbed me when I reached out to touch the wall."

I remembered the feel of that biting cold from the first time I'd seen the demoni. Bressen had summoned them after the coup in Gendris to come for Glenora. I'd tried to get to him, and the smoke surrounding him had been cold enough to burn my skin.

The demoni that sat on my shoulder now was cold, but not nearly as frigid as what I'd felt that day in Gendris. Perhaps the demoni were warming up to me, literally, or maybe I was acclimating to them.

We began to descend the stairs toward Clarice's cell, and Axenus pushed past Serise to press in next to me.

"What do you need Clarice for?" he asked in a low voice.

"She knew Magdalene," I said. "She may know how to find her."

"Do you intend to hurt her?" he asked.

"If I need to."

"Cyra, please."

I stopped and looked at him, which caused Surgeon and Serise to pull up short to avoid colliding with us on the stairs.

"Why do you care if I hurt her?" I asked him. I was genuinely curious. According to Bressen, Axenus had tried to drown Clarice the last time he'd been here, but he'd eventually stopped. I didn't understand why.

Axenus glanced at the two gargoyles, and I knew this wasn't a conversation he wanted to have here of all places, but there wasn't anywhere else for us to go. In Revenmyer, the walls literally had ears.

Axenus looked back at me, and I was momentarily held by the piercing cerulean of his eyes. They were similar to Bressen's in their strikingness, and the knot in my stomach pulled tighter.

"I don't care what happens to Clarice," Axenus whispered, leaning in so only I could hear. "I care what hurting her will do to you. Don't let her or Magdalene turn you into a monster, Cyra."

I pulled back as if he'd slapped me, but his expression was unapologetic.

"Stay outside if you want," I told him. "You don't need to see what I do if you don't want to. Then you can continue to pretend I'm as sweet and innocent as you want."

I turned away from him so quickly that Blink had to grab a lock of my hair to keep from being pitched off my shoulder. I could practically feel Axenus's hurt and disappointment at my words, but I couldn't deal with him at the moment. Not when I didn't know what was happening to Bressen right now. My sole focus was getting to him before…

No one else spoke as we arrived at Clarice's cell door and Hettie opened it. I strode inside, but I didn't immediately see Clarice. The cell was darker than the hall, and it took my eyes a moment to adjust before I saw her facing the wall at the far end of the cell. An oval frame hung there, like the kind that might contain a mirror, but this one was empty. Nevertheless, Clarice looked into it as if she could see her reflection.

She jumped back a second later as several pairs of red eyes popped into the frame, followed by the faces of their demoni.

"Clarice," I said, and she swung around. Her face seemed to brighten as she saw me.

"You came back," she said. "Did you bring…?"

She looked around, presumably for Bressen, but her eyes widened, and her lips parted as her gaze lit on someone behind me. I knew who I'd see as I turned to confirm Axenus had followed me into the cell.

"Axenus," Clarice breathed. Her eyes traveled up and down his body, and I had the urge to burn them out of her head.

For his own part, Axenus had frozen in place. His jaw was clenched tightly, and a muscle ticked wildly just under his ear.

The start of a smile hitched the corners of Clarice's mouth, and she stepped forward, but I blasted her with a forcefield that threw her back against the wall.

"Cyra, no!" Axenus shouted. He wrapped his hand around the wrist I still held out toward Clarice.

"Please don't do this," he said.

"You should have drowned her," I said.

He flinched, but his expression hardened. "If I'd done that, she wouldn't be here for you to question now. Ask her what you came here to ask and let's go."

I tugged on my hand, and he let go of it. Then I turned to Clarice.

"I need some information from you about Magdalene," I told her.

Clarice tore her eyes from Axenus and met mine. Slowly she picked herself up off the floor.

"I'll tell you anything you want," Clarice said, "but I want something in return."

I raised a brow. "Oh? And what do you want?"

Her gaze shifted back to Axenus. "I want five minutes to catch up with him," she said silkily, and my stomach churned.

Axenus didn't move, but his lips curled in disgust.

Clarice stepped up in front of me, and I was annoyed to find I had to look up at her. I knew she was taller than me when I'd first encountered her in Axenus's dream, but it had been the least of my concerns at the time. I'd been more focused on the smugness in her expression and how she looked at Axenus as if he belonged to her. I saw that same smugness in her expression now.

"Convince him to see me for five minutes alone, and I'll answer any questions you want," Clarice said.

There was silence behind me as I met her eyes. Surgeon and Serise had entered the cell as well, and, with their mind shields down, I felt their curiosity about why Clarice was so interested in Axenus. I also felt Axenus's own acquiescence. He'd do it. He'd put up with this woman alone for five minutes to give me the answers I needed.

Luckily, he didn't have to.

"You misunderstand me," I said to Clarice. "I don't need to ask you any questions."

I reached forward and fastened my hand on Clarice's forehead. I had to reach up, but she screamed and dropped to her knees as I seized her mind. Axenus yelled behind me, but there was a scuffle, and I knew Surgeon and Serise had grabbed him to keep him from trying to stop me.

Clarice continued to cry out as I dug myself into her mind the way I might twist a corkscrew into a bottle of wine. She couldn't put up much of a mind shield here in her cell, and I could've made this easy for her, but I didn't want to. I tore into her mind brutally, relishing her pain as I sifted through her memories and her knowledge of Magdalene.

Bits and pieces of Axenus's time with her surfaced occasionally as well, but I pushed those back down, not wanting to see the details of what she'd done to him. Even so, I couldn't fully block them out, and bile rose in my throat several times at what I saw. She hadn't just used him herself. She'd let dozens of others use him as well – men and women alike – and a burning hatred rose in me as I broke off the connection.

I shoved Clarice away from me, and she crumpled onto her hands and knees as she whimpered softly.

"Let him go," I said without looking behind me, and there was more shuffling as Axenus freed himself from the twins' hold. I turned and found him right behind me. His brows were pinched in anger, and I felt it radiating off him.

"Did that make you feel better?" he asked, and I didn't blame him for the bitterness I heard in his voice.

I shook my head. "No. But I didn't expect it to. She had information I needed, so I took it."

"You enjoyed hurting her," he accused. "You could've read her mind without pain, but you didn't."

"And she could've let you go without hurting you, but she didn't," I snapped back at him.

He jerked away from me, eyes wide. He started to speak, but before he could, I was shunted out of the way as Clarice pushed herself between us. She grabbed Axenus's shirt as she pressed herself against him, and he froze again as his eyes flew even wider to have her touching him.

"Axenus, tell her the truth," Clarice begged him. "Tell her how you enjoyed your time with me. Tell her I don't belong in here."

Axenus blinked and grabbed her wrists to pry her hands from his shirt, but she seemed to have an inhuman hold on him.

"You wanted me," she insisted. "You wanted everything we did."

She released his shirt, and he let go of her wrists to push her away, but she threw herself back against his body. She wrapped one hand around the back of his neck while reaching for the buckle of his belt with the other. He tried to pull her wrist away again to stop her, but she only moved the hand on his neck down to work at the closure. It was like fighting the flailing limbs of the kraken all over again.

Alarm crossed Axenus's face as Clarice fought to get to his pants. His skin had gone paler than I'd ever seen, and fury like I'd felt when Talyn had kidnapped Bressen surged inside me, nearly making me dizzy.

No, not fury. Wrath.

"Let me remind you how good it was between us," Clarice pleaded with Axenus. "Don't you remember the pleasure of being between my thighs? You always climaxed. I was always filled with you by the end of the night, your seed dripping from-"

She didn't get to finish the thought as I pressed a hand to her shoulder, and her body burst into a thousand blue butterflies that scattered madly in all directions, filling the room with a tempest of fluttering wings.

Sheer chaos reigned for several seconds as the demoni thrashed within the walls, and the blinking red glow of their eyes jumbled with the hectic flap of blue wings to create a disorienting kaleidoscope of colors. Even Blink leapt away from me to join the pandemonium as Axenus, Hettie, and the twins all threw up their arms to cover their heads from the swarm of butterfly wings buffeting them.

Almost as quickly as it started, it ended. The butterflies lost their ersatz life and fluttered to the ground where they lay motionless like a carpet of leaves on a forest floor. The demoni settled as well and faded back into the walls as their red eyes flickered out like candles to leave the room in near darkness again.

I lowered my hand from where I'd been touching Clarice when I transfigured her. I'd turned living things to lifeless objects twice before — the bear and the kraken — but both times had been accidents.

This time had been on purpose.

At my command, the butterflies — nothing but paper imitations of life — flared up in fire all around us and curled to ash. In the brief flash of light they provided, I saw the horror on Axenus's face at what I'd done.

A small part of me had expected to see relief, and I was disappointed at not getting the reaction I'd been hoping for. I wanted Axenus to be at peace knowing Clarice was dead, but it wasn't peace I saw in his face.

No matter. Clarice had deserved death, and a far less easy one than I'd given her. Her death was the will of the Nemesis, and I was responsible for enacting that will in the human realm.

Without another word, I stepped around Axenus and left the cell.

Chapter 25

Cyra

I was most of the way back down the hall when Axenus caught up and stepped in front of me again. He was breathing hard, and I couldn't help being momentarily mesmerized by the way the light from the torches made his iridescent skin shimmer with the movement.

Axenus was beautiful, much like Bressen was, but I couldn't recall ever hearing him talk about relationships he'd had. Bressen and Samhail could be blunt and even bawdy about their past conquests, but I knew nothing about any past lovers Axenus may have had, either before or after Clarice. It was possible he just liked to keep that part of his life private, but I had to wonder if he shied away from intimacy in general since his ordeal with her. Perhaps he eschewed any opportunity for love because she'd broken something in him.

The thought alone made me want to kill her all over again.

"What did you do?" Axenus asked me, his voice shaking. "Cyra, what in the three hells did you just do?"

I cocked my head at him. "You know very well what I just did. And you're welcome."

I tried to move past him, but he grabbed my arm.

"I didn't ask you to do that," he said through gasping breaths. "I would never ask you to do that."

"I know. Which is why I did it without you having to."

His face fell. "Cyra."

My stomach twisted at the disappointment in his voice, and I cursed myself for caring so much about his opinion of me. Clarice had deserved to die, so why was I frustrated it hadn't made Axenus happy?

"What's done is done," I said. "Mourn her if you want, but I don't have time to shed tears. I need to find Bressen, and I don't know if anything I got from Clarice will be useful. I need to speak to Glenora."

I pushed past him and started toward the stairs again. Hettie had gotten ahead of us while we'd spoken, and she led the way while the twins brought up the rear.

"And do you actually intend to talk to her?" Axenus asked as he took the stairs a step behind me. "Or are she and her child going to end up like Clarice?"

"That depends entirely on how cooperative she is," I said.

Angry as I was, I didn't think I had it in me to kill Glenora's child, even if I didn't mind seeing her herself die, but I didn't feel like explaining that to Axenus. Despite what Magdalene had claimed, and despite what Axenus seemed to fear, I wasn't a monster.

I was *not* a monster...

My legs burned from the climb by the time Hettie stepped out of the stairwell. The floors all looked much the same in Revenmyer, save for the amount of light each got, so I had to trust we were in the right place. While Clarice's cell was belowground somewhere and had no windows, Glenora's was near the top of the prison and had one small window that let in outside light, even if that light was often dim from the constant clouds that plagued the area.

The upper levels also had windows at each end of the corridor, and the demoni that surfaced out of the stone every now and then seemed to avoid the area of floor just below them where the muted light touched down. Even with these windows, the inside of the prison was dark enough to need torches on the walls.

Hettie unlocked the door to Glenora's cell, and I strode in with Axenus and the twins in my wake. I felt Axenus directly behind me, so close he nearly touched me. Had he not been a merman, I might've been able to feel his body heat, but Axenus's body temperature ran cooler than a normal human. His skin wasn't cold per se, but he wasn't as warm as Bressen and Samhail.

I knew he was determined to stay near me, although what he thought he could do if I decided to kill Glenora, I didn't know.

The former Lady of Polaris stood at her window today, but she turned when we entered. I couldn't read the range of emotions that crossed her face as she took us all in, but I was sure I wouldn't have liked any of them.

"Back so soon, my dear?" she asked. She surveyed Axenus and the gargoyles. "And who have you brought with you this time?"

Her eyes fell on Axenus, and she cocked her head. She came forward and stopped in front of him to look him over. After a moment, she gave him a small sniff.

"I thought I smelled fish," she said with a quirk of her lips. She looked back at me. "He does look rather delicious, though. Have you taken this one to your bed as well, or just the gargoyle?"

I felt the color drain from my face as I realized neither Axenus nor the twins knew I'd taken Samhail to bed. I tried to tell myself it didn't matter. Bressen wouldn't care, but I didn't know how Samhail might feel about Axenus and his siblings knowing about us.

Unfortunately, Glenora noticed me go pale, and her eyes lit up.

"They don't know, do they," she said.

"Don't speak about things you don't understand," I told her.

I willed her to stay quiet, but I knew she wouldn't. Glenora had spent her life reading people, always looking for evidence they might be trying to get around her ability to see their lies. It had made her a sharp observer, and she knew how to use those observations to her advantage.

Glenora eyed the two gargoyles. "Relations of Samhail?" she asked.

I didn't answer. Gods damn it. Why hadn't I anticipated this?

"Do they know you've taken him between your thighs?" she went on.

I glanced at the twins. Both looked at me with wide eyes, but I didn't bother denying it. It was none of their concern who I fucked, and if they tried to take it up with Samhail, he'd set them straight.

I frowned as some kind of mark glowed gold on both of their foreheads all of a sudden, but it was there and gone in an instant, and I wondered if I'd imagined it.

I turned back to Glenora as her sharp gaze swung to Axenus. "The merman didn't know either," she observed. She narrowed her gaze in consideration. "But he's only surprised, not jealous. Perhaps you have yet to let him fuck you."

I refused to look at Axenus to see his reaction.

"Why such concern with who I take to bed?" I asked her. "You seem determined to shame me, but that didn't work out for you with Bressen."

Glenora's gaze turned cold. "You're right. You don't seem to have any shame," she said. "It wasn't enough for you to have one Triumvirate lord. You had to have two, plus the gargoyle."

I furrowed my brows. "Two lords? What are you talking about?"

"I'm talking about how I spent years seducing Jerram, and even more years fucking him until he was willing to do anything I wanted. Then you walked through the door, and it took him all of a week to decide he wanted you instead. You don't think I know he would've betrayed me and taken you as his consort if you'd agreed to it? You don't think I know he tried to fuck you on the Harmilan?"

"Tried and failed," I said. "Don't blame me for Jerram's fickleness."

She gave a bitter laugh and turned away to go back to her window.

"I have more questions for you," I said to her.

Glenora didn't say anything, but she began to hum as she looked out the window. I recognized it as the song I'd learned from my mother, and I resisted the urge to make her stop humming it.

"Where does Magdalene live?" I asked her, gritting my teeth and trying to ignore the song.

She didn't respond.

I strode toward her. "One way or another, you're going to answer my questions," I said.

I jerked to a halt as Axenus grabbed my wrist.

"Cyra, don't do what I think you're planning to do," he said.

"I'm planning to make her talk," I said.

He shook his head in warning, but I wrenched my hand free and rounded on him.

"I don't have time for this!" I yelled at him. "Don't you understand that Sandrian and Magdalene could be torturing Bressen to death right now? We need to find him!"

Tears welled in my eyes, but I froze at the noise of delight behind me.

"The Nemesis Incarnate has been taken?" Glenora asked.

I swung around to find her grinning broadly.

"You should have led with that," she said.

My brow furrowed. "You'll help me find him?" I asked.

Glenora laughed merrily, a hideous sound coming from her.

"No, of course not," she said. "But I would dearly love to hear all about how you lost the lord."

I screamed and launched myself at her. I was nearly to her when I was hit by a wall of water that swept me back all the way out of the cell. I found myself in the hallway as I hit the opposite wall and fell to the floor, sputtering for breath. Axenus stood over me, and I was momentarily confused at how he'd used his powers until it hit me that he'd left the cell when I charged Glenora in order to get them back.

I glared up at him as I got to my feet. "You overstep, Axenus."

"You know Bressen wouldn't want you to do this," he said.

I started to raise my hands, to do what I wasn't yet sure, but Axenus was faster. A huge wave crashed into me as water filled the corridor before I could do anything. I had to clamp my mouth shut to avoid gulping it in as I was swept all the way down the hall and into the stairwell. I heard Surgeon and Serise shout, but they could apparently do nothing as the deluge washed me down the stairs. I expected to crash into the stone walls, but Axenus's water magic swept me down the center of the stairwell, although I did bump and scrape against the stone every now and then.

I considered porting, but I had only a limited range, and there weren't many places I could go unless I wanted to port into one of the cells and take my chances with whatever prisoner was inside. I could try to fight

Axenus's water magic, but even with my enhanced syphon powers, he had far more practice with and control over that element than I did.

I was dizzy and nauseous when I finally washed through the atrium and found myself pressed hard against the bars of the gate to the foyer. I ported outside onto the landing at the bottom of the stairs near the stone path and took a moment to collect myself. I'd had to use my air magic to breathe as I was swept down the stairs, and I gasped in a breath as the last of Axenus's water washed into the bay.

I picked myself up off the stone and looked up to see Axenus striding toward me out of the front door and down the stairs.

I'd underestimated the strength of his powers. I'd only ever seen him manipulate relatively small amounts of water, but it appeared his control of the element was more prodigious than I'd realized, and – more surprisingly – he was willing to use the full might of it against me. I wasn't sure whether to be impressed or furious.

"How dare you!" I snapped, opting for fury at the moment. "You just attacked the Lady of Hiraeth."

Axenus's expression remained hard, and I had a feeling he'd made his peace with that when he'd decided to act.

"I stopped a friend from doing something she'd regret," he countered as he came to stand in front of me. "I know that's not how you see it, but I'm prepared for the consequences of my actions."

"Where are Surgeon and Serise?" I asked.

"Fighting a riptide back up on Glenora's floor," he answered. "You and I need to talk."

"I told you, I don't have time to talk!"

"Hurting Glenora isn't going to get Bressen back," he said. "You heard her. She's not going to help. She'll only take pleasure in needling you and pushing you into doing something you'll regret. I've only known her a few minutes, and even I can see that."

"She knows something!" I insisted. "And I'm going to find out what."

I lifted my hands and sent a forcefield at Axenus to push him aside, but he was fast, and he threw up a wall of water to block it as he'd done once before when we'd first started my training. It occurred to me that he'd probably trained with Samhail before and knew how to counter forcefields well.

"Merman!" Surgeon's enraged voice echoed in the atrium before he and Serise emerged from the prison onto the front terrace. A containment bubble appeared around Axenus a moment later.

The twins looked thunderous as they stalked toward us, Hettie on their heels.

Axenus shouted in alarm as the bubble he was in began to shrink.

"I should crush you to death!" Serise roared as she closed the bubble in on Axenus.

Axenus dropped into a crouch inside it as he tried to pull back from the walls closing in around him.

"Stop," I said. "Let him out."

"But, my lady-" Serise tried to argue.

"Let him out," I repeated. "If anyone gets to punish him, it's me."

Serise grumbled something under her breath but lifted the bubble just as it closed in around Axenus. He collapsed out onto the ground in a sprawl as the bubble disappeared.

I tried to get my rage under control as Axenus got to his feet again.

"Cyra," he said.

"You're my friend!" I yelled at him as my frustration boiled over. He was supposed to be helping me find Bressen, not hindering me.

"Yes, and as your friend it's my responsibility to keep you from doing something you'll regret," he answered.

"It's your responsibility to support me!"

"Not blindly. I won't support or condone you hurting Glenora."

"Because she's pregnant?" I spat out.

"Because she's human, and I don't want to see you become a cold-blooded murderer."

I huffed a laugh. "It's too late for that."

I saw the crushing truth of that statement in his face, but I couldn't bring myself to care. Every second I spent here arguing with him was another second Bressen could be in pain, another second he might be closer to death. I was going out of my mind with worry for him. I had to believe he was still alive, but I didn't know for sure, and the uncertainty was killing me. If he was dead, I just needed to know.

Because if he was dead, I'd destroy this world.

"I'm going back to question Glenora," I said as I headed inside again, "and if you really are my friend, you'll let me do it."

Axenus glanced at the water behind me in the little bay that surrounded the prison. I looked as well and frowned as the tide seemed to swell before me.

My gaze snapped back to Axenus, and I saw the resolve in his face.

"I'm sorry, Cyra," he said, and then he launched himself at me.

I'd barely raised my hand to defend myself before Axenus's hard body hit me and the breath punched out of my lungs. Then I was falling backward with Axenus wrapped around me.

My back stung as we hit the cold water of the bay, and I took in a mouthful of it before I had the wherewithal to shut my lips. The shock of the icy water as it closed around us left me paralyzed as my mind tried to make sense of what was happening. I felt Axenus's body moving against mine, and it gradually occurred to me he must be swimming. I felt the pressure of the water increase, and somewhere in the back of my mind I realized we were going deeper below the surface.

My mind cleared suddenly, and one thought rose above the others.

Axenus was trying to kill me.

Chapter 26

Bressen

I had no idea what time it was when the door to my cell swung open so silently I almost thought I'd imagined hearing it. Even without my mind power, though, I felt the presence.

Talyn had come to see me earlier, to explain why she'd kidnapped me, and I'd been surprised to learn she had a relatively good, almost forgivable, reason for doing so. Her actions were ill-advised to be sure, but truthfully, I couldn't say I wouldn't have done much the same under similar circumstances. Even more surprisingly, I'd found myself agreeing to help her, if only because our purposes were partially aligned. She wanted Morland, and so did I, and if we worked together, we might actually get him back to Thasia.

She'd even given me a hairpin to work on unlocking my caronium cuff, and I'd spent most of the evening practicing. My results were inconsistent at best – sometimes it took me several minutes, sometimes only a few seconds – but I could at least get the cuff off regularly. It hung unlocked around my wrist now, and I readied myself to move if needed.

I didn't open my eyes just yet. If it was Morland or Sandrian in my cell, they likely would've made their presence known loudly and immediately, would've delighted in disturbing my sleep in the dead of night before they tried to beat me again. Stealth meant one of two things. Either someone had crept down here in the hopes of slitting my throat while I slept or…

"Your breathing isn't even enough for you to be asleep, Lord Bressen," came the assassin's low voice, "and I'd rather not have your hands around my throat again since I'm here to help you."

I opened my eyes and turned my head to look at the woman standing in the doorway. She hadn't closed the cell yet, likely so she could make a quick escape if she needed to. She held a lantern turned down low in one hand and a cloth sack in the other.

"You're not here to slit my throat?" I asked.

She smiled. "Not tonight."

I winced as I sat up and swung my legs around to hang them over the cot. Every part of my body still hurt from the beating I'd taken earlier, but at least I was still alive. That was more than I'd expected at this point.

The cell door finally clicked shut behind her as she stepped further inside. It briefly crossed my mind that she must have the key on her somewhere, and I could try to take it, but I dismissed the thought. I'd tried to get the upper hand on her when she'd visited me earlier, and she'd quickly turned the tables on me. She was a good fighter, and I was in no condition to test her again. For now, I'd have to trust her.

"You came back," I observed.

She'd promised to get the caronium tip from the crossbow bolt out of my shoulder, but I'd been cynical of her return. She'd been true to her word, though.

She looked at me in annoyance. "You doubted I would?"

"I was starting to wonder."

"I would've come sooner, but I had to wait for Morland to make his move. I couldn't chance he'd come looking for me while I was down here," she said.

"He tried to attack you?"

"He broke into my room with some rope and a caronium cuff," she said, and I felt my blood boil in my veins. It didn't take much imagination to guess what he'd intended to do, and while I didn't have any love for the assassin, I certainly didn't condone what Morland had been planning.

"Take your shirt off," Talyn ordered as she turned the lamp up and set the cloth sack down next to me on the cot.

I raised a brow. "That's awfully forward of you," I said. "I thought Samhail was more your type."

She gave me a look that said she didn't find my attempt at humor amusing, so I gave up and gingerly pulled my shirt over my head.

"Sweet gods!" Talyn hissed under her breath as I laid the shirt down next to me.

I looked down at my chest and grimaced at the mass of purple and black bruising that covered most of it. It looked about how I expected it to. It really was a wonder Morland and the guards hadn't broken or ruptured anything besides my nose.

"It's fine. It feels worse than it looks," I said, and she rolled her eyes.

I should probably stop before she got fed up and left me here in pain, but joking about the situation was the only thing keeping me sane right now. Talyn had promised she'd protect me while we were here, but it was a miracle Sandrian and Morland hadn't killed me the second the portal closed behind us.

I also imagined Cyra was going out of her mind with worry right now, and I wished I had a way to assure her I was at least alive, if not well.

"I can't do anything for the bruises," Talyn said, "but I can at least remove any caronium left in your wound and stitch it up."

She began to pull the dressing off the wound. No one had bothered to treat it, so I'd had to clean it myself as best I could. I'd ripped part of the bottom of my shirt off in order to tie a cloth in place over it to stem the bleeding.

Talyn frowned as she looked down at the hole in my shoulder.

"This will be easiest if you lay down," she said.

"What makes you think there's still a piece of caronium in it?" I asked.

"Samhail and I were attacked in the woods while we were traveling, and the men had crossbows with caronium-tipped bolts. Samhail was shot twice, and in both cases the tips of the bolt stayed lodged inside him when he pulled them out."

"Samhail was shot?" I asked in surprise.

"They snuck up on us."

I narrowed my eyes. "Snuck up on you while you were…doing what exactly?"

Talyn didn't say anything as she pulled items out of the sack and laid them on the one chair in the cell. Even in the lantern light I could see the blush that reddened her cheeks.

"Samhail was shot because he was too busy fucking you?" I guessed.

Talyn's head jerked up, and anger flashed in her eyes. "No, he wasn't fucking me," she snapped. "He was-"

She clamped her mouth shut, biting off the retort, then shook her head. I frowned as I thought I saw pain cross her features.

"It doesn't matter what we were doing," she said. "We weren't paying attention, and the men got the drop on us. Samhail took the first shot in his armor, but they hit him in the side and stomach when he reached up for his swords."

"How many men?"

She shrugged. "A little over a dozen or so?"

"How did you get away?" I asked.

She looked at me as if the answer was obvious. "I killed the men and got Samhail to the nearest village."

Of course. How foolish of me for not guessing as much.

"We got lucky and happened to find one with a perimortal healer," she went on as she doused a clean cloth in alcohol. "But the healer was delivering a baby at the time we arrived, so I worked on getting the caronium tips out of Samhail's wounds until the healer could get to us."

"So you've done this before," I said.

"Once. This may hurt a bit."

I lurched back as she reached for my pants and began to unbuckle my belt. It was on the tip of my tongue to ask her what in the three hells she was doing, when I realized her intent. She whipped the belt out of the loops and folded it twice before handing it back to me.

I scowled at her but put the belt in my mouth and lay back on the cot as she began to clean the wound with the alcohol-soaked cloth.

I pulled the belt out of my mouth. "Why would you help Samhail?" I asked. "According to him, you were his prisoner. You could've left him to die in those woods and been free. Why didn't you?"

Talyn's hand went still over my wound, and for a moment I could tell her mind was far away.

"There was a man in the town where I grew up who owned a hilynx," she said. "Are you familiar with those?"

I nodded. Hilynxs looked a bit like white jaguars with tufted ears, but they were bigger, and their fangs were venomous. They were rare, and it was believed the only remaining ones in the world were in captivity. The occasional traveling circus might have one, but they were entirely too dangerous to keep as pets.

"Everyone believed the man was crazy for keeping the thing, especially since he let it roam free around his house," Talyn said as she held a pair of tweezers over the fire and then dipped them in the alcohol. "I asked him once why he kept it. Wasn't he afraid it would kill him?"

"And what did he say?" I asked.

"He admitted he was in fact afraid of the thing. He knew it could easily turn on him and kill him at any point, but for him, that was part of its appeal. The hilynx is one of the most impressively lethal animals in the world, and it gave him an immense sense of power to be near it and not have it kill him."

I furrowed my brows. "So…you saved Samhail's life because he's like a hilynx, and you…felt powerful every day he didn't kill you?" I guessed.

She met my eyes then. "I saved his life because it would've been a travesty to let such an impressively lethal man die at the end of a crossbow bolt fired by cowards looking to claim a reward. That hilynx was wasted, living tucked away in that man's house when it could've been out in the world being what it was meant to be. An apex predator."

I was silent a moment. "And that's why you saved him?"

She shrugged. "That, and I was sure you and Cyra would hunt me to the ends of the earth if I let him die."

I nodded. "Very true."

She pointed to the belt, a silent order to put it back in my mouth.

"What happened to the hilynx?" I asked.

Her face hardened a bit. "It got upset at the man one day and tore him to shreds. After that, the city guard put it down. They shot so many arrows into it that it looked more like a giant porcupine by the end."

I blinked. That wasn't quite the ending I'd expected. But then, that seemed to be her point about Samhail.

"Belt," Talyn said, and I lay back again and clamped my teeth down on the leather.

I grunted loudly and grabbed the sides of the cot as Talyn dug the tweezers into my shoulder. The woman was certainly no healer with a gentle touch.

"I feel it in there," she said a few seconds later.

I tried to let my mind drift to other things as Talyn worked on me. Whether she realized it or not, her story of the hilynx was more applicable to her than to Samhail. She herself was an impressively lethal woman who'd spent weeks prowling around my home. The only difference was that – unlike the man in Talyn's town – I hadn't suspected the danger that lurked so close.

Now that I knew about it, though, I wasn't sure I wanted to let it go either. Samhail was right. Talyn's unique set of skills made her an extremely valuable asset. Some rulers might be interested in her power to kill, but information could cut deeper than a sword. Her ability to camouflage herself in any household and report back what she learned was worth infinitely more than her abilities as an assassin in my book. The question was whether I could trust her enough after all this to bring her into my inner circle. Could I trust her around Cyra? Or would we one day find ourselves torn to shreds by the creature we'd let in by the front door?

"Got it," Talyn said, and I grunted in pain as she withdrew the tweezers from the hole in my shoulder. My body tensed, then relaxed as she laid the bloody tip of metal on the chair beside us.

I looked over at the small tip. How could something so little cause so much trouble?

My wound was bleeding again, and Talyn pressed a clean cloth down onto it hard.

"Hold that there while I get the needle and thread ready," she said as she grabbed my hand and laid it over the cloth.

A smile twitched at my lips at how she ordered me around like I wasn't one of the most powerful rulers on the continent. She and Samhail really were cut from the same cloth.

You haven't earned the answer to that question yet, my lord. That's what she'd dared to tell me when I'd first asked her who she was. I might've been impressed if I hadn't wanted to kill her at the time.

I considered if I was still angry enough to want her dead. She spied on us, planned to kill us, then kidnapped me and dragged me into the middle of my greatest enemy's stronghold for purely selfish reasons. Granted, I could almost empathize with why she'd done the last, but she'd been reckless with both my life and her own.

"It was you who set off the wards that night?" I asked as she pulled my hand off my chest and removed the cloth.

"Yes." No pause.

"You realized you set them off and ported back down to your room before my power pulsed."

"I didn't quite make it back to my room," she said. "I made it to the first floor, but I had to shift into a guard when the rest of the guards came rushing into the house."

"And you were outside our room a week or so earlier in the middle of the night. Samhail caught you in the hall. What were you doing up there that night?"

This time there was a pause. "Actually, I was inside your room that night deciding if I should just kill you and be done with it," she said.

I leaned up on an elbow. "What?"

Talyn sighed and met my eyes. "I was tired of waiting for Sandrian to tell me what he wanted me to do, so I crept into your room that night.

Cyra woke up from a nightmare while I was standing at the foot of your bed. I could've sworn she caught a glimpse of me before I ported across the room to hide, but she must have thought I was part of her dream."

I fell back against the cot as my insides went cold. Nemesis take me. Cyra and I had been closer to death than we'd ever realized.

Talyn repositioned the lamp as she leaned over me with her needle. I winced as she pushed it through the first piece of skin.

"Why didn't you kill us that night?" I asked.

"I hadn't been ordered to yet," she said. She let out a heavy breath. "Truthfully, I was having trouble convincing myself Cyra needed to die as Sandrian suggested."

I raised a brow. "Just Cyra?"

She smiled down at me before pushing the needle through again. "Just Cyra," she confirmed. "I was counting the days until I could kill you."

"I have that effect on people."

She huffed a small laugh.

"And now you no longer want to kill me, or are you just waiting until I've outlived my usefulness to you?" I asked.

She shrugged again. "You agreed to help me when you didn't have to, when you in fact have every reason not to. I still think you're an arrogant ass, but I don't particularly have any desire to kill you anymore."

I chuckled. "Be careful, assassin. Next you'll be declaring yourself the head of my fan club."

"Don't you already hold that position?" she asked, and I couldn't help the bark of laughter that jumped up my throat.

I groaned as the movement stabbed Talyn's needle into my shoulder.

"No more talking," she declared, glaring down at me. "I need to finish this and get back to my room. I can't be caught down here."

"Do you have a plan yet?" I asked.

"Not yet, but I'll try to think of one tonight. It's not safe for either of us to stay here very long. Morland knows why I'm here, and so does Magdalene, for that matter."

I lifted my head. "What do you mean she knows why you're here?"

"She knows I'm here to kill Morland," she said. "Luckily, she doesn't seem to care all that much if I succeed."

That was certainly interesting news.

I remained quiet the rest of the time as Talyn finished stitching up my wound. She put a clean cloth over it again and rewrapped it with the piece of my shirt. We tried to make it look as much like I hadn't been given any medical treatment while still keeping the wound clean so it would heal.

Then she gathered all her things back into the cloth sack and headed for the cell door.

"Have you been practicing with the caronium cuff?" she asked as she reached outside the cell to unlock it with a key she retrieved from between her breasts.

"It takes me a while sometimes, but I can do it," I said.

"Keep practicing," she said. "You need to be able to do it fast."

I nodded, and she slipped quickly out of the cell before closing it behind her and heading back upstairs.

Morland was the issue. Talyn and I could escape easily enough, but finding a way to bring Morland with us was the trick. Regardless of what Talyn wanted him for, I needed to get Aidan's body back to Callanus. Eventually his people would start to wonder where he was, and we needed him close if we were going to find a way to get Morland out of him.

In a strange way, I was actually grateful Talyn had brought me here. Who knows how long it would've taken us to find and get Aidan back if she hadn't. If we could just get him out with us, then we could focus on removing Morland from his mind.

I already had one possible idea about that. If the memory that had come crashing back to me after Magdalene had invaded my mind was true, then I knew just the person who might be able to help us.

Chapter 27

I barely had time to gasp in air before the icy chill of the ocean water sent needles of pain through my body. The shock of it left me dazed for several long moments as my mind reeled, trying to understand what had just happened as I took stock of my situation.

Axenus had grabbed me and was now dragging me down into the depths of the ocean. Fast, if the water rushing over my body was any indication. Faster than I would've thought possible. Was he really trying to kill me?

No, Axenus knew I could survive underwater. He was trying to get me away from the prison.

A strange mix of fury and relief hit me, and my mind cleared. My magic had already begun to do all the things it needed to do to keep me alive, such as filling my lungs with air, warming the water around me, and relieving the depth pressure.

Axenus's strong arm was like a band of iron around my waist, but now that I had my bearings, I ported out of his grasp.

It took me a moment to orient myself when I reappeared in the vast nothingness of the water, though. Axenus must've expected the port because it seemed like only a second before his hand closed over my ankle, and he yanked me back down against him to continue swimming.

I considered porting again, but I realized the futility of it. Porting required me to imagine my destination within a frame of reference, and I had none down here. On land, you ported next to a tree or onto the other side of a door. The tree and the door were spatial references that helped the power determine where to make a person appear. Down here, the only thing I could use as a spatial reference was Axenus, and – to a degree –

the surface, but that didn't seem to be enough for the magic. I could probably do better with some practice, but I didn't have time for that now.

Moreover, now that we were no longer in the prison, I was starting to lose my anger, and with it, my desire to fight Axenus. The deeper we got, the more I also needed to concentrate on keeping myself alive, so I stopped struggling.

I felt the tension in Axenus ease as my body relaxed against him.

"I'm sorry, Cyra," he said, and his voice was garbled through the water. "This was the only thing I could think of to stop you."

I didn't respond. I could've tried to break through his mind shield to seize control and make him bring me back to the surface, but I was tired. I didn't want to fight him. Whatever plan he had, I'd let it play out.

I lost track of how long we swam into the depths, and I was about to break my silence when Axenus finally slowed. The pale blue glow of phosphorescent light appeared before us, and I made out the dark outline of an underwater rock formation. Axenus swam straight for it, and I saw what looked like the opening of a cave.

Panic surged again at the thought of him dragging me into a dark enclosed space, and I pulled at his arm with a muffled scream of protest.

"There's a large cave inside," he assured me. "Don't worry. It's safe. We just need a place to talk."

I stilled against him, but the tension in my body didn't abate as he swam us through an opening just barely large enough for both of us to pass. Nausea turned in my stomach as claustrophobia took hold of me, but it eased slightly as the phosphorescence illuminated a wide-open space inside the stone.

"I'm going to push the water out of the cave," Axenus told me. "I need you to fill the space I make with air."

I nodded.

All around us the water started to flow out the way we'd come in, and I immediately filled the space with breathable air. About a minute later, my feet touched down onto rock as the water withdrew, and several seconds after that, my head was above the surface.

I gulped in a huge lung-full of air. Axenus's arm was still around me, and he was standing as well. He'd apparently shifted out of his merform because he held onto me until I was steady enough to stand.

"Are you alright?" he asked as he eased his hold on me.

I stepped away from him.

"You mean aside from the fact you tried to drown me, and I'm now trapped on the bottom of the ocean somewhere?" I asked.

Neither was true, but I wasn't above hyperbole right now.

I stepped back some more and saw Axenus was still wearing his clothes, but the seams of his pants had been torn when he shifted, and they now hung around his waist like a tattered skirt.

At least he wasn't naked.

"How long do you intend to keep me down here?" I asked.

"Until you feel it's safe for you to go back up," he said.

"And if I told you I feel it's safe now?"

"I'd ask you if you really believe that."

I pushed out a breath. I wouldn't admit it out loud, but he was right. I wasn't ready to go back up yet. I *shouldn't* go back up yet. It was just now hitting me that I'd killed Clarice, not in self-defense, but out of wrath.

I looked around, but there wasn't anything to sit on, so I eased myself down onto the hard stone floor. The faint glow of phosphorescence still dimly lit the space from under the water at one end of the cave, so I let a small fire flare to life on the stone. It didn't actually burn anything, so there was no smoke, but I still wasn't sure it would be safe to stay down here for long. I also warmed the air in the cave, and the chill from our little swim began to seep away.

Axenus sat on the ground across from me, and for a long while, neither of us spoke. His lightly iridescent skin shimmered in the firelight, and his garnet-colored hair hung over his shoulders, dripping beads of water. His shirt clung to his body showing each muscle of his sculpted chest, but I wouldn't let myself see him as an object of desire as I once had. I knew too much about his past.

Finally, I couldn't stand the silence any longer.

"Do you wish you'd killed Clarice instead of me?" I asked. My voice was overly loud as it bounced off the walls of the cave, and both Axenus and I winced at it.

"I had my chance to kill Clarice years ago, and I chose not to," he said. "I wish you'd chosen the same."

The resignation in his voice was worse than any anger, and my face flamed with shame.

"Why didn't you kill her?" I asked, anger rising to mask the shame. "She deserved to die for what she did."

He looked me squarely in the eye, and I had the urge to shrink back from his stare as his expression made me shudder.

"You don't even know half of what she did," he said, and it sounded like he was barely holding onto his composure. "You killed her because you wanted to kill someone, not because she may or may not have deserved it."

"I killed her because she put her hands on you," I said.

"It's not your job to protect me."

"No, but it is my job to punish," I said, standing. "I don't understand why you let her live."

Axenus heaved a deep sigh. He remained seated, his legs stretched out in front of him, crossed at the ankle.

"I couldn't kill her," he said. "Not without risking my own humanity, my own sense of self. I didn't want to let her take that from me."

"Have you never killed anyone before?" I asked, a bit surprised.

"I have," he answered, "but when Bressen brought me to see Clarice and told me he wouldn't stop me if I wanted to kill her, it wasn't the same. When I started to drown her, she wasn't a soldier on a battlefield. I wasn't defending myself or trying to save someone else. I was murdering a woman in her prison cell. I didn't like what I felt, so I stopped."

The memory of almost killing Eddin in his prison cell came back to me. Bressen had brought him to Tide's End, and I'd nearly killed my former lover before my healer magic had kicked in and tried to counteract what I was doing.

"Well, I took care of her for you," I said stubbornly to Axenus.

He finally rose to face me. "Do you think I wanted to see you become a murderer?" he said harshly, and the words struck home. My stomach knotted at the accusation in his voice.

"I'm the Hand of the Nemesis!" I shot back. "It's my job to punish."

"The Nemesis decides who lives and who dies, not you," he said.

"Maybe the Nemesis decided Clarice should die and that's why I had the urge to kill her."

"Or maybe you were angry and scared that Bressen was taken, and you were looking to lash out at someone," he said. "Clarice was just a convenient surrogate for the person or people you really want to hurt."

I turned away from him, not willing to let him see just how right he was. I shook my head.

"It's not fair," I said. "When bad people hurt us, we're expected not to retaliate out of some misguided sense that doing so will make us as bad as or worse than them. Why do others get a pass – get to live – when they do horrible things, but if I kill someone in retribution or punishment, I risk being branded a monster?"

"Cyra, killing is a slippery slope," he said. "You told yourself Clarice deserved to die – and maybe she did – but then that wasn't enough for you. You went after Glenora next. And yes, maybe Glenora deserves to die as well, but her child doesn't, and you were willing to sacrifice that baby for your vengeance. That wasn't your choice to make. That's not a soul that deserves punishment. If I'd let you kill Glenora, how many more people would you justify killing to get the answers you want?"

I clenched my teeth together. I didn't have a response to that, and once again, I knew he was right.

"So what am I supposed to do?" I yelled. I closed the distance between us and pushed on his chest with both hands. "Am I just supposed to sit here and do nothing while Magdalene and Sandrian do the gods-only-know-what to Bressen?" Angry tears sprung to my eyes. "What if they're torturing him? What if he's hurt badly? What if…what if he's already dead?"

I clenched my teeth even tighter to keep the sobs in, but I couldn't stop the tears from rolling down my cheeks. Nemesis damn me, I didn't have time to be this weak right now. I had to keep my head on straight for Bressen's sake, and my body shook with the effort of trying to hold my bone-deep panic at bay.

"Cyra." A look of compassion overtook Axenus's face.

I shook my head. "No," I managed to say. I couldn't handle his kindness right now. I didn't want his understanding.

He stepped toward me, and I took an answering step back. He kept coming, though, until he'd wrapped his arms around me and pulled me against him.

I broke. I sobbed into his chest as the weight of everything finally came crashing down on me. The things Magdalene had told me shook me to my core, but they were so much worse because Bressen wasn't here to help me pick up the pieces. He himself might be in mortal danger right now, if not dead already.

No. I held on desperately to the belief that I'd know if Bressen were dead. I'd just know. I'd feel it in my soul. In *our* soul.

I curled my hands into fists in Axenus's shirt. It was still wet, so my tears couldn't do it much worse.

It was a long time before I finally let go of him. He hadn't moved, and he didn't release me until he felt me pull back. His arms slipped away as I wiped at the moisture on my face, which was a pointless endeavor. We were both still wet from head to toe, so trying to dry anything would be futile until we got to the surface.

"Are you ready to go back up?" he asked me quietly.

"Do you think it's safe for me to go?" I asked.

"I can't know your heart and mind, Cyra," he said. "You're ultimately the person who needs to live with your actions. Are you ready to live with whatever happens if we go back up?"

I nodded. Whatever lust for wrath or vengeance had gripped me before was gone, washed away by either ocean water, or my tears, or both.

I looked at Axenus. Or maybe it was the unwavering caring and compassion of this man I now considered among my closest friends. He'd been called in to train me to use my magic, but he'd taught me so much more in the short time I'd known him.

"I'm sorry," I said. "I shouldn't have killed Clarice, and I shouldn't have made you face her to begin with."

"You didn't make me do anything. If I hadn't wanted to see her, I wouldn't have stepped inside that cell." He exhaled deeply. "Part of me wanted to see what Revenmyer had done to her." His eyes locked with mine. "And yes, part of me is…grateful she's dead."

I knew it wasn't supposed to be a thank you, at least not in the truest sense, so I didn't say anything. I just nodded my understanding.

"I think it's time to go home," I said. "We need to try whatever else we can to find Bressen."

Axenus nodded. "Cyra, you know we'll all do everything in our power to get him back safely."

I smiled weakly. "I know."

I turned away from him to draw a portal back up to Revenmyer, and it opened in front of the prison. Since we'd left the area inside the wards, we'd have to be let back in if we still had business there, but I was content for the moment to return home.

I closed the portal behind us after we stepped through and looked around for Surgeon and Serise. I doubted they would've left without me, but I didn't see them.

There was no warning when they attacked, but Axenus threw himself to the ground and rolled out of the way just as both gargoyles came streaking out of the sky for him. He was on his feet a second later with his dagger in his hand, which had somehow stayed on his belt.

"No!" I yelled as Surgeon and Serise banked around for another try.

I jumped in front of Axenus and hit Surgeon with a forcefield to send him veering off course just in time as he came in for another attack.

"Stop!" I said, throwing my hands out to ward off my protectors. I knew they were furious with Axenus for what he'd done, but they'd have to shelve their pride for the moment.

Surgeon and Serise landed in front of us, swords drawn.

"Step away from him, my lady," Serise said, "and let us filet the fish."

"Stand down," I told them, and they both looked at me in shock. "Axenus isn't to be harmed. He did what he thought was right, and he didn't hurt me. We're going to let it go this time."

"My lady," Surgeon said incredulously.

"Stand down," I repeated.

The twins exchanged glances, but they finally lowered their swords.

"Are you sure, my lady?" Serise asked as she glared at Axenus.

"I'm sure," I said. "It's time to go home."

For as much as a place without Bressen could be considered home.

Chapter 28

Cyra

I opened a portal back to my bedchamber at Tide's End, and we all stepped through. Surgeon and Serise continued to glare at Axenus, but he ignored them.

"What do we do now?" the merman asked gently.

"We figure out how to rescue Bressen," I said. My entire body seemed numb except for my heart, which was twisted in knots in my chest. I could barely breathe now that I'd regained some semblance of myself.

Samhail? Are you here? I called into his mind. He normally left a sliver of his shield open for both me and Bressen in case we needed to send him a message, and I hoped that was still true.

I opened my mind to search for a response and jumped when Samhail's voice boomed through my head.

Cyra! Where have you been? Where are you?

I'm in my room, I answered.

Don't move, he said.

"Samhail's on his way," I told the others.

I went into my closet and stripped off my wet clothes as Axenus went down to his own room to change. I put on a dry pair of pants, a sweater, and some shoes. I was trying to run a brush through my damp hair when Axenus returned, and the rustle of leathery wings sounded from out on the balcony.

Something big landed hard on the stone, and we all turned to see Samhail stalk into the room. He tucked his wings back against his body, but he didn't fully dispel them. He'd obviously been out looking for me, and I now felt guilty for leaving without telling him. Not only was Bressen gone, but then I'd disappeared on him as well.

I frowned as some kind of mark glowed gold on his forehead like the one I'd seen on the twins' foreheads. This time I was able to get a better look at it. It appeared to be three interlocking triangles above three radiant lines that extended down like sunbeams, but it was again there and gone before I had time to consider it. I remembered seeing the interlocking triangles on the altar in the Priory just before Bressen and I had made love on it weeks ago — a symbol of the Trinity, I assumed — but I wasn't sure what the radiant lines meant.

"Where the fuck did you all go?" Samhail thundered, looking from the twins to Axenus. He stopped in front of me and grabbed my arms. "Are you alright?" he asked as he looked me over.

I didn't know how to answer that. Physically I was unharmed. In every other way, I was half a second from either disintegrating into smoke or exploding into fire.

"I'm fine," I said finally. "I…went to Revenmyer."

Samhail went still, and his expression grew serious as he searched my face. I took the opportunity to look for the symbol I'd seen on his forehead before, but there was no trace of it.

"Why did you go to Revenmyer?" Samhail asked warily.

I gave him a very abbreviated version of what happened, then had to spend several minutes calming him down as he admonished me for being so reckless as to go to Revenmyer without Bressen.

I apologized, but he only turned his attention to Axenus and spent several more minutes laying into him about taking me below the water while the merman stood stoically with his arms crossed.

"Feel better now?" Axenus asked when Samhail finally wound down.

The answer was apparently no, because Samhail then turned to Surgeon and Serise to unleash his rage on them, the merman's casual dismissal of his displeasure renewing his fire. While Samhail wouldn't touch Axenus, I knew he had no such boundaries where his siblings were concerned, so I finally put a stop to his rant when he stalked toward them, seemingly intent on thrashing them both.

"Samhail," I said, taking a page from Bressen's book when it came to an authoritative tone.

To his credit, Samhail stopped immediately, although his face remained a mask of fury. I considered letting him get into a fight with the twins, only because I knew they could handle themselves, but I decided against it. I felt like a hypocrite, given that venting my own rage earlier had involved Clarice's death, but I needed my gargoyles healthy and whole on the chance we got news of where Bressen was.

For that matter, it was unusual for Samhail to show quite this much anger. His rage usually simmered just below the surface, and it was cold and calculated when he did release it. To see him storm around like this with his emotions so close to the surface wasn't something I'd ever seen before. Was he as worried about Bressen as I was? Or was his lack of control a consequence of something else?…Like strong feelings of another kind for the fiery assassin who'd betrayed us. Betrayed *him*.

When Samhail finally calmed down enough that I was reasonably certain he wouldn't attack anyone, we moved into Bressen's study, and the five of us spent the rest of the day fruitlessly trying to figure out a way to find Bressen. I could usually find him through our bond, but something was blocking it now. My seeker power couldn't locate him – I knew it wouldn't, but I'd tried anyway – and we eventually called in Phaedrus to see if there was anyone at the Priory who could help.

No such luck. Not even the priestess who I'd originally syphoned the seeker power from could find Bressen.

We stayed awake late into the night until Axenus gently suggested we all needed to get some sleep so we could start fresh the next morning. I agreed reluctantly, although I was sure I wouldn't be able to sleep.

Cyra

I laid awake in bed for at least an hour as my mind juggled thoughts of Bressen, Revenmyer, Clarice, and Magdalene.

I wasn't truly sorry I'd killed Clarice, only sorry my actions had upset Axenus. He was right that I'd gone too far, and he was right to stop me from hurting Glenora, but the one light spot in my world right now was that the woman who'd kept him as a slave was gone. He'd never thank me for it, but I didn't need him to. I'd caught glimpses of Axenus's past a couple times in Clarice's mind, and I knew I'd killed a monster today.

When I couldn't stand being in my own head any longer, I swung my legs out of bed, put on my robe and slippers, and left my room. It was too empty without Bressen, the bed too large and too cold.

I walked down to the third floor, hesitated, then knocked quietly on Samhail's door.

I wasn't completely sure if I wanted him to hear me or not, but I was relieved when he opened the door a few seconds later wearing only a loose pair of black pants. He and I looked at each other for a few long moments.

"Couldn't sleep either?" he asked, and I shook my head.

Another long pause.

"Do you want to come in?" he asked.

"Just to sleep," I assured him. "I…just don't want to be alone. I need to be near someone."

A shorter pause before Samhail opened the door to let me pass.

I'd thought long before deciding to come down to Samhail's room. My other option had been to open a portal to Gendris and wake Raina, but I didn't want to drag her into all this, no matter what she'd said earlier.

I also couldn't deny I found something especially comforting about being near Samhail. He'd been my friend and my protector for less than a year, but we'd grown exceptionally close in that time, and there was something about him that always made me feel safe. I also knew Bressen trusted us together.

I removed my robe and kicked off my slippers before climbing under the covers on the side of his bed that looked less slept-in. Samhail climbed back in on his side, still in the pair of loose pants he'd worn to answer the door, and I wondered if he actually slept in them, or if he only wore them now for the sake of propriety. I'd never actually been in his bed when he slept. He'd always come to me and Bressen's bed, and it suddenly felt strange to be here.

We lay on our sides looking at each other for a while before I spoke.

"Are you alright?" I asked him.

I saw his frown, even in the dark.

"Why wouldn't I be?" he asked.

"I've never seen you quite as riled up as you were today."

"My best friend is in the hands of our enemies, including two sadistic bastards with a grudge and one bitch who likes to ra-"

He cut himself off before finishing the thought. I wasn't sure if my horror showed in my face or not, but he shook his head.

"I'm sorry," he said. "I'm just worried about him."

I nodded. "And…what about Talyn?"

His scowl was again easy to read in the dark.

"Am I worried about Talyn?" he asked incredulously. "The woman who deceived us and took my friend?"

"I'm not asking if you're worried about her. I'm asking if…" I trailed off, not sure how to say it.

Samhail lifted himself up on an elbow. "If I'm what?"

I shrugged against the mattress. *If you're heartbroken*, I wanted to say, but he'd scoff at that.

"It just seems like you and Talyn had grown close," I said. "I was wondering how you felt about her betrayal."

He grunted and turned onto his back. "Talyn is nothing to me. I don't feel betrayed. I feel stupid for having trusted her, and angry at myself that my lapse in judgement put Bressen in danger."

I was the one to sit up this time, and I let a small flame flare to life in my hand. The red 'glow' I usually saw when someone lied wasn't a real glow, so I couldn't see it in the dark. It was more of an aura, and I could see it now clinging faintly to Samhail's skin in the light of my fire.

"You're lying," I said. "You care for her."

A muscle twitched in his jaw. He wanted to deny it, but I'd see the lie.

"It doesn't matter," he said without looking at me. "She was probably working for Sandrian the whole time."

I closed my hand to extinguish the flame. "She tried to save me when I was fighting Magdalene," I pointed out.

He didn't say anything, and I laid back down. Even with his mind shield up, I felt the conflicting emotions roiling within him. He wanted to believe Talyn hadn't been working for Sandrian, but he couldn't reconcile her actions today.

Neither could I. Bressen and I had both read her mind before we'd agreed to let her help us trap Sandrian and Magdalene, and we'd seen nothing but pure intentions. She'd been committed to helping us, at least at first, but something had changed at some point.

I wasn't sure why I was looking for reason in Talyn's actions or defending her to Samhail. Part of me wanted to kill her for taking Bressen – a large part – but a tiny sliver of me, like Samhail, wanted to believe there was more to why she'd done what she'd done.

We didn't say anything more, and I closed my eyes to try and sleep. Samhail's presence next to me made a difference, and I finally fell asleep a few minutes after his own breathing became deeper.

Cyra

I was in the middle of a forest without any memory of how I'd gotten there. The feeling was familiar. It's how I'd ended up in Axenus's nightmare weeks ago.

I looked around for an indication I was once again dream walking and found it immediately.

Two women faced off against each other near a small cottage that stood in a clearing in the trees. One woman seemed ancient. Her long gray hair was tied back in a loose knot at the nape of her neck, but she stood straight despite how thin and delicate her body looked. The other woman had her back to me, but I could tell without seeing her face who the petite blonde was.

Magdalene.

"What are you doing?" Magdalene asked the woman warily.

The older woman smiled. "Going where you can't follow," she said. "Or where you *won't* follow."

She put a hand to the center of her chest and the spot glowed, as if she were channeling magic into herself.

"No!" Magdalene screamed. She lunged forward, but the woman's body was suddenly engulfed in flames, and I clamped a hand to my mouth to stifle my scream.

I stared in horror as the woman's body burned, yet she didn't seem to be in pain. If anything, she wore a faint smile, as if she were savoring Magdalene's obvious misery.

Magdalene continued to scream as she tried to get close to the woman, but the heat of the flames kept her back. She seemed to be trying to use her frost power to counteract the fire, but it had no effect, and a second later, the older woman's body turned completely to ash and collapsed to the ground in a pile. The flames died, and ash puffed into the air as the woods once again went silent.

Magdalene sank to her knees next to the ash. She looked as though she wanted to reach out and touch the pile, but I stepped forward, unexplainable anger surging through me at the thought of her touching what remained of the woman.

"Magdalene!" I yelled.

Magdalene started and spun around. She stood quickly as she saw me.

"Cyra?" she asked, cocking her head in question. "How are you…?" A look of understanding passed over her face. "You can dream walk. I'm jealous. That's a power I never managed to pick up."

"What did you do to that woman?" I asked, my voice full of menace.

Magdalene huffed a laugh. "I did nothing. She did that to herself."

I blinked. "What? Why?"

"To escape me," Magdalene said. "It was her only way out."

"She killed herself just to escape you?" I said incredulously. "Why? What were you planning to do to her?"

A grin crept over Magdalene's face. "You don't know who she was."

"Should I?"

Magdalene's grin grew wry. "In a way, she was your mother."

I blinked again. "What in the three hells are you talking about? I already have two mothers, and she isn't one of them."

"Her name was Crissail," Magdalene said. "She was the Hand of the Nemesis before you, and she died so you could be born. She knew the only way to escape was to pass the power of the Nemesis on to another."

My mouth hung open in disbelief, but I was incapable of shutting it.

"It was twenty-two years before you finally used that power yourself and allowed me to sense you," she said. "Unfortunately, the Triumvirate got ahold of you before I was able to find you."

I couldn't move. Not only had I just witnessed the death of the last Hand of the Nemesis, but somewhere across the world, her power had just passed to me as I was being born.

Well, not really. This was a dream, but it was nevertheless the memory of how I'd been created.

"It was noble of her," Magdalene went on, still oblivious to my shock, "and she bought the world a couple decades, but her sacrifice was ultimately in vain."

Magdalene smiled as she rushed toward me, her hand outstretched as if she meant to touch me. I tried to step back, but I didn't react fast enough to avoid her.

It turned out to be moot. Magdalene's hand passed right through me, and her eyes widened in surprise.

I smiled as my shock finally wore off. "We're in a dream," I reminded her, "and by your own admission, I'm the only dream walker here. You don't control what happens. I do."

I held out a hand and sent Magdalene flying backward with a forcefield. She landed hard against a tree and crumpled to the ground.

It had been an experiment. I wasn't entirely sure I could affect her here, but apparently I could.

Magdalene's eyes narrowed as she pushed herself to her feet and threw her hand toward me, likely trying to use her frost magic.

Nothing happened.

She tried again, but I only stood there, untouched by any power.

I used my sunfire next, and Magdalene screamed as she writhed on the ground in pain while the phantom flames burned through her, leaving her flesh uncharred. The feeling of being able to hurt her without fear of her returning the favor was heady, and I wondered what effect, if any, this was having back on the real Magdalene in her bed.

"Where is Bressen?" I asked, releasing her from my sunfire. "Tell me where you're keeping him, and maybe I'll let you live."

Magdalene shook her head as she lay on the ground panting. "You can't kill me through a dream."

"Are you sure about that?" I asked. "If I will you to die, are you sure your mind won't obey me, dream or no?"

Her eyes flared. "Kill me and you'll never find him."

"I've learned that the mind is a powerful thing," I said, stepping toward her. "I've been told I can use my dream walking to make people live their worst fears. Shall we figure out what yours are?"

A low growl sounded from somewhere between the trees, and Magdalene's head jerked to the side to see what had made it.

A huge cat stepped into the clearing. Its coat was pure white, and tufts of black fur topped its ears. Long, sharp fangs hung from its top jaw as it opened its maw wide to snarl at Magdalene. It was like the one I'd seen in Clarice's room chained to the wall when I'd dream walked into Axenus's nightmare.

Another growl sounded from Magdalene's other side as two more giant cats emerged from the brush, and her eyes flew to me in panic.

"Tell me where Bressen is before they tear you apart," I said.

"This is only a dream. They can't hurt me," Magdalene said, but she sounded far from convinced.

The first cat lunged for her and swiped out with razor-sharp claws. She screamed and fell to the ground as it ripped her calf open. I couldn't see exactly what her leg looked like under her dress, but a copious amount of blood stained the skirt, and whatever was beneath it now looked rather lumpy, as if flesh had been torn from bone.

The other two cats closed in, and Magdalene tried to repel them back with her power, but this dream wasn't under her control.

"Tell me where he is!" I yelled at her.

Magdalene looked at me with defiance. "Come find him in time if you can," she spat out, and her eyes began to flutter.

I didn't understand what she was doing at first, but then it hit me. She was trying to wake herself up.

"No!" I yelled, and I sent all three cats surging for her. I wasn't sure if having them attack would help or hurt, but I had to do something to keep her from escaping.

One cat sunk its fangs into her thigh while another went for her throat. I prepared myself for her screams of pain, but they never came. Instead, everything went quiet as darkness crept in around me.

My eyes popped open, and I sat up slowly in bed. It took me a moment to realize I was in Samhail's room as his warmth drifted across the bed to me from where he lay on his side facing me, his chest rising and falling with the steady rhythm of sleep. One of his arms stretched out between us as if he meant to wrap it around me, but I knew instinctively it wasn't *my* body he sought in unconsciousness.

I lay back down as bile tickled the back of my throat. I'd let Magdalene escape without learning where Bressen was. Worse yet, if I'd angered or frightened her, she might take her fury out on Bressen, and I swallowed down the urge to vomit.

I had to find Bressen. I had to.

I lay awake for at least another hour before exhaustion finally overtook me again. I wanted to wake Samhail to keep me company, but I envied him his oblivion, and I wouldn't take it away from him.

If something did happen to Bressen, I doubted either of us would ever sleep well again.

Cyra

I woke before Samhail the next morning and went back to my own room. It was unbearably quiet and empty there, and I fought back tears as I dressed and went down to the dining room for breakfast.

Axenus was already at the table, and Samhail entered about a minute after I did. None of us spoke, and my plate trembled in my hand as I tried to fill it. I wasn't hungry. I'd barely forced some food down at dinner yesterday, but for the sake of keeping up my strength, I'd try to eat. If we found Bressen, I'd need-

Energy suddenly surged through my chest, and I dropped my plate so it crashed on the floor and shattered, sending food scattering everywhere.

"Cyra? Are you alright?" Samhail asked, setting down his own plate.

I planted my hands on the table and leaned over it as I tried to steady myself against a wave of lightheadedness. At first, I didn't understand what I was feeling, but joy flooded my veins a second later as I realized I could feel Bressen again. His voice filled my mind, rising like the chorus of a song, but sweeter than any melody I'd ever heard.

I need you, my love. Come find me.

Chapter 29

Cyra

"It's Bressen! I can feel him again!" I said as Axenus and Samhail both crowded in to see if I was alright.

I let my power reach out to look for Bressen, and this time it latched onto him. The relief I felt at learning he was alive was dizzying, but I forced myself to focus. He wasn't out of danger yet.

"Where is he?" Samhail asked urgently.

I drew a small circle in the air, and a miniature portal flared to life. I'd purposely made it just big enough to see through, but hopefully not big enough to draw attention if anyone was around. Samhail, Axenus, and I all peered through it to see what was on the other side.

The portal had opened outside an old castle, part of which was nothing but rubble. Most of the castle still stood, but one corner of the keep and part of the battlements had fallen down, as if they'd sustained damage in an attack and no one had bothered to fix them.

"There are wards," I said. I could feel them now, and that's likely why the portal had opened outside the castle instead of inside it. I was able to feel Bressen again for whatever reason, but the wards still prevented me from opening a portal directly to him, and they might hinder us from getting into the castle from the outside as well.

"What's the plan?" Axenus asked.

The rumble of heavy footsteps sounded in the hall just before Surgeon and Serise burst into the dining room in answer to the mental message I'd sent them.

"Axenus, you may want to get a weapon," I said before turning to the gargoyles. "You three should shift as soon as we're through. We attack in two minutes. I'll see what I can do about getting the wards down."

Axenus nodded and sprinted toward the armory as Samhail, Surgeon, and Serise all began to undress in preparation to shift. It was a testament to just how much my life had changed in the last several months that the sight of three huge warriors getting naked in my dining room didn't phase me in the slightest.

Axenus was back in a minute and a half with a longsword in hand. He also carried a sheathed dagger attached to a belt that he quickly fastened around my waist.

"Ready?" I asked, and everyone nodded.

I threw the portal open wide, and the gargoyles barreled through it, shifting as soon as they got to the other side. Axenus and I followed, and I closed the portal quickly behind me before turning to the wards.

The gargoyles had found the edges of them, but they couldn't get past. While we'd waited for Axenus to arm himself, I'd tried to get a sense for the wards and the best way to break them down, but if Magdalene had put these up – which she undoubtedly had – that would be easier said than done.

I put out my hands and sent my power into the wards with a command that they lower for me. Instead, I was thrown back as they rebuffed my attempt. Luckily Axenus was behind me, so I only slammed against his chest, and he steadied me.

Inside the castle, I felt Bressen's urgency, his conviction that he needed to get out of there right away, and his determination spurred my own. I pushed forward again.

"See if you can hold me steady," I told Axenus, and he stepped up behind me to act as a brace for when the wards tried to throw me back.

A day ago on that field with Magdalene, I'd been able to combine several powers at once to create a singular destructive force, but there'd been more to it than that. The powers had been held together and amplified by something I was starting to realize was specific to me as a syphon, a power attuned to the Nemesis.

I drew on that power now, letting it mingle with my fire and forcefields and any other magic I had that might break through, and I sent it battering into the wards. I was thrown back again, but Axenus was there this time, and he put his weight behind me to help keep me upright.

The entire ground shook as the wards quivered, and I redoubled my efforts, throwing everything I had at them in an attempt to overload them, to break them down. Anything to get them out of my way. They were between me and my mate, me and the other half of my soul.

Three other blasts hit the wards, and I saw the gargoyles were all aiming their powers at the magical barrier. They were fighting against something that tried to throw them back, but in their stone forms, they weren't so easily moved.

I sent a blast of elemental power shooting through the ground, and ripples of earth tore forward to slam into the barrier. The wards flickered, and I sent another blast of my combined powers into them. I'd never used this much power before, not even after the gods had boosted them at the Priory, but I needed to get to Bressen, so I had to push beyond my normal limits.

I'm coming, my love. I sent the message into his mind to let him know I was here and trying to get to him.

More power suddenly streamed through me as Bressen added his own to my efforts, and I harnessed it to send it blasting into the wards.

A second later, the wards shattered, and the gargoyles surged forward. Their huge stone-like wings beat, kicking up dirt and debris as they took to the air with roars of triumph to head for the castle.

I drew another portal, and this one opened inside the battlements. Axenus and I stepped through it just as the gargoyles landed in the courtyard with enough impact to crack some of the stones of the terrace.

The doors of the castle flew open as dozens of guards poured out, their blue symbiotic shells spreading out over their bodies. The gargoyles all roared and met the creatures before they finished descending the stairs. Samhail and the twins threw the guards back with forcefields or just knocked them to the side with huge stone-like fists, tails, and wings.

Axenus and I hung back and tried to deal with any guards who broke through. He swept them back with blasts of water while I used my own forcefields to try and clear a path. We used our blades when we couldn't help it, but Axenus and I at least tried to avoid killing the symbionts whenever possible.

"We need to get inside and find Bressen!" I yelled to Axenus.

He was about to answer when his eyes flared. "No, we don't! Look!"

I looked to the front doors of the castle where Axenus pointed. Bressen was running toward us with someone in his arms, and I recognized Talyn's coppery hair. She looked only half conscious, but how or why Bressen had chosen to slow himself down by bringing her back with him, I wasn't sure.

"Bressen!" I yelled in relief.

A golden glow like the one I'd seen on the gargoyles' foreheads flashed on Bressen's, and I paused briefly to wonder once again what in the three hells the mark was and why I was only now seeing it.

I didn't have time to dwell on the thought, because a moment later I saw Aidan running behind Bressen, not chasing him, but following him. Had Bressen somehow managed to get Morland out of Aidan?

My relief at seeing Bressen alive was fleeting as I realized he ran barefoot over the cold stone, and my magic recognized the pair of pants he wore as a glamour.

Nemesis take me, why was he naked and barefoot?

I didn't see the bruises and slashes on his face and upper body until he got closer, and then rage flooded me.

"Magdalene!" I growled as the woman appeared in a portal at the top of the stairs, and our eyes met.

"Not now!" Bressen yelled. "Open a portal and get us out of here!"

I hesitated only a second while my need for vengeance warred with common sense, then common sense won out. Bressen was alive and he had both Talyn and Aidan with him. It was more than we could've hoped for, and I'd be foolish not to take this small victory.

I turned and opened a portal just in time for Bressen to fly through it with Talyn in his arms and Aidan on his heels.

The gargoyles roared and turned their attention to Sandrian and Magdalene, but Bressen was right. Now was not the time for this fight.

"Retreat now!" I yelled to them, and they all turned to follow me and Axenus back through the portal.

Samhail ushered Surgeon and Serise through before him, then dove through himself, and I slammed the portal shut just as a bolt of Sandrian's lightning came streaking toward the opening. A small zap of it slipped through and crackled the air, but it dissipated quickly without access to its source, and I let out the breath I'd been holding.

My eyes sought Bressen, and I found him kneeling by a pillar where he'd set Talyn down. I'd brought us to the Great Chamber of the Citadel without really thinking about it, but this was the best place to come with Aidan, I realized.

I took a good look at Bressen's body then, and my stomach bottomed out. He was covered in blue and purple bruises as well as multiple cuts that still bled down his back, arms, and chest.

"Sweet gods! What happened?" I cried as I knelt next to him. "Bressen." I laid a hand on his cheek, and he covered mine with his own.

"I'm alright," he assured me.

No, he wasn't, and I remembered whose fault that was.

My head jerked to Talyn as all my rage from yesterday sparked again. "You!"

She jolted to see the red I was sure had just flashed in my eyes.

"Time for you to die!" I said as I reached a hand toward her, but Bressen grabbed my wrist.

"Cyra, wait-," he started to say, but his words were cut off by a roar that shook the room and made him jump.

We both turned to see Samhail just shifting back to his human form. A second later he charged at Talyn.

I moved back out of his way, content to let him exact his revenge for both of us. Last night I'd almost been willing to give Talyn the benefit of the doubt, but seeing the state Bressen was in had banished any leeway I was willing to grant her.

"Samhail, no!" Bressen yelled as he tried to position himself between Talyn and the charging gargoyle, but he and I were both surprised when Samhail's forcefield pushed him aside.

Talyn's eyes widened with fear, and she seemed unable to do anything as Samhail's hands closed around her throat.

"Samhail, let go of her!" Bressen shouted, but Samhail didn't seem to hear as he squeezed harder.

Talyn clawed at his hold, but Samhail was either drawing out her death, or he was more conflicted about killing her than even he realized. I'd seen him rip Jerram's head off with little effort.

Samhail froze just as Talyn's eyes began to roll back in her head and her eyelids fluttered. Then she gasped and sucked in a lungful of air as Samhail dropped his hands from her neck.

I looked at Samhail, but his face was placid, his eyes glassy. I recognized the look. Bressen had control of his mind.

Samhail snapped awake a moment later.

"What did you do to me?" Samhail asked Bressen, rising to his feet.

Bressen stood as well. "I stopped you from making a big mistake," he said. "Talyn is the only reason I got out of there alive and with my body parts intact."

Tandem Read: Go to *Clash of Stone and Steel* (Bk 3), Chapter 37-38

Chapter 30

Bressen

It had been a long day back, mostly because I was away from Cyra for much of it. The second I returned I'd wanted nothing more than to sequester myself with her in our room, but I had responsibilities I couldn't shirk, especially given recent events.

First, I'd secured Talyn and Morland in dungeon cells below the Citadel. Both had gone willingly, Morland because I still had control of his mind, and Talyn because she'd agreed to be locked up with him until we figured out how to remove him from Aidan's body.

Then I'd met with Samhail and Axenus. We needed to stay at the Citadel for the time being, mainly because I couldn't keep Aidan, or at least his body, locked up in Hiraeth. This meant moving the household back to Callanus for the time being.

I also met with Jasper and Maziren. Thank the gods they'd both already known about Morland's takeover of Aidan, because I would've had an interesting time explaining to them why I'd locked up the Lord of Derridan otherwise. The bigger issue was how we'd handle Aidan's absence from the palace in Seatherny.

So far, Aidan had only been gone for about two days, and Jasper had told the palace staff that Aidan was simply taking a much-needed break. It was believable enough given that most of the servants and guards had started to notice the change in their lord's demeanor over the last week, but we needed a more solid plan moving forward. We could stall for maybe a week, but we'd eventually need to come up with a more permanent explanation for Aidan's absence.

Lastly, I began making plans for another ocean voyage. I'd lifted the memory block on Cyra and Axenus, and they'd both been shocked to remember being on the island near where we'd found *The Stalwart*.

Flynt, one of the warriors freed from the necklace, had insisted Praya was still alive, and we were almost certain one of the women we'd met on the island must be her. Someone there had gotten into our heads – into *my* head – and planted a memory wipe so deep it had taken Magdalene's incursion to jar it loose. Perhaps it was hubris, but the only way I could explain that was the presence of another syphon.

I'd promised Talyn we would get Morland out of Aidan so she could kill him, and Praya's assistance was the only option we had right now to do that. It was a long shot, but it was our only one. Regardless of Talyn's vendetta, we needed to extract Morland and get Aidan back to ruling Derridan. If we couldn't, then we had a whole new set of problems.

As it was, it was a miracle nothing catastrophic had happened the last two days with, not one, but two Triumvirate lords missing. Cyra and I would need to make our journey to the island as quickly as possible because we'd essentially be leaving Thasia with only the High Council of Polaris in charge, unbeknownst to them.

I trusted Samhail and Axenus to keep things running in Hiraeth while I was gone, and Jasper and Maziren were competent enough to keep things under control in Derridan, but I didn't want to tempt fate. We had to get back before Sandrian and Magdalene realized we were gone. I assumed they'd be busy moving their headquarters now that we knew where they were, but I wasn't betting on anything.

It was late when I finally got back to the room I shared with Cyra in the Citadel, and I opened the door quietly in case she was already asleep.

I wasn't surprised to find her awake, sitting by the fire reading. She looked up when I entered and closed the book. For a few seconds, we just looked at each other across the room, the distance between us more than physical.

I'd already felt the change in her when I returned, but it had broken my heart when Axenus told me what had happened at Revenmyer. In killing Clarice, I was afraid Cyra had taken another step down a very slippery slope.

I crossed the room to Cyra in a few strides. She set her book aside and stood to meet me. Part of me wanted to crush her body against mine, to claim her so thoroughly she'd wonder how she ever survived without me inside her, but another part of me urged patience.

That other part remembered sitting in a dungeon cell wondering if I'd ever see her again. It remembered being stripped naked and facing Morland's threats of removing my cock so I'd never again be able to bury myself inside my wife. That part of me had promised if I ever saw Cyra again, I'd savor every second with her. I'd take things slow and draw out our time together as long as possible as a reminder of what I'd almost lost.

Cyra looked confused when I stopped just in front of her and lifted my hands to cup her face rather than dragging her against me. I kissed her forehead, and she blinked at me.

"Bressen, what are you-"

I slipped one arm around her waist and pulled her gently to me before I silenced her question with a long, sensual kiss. The fingers of my other hand threaded through her thick, dark locks as I held her in place, not roughly, but just firmly enough so she couldn't move.

I deepened the kiss as my mouth continued to move over hers, and when I finally pulled away nearly a minute later, Cyra was breathless.

We were normally ravenous around each other, and it had been a long time since I'd simply kissed her slowly and deeply like that.

"Bressen," she breathed.

There was one thing I needed to talk to her about before we went any further, though.

"I spoke to Axenus," I said, and her body tensed against me.

She raised her eyes to meet mine. "I'm not sorry I killed her," she said. "You killed that man in Bronwyn when I was threatened. Well, Clarice threatened Axenus."

I raised a brow, and she looked back at me defiantly. We both knew the situations weren't the same, but I wasn't going to argue with her now.

"I don't want to lose you," I said quietly, and her face softened.

She knew what I meant.

Cyra's expression turned sultry. "Do you want to punish me for what I did?" She bit her lip, and my cock went hard.

Fuck.

My punishments were never really punishments. Cyra enjoyed it far too much when I was rough with her, and maybe I enjoyed it a bit too much as well.

Thoughts of pushing her to her knees and fucking her mouth until she choked around my cock flitted through my head, but I pushed them away. Ironically, if I really wanted to discipline her for killing Clarice, the best way was not to give her the punishment she wanted.

I swallowed hard and willed the traitorous appendage between my legs to calm down.

I shook my head. "Not tonight," I said, my voice graveled with need. "Tonight, I plan to take my time with you. To use a slow hand."

She only blinked at me as I trailed my hand down her face until my thumb brushed her lips.

"All I could think about while I was gone was how much I neglected these lips," I whispered. "I should've spent so much more time kissing you than I have. I promised myself that, if I made it back to you, I'd rectify this grievous mistake."

I lowered my head toward hers ever so slowly. Her lips parted in anticipation, and her chin tipped up to meet me. I paused just as my lips touched hers, and I heard her stuttered inhalation.

I could fuck my wife easily enough. At least once a day I bent her over a table or pushed her legs open and had her wrap them around me. We'd fuck hard and fast until we were both panting with the effort and covered in a film of sweat.

But that's not what I wanted now.

Right now, I wanted to make love to my wife. I wanted to seduce her, to make her pant not from physical exertion, but because I'd driven her so close to the brink of madness that she couldn't remember how to breathe. I wanted her body to be so sensitive that I could make her come just by blowing softly on the right spot. And I wanted her so drunk on what I was doing that her world narrowed to the existence of us and us alone, and she forgot every pain and worry she'd felt the last few days.

"Did you miss me while I was away?" I asked.

A stupid question. She'd killed a woman when she'd woken to remember I was gone, but I still needed to hear her say it.

"I burned half the woods down near that clearing when Talyn took you," she said. "Does that count?"

I smiled. "Only *half* the woods?" I asked. "I suppose that's a start."

She started to smile, but it faltered.

"What's wrong?" I asked.

"I…slept in Samhail's room last night," she said, then went on hurriedly. "Just slept. We didn't touch each other. I couldn't be in here alone. The room was too cold and empty without you. I needed to be near someone, and Samhail…" She trailed off.

"Was someone?" I finished for her with the hint of a smile. "Did you think I'd be upset?"

She let out a relieved breath. "I hoped not."

"Cyra, I know you and Samhail are close, and I trust you both," I said. "To be honest, if I couldn't be here to protect you, I'm glad he was. I'd rather have you climb into bed with him and feel safe and comforted than have you lay up here feeling cold and alone." I paused. "Did sleeping next to him help?"

She hesitated before nodding. "It wasn't the same as having you here, but I could at least fall asleep with him close by."

"Then you have nothing to worry about," I said.

Her mouth tipped up into the hint of a smile. "Are you sure you don't want to punish me?"

I gave her an indulgent smile of my own. "Actually, I think I will."

She let out a squeak of delight as I scooped her up in my arms and carried her to the bed. I laid her down in the middle of the mattress, then rolled her onto her stomach. I stretched out alongside her and gathered her hair to pull it away from her back and neck.

"I call this first part 'Death by a Thousand Kisses.'" I said.

I kissed the bare spot at the base of her neck. "One," I said. Then I opened two of the buttons at the back of her dress and kissed the patch of skin they revealed. "Two."

I popped open two more buttons.

"Bressen," she said, her tone a playful admonishment.

"Sshh. Don't distract me," I said. "If I lose count, I'll have to start over." I kissed the newly uncovered spot, then added an extra for good measure. "Three. Four."

She fell silent, and I resumed my task of opening her buttons two at a time and planting kisses as I went. My cock was still hard, but my need was manageable at the moment. We'd see who broke first, her or me.

Cyra

I savored the feel of Bressen's lips pressing lightly to my back as he slowly undid the fastenings of my dress, even if he was driving me mad. Not being able to see him for much of the day had been torture, but this was its own special hell. Bressen wanted to take his time, but I was dying already, and he'd only gotten up to seventeen kisses so far.

What I wouldn't give to have Maziren's strength back for just a few minutes so I could toss Bressen onto his back, rip his pants open, and ride him until our screams of pleasure brought the Citadel guards running to see what was the matter.

He finally reached the last of the buttons, and my breathing shallowed as I waited to see what he'd do next.

His hand moved down to the skirt of the dress, and he pulled it slowly up my legs. He shifted his body down the bed, and I felt his hands on the backs of my thighs as he slid the fabric the rest of the way up over my backside. Then he looped his fingers over the waist of my undergarment and pulled it down my legs, each move achingly slow and deliberate.

There was a pause when I didn't hear or feel anything until he shifted again so he was kneeling near my legs. He lifted one of my feet back so my leg bent at the knee, then he kissed the top of the foot before kissing a trail around my ankle.

"How many is that now?" I asked.

"I lost count," he said. "I'll have to start over." He kissed a path along the back of my calf. "One…two…three…"

"We do have to sleep sometime tonight," I teased.

"Do you want me to stop?" he asked. He put my foot down and straddled my calves. I felt his next two kisses on the backs of my knees before he kissed a new path up my thigh.

My breath hitched as he got closer and closer to the apex of my legs. I jerked in surprise as he ran his teeth over one buttock, then nipped at the cheek. He did the same to the other.

I was panting as his body moved higher. He lowered himself down so his bare chest grazed my back, and I realized he'd taken his jacket and shirt off at some point.

He resumed kissing my back, but I cried out when he moved his hand between my legs and slipped a finger inside me. I arched my ass up into him, chasing his touch and pushing him deeper.

He groaned against my ear. "Fuck, Cyra. You're so gods damned wet. How am I supposed to keep things slow when your body is begging me to fuck you?"

He pushed a second finger inside me and moved them in and out. I moaned and writhed beneath him like a wanton, needy little creature. One might've thought I hadn't been touched in weeks. I opened my legs to give him better access, and I rode his hand as best I could with half his weight pressing down on top of me.

"Bressen…please," I begged.

"Not yet," he said, and he lifted himself off me.

I made a sound of frustration as he withdrew his fingers. He grabbed the shoulders of my dress and pulled them down so they were at my elbows, then he flipped me over on my back. This left my breasts exposed, but it also pinned my arms to my sides. He was on top of me again, his hips cradled between my legs.

"What are you doing?" I asked, a note of desperation in my voice.

He didn't answer but instead kissed a circle around one nipple before biting it gently, then sucking it into his mouth.

My body nearly combusted as the feel of his mouth on my breast almost pushed me over the edge. I bucked beneath him and tried to grind my clit against his torso, desperate now for a release. He switched his mouth to my other breast and sucked hard, and I screamed as my climax exploded through me. He didn't let up, and my body rocked and shuddered beneath him as I fisted my hands in the covers and let the aftershocks roll over me.

Bressen moved back up and planted gentle kisses along my face and neck as I lay panting beneath him, barely able to move.

"Better?" he asked, and I could only nod as words failed me.

Gods, he hadn't even done that much to me, but my body didn't care. Maybe I'd missed him that much, or maybe those gentle kisses all over my skin had done more than I thought.

"I don't think we got to a thousand kisses," he said. "You're making this too easy on me. I guess we'll just move on to the next part."

He lifted himself off me but continued to trail kisses down between my breasts.

"Get this dress off me," I said as I tried to wriggle it up my body.

Bressen sat back on his knees and looked down at me. There was a hint of a smile on his lips as he watched me struggle with it.

"I may not have the use of my arms, but I still have my magic," I warned him.

He held his hands up in surrender and helped me pull the dress over my head before he pushed me back down.

"I call this next part a 'Tongue Lashing,'" he said as he moved back and started to lower his head between my legs.

"Oh no you don't," I said, sitting up.

I quickly unfastened his pants and pulled them down to his thighs. Then I wrapped my hand around his cock to give it a long stroke. He swore, and I grabbed his hips to pull them forward so his groin was level with my face. Before he could protest, I slipped my mouth over him.

His hips jerked forward as he groaned loudly, and I had to relax my throat as the length of him almost choked me.

Bressen gathered up my hair in one hand and hissed out a breath as I pulled back and let my tongue circle his head. "Fuuck," he said, drawing out the word.

I pushed my mouth down on him again and sucked in my cheeks as I began to move my lips over him in an increasingly faster pace. His hand tightened in my hair as he tried to slow me down. He really was committed to not letting us go too fast, but I wanted to make him fall apart as he'd done to me.

I dug my fingernails into his hips and pulled him toward me as I fought against his hold on my hair. The next time I took him deep, I swallowed around his cock, and he let out a roar of pleasure. His hand tightened even more in my hair, almost painfully, and he pulled his hips back so his cock popped out of my mouth.

"That's not the way this is going to work," he said as he pushed me back down against the mattress. He looped his arms under my knees and pressed his body over mine so my legs were pinned back against my chest and I was nearly sandwiched in half beneath him. "I'm coming between your legs, not inside your mouth," he growled. "I want to see my seed dripping out of you when we're done."

The head of his cock pushed between my folds, and I arched against him with a moan as he slid slowly inside me. He went still when he was fully seated, and I whimpered at the exquisite feeling of being filled by him again. I was about to start squirming beneath him to get some friction, but he moved then, taking long, slow strokes that let me feel every inch of him as he withdrew then slid back in.

"Bressen," I mewled as he continued his languid thrusts.

He leaned forward and captured my mouth for a searing kiss as he pushed in, and I whimpered again. I loved it when he took me hard and fast, but gods, there was something to be said about the way he moved now, so gentle and unhurried. It was primal and hungry when he was driving into me, but there was a certain beauty in what we did now, a cognizance of how perfectly our bodies responded to each other that made me remember just how much I loved this man.

"Bressen," I said again when he lifted his lips. This time it wasn't a plea or a mewl but a whispered benediction. Trinity forgive me, but this man was my god.

I wrapped my arms around his neck and pulled him back down to kiss me again. He accepted the invitation gladly, and my mind soared somewhere above our bodies as I let the exquisite tensity build between us. I hoped he was close to his release, because I didn't know how I was still holding on.

"I can't hold out much longer," he said as if he'd read my mind.

"Then come for m-"

My command was usurped by the cry of release that barreled up my throat. Bressen brought his mouth down on mine to drink in my pleasure, and my inner walls spasmed around him. He let out a long, low groan, as he continued to move, driving slow, but deep. A few thrusts later, he buried himself into me as far as he could, and I felt the pulse of his release inside me as he groaned loudly. I'd felt him release before, but it seemed so much more intense this time, so much more noticeable as my body clamped down around him.

"Good girl," he whispered against my lips. "Take all of me."

I let out a noise that was half agreement, half moan, and Bressen relaxed above me. He stayed there a moment to catch his breath before he pushed himself off me, and I unfolded my body. His attention was focused between my legs where I felt his seed drip out of me, and a look of satisfaction stole over his face.

"You look entirely too pleased with yourself," I teased.

He smirked at me and reached between my legs to swipe two fingers through the mess he'd made. "I'll never get tired of seeing you like this, glowing after being freshly fucked and anointed in my seed."

He reached up to run his fingers down the center of my chest, but I grabbed his hand and brought the fingers to my mouth instead. I sucked them in and ran my tongue around them before swallowing down the salty substance on them.

He groaned again. "You're going to be the fucking death of me, Cyra."

I grinned at him as I summoned a small towel to clean myself up. "At least you'll die happy."

He kissed me. "That I will."

Tandem Read: Go to *Clash of Stone and Steel* (Bk 3), Chapter 39-42

Chapter 31

Bressen

The small boat carrying me and Cyra cut through the water toward the island, propelled by Cyra's water magic. Surgeon and Serise soared above us, still in their human forms, but wings outstretched as they circled overhead looking for danger. We'd left any sailors behind on the ship this time since they wouldn't do us any good. If the four of us couldn't handle the two people on the island, mortal sailors wouldn't make a difference.

For that matter, it was questionable how useful Surgeon and Serise would be if things went wrong. If one of the women on the island was who we suspected she was, the gargoyles wouldn't be able to attack her. It would be up to me and Cyra to handle her while the twins took on whoever the other woman was.

We'd debated whether or not to land at night to take them by surprise. Surgeon and Serise were all for a stealth arrival, but Cyra reasoned we'd be starting off on the wrong foot by taking a hostile approach. We were, after all, on a diplomatic mission, and sneaking onto the island in the dead of night to surprise its inhabitants wasn't the way to build trust before we asked for a favor. They'd left us alive last time, after all, just without our memories of having ever landed there.

A surprise arrival turned out to be impossible anyway, since the portals Cyra had tried to open failed. She'd tried one from Tide's End, but it was likely too far. Her portal from the ship had failed as well, though, so the island was undoubtedly blocked by warding that prevented them.

"On the beach," Surgeon called down, his tone warning.

I looked over the water to see two figures walking out onto the sand where it became more compacted by the surf. They stopped, and we all waited to see what they'd do. If either of them had powerful elemental magic, they could have the ocean try to swallow us before we reached the island, but nothing happened.

The figures, two women, didn't move as our small boat ran aground on the beach, and Surgeon and Serise landed next to us. The gargoyles each grabbed the prow of the boat and pulled it further ashore until it was fully out of the water.

I stepped out and held out a hand to help Cyra, but she ported to my side instead, and I lowered the hand.

"It's hard to play the gentleman when your wife is so self-sufficient," I teased her.

Her look was serious when she turned to me, but she must've realized it, because her face softened a moment later, and she wove her fingers into mine.

A pang of regret hit me. Cyra was different since I'd returned from my captivity. She was harder, her edges sharper. Having to accept she might now be as jaded as me was a bitter draft to swallow, but I couldn't blame her. I was ruthless with those I considered a threat, especially a threat to her. I'd wanted to preserve her innocence as long as possible, to help her hold onto her humanity, but I felt her slowly slipping away, and I didn't know how to stop it.

Killing Clarice wasn't the only reason she was different, though. Something else had happened that she wasn't telling me. I wouldn't push her. Not yet, but I had a feeling something else of critical importance had happened, either on that field or while I was gone.

Cyra and I stopped in front of the two women on the beach, who stood silently as Surgeon and Serise flanked us.

"We assume one of you is Praya of Gonderil," Cyra said.

The woman with chestnut skin and grey-streaked black hair who'd introduced herself as Miranda last time sighed.

"Yes, I'm Praya," she said, "and I'm sure you remember my wife Ariel." She gave a small smile. "Or at least, you do now."

The tall, pale-haired woman inclined her head.

"Lord Bressen of Hiraeth, if I recall," Praya went on, nodding at me. She turned to Cyra. "And Lady Cyra…Hand of the Nemesis."

Cyra sucked in a breath. "Did you know that before?" she asked.

Praya inclined her head. "I did. You're probably too young to feel it, but the longer you live, the more in tune with the Trinity you'll become, and you'll start to sense these things."

"If you knew who I was, why did you erase our memories when we came here last time?" Cyra asked.

"*How* did you erase our memories?" I asked.

Maybe it wasn't the most important question, but it had shaken me that Praya had been able to get into my mind and remove several hours from my memory without me realizing it. Not just remove the memories, but plant false ones as well.

Praya sighed again. "You might as well come up to the house so we can speak. I was expecting you back at some point."

Without waiting for us to agree, Praya turned and walked back toward the house that I now remembered from the last time we were here. Ariel hesitated a moment, as if she was unsure about turning her back on us, but then she followed Praya, and the four of us did the same.

Inside the house, Cyra and I took seats on a couch – the one we'd sat on during the previous visit – and I had the oddest sense of having done all this before, even as it still felt like I was doing it for the first time.

Praya pulled over a chair from the small table, but Ariel remained standing behind her. Meanwhile, Surgeon and Serise took up posts at either end of the room, with Serise right behind Cyra. They'd stowed their wings, but their hands rested on the hilts of their weapons.

"I see you've acquired some gargoyles since we last met," Praya said.

Cyra raised a brow at the phrasing. "Something like that," she said. "Ajax also seems willing to serve me, although we didn't bring him along."

Praya frowned. "Ajax?"

"The gargoyle you imprisoned in the necklace," Cyra said.

Careful, I warned into her mind. Her tone had been almost accusatory, and we needed Praya on our side.

Praya looked shocked. "You freed the warriors from the collar?"

"It was an accident," Cyra said, "but yes. Just as a forewarning, they aren't very happy with you."

To my surprise, Praya laughed. "No, I don't imagine they would be."

"You left them at the bottom of the ocean to die," Cyra said, and this time there was definite accusation in her tone, but also a question and a bit of pleading. She didn't want to believe Praya could be that cruel, and hope swelled in my chest that Cyra was still herself.

Praya exchanged an odd look with Ariel, and I ached to push past their mind shields to know what was behind it. There was something akin to either relief or compassion in the look. Maybe both?

"It…it was a dark moment for me," Praya said finally. "I serve the Creator, so using my powers to destroy – to kill – is to be avoided at all costs unless absolutely necessary. I was angry, though. I'd trapped those warriors in the collar, but more kept coming. We were fending off assassins sent by rulers on the continent almost weekly, and Magdalene continued to try and get to me. Ariel and I finally decided to flee, to leave our home and everything we'd ever known. When we were far enough out on the ocean, I created the storm that sank *The Stalwart*, but by then my bitterness at having to leave everything behind had eaten away at me."

Praya's gaze was far away, as if she was seeing through us to the past.

"I should've left the collar behind when we fled, but I didn't," she said. "I realized too late I couldn't bring it with us to the island. If I died before Ariel, the warriors would've been released, and Ariel would've been left alone here with three highly-skilled and angry killers. We…I decided the only thing to do was let the collar go down with the ship. I knew the fate I was consigning those warriors to, but part of me didn't care."

"What happened to the sailors on the ship?" I asked.

"They survived," Praya said. "When the storm started, I took over their minds and made them lower the lifeboats to abandon the ship. Someone had to make it back to land to carry the story that I'd died at sea, so I made sure their boats were swept far away from the ship before I sunk it. It didn't occur to me until the crew was already gone that I could've given them the collar to take back with them." She paused. "To be honest, I'm relieved you found it and brought it back up. One of my nightmares is seeing those people dying at the bottom of the ocean."

Ariel put a hand on her wife's shoulder. The bandage she'd worn on her forearm the last time was still there.

"How did you know this island was out here?" I asked. "It's not on any maps."

"It wouldn't be," Praya said, "because I didn't find it. I created it."

Cyra's eyes widened. "You created this whole island?"

Praya nodded. "It's a benefit of being the Hand of the Creator."

"And you've been here for four hundred years," I said.

"That sounds about right."

"You clearly didn't want us to remember we'd found you," I said, "but you weren't willing to kill us?"

"I couldn't kill you," Praya said. "Not without facing severe consequences. The Hands of the Gods are given powers specific to their god, and there are repercussions for straying too far from those powers or trying to use powers that aren't theirs by right. As the Hand of the Creator, my power to destroy is limited. I couldn't kill the warriors directly, but I could leave the collar at the bottom of the ocean and let fate take its course." She smiled. "Although apparently fate had other plans."

"So you can't defend yourself if attacked?" Cyra asked.

"I can," Praya said, "but if I choose to kill, it must be a last resort."

"Luckily, I can kill without consequence," Ariel added. "The mate of a Hand isn't held to the same standards."

Ariel's eyes drifted to me, and once again I had the urge to read her mind, but I held back. We still needed Praya, and I didn't dare do anything yet that might make her angry enough to refuse. I'd never dealt with a perimortal as powerful as Praya – a woman who'd been able to break into my own mind, which I hadn't thought possible.

"Your arm is still injured," Cyra said, eyeing Ariel's bandage.

"And it will be forever," Ariel said. "The cut was made with a sword Praya created, the wounds of which don't heal."

Ariel unrolled the bandage to show us the neat stitches that held the two sides of the three-inch cut together.

"We've heard of the sword," I said. I looked at Praya. "The legends claim you destroyed it when your husband cut himself and bled to death."

Praya chuckled. "I never had a husband, but it's true Ariel cut herself with the sword, and we couldn't heal the wound. Thankfully it wasn't a bad cut, so we've been able to manage it with careful cleaning and restitching every so often."

"As for the sword," Ariel said, stepping toward a closet, "I wouldn't let her destroy it."

She opened the closet and pulled out something long and thin that was wrapped in a soft leather hide. She peeled back the hide to reveal a beautiful sword in a black leather scabbard. It had a large obsidian cabochon embedded in the hilt, and the scabbard was adorned with smaller stones, as well as an intricate pattern of stamping in the leather. She pulled the blade out a few inches to reveal black marbling in the steel that I suspected was caronium, or perhaps an alloy of it.

On either side of the room, Surgeon and Serise shifted to get a better look. I couldn't see Serise from where she was behind us, but Surgeon's face held a distinct look of longing.

Rather than putting the sword away, though, Ariel finished drawing it the rest of the way and took a fighting stance.

Every muscle in my body tensed. On either side of the room, Surgeon and Serise both tensed as well, and their blades were out of their sheaths before I could wrap my head around how quickly things had taken a turn.

"Now that we've gotten all that out of the way," Praya said, "let's talk about why you returned. Did Magdalene send you? Because if she did, then you've made a grave mistake."

Chapter 32

Bressen

Serise held her sword out as she put herself in front of Cyra, and across the room, Surgeon snarled as he took a step forward.

Cyra and I were both on our feet a second later, but it was Cyra who got the denial out first.

"Stop!" Cyra said. "We're not working with Magdalene. She's part of the reason we're here, but she didn't send us."

Praya hadn't moved yet. "Only part of the reason?" she asked.

"We have a problem we think only you may be able to fix," I said quickly. "Please hear us out. We mean you no harm."

Praya nodded. "Go on."

"If you're familiar with the Triumvirate of Thasia," I said, "you know I rule one territory of the country, and I have two counterparts who rule other territories. Unfortunately, one of those counterparts, Lord Aidan of Derridan, has had his mind…uh, usurped by someone else."

Praya cocked her head. "Usurped?"

"Along with the collar, we also found your rings when we went down to *The Stalwart*," I explained. "We had a confrontation with Magdalene and some of her allies a little while ago, and – to make a long and complicated story short – Cyra accidentally transferred the mind of one of our enemies, a man named Morland, into the body of Lord Aidan. Lord Aidan's mind is still in his body, but Morland somehow suppressed it and has taken over."

Praya's eyes had gone wide, and she blinked at us. "I…I didn't know that was possible. You're sure?"

"Positive," I said. "I've been in his mind and seen it myself."

"And how do you see me helping with this?" Praya asked.

"We think Cyra may be able to pull Morland's mind out of Aidan again using the rings, but we have nowhere to put him," I said. "The collar we retrieved was destroyed, and we don't have a comparable magical object we can use. We could try transferring Morland into another body, but we'd need a live one, and all the available ones are already occupied."

"You want me to create a vessel into which you can put this man's mind," Praya concluded.

"Yes," I said. "We assumed you created the collar. You could do something like that again…although putting him into an actual body would be better."

Praya took a long look at us. "Morland is your enemy. What will you do with him once he's out of Lord Aidan?"

Cyra and I glanced at each other. This would be the tricky part.

"Ideally, we'd kill him," I admitted.

Praya was quiet a moment. "So to be clear, you want me to create a vessel – preferably a human body – so you can move this man's mind into it and kill him? You want me to create a body you can destroy."

I opened my mouth, closed it, then opened it again. "I know this sounds bad, but I can assure you, Morland isn't just an enemy. He's a stain on humanity. We've promised his death to a woman whose sister Morland brutally raped, tortured, and killed, along with several other women."

I blinked as I thought I saw a flash of green light in Praya's eyes. Something had shifted in her face, a subtle change in the set of her jaw and the slight drawing in of her brow, and I had my first glimmer of hope she might help us.

"I knew Morland twenty-five years ago during the war…uh, during a war between Rowe and Thasia," I corrected, realizing Praya wouldn't know the history. "He was a cruel bastard even back then, although we're only now learning the extent of his atrocities. A friend of ours actually killed him in the war – or thought he did – but it turns out that was the first time Morland managed to jump bodies. He was a mind wraith back then, like me, and somehow he was able to jump out of his body just before it died. He should've died then, but he escaped and hid in a mortal body until recently."

Praya's interest had perked by the time I finished speaking, and I motioned for Surgeon and Serise to stand down. They did so reluctantly, returning to their positions as Cyra and I once again took our seats. Ariel's own stance had eased somewhat.

"Morland's body was killed twenty-five years ago?" Praya asked. "Where is it now?"

I raised a brow. "His original body? I'm not sure. I think he was buried on the battlefield with the other dead. Why?"

"Because the best solution to your problem is to put him back into his original body and then kill it all over again," she said.

"I…don't understand," Cyra said. "He'd be nothing but a skeleton by now. How could we do that?"

Praya exchanged a look with Ariel, who had let her sword fall to her side finally. Ariel gave her a resigned shrug.

"If you were able to find at least one of Morland's original bones," Praya offered, "I could…regrow his body for you."

It was Cyra and I who exchanged looks this time.

"Would you do it?" Cyra asked eagerly. "Would you come back with us to regrow Morland if we could find one of his bones?"

Praya looked alarmed. "Go back? No, I can't go back. You'd have to bring the bone here."

"That would complicate things," I said, "and we were really hoping you'd also consider coming back with us to help fight Magdalene."

Praya was shaking her head before I'd finished speaking. "No, I'm sorry, I can't go back," she said.

"We can help protect-" I started to say, but her bark of laughter cut me off.

"You think I need protection?" she asked. "You think that's what I'm worried about?"

I frowned. "Then what *are* you worried about?"

Praya laughed again. "I'm worried about what will happen when Magdalene succeeds in getting the three of us together." She gestured to herself and Cyra. "Do you have any idea what she wants to do?"

"She plans to syphon our god-specific gifts and use them to kill mortals, then take over the continent," Cyra answered.

Praya blinked at her in surprise. "She told you that?"

Cyra nodded. "Something to that effect. Can she do it?"

Praya sighed. "I'm not sure, but I don't plan to find out."

"What about normal powers?" I asked. "Can syphons take powers from each other?"

"No," Praya said. "For syphons, their base power is the ability to syphon. They can't take that from each other because they already have it. All their other powers are secondary, and they can't syphon those from each other. They also can't syphon powers from the mates of other syphons." She looked at me. "While I can and have syphoned mind abilities from another mind wraith, I can't syphon them from you, Lord Bressen. I'll therefore never have your level of abilities, although, for that matter, no other mind wraith ever will." She turned back to Cyra. "Likewise, you can't syphon Ariel's ability."

Cyra and I both turned to Ariel expectantly, but she didn't offer an answer to our unspoken question of what her power was.

My mind reeled as I let the rest of what Praya had said sink in, and one thing caught in my head.

"Why don't you think any other mind wraith will ever have my level of power?" I asked. Of all the things she'd said, I wasn't sure why I'd fixated on that, but it struck me as important for some reason.

"Checks and balances," Praya said. "For every powerful force in nature, there needs to be something that can hold it in check. Being of Thasia's Triumvirate, you should understand that better than most. That government structure is built on the idea of the balance of power."

I frowned. "I'm not sure I know what you mean," I said. "How does that apply to me?"

"Cyra is one of the most powerful beings in the world, but there must always be something – or someone – to check her power," Praya said. "As her mate, part of that job falls to you. You're powerful because she is, and you're as strong as you are because you need to be. The mates of syphons are powerful in their own right because they're the counterbalance to their mates. Just as you balance Cyra, Ariel balances me."

I blinked at her as my entire existence up until now seemed to flash before my eyes. I'd never even thought to consider why I – of all people – had been given gifts that made me one of the most dangerously powerful people in the world. A lesser man might have balked at the idea he'd been granted such immense power, not because he was special himself, but because he was the mate of an even more powerful being. Perhaps I had a flicker of self-doubt, but it vanished quickly enough.

In some ways it was almost comforting to know my power had a very specific purpose, and so much made more sense now. As much as Cyra and I practiced her mind powers, she'd never been able to fully keep me out of her head, and she'd never been able to break into my own mind when my shield was at full strength. No one had ever been able to keep me out of their mind if I really wanted to get in, but part of me always believed Cyra would be able to match my mind powers eventually.

If what Praya said was true, though, it seemed as though Cyra wasn't meant to. I always needed to be a little stronger than her in this one thing, just in case.

A voice in the back of my head reminded me we'd already had just such a scenario a few months ago. I'd had to break into Cyra's mind to stop her from killing those men in Fernweh.

"What else can you tell us about syphon powers?" I asked. "We know very little about them back on the continent. You were the last known syphon to exist, although it now appears Magdalene has been hiding in plain sight for centuries."

"As was the woman I replaced," Cyra added. "I saw her in a dream the other night. In Magdalene's dream."

I stared at Cyra. She hadn't told me she'd dream walked again, let alone into Magdalene's dream. For that matter, I'd also forgotten that for her to be a syphon, she'd had to replace one who died.

Praya smiled sadly. "Your predecessor's name was Crissail, and she was my mentor." She sighed heavily. "I suspected she died. I thought I felt her death a couple decades ago, but I didn't know for sure until you landed on our island, and I sensed who you were."

I felt Cyra's stab of grief and sympathy for Praya.

"I'm sorry," Cyra told her. "I didn't realize."

Praya waved a hand. "I made my peace with never seeing Crissail again when Ariel and I fled. She was almost eight hundred, so it was likely just her time. I trust the Nemesis is rewarding her justly for her service."

Cyra's mouth worked for a moment before she finally spoke. "Actually…I saw Crissail's death in the dream," she said quietly. "She killed herself to escape Magdalene. Magdalene said that Crissail knew the only way to escape her was to pass the power of the Nemesis on to someone else. She died to pass it on to me."

Both Praya and I stared at Cyra.

"Magdalene was there when Crissail died?" Praya asked softly.

Cyra nodded. "Crissail put a hand on her own chest and used what I assumed was her Nemesis power to…" She trailed off before adding reluctantly, "She burst into flames and then turned to ash."

There was a protracted silence before Praya spoke again. "Thank you for letting me know," she said, but her voice was strained.

"I feel like I should've let you believe she died peacefully as you assumed," Cyra said apologetically.

Praya shook her head. "No, I'm glad you told me of Magdalene's involvement."

"Magdalene said she's been experiencing side effects with her powers," Cyra said. "It's why she wants to syphon ours. Do you know what she meant by side effects?"

Praya shook her head again. "I'm not sure."

"I'm worried I might be experiencing side effects as well," Cyra said.

"How so?" Praya asked.

"I syphoned physical strength from Lord Aidan's Captain of the Guard at one point, but I only had it briefly. I can't seem to access that power anymore. Is there a reason I lost it?" Cyra asked.

"I can't say for sure," Praya said, "but that's not necessarily a side effect of anything. There are a number of factors that go into which powers we can acquire, which ones we use well, and which ones we may lose over time. For instance, you'll obviously wield the power your mate has very well, and you'll never lose that. Likewise, there are powers that are more closely aligned with each of the gods, and you'll find it easier to syphon and keep powers associated with the Nemesis. Strength is a power usually associated with the Protector, so that may be one of the reasons you found it hard to hold onto."

Cyra and I exchanged glances, and I knew we were both thinking the same thing. Some of the powers Cyra wielded the best and most often were ones she'd gotten from Samhail, who – as a gargoyle – was a servant of the Protector.

The look didn't go unnoticed by Praya.

"You wield a power you think must be associated with one of the other gods," Praya guessed.

"One of the first abilities Cyra syphoned, and one she uses well, is from a friend of ours," I said. "Another gargoyle. Based on what you said, that seems like a power she shouldn't wield well."

Praya waggled her head to indicate that wasn't exactly the case.

"You say this gargoyle is a friend," she observed. "Sometimes a syphon's ability to take and keep a power depends on how close they are personally to a source and how much they want to have that power." Praya paused and turned to Cyra. "Are you close to this gargoyle?"

I sensed rather than saw Surgeon and Serise shift where they stood.

Cyra leaned back in her chair and nodded. "Yes. This all makes sense. Samhail is a very good friend, and I rather like that particular power. On the other hand, I'm not close to the woman from whom I got the strength, and I was a bit worried about having her power, to be honest. I was afraid I might spend a few weeks breaking things before I got used to having her strength. It was actually a relief when I realized I no longer had it."

Praya nodded in understanding. "Yes, that might explain why you no longer have the strength, but you do still have the power from this other gargoyle." She paused. "Is there anything else?"

I exchanged a look with Cyra, and she gave me a nod.

"Agree to come back with us," I said to Praya. "We understand why you fled, but Magdalene has become a threat you can no longer ignore. We need your help. Please."

Chapter 33

Bressen

Praya shook her head again. "I'm sorry. I can't. If Magdalene ever managed to get us together and draw the powers of the Creator and Nemesis out of us, it could be catastrophic. She could kill millions."

"She already has the power to kill millions," Cyra said, standing.

I sensed her frustration with Praya.

"She's somehow created creatures, parasites, that bond with humans and take over their bodies," Cyra said. "I'm not sure how many she has already, but I've seen a vision where she has thousands of them, enough for an entire army."

"What?" It was Ariel who spoke this time as she pushed off the wall where she'd been leaning.

"That's impossible," Praya said. "Magdalene doesn't have the power of the Creator. She couldn't…"

"She can and has," I said, rising as well. "Let me show you."

Reluctance crossed Praya's face.

"Please," I said. "Let me show you what we've been dealing with."

"Show me," Ariel said, stepping forward. She sheathed her sword finally and set it aside.

"Ariel," Praya warned.

"Let him show me," she said to Praya, "and if it's worth seeing, I'll show you."

It was a few seconds before Praya finally nodded.

I felt Ariel lower her mind shield, and I sent the images of the symbionts into her head. I showed her the scene at the gambling den when we'd first fought the creatures, and I let her feel what I'd felt when I'd been wounded, and the thing had tried to crawl its way into me. I showed her our confrontation with Magdalene and Sandrian at the temple and the vision Cyra had stolen from Magdalene of the army of symbionts stretched out across the land.

If possible, Ariel looked even paler than normal when I finished.

"That's all true?" she asked. "Everything you showed me is real?"

"Yes," I said. "Everything but the vision, which has yet to pass."

Ariel turned to Praya. "You need to see this."

There was a long pause as Praya presumably read her wife's mind to see everything I'd just shown her.

Praya closed her eyes and shook her head. "That shouldn't be possible. How could she have created those things?"

"Praya," Ariel said seriously, "I think we should-"

Praya held up a hand, and Ariel immediately fell silent. Praya rose and went to stand in front of her wife. There was a long silence as the two presumably had a mental conversation about what to do.

I didn't try to read their minds, but I could see clearly enough how the conversation was going in their faces. Praya's face showed signs of fear, and there was a look of pleading in her eyes. Ariel's face was resolute, only breaking now and then into a frown at something Praya must've said. I saw the moment Ariel won their argument, because Praya's lips pursed in resignation, and she gave a short, unhappy nod.

Praya turned back to us, and her attention jumped from me to Cyra before she heaved a deep sigh. "Ariel and I will return to the continent with you. I'd hoped that putting myself out of Magdalene's reach might dampen her ambition, but it seems she's found a way around that, and we can no longer in good conscience remain in hiding."

The tension in my shoulders released. Even though I'd seen the outcome in their faces, I hadn't let myself believe it until just now. I was surprised at how relieved I was they'd agreed to come back.

"Thank you," I said. "We understand the sacrifice we're asking you to make." I paused, not sure I should say the next part, but I decided to err on the side of honesty nevertheless. "I should remind you that the three warriors you imprisoned are now free and looking for retribution, but we'll do everything in our power to keep your return a secret from them and to protect you from any harm if they do learn you've returned."

Praya's face faltered, and I guessed she'd forgotten about the warriors, but she nodded.

"We appreciate your forthrightness as well as your assurances of our safety," she said. "With any luck, we can deal with Magdalene and return here before the warriors are any wiser. Just give us a few hours to pack some things and prepare the house to be vacant for a while."

I nodded. "Let us know what we can do to help."

"Can we portal back to the continent from here?" Cyra asked.

Praya shook her head. "It's too far. We'll have to get closer to land before we can portal anywhere."

"There's a stop we should make before we head back to Tide's End," I said. "We need to go to the battlefield on the border of Derridan and Rowe to see if anything of Morland's body is still there." I turned to Praya. "You'll help us get Morland out of Aidan as well?"

She nodded. "Regardless of his crimes, the man should've died years ago. The Nemesis doesn't take kindly to being denied the souls it's due."

Cyra and I exchanged a relieved look.

"I'll start packing," Ariel said as she turned toward where I assumed the bedroom was.

"I'll help you," Cyra said.

I started to offer my assistance as well, but I was cut short when Praya laid a hand on my arm.

"Lord Bressen, might I have a quick word with you alone?" she said as Cyra and the gargoyles followed Ariel into the back of the house to help pack. She cocked her head toward the front door, indicating I should follow her outside, so I did.

"What can I do for you?" I asked when we were alone.

"You can promise to be vigilant," she said seriously.

I cocked a brow. "I'm always vigilant."

"Not where Cyra is concerned. That's how I was able to wipe your memory. Given how powerful you are, I shouldn't have been able to get into your mind, but Cyra's mind magic is less powerful and less practiced than yours, so I slipped into her mind first. From there, I got into your mind through your connection with her because you were both too distracted by me kissing her."

My mouth slowly dropped open as she spoke. It hadn't even occurred to me it was possible for someone to get into my mind through Cyra, but I supposed the situation with Morland had opened up a whole new realm of possibilities regarding mind magic that I'd never considered before.

"She's your weak spot," Praya went on, "but you can't let her be. I told you the mates of syphons are made to be their counterbalance, and that comes with responsibility. Yours is heavier than most because the Hand of the Nemesis has always been the most dangerous of the three syphons. There are ultimately consequences if any of us abuse our powers, but for Cyra, those consequences can be far more destructive and deadly."

I was careful to keep my face as neutral as possible. One could argue Cyra had already abused her powers twice now, once with deadly consequences. In truth, she didn't do anything I myself hadn't done in the past and much worse than her, but that only emphasized the truth of Praya's words even more. If it was my responsibility to keep Cyra in check, maybe it was her responsibility to do that for me now as well.

Praya angled her head to eye me. "Something you'd liked to share, Lord Bressen?"

Whether she'd read something in my face or in my mind, I wasn't sure, but I gave her the barest hint of a smile.

"No," I said. "Not at this time. Do you still have a channel into my mind?" Even as I asked, I let my powers search for possible incursions.

"No," she said with an apologetic smile. "I was lucky to do it the first time. I wouldn't dare try again."

"While I have you," I said, "maybe you can answer a couple more questions about syphons and their mates."

"I will if I can," Praya said.

Her eyes widened and she started to object as I pulled the front of my shirt out of my pants, but then she realized what I wanted to show her.

"Ah, the mark," she said, looking at the crescent moon around my navel. "I suppose that showed up after you consummated your union?"

I smiled. "Sometime around then."

Praya untucked her own shirt and showed me a ring of pale skin around her navel, not solid like the sphere Aidan had shown Cyra, but just the outline of a circle.

"You and Ariel have them as well," I said, surprised.

"All syphons and their mates have them," she said.

I frowned and shook my head. "That can't be right. Lord Aidan and his husband have these marks as well, or similar ones in any case. Theirs are a solid circle."

It was Praya's turn to frown. "What? That's not possible. I was told only syphons have these marks. Are you sure neither Lord Aidan nor his husband are syphons?"

"I'm fairly certain Aidan isn't. His power is transfiguration. As for Aidan's husband, Jasper is mortal."

Praya's brows shot up. "The Soul of the Sun mark appeared on a mortal? Are you sure?"

I paused. "Well, I haven't seen Jasper's mark myself, but Aidan says it's there. I've only seen Aidan's mark firsthand."

Praya bit her lip as she considered this.

"You don't know what it means?" I asked, and she shook her head.

"There's something else I don't understand about the marks," I said. "I'm almost a hundred and eighteen years old, and Cyra will only turn twenty-three soon, but according to the legend one of our priests told Cyra, the Souls of the Sun, Moon, and Earth were once singular beings that were split in two. How is that possible?"

Praya smiled. "Remember that myths and legends are really just fanciful ways to explain things we don't understand," she said. "They're largely metaphorical and shouldn't necessarily be taken at face value."

I nodded. "Fair enough. But even so, is it normal for syphons and their mates to be born so far apart?"

Praya shrugged. "Ariel is nearly seventy years younger than me," she said. "Mates are meant to find each other when they're ready to be together. Can you honestly say you would've been the man Cyra needed you to be for her if you'd both met at twenty-two?"

I balked at the thought. Gods no. I'd been an arrogant idiot sowing his wild oats at that age. Chances are I would've fucked Cyra and moved on to my next conquest. Part of me hoped I would've known better, but I remembered all too well what I'd been like at that age.

"So if Cyra couldn't become a syphon until Crissail died, and I was meant for Cyra, doesn't that mean…" My mind reeled as I tried to wrap my head around the implications.

"That the gods always planned for things to work out just as they did?" Praya finished for me. "It seems that way."

Then something else hit me.

"Does Magdalene have a mate?" I asked. "If she's a syphon, wouldn't she also be either a Soul of the Moon or Earth?"

Praya's expression went grim.

"Magdalene had a mate, but she killed him," she said. "He tried to check her power when she got ambitious and began to get out of hand, as was his responsibility, and she killed him for his efforts."

"Gods above," I said quietly.

"Remember what I said about your responsibility, Lord Bressen," Praya said as she looked at me seriously. "The other two syphons are also supposed to help check each other's powers, but Magdalene has already gone rogue, and there's not much I can do on my own against a Hand of the Nemesis. You're the only real protection the world has against Cyra if she…if things go wrong with her."

I paused, choosing my words carefully. "Cyra has had a lot thrown at her in a very short time. I think she'll be the first to admit she hasn't always handled things well in some cases, but she isn't an evil person. I trust her to make the right decisions when things are on the line."

Praya gave me a small smile. "I'm sure you're right and my concerns are unfounded," she said.

She's lying. Whatever Praya just said to you was a lie. Cyra's voice sounded in my head suddenly, and I looked over Praya's shoulder to see her standing in the doorway watching us.

What did she say? Cyra asked.

I'll explain everything tonight when we're alone, I replied into her mind. *I've learned a number of other things you should know.*

Praya caught where my attention had gone and looked behind her.

"Ah, come to reclaim your husband I see," she said to Cyra with a smile. "I suppose I've monopolized him enough for now. I should go help Ariel pack anyway."

Praya turned and went back into the house. Cyra moved out of the way to let her pass and came straight to me.

"What did she lie about?" she asked again, and I sighed. She wasn't going to let it go until I told her.

"Praya has some concerns about you and your powers," I said. "There's a lot we need to discuss, though, and I don't want to do it here. We'll talk tonight."

"Do you share her concerns?" she asked, and I closed my eyes. I didn't want to answer that just yet, but I also couldn't lie.

"I…have *some* concerns we can discuss tonight," I said looking down at her again, "but mine aren't the same as Praya's."

I felt her twinge of hurt.

"I told Praya that you've been going through a lot lately, but that I trust you to make good decisions," I assured her, and her expression eased. "My concern is more for your well-being." I paused. "There's something you're not telling me, and I need to know what it is."

Cyra pursed her lips. "You're right. We should talk tonight," she said.

I wasn't sure whether to be amused or concerned that she suddenly wasn't quite so eager to speak now that I'd called out her own secret keeping. I lifted a hand to brush my thumb over her lips, and she kissed the pad of it. Before I knew it, my mouth was on hers, kissing her hungrily.

I pulled back before my cock hardened too much. This wasn't exactly the time or place to fuck my wife, but apparently Cyra disagreed.

"Let's go into the trees," she said softly. "There must be some place we can go for a few minutes before we're missed."

That's all it took to bring my cock the rest of the way, and I had to adjust my pants to ease the strain against my groin.

"Fuck," I muttered. "You're a gods damned temptress."

"And you're so easily led into temptation," she countered, smiling.

I let my wings unfurl from my back as I grinned and pulled her against me. "Who needs to be led? I find it just fine on my own."

Chapter 34

Bressen

It was almost dark when we returned to the ship, this time with Praya and Ariel accompanying us. We'd taken the rowboat to get to the island because the wards didn't allow us to portal, but there was no need to take the boat all the way back. Praya dropped the wards long enough for Cyra to create a portal from the beach onto the ship, and we dragged the boat back through after we were all on board.

We settled Praya and Ariel in a cabin after they'd taken a long last look at the island that had been their home for the last four hundred years, and then I went to check in with the captain.

Cyra veered off toward the prow of the ship, and I kept half an eye on her while I spoke with the captain about how long it would be until we were home. With Cyra's ability to control the wind and water currents, we'd been able to get out to the island far faster than an unassisted vessel would've been able to, but the journey had still taken several days.

When I was finally finished with the captain, I headed toward the prow. I stopped several feet behind Cyra and just watched her for a moment. What I felt for her always made it harder to breathe, and I just watched her now, transfixed by the way the wind blew her hair out behind her as she stood up straight at the railing looking out over the ocean.

She'd been quiet since she'd found me talking with Praya, but whatever she wasn't telling me, I'd get it out of her tonight.

I let my mind slip into hers, careful not to disturb her thoughts. She stared into the dark water as the ship cut lithely through it, and I frowned at the seriousness of her mood. She was recalling the last time we were here when she'd been down under those waves with Axenus, far below the surface in the icy, inky depths of the water. I felt the chill and the nearly crushing weight of the water as her power left her while she fought the kraken. I felt her ready herself to succumb to the oblivion of death.

No, not succumb. Embrace...

I surged forward and grabbed her around the waist to pull her away from the railing. She shrieked in surprise as I spun her around, but her body eased as she realized it was me.

Her hands wrapped around my biceps to steady herself. "Bressen, what are-"

"Cyra, what in the three hells are you doing?" I interrupted her. My heart thundered in my chest as I realized she'd been considering what it might be like to jump into that black water and...

She couldn't be thinking what I was afraid she'd been thinking. Axenus had taken her down into the water again recently, so perhaps she'd just started to enjoy the feeling of being down there, of the calmness beneath the churning ocean. I held desperately to the thought.

"Answer me," I said, shaking her. "What were you thinking of doing just now?"

The look of guilt on her face told me everything I needed to know, and I crushed her to me.

"Don't you dare," I whispered, wrapping my arms tightly around her. "Don't you fucking dare."

"I...I wasn't going to," she said, so softly I could barely hear her.

I pulled back to look down at her. Tears glistened in her eyes.

"We need to talk. Now," I said. "It's time for you to tell me what happened, what you've been hiding."

I'd pry her mind open if necessary. I didn't tell her that because threats wouldn't help right now, but I'd do it.

I took Cyra's hand and pulled her toward our cabin. She didn't resist, and I tried not to drag her across the deck in my eagerness to get her below, away from the pull of that water, away from danger.

I locked the door when we were alone in our cabin and turned to her. She stood in the middle of the room, arms wrapped around her shoulders.

Gods, I was an idiot. She was cold. She'd been standing at the prow of the ship without a cloak on. She hadn't worn one onto the island, but it had gotten colder out with the sun down.

I went to the chest at the foot of the bed and pulled a blanket out. I wrapped it around her shoulders and settled her on the bed before I sat down next to her.

"Cyra, what's going on?" I asked. "You haven't been the same since I got back. What happened while I was gone? You need to tell me."

Her mouth worked as if she were trying to force the words up her throat, but they wouldn't come.

"What happened in that battle, Cyra?" I tried again. "You found Magdalene, didn't you. What did she say to you?"

Whatever it was, it had to do with Magdalene. I knew that much. We'd been separated during the battle, and we'd heard Cyra scream, but no one had seen what happened to her.

Samhail told me Cyra had incinerated the area after Talyn had taken me, and yes, Cyra would've been angry, worried about me, but her reaction still seemed far too extreme. The last time Cyra had been that destructive, she'd been in pain.

I reached across and took her hand in mine. "Cyra, please."

Her eyes were wet with tears again when she looked up at me.

"I killed Aramis," she said, barely above a whisper.

I let out a deep breath. "Cyra, you can't blame yourself for Aramis's death. Magdalene-"

"Magdalene didn't kill him," she cut in. "I did. My lightning killed him. That's what Magdalene told me."

I couldn't speak for a moment as I just stared at her. Then I shook my head. "No, she's lying. We saw the frost-"

"She wasn't lying," Cyra said. Her voice cracked as the sobs started to break through. "Trust me, I looked for any hint of a red glow on her skin, any flush of color whatsoever. She wasn't lying. She told me she iced over his body after he was…already dead because she knew I'd come looking for her. It was her way to get me to come to her."

She was nearly choking on her tears by the time she finished, and I pulled her onto my lap to cradle her against me. She buried her face in my chest, and her hands fisted in my shirt as she sobbed uncontrollably. I rocked her gently as she repeated, "I killed him. I killed him," over and over again.

My heart cracked open at her pain, and I felt every stab of guilt and grief she did. It was a familiar pain given that I still blamed myself for my own father's death, for not telling him sooner what my mother had been doing behind his back. I'd figured it would hurt him more to know the truth, but in the end, my silence had killed him.

I pulled Cyra tighter and laid my head on hers.

"It was an accident," I said. "You couldn't have known."

Cyra lifted her head from my chest. "Couldn't have known what?" she said. "Couldn't have known that when I sent an entire storm's worth of lightning through an enclosed space I might hurt someone? Might kill someone?"

She launched herself off my lap. I grabbed for her, but she pulled away. I stood as well, but she stepped back from me.

"Do you know what else Magdalene told me?" she asked. Her voice still shook, but it had grown harder.

"Cyra," I said placatingly.

"Do you remember that army of symbionts?" she said. "She told me that was only one part of the vision. She let me see that part, but there was more. She left out the part of the vision where I kill them all."

She spat the last part out as if she had something bitter in her mouth.

"She let me see the rest of it that day in the clearing," she said. "She showed me that I kill them all."

I shook my head. "You're not a killer. Not the kind of killer who would murder thousands for no reason," I corrected when she opened her mouth to remind me she had in fact killed before.

"Maybe there's a reason," she said. "Maybe it's the only way to stop the army." She shook her head. "Or maybe I finally snap at some point and become more of a monster than those creatures ever were."

I closed the distance between us in two strides and grabbed her upper arms. She winced at the force of my hold, but I couldn't loosen my grip.

"Listen to me," I told her. "You're not a monster, and you never will be. We've learned by now that these visions never work out the way we expect them to. There has to be some kind of catch, something that explains what you saw."

"Or maybe this time, what we see is what we get," she said quietly.

"I refuse to believe that."

"She's counting on me to kill them," Cyra went on. "It's part of Magdalene's plan to wipe out as many mortals as she can, and she wants to use me to do it."

I let go of her and raked a hand through my hair. There had to be more to Magdalene's vision than what she'd shown Cyra, or there was some trick to the vision we weren't yet seeing, but I'd be damned if I could figure out what it was.

"At the railing, when I was looking down into the ocean," she said, staring at the floor as if she was again seeing that black water, "I just thought…maybe if I wasn't here, she couldn't use me. Maybe…"

It would have hurt less if she'd stabbed me in the heart. I pulled her against me again, crushing her body to mine so hard I heard her breath punch out of her.

"Don't you ever think anything of the kind," I said, and this time I let her hear the threat in my voice. "Don't you ever fucking think this world would be better off without you."

"Bressen, I-"

I moved my hands up so I gripped her face between them, and I forced her to look at me.

"Don't you dare fucking leave me like that," I said, and now my own voice broke. "Not after I just found you. Not after I waited over a hundred years to finally feel whole. Don't leave me alone in this world again, because I won't survive. Please."

I barely managed to get the last word out before my voice failed. Tears poured down my own cheeks as I laid my forehead against hers and tried not to consider what a world without Cyra would be like. The third level of hell would be nothing compared to such a place.

"Please," I said again, forcing the word up my throat and past my lips on a whisper of air.

She shook her forehead against mine. "I won't. I promise."

Cyra

Bressen's relief came out in a stuttering exhale as he held my head against his, and his maelstrom of emotions overwhelmed me.

I hadn't seriously considered jumping into the ocean earlier. Or I didn't think I had. It had simply occurred to me that Magdalene's vision couldn't come true if I wasn't here. In that moment, I understood why Praya and Ariel had fled, and part of me now regretted convincing them to come back with us. Maybe it was a mistake for them to return to the continent, to put both me and Praya where Magdalene could get to us.

Axenus had taken me down far under the ocean up at Revenmyer to keep me from hurting or killing anyone else. It hadn't been a bad plan. When I'd thought earlier about that vast blanket of water over me, I hadn't been thinking of my death so much as…my entombment?

"I wasn't thinking of killing myself," I said, and I was at least fairly certain that was true. "Praya sequestered herself on an island to keep Magdalene from being able to use her. I was just thinking maybe the safest place to keep me is deep under the ocean where I can't hurt anyone."

He pulled back to frown at me. "So you plan to live underwater?"

I sighed. "It wasn't really a serious plan. I just…I was just wondering what it would be like, to never see the surface again. To never…"

I shuddered, and Bressen pulled me into his arms again. I rested my head against his chest and inhaled his musk and hot cinnamon scent. The smell of him wound its way into my brain, and my body relaxed of its own accord. There was nowhere in the world I'd rather be at any given time than in Bressen's arms, feeling his body against mine, letting his warmth soothe away every hurt and fear.

"I need you to listen to me, Cyra," he said quietly. "Do you remember how I told you Praya had some concerns about your power?"

I huffed a laugh. "That's what started this conversation, wasn't it?"

Bressen pressed me gently away from him so he could look into my eyes. He took my chin between his thumb and forefinger.

"I'm going to give you the cold, hard truth right now," he said, "but I want you to hear me out. I want you to hear everything I say."

I nodded.

"It's true that you have the potential to be dangerous," he said, and a knot twisted in my stomach.

"Listen to me," Bressen said, tightening his hold on my chin, and I nodded again.

"Praya told me that all the Hands of the Gods have the potential to be dangerous, but your affiliation with the Nemesis makes you more dangerous than most. You know that. You have the power of death."

I bit my lip. I wasn't sure where he was going with this. I needed to hear the "but."

"But Praya reminded me that it's my responsibility to balance you. If you snap, it's my job to tie you back together. If you stray, it's my job to bring you home. If you lose yourself, it's my job to find you."

I looked at him. I knew what he wasn't saying, so I said it for him.

"If I go too far and can't be brought back, it's your job to end me."

His face hardened. "No," he said. The word was forceful. Final. "It's true that's what Praya hinted I'd need to do, but I know you, and I know it'll never go that far with you."

"You can't know–"

"I can," he interrupted. "Would you ever kill me?"

I blinked at the pivot in topic. "What? No. Of course not."

"Magdalene had a husband," he said. "Praya said she killed him."

My mouth fell open. "What?"

"According to Praya, he tried to stop Magdalene when her ambition grew dangerous, and she killed him for it."

I furrowed my brow, trying to understand his point. "And you think because I won't kill you…?" I left the question open for him to fill in.

"If you can't kill me, you can't ever get to the point where I would need to 'end you,'" he insisted.

I shook my head. "None of this makes sense. Why would the mates of Hands be the ones responsible for keeping them in check? Doesn't it seem more likely that the mates would, or should, support the Hands? We've merged our powers before. If I'm dangerous on my own, how dangerous are you and I together? Who keeps the two of us in check?"

Even as I spoke the words, something my father said to me at my wedding drifted back to me. I'd balked when Aramis had talked about how much power I had over Bressen, how I kept him in line.

Aramis had said, *There are very few people or powers in this world that can keep a man like Lord Bressen in check, but it's good to have at least one thing that makes him pause, and you're that one thing for him. Don't regret that. Embrace it.*

Was Bressen the one thing, the one person, who could make me pause? Yes, mates supported each other, but perhaps they also tempered each other as well. Bressen would fight for me and protect me from outside dangers with his dying breath, but when I'd tried to go too far in Fernweh, he'd done what needed to be done to stop me.

I remembered the day in Gendris, the day of the coup. I'd seen Bressen with all his angelus power as he'd called the demoni to swarm Glenora. I hadn't been fully aware of it at the time, but I'd felt his anger, felt how untethered he was, and I'd been determined to bring him back. I remembered thinking the darkness was trying to take him but that I wouldn't let it have him.

"We keep each other in check," Bressen said, voicing the conclusion I'd already come to.

Maybe it wasn't a perfect solution, but it had worked so far, and I found the idea unexpectedly comforting.

"I needed you," I said softly. "I needed you after Magdalene told me all those horrible things, but Talyn took you away, and then I was terrified of what might happen to you." I started to speak faster. "I thought I'd feel it if they killed you, but I didn't know for sure and-"

He pulled me against him again, and I cut off my panicked rambling.

"I know," he said. "I'm sorry I wasn't there for you."

"I'm sorry I couldn't find you sooner," I whispered. "I tried. I tried so hard to sense where you were, to use my powers to find you, but nothing worked."

I started to cry again, and he stroked my hair gently.

"It's not your fault," he said. "Your powers do have limits, but the gods were with us, and we were able to get out relatively unharmed. As a bonus, we got Aidan back as well. Or at least his body."

I lifted my head again to look at him.

"You're not angry at Talyn for what she did, are you," I said. A statement, not a question.

He sighed. "I'll admit there were several hours after she took me that I happily would've killed her as painfully as possible, but…I suppose I understand why she did what she did. And ultimately, she kept her promise to get me out of there safely. Let's just say I no longer put her in the same category as Sandrian and Magdalene."

I looked into his eyes, those beautiful turquoise pools that always made my knees weak, and I saw the rest of what he didn't say.

"You're considering asking her to work with us," I said.

He paused. "I already suggested it actually. Before the battle. She wasn't inclined to accept at the time, but I haven't taken the offer off the table. Would it bother you if she did work with us?"

I considered this. My feelings about Talyn were…complicated at best, but as long as she could be trusted, I could live with having her around.

"Samhail seems to like her," I said, evading the question.

He chuckled. "Samhail more than likes her, although I doubt he's ready to admit how much, especially now. Does that bother you?"

I honestly didn't know. Samhail and I would never be lovers again, and I'd accepted that. To see him with another woman so soon, though, particularly one we had such a fraught relationship with, was unsettling, to say the least. But I wasn't sure it bothered me per se.

"No," I said, then corrected myself at Bressen's dubious look. "I don't think so anyway."

He kissed me on the forehead. "It's fine if it does. I don't expect you to get over your feelings for Samhail so soon, if ever."

"I love you," I told him.

"I know you do, and I love you too," he said, "but that doesn't mean you can't feel something for him as well. Human emotions can be complicated fucking things."

I smiled. "I need to go to bed. It's been a long day."

He kissed my forehead again and released me so I could change into my nightgown.

Minutes later, we were in bed with his large, strong body curled protectively around mine. His arm wrapped around my waist to pull me close, and I savored the feel of his warm breath as it ghosted over my ear. We were both too tired to do anything more, but we'd make up for it in the morning. For now, being together like this was enough.

Here in Bressen's arms, nothing could hurt me.

And I couldn't hurt anyone else.

Chapter 35

Cyra

The verdant meadow Bressen, Praya, Ariel, and I stepped out of the portal onto days later was a far cry from the killing field it had been a quarter of a century ago. The only battle raging now was between the new grass that fought for space with early spring flowers like snowdrops, crocuses, and maidenfairs. The place even smelled like new life, fresh and clean, despite the death and decay that lay not far beneath the surface.

I closed the portal behind me. The ship was still a couple days out from the mainland, but we were close enough now for me to get us to this battlefield where Morland's bones supposedly rested.

At the thought of what lay buried here, the hint of something dark tingled over my skin. I looked around, trying to figure out why every nerve suddenly seemed to be alert and why every hair on my body stood on end.

Praya caught my eye as I surveyed the area. "You feel it, don't you."

"I feel something," I said. "What is it?"

"Death," she said. "You're becoming more attuned with the Nemesis. You can feel what happened here."

I knew instantly she was right. I definitely felt some kind of force, something that – ironically – seemed to pulse over the land like a heartbeat. I let a few tendrils of my power reach toward it, and I jumped when something like a static electric shock hit me.

I opened my mouth to say something about it, but I let out a yelp and stepped back instead as I saw a man only feet away, watching me.

He was young, likely in his late teens and certainly no older than me. His dark brown hair was longer on top and seemed to blow in a breeze I couldn't feel. His clothing looked like a uniform, but his face was passive, and he stood still and silent between the four of us.

"Who are you?" I asked. I raised my hands, ready to send him blasting backward with a forcefield, but he didn't move.

"Cyra?" Bressen asked, brows pinched. "Who are you talking to?"

I turned to him but stumbled back a few steps more when I saw two other men standing next to him, one short with light brown skin, and another tall and lanky with pale skin and shockingly red hair. I spun around, and panic sent a lump up my throat. We were suddenly surrounded by dozens of young men, all standing quietly.

"Where did they come from?" I asked as I spun in a circle. We were surrounded.

Praya looked around as well. Next to her, Ariel had drawn her sword, the one with the black marbling in the blade, but she didn't swing it, even though there was a man standing right in front of her. Indeed, she seemed to look right through him. I raised my hands, ready to fight if the men proved to be a threat.

I cried out as a hand closed over my arm and turned me around, but it was only Bressen. He gripped my shoulders tightly.

"Cyra, what's wrong? What do you see?" he asked urgently.

I looked at him incredulously. "Don't you see them all?" I asked, trying to watch for movement, for an attack. "They're-"

I looked around, intending to point out the men, but my words cut off as I saw the field was suddenly empty again, save for us. I whipped my head around, but there was nothing.

"Cyra?" Bressen prompted.

"There were…I saw men. Dozens of them standing around us," I said. "I don't understand. They're gone now."

"You likely have spirit anchor power," Praya said knowingly. "You'd be more susceptible to it as Hand of the Nemesis, but it's not innate. You would've had to pick it up somewhere."

"Spirit anchor power?" Bressen questioned. "I've never heard of it."

Praya smiled. "You probably have, Lord Bressen, but you dismissed it. People who claim they can see and communicate with the dead are often dismissed as frauds. Granted some of them are, but spirit anchors are real perimortals who can see and communicate with the dead when they're in close proximity to the person's body or an object that was important to them. If there really are hundreds of bodies buried here, Cyra probably anchored some of their spirits unwittingly."

"Why are spirit anchors dismissed as frauds?" I asked, although I thought I knew. We occasionally had traveling mystics come through Fernweh who claimed they could commune with the dead, but many people decried them as charlatans.

"It's not a visible power," Praya said. "Only the anchor can see and hear the spirits, so no one can confirm they're actually doing anything, and many people aren't willing to believe something exists unless they can see and hear it themselves." She shrugged. "Then of course, some people who don't actually have the power use this to their advantage if they're clever enough."

I tried to remember the times mystics came through town. I usually stayed away from them, but if one of them was actually a spirit anchor, perhaps I'd touched them inadvertently. It was the most logical reason for why I had the power. Or perhaps I'd picked it up at the Priory one of the times I'd been there. Surely one of the priests or priestesses had it. It must be new since this was the first time I'd seen-

My eyes widened as a memory burst into my head, the vivid image of seeing my mother the night after she'd died. I'd been at the kitchen window, and I'd found one of her bracelets sitting on the counter. My mother didn't wear much jewelry, but this piece had been an anniversary gift from my father. She often took it off to clean or cook so it didn't get dirty or damaged, and she must've forgotten to put it back on the last time she took it off.

The bracelet had sent a wave of grief through me, and I'd looked up to see my mother outside the window standing at the edge of the vineyard. She'd started walking, and I'd rushed out of the house and after her down a row of grapevines until she vanished. I'd searched frantically for twenty minutes for her before sitting down in the middle of a row, just hoping she'd reappear.

Jaylan and Brix found me still sitting there later that night when they realized I was missing. Jaylan had humored me when I told him I'd seen our mother, but I knew he thought grief was making me imagine things. Nevertheless, he'd gone back to the house to get blankets, and the three of us had slept out under the stars, waiting for her to come back.

Was it really possible…

"Cyra," Bressen's voice was gentle, and I knew he must've seen the memory. It was a powerful one, and my mind was open to him.

I leaned forward, and Bressen gathered me into his arms. I laid my head on his chest and willed the wave of pain at the memory to pass. When I lifted my head again, Praya and Ariel stood patiently waiting for me to pull myself together.

"I'm sorry," I said. "I just-"

"No explanation needed," Praya said.

I pulled back, and Bressen kissed my forehead before letting me go.

"I'm ready," I said.

He nodded, and I let my seeker power reach out across the field. Bressen couldn't remember exactly where in the area Morland had been killed – or almost killed – but my power knew immediately. The tug in my chest pulled me to the left, and I walked toward it as Bressen, Praya, and Ariel trailed behind me.

The tug grew incessantly stronger until I crossed a particular spot, then it suddenly shifted downward, as if it might root me there.

"Here," I said. I stepped back and let my hand hover over the spot. The sensation told me we were in the right place.

I held up my other hand as well and let my earth magic work. In front of me, the ground peeled back as layer upon layer of dirt lifted away to pile on either side of the spot my magic had isolated. When the hole was several feet deep, I saw the shapes of bones appear at the bottom.

Bile rose up my throat at the sheer volume of skeletons piled on top of each other in a mass grave, their once white bones discolored from decades under the dirt. My hand went to my stomach as nausea overtook me, and I swallowed hard to keep from vomiting.

A gentle hand landed on my waist as Bressen pressed his body to me from behind. He'd sensed my distress, and I knew the sudden lessening of my queasiness was his doing. I wasn't sure if I was grateful for his help or annoyed that he was taking away this feeling that part of me believed I should experience.

"It's an unfortunate reality of war," Bressen said softly in my ear. "Hundreds, even thousands die, and most are buried where they fall."

"Especially the enemy?" I asked.

I felt his exhale on my cheek. "Especially the enemy."

You'll kill tens of thousands before this is over.

Magdalene's words rose up in my mind, and I swallowed again. Would someone else a few decades or even centuries from now dig up a field and find the bodies of the thousands I'd killed?

I shook the thought away. Bressen was adamant Magdalene's vision wouldn't play out the way we feared it would, and I had to believe that.

I extended a hand over the hole and called on my summoning power. The bones at the bottom began to shudder and rattle, and I clamped my teeth shut to keep them from doing the same.

Just when I wasn't sure I could take it anymore, something came shooting up out of the hole into my hand. It smacked hard against my palm, stinging it, and I closed my hand around it. It was an ulna, an arm bone. I knew that from studying anatomy during my healer training, and my stomach lurched all over again as I held the dirt-covered bone.

I turned to Praya. "Will this do?" I asked, and she nodded.

I handed the bone to Bressen, and he wrapped it in a cloth we'd brought. I turned back to the hole to fill it in, but my eyes widened as a ghostly white arm reached up out of it and dug its fingers into the ground.

For a second or two I assumed it was another spirit I'd accidentally summoned, but then a head rose up from the hole, and I gasped. It had only the vague impression of facial features, and there were dark voids where its eyes should be.

I grabbed Bressen's arm. "Please tell me you see that."

He followed my point and jolted. "Fucking hells! What is that?"

"Reapers!" Ariel shouted. "Praya, get behind me!"

"What in the three hells is a reaper?" Bressen asked as he drew his sword. Praya and I drew our blades as well.

Cold dread pooled in my stomach as I looked around the field and saw pale, humanoid creatures crawling up out of the ground all around us. There had to be close to twenty of them. Their bodies rose up from out of solid earth, but once above the ground, they planted their hands and pushed themselves up the rest of the way. Some kind of mist or smoke trailed off them as they moved.

I felt something solid grasp my ankle, and I screamed as one of the reapers pulled itself from the ground just at my feet. I slashed at it with my sword, but the blade slid through it as if nothing was there. Luckily, this also meant its hand on my ankle became phantasmal as well, and I freed myself from its grasp.

Bressen grabbed my arm and pulled me behind him before he swung at another reaper that was closing in on us.

"What do they want?" Bressen yelled to Ariel, who swung her sword at two other reapers. The sword passed right through them.

"They guard places like cemeteries and battlefields where the bones of many dead lie," Ariel shouted back. "They help usher the souls of the dead into the afterworld and then watch over their remains. Gods damn me, I should've remembered they'd be in a place like this. They don't like that we disturbed the bones."

"What can they do to us?" Bressen asked as he swung his sword at an approaching reaper. The thing looked solid enough at first, but just before his sword reached it, its body turned transparent, and the sword passed through it without doing any damage.

"Don't let them near you!" Ariel shouted. "They can reach inside your chest and stop your heart."

"What!" Bressen and I shouted together as our attention whipped toward her.

I saw the threat a second too late.

"Ariel! Behind you!" I shouted.

Ariel spun around, but the reaper was on her, and her eyes flew open wide as its hand reached straight through her chest. Her body jerked as the thing seized her heart, and both Praya and I screamed.

Ariel cried out in pain as her sword fell from her grasp. She put her hand on the thing's chest to push it away, but it wouldn't budge.

She couldn't move it, but it was at least corporeal at the moment.

"Praya," Ariel croaked. "Its head."

Praya seemed to know exactly what Ariel meant, because she drew back her sword to take a mighty swing.

A strangled scream pried its way up my throat as Praya swung her sword at the back of the reaper's neck. If the reaper went incorporeal again, Praya's slash would cut straight across Ariel.

Everything seemed to slow as the blade cut the air. It sliced through the reaper's neck in one quick pass, sending its head tumbling. Before either head or body could hit the ground, though, the reaper disappeared in a cloud of white smoke.

My eyes were frozen open as Praya didn't even try to slow the follow through of her swing, but my scream choked off as her blade passed straight through Ariel's own neck.

I blinked, letting my mind catch up to what I thought I'd just seen. Like the reapers, Ariel's body had gone suddenly incorporeal, allowing Praya's blade to pass through her harmlessly.

Bressen and I stared as Ariel let out a ragged breath. Praya threw herself at Ariel, and the taller woman pulled her wife in for a deep kiss.

"Good job," Ariel said to Praya when she let her go.

I knew both Bressen and I wanted to question what in the three hells we'd just seen, but there was no time. The other reapers were on us, and we both swung our swords wildly at them, if only to keep them from being able to touch us.

"How do we stop them?" I shouted.

"The only way is to cut through them when they're solid," Ariel said, "but it's getting them to stay solid that's the trick."

Bressen swore loudly next to me as his sword passed harmlessly through another reaper. They were closing in on us.

I saw movement in my periphery and turned just in time to dodge the swipe of an incoming reaper. A second later, I felt something solid on my shoulder. I was ready to scream again when I realized it was Blink.

The little demoni lurched forward on my shoulder and hissed at the reaper who, amazingly, reared back in fear.

"Bressen! They're afraid of demoni!" I shouted. "We should call the wrath."

Bressen met my eyes, and I saw the question there. *We?*

Amidst everything else, I'd forgotten to tell him I'd called the demoni during my fight with Magdalene.

He didn't wait for an answer, though. His eyes went red as his wings sprung out from his back. His feet lifted off the ground to hover just above it as black smoke curled around him.

I felt something stir within me as well, as I had with Magdalene, and I was certain my eyes must now be glowing red too. My body went rigid as my arms lifted at my sides, and I heard the clamor of the demoni through the smoke that rose at my own feet. On my shoulder, Blink shifted excitedly as his brethren began to emerge from the black smoke.

All around us, the reapers had stopped attacking and were backing away. I felt Bressen next to me, both of us with eyes glowing and arms outstretched as the demoni swarmed around our feet. I felt the power pass between us as if it wasn't *my* power or *his* power, but *our* power.

The reapers continued to back away. With each step, they sunk back into the ground, their heads bowed as if in deference, but Bressen and I didn't let up until the last one had disappeared. I reached out, and my elemental power willed the earth to slide back into the hole I'd made to dig out Morland's bone.

When everything was once again quiet, Bressen and I both pulled back our power. One of us probably would have been enough to call the demoni and push the reapers back, but I'd wanted to share this with him, to work together and feel our powers merge. Ever since finding out we were a Soul of the Moon, I'd felt more and more drawn to him, and that pull had returned twofold after we'd been separated then reunited. Being away from Bressen would've been painful regardless, but I wondered if it was worse because of our soul bond.

Bressen's feet touched back down and the fire in his eyes cooled, although he left his wings out, slightly splayed at his back. I assumed my own eyes must have gone back to normal as the smoke disappeared from around my feet. The demoni had receded along with the smoke. All but Blink, who still crouched on my shoulder, one hand wrapped in my hair for balance.

"Thank you," I said softly to the creature, as much a dismissal as an expression of gratitude. The demoni took the hint, and its weight lifted from my shoulder as it departed in a swirl of smoke.

Bressen and I turned to look at Praya and Ariel, and the four of us stared at each other for several long moments.

"That's a neat trick," Bressen said to Ariel.

She cocked her head at us. "Likewise."

Praya eyed me curiously. "I knew dark angelus could call demoni, but I wasn't aware the Hand of the Nemesis could do it. I never saw Crissail do it, in any case," she said.

I wasn't aware the Hand of the Nemesis could do it either, Bressen said into my mind, and I started.

I gave him an apologetic look. *I'm sorry*, I said back. *I meant to tell you I did it against Magdalene, but it slipped my mind with everything else going on. It's why she called the retreat.*

Bressen's brows rose with a look that said we'd certainly talk more about this later, but he let it drop for now and turned back to Ariel.

"Your power is to make yourself insubstantial," he said to her, and she nodded.

"It's phantom power," she said, "and it's definitely handy in a fight."

"Does your body do it automatically?" I asked. She was Praya's mate, so I couldn't syphon the power from her, but I was curious to know more.

"Not exactly," Ariel said. "I do need to think about it, to command my body to become incorporeal, but after about four hundred and fifty years of practice, it does become somewhat automatic."

As if all four of us had the same thought at once, our eyes dipped to the bandage on Ariel's arm.

Her smile was wry this time. "I made the mistake of letting my mind wander to places I shouldn't have let it wander when sharpening an incredibly powerful and lethal blade." She glanced at Praya, and the direction her mind had wandered that day became very clear.

"Does the sword have a name?" I asked, recalling the conversation I'd had months ago with Samhail about whether his blades had names.

Ariel huffed a small laugh. "Not officially," she said. "Unofficially I've been calling it Dangerous Daydream."

I pursed my lips to hide my smile as Bressen let out a quick bark of laughter next to me.

"An aptly named sword indeed," he said, "but we should probably leave before those reapers decide we've overstayed our welcome again."

Bressen nodded to me, and I opened a portal in front of the small house where my father had lived until recently.

We'd agreed earlier that's where Praya and Ariel could live while they were with us. Staying in the manor itself wasn't an option with all the servants. We'd tell Samhail and Axenus eventually the women were here, but otherwise Praya and Ariel wanted to keep their presence on the continent a secret for as long as possible. Aramis's house was just outside of Tide's End, so staying there kept them close, yet hidden enough that Magdalene hopefully wouldn't learn they were back.

Bressen and I would return to the ship with Praya later tonight to pick up Serise and get the things we'd left on board when we portaled here. We'd left the gargoyle behind to keep an eye on the crew, while we'd sent Surgeon back here to Solandis to prepare Aramis's house for guests.

Praya would also wipe the memories of seeing her and Ariel from the minds of the crew.

I didn't like the idea of playing with their memories again, but we couldn't take the chance any of them would mention what they'd seen. As far as they'd remember, they'd taken Bressen and I out with our guards for a long cruise, and we'd returned to land early by portal.

No, the captain and sailors of *The Maidenhead* would never know their ship had carried the infamous syphon, Praya of Gonderil, Hand of the Creator, back to the continent after four hundred years of self-exile.

Tandem Read: Go to *Clash of Stone and Steel* (Bk 3), Chapter 43

Chapter 36

Cyra

The next morning, I stepped inside the room next to the training yard to find Praya and Ariel already waiting there. The Citadel guards often used the room if they needed to change before training or store any of their gear, but we'd made sure it was empty earlier, and Bressen had used his mind power to clear everyone out of the area until we were done.

"Are you ready?" I asked Praya. "Do you have everything you need?"

"The only thing I need is the bone," she said.

"How close do you have to be?"

"Not close," Praya said. "Probably thirty feet. You can put up an obfuscation glamour so no one will see us?"

"Bressen will do it," I told her. "He's better at them than I am."

"Then I'm ready whenever you are," she said.

I nodded then paused. "I…have something to ask you," I said.

Praya sighed deeply, as if she already knew what I was going to ask. I went on anyway.

"My father," I started, but she cut me off.

"Cyra, I can't bring your father back," she said.

I'd spoken with Praya a lot on the trip back from the island. She was a good listener, and I'd told her most of my story by the time we got close enough to land to portal, so she knew I'd recently lost Aramis. What she didn't know was that I still had a piece of him.

"But you can," I insisted.

I fished quickly in the pocket of my pants for the paper butterfly I always kept with me now. I'd had a small leather wallet made for it, only a couple inches with a pocket inside to keep the butterfly from slipping out, and I carefully removed the paper to hold it in my palm.

"This is a piece of my father," I said. "I transfigured his body when we had the funeral. If you need me to, I can change it back into…"

I trailed off. Into what? It had never occurred to me to think what piece of my father this had been. If I tried to change it back, would the thing change into a fingernail? A piece of his liver? An eyeball? Some skin?

Thinking about it suddenly made me a little sick, but I took a deep breath to quell the nausea and looked at Praya.

"Please," I said softly. "It's my fault he's dead."

She gave me an empathetic look.

"Cyra, even if I could recreate your father's body, there's no mind or soul to put into it. Your father's spirit has passed on."

My stomach turned to lead, and tears sprung to my eyes, but I blinked them away.

"But maybe-"

"Cyra," she cut in gently, "even if there was a way to fully restore your father, I wouldn't do it. Once the Nemesis has taken a soul, that soul can't return. There would be grave consequences for bringing back a soul the Nemesis has already taken. The Nemesis wouldn't react kindly to us meddling in this."

"I'm bonded to the Nemesis," I said. "I'm sure I could-"

"No, you couldn't," she said, exasperated now. "I understand you're in pain and you think bringing your father back will fix what happened, but it won't. There are rules to the natural order, and I won't break them."

"Aren't we breaking them to bring back Morland?" I asked.

"No, we're actually setting things right," she insisted. "Morland was the one who broke the rules when he refused to fully die. The Nemesis tried to claim him over twenty-five years ago, but Morland defied that claim. His continued existence is an afront to the gods. The only reason I agreed to help you is because bringing Morland back now to kill him fixes a mistake that was made a quarter century ago."

A feeling of stone crept up my throat, much like Samhail's gargoyle form crawled over his skin when he shifted. I tried to swallow down my grief, but I couldn't.

"I brought Bressen back from the dead," I told her. Tears broke free from my eyes and trickled down my face. "Sandrian struck him with lightning, and he died. He wasn't breathing. His heart wasn't beating, but I revived him. He came back."

My voice was drenched in desperation. Praya closed her eyes, and I knew she was losing patience with me, but I had to try one last time. If what she'd said was true, I wouldn't have been able to bring Bressen back.

"I don't profess to be a healer or to know everything about the line between life and death," Praya said, "but as I understand it, the soul doesn't leave the body immediately upon death. In most cases, there's a short period where the body, mind, and soul all still live, even if the heart no longer beats or the person no longer breathes. It's possible Bressen wasn't fully dead when you revived him."

She gave me a firm look, and the resolution in her eyes shattered me. I let out a sob, but Praya was no longer in the mood to be merciful.

"Your father is dead, Cyra. Fully dead," she said. "He belongs to the Nemesis now, and I won't take what the Nemesis has claimed. Nor should you try. You especially. If you attempt to go against the Nemesis, you risk severing your bond with it, and the consequences could be severe."

I pursed my mouth and tried to get control of myself, but my lips quivered with grief. That had been my last hope.

Praya clasped her hands on my shoulders, and I looked at her through bleary, tear-filled eyes. Her face had finally softened.

"Please, Cyra," she said, a modicum of compassion returning to her voice. "I know you're in pain, but take it from someone much older and more experienced than you. Being a syphon doesn't mean unlimited power or the latitude to do whatever we want. Our positions come with a heavy responsibility, and there are penalties for not heeding that."

I nodded, not because I understood or agreed, but because I couldn't bear to discuss it anymore. I closed the butterfly back in its wallet and slipped it into my pocket again. I wiped my eyes to dispel the last of my tears and blew my nose into a handkerchief Praya handed me.

Bressen appeared in the doorway of the room.

"Are we ready?" he asked. "Everyone is…"

His words fell away when he saw my face.

"Cyra, what's wrong?" he asked, striding toward me. He looked sharply at Praya. "What did you do?" he snapped at her.

"Nothing," I cut in quickly. "She didn't do anything."

Or more specifically, she *wouldn't* do anything, and that was part of the problem. My breath stuttered in my chest as I exhaled deeply.

"I just…" I broke off and threw myself against Bressen's chest. He wrapped me in his arms, and I gave in to silent sobs.

I felt the anger roiling inside Bressen and knew he was likely still glaring at Praya, but I spoke into his mind.

I wanted to bring Aramis back, but it's not possible, I said to him.

The tension in his body eased as understanding sunk in, and his arms tightened around me.

When I pulled away a minute or so later, Praya and Ariel were gone, having left to find a place to wait while I pulled myself together. Again.

Gods, I was so tired of crying.

"You don't have to be here when we do this if you don't want," Bressen said quietly to me.

"Yes, I do," I said. "Samhail and Talyn need to believe I'm the one working the magic that restores Morland's body. I doubt they'll believe you can do it."

Bressen canted his head to concede the point.

"Besides, I need to see this through," I said. "I need to be sure Morland is gone once and for all."

He sighed. "Very well. Praya and Ariel should be in place now. I put the obfuscation glamour on them the second they left the room."

I nodded. "Let's go then."

Bressen turned, and I followed him out of the room, down the hall, and out into the training yard. Surgeon and Serise had been stationed just outside the entrance to the yard, and they fell into step behind us now.

I took in the scene that awaited us. Morland stood silently in the yard, while Samhail and Talyn stood a few steps away from him, both of them looking rigid and anxious. I took note of how closely they stood to each other and how Samhail had positioned himself between Talyn and Morland as if to shield her from him.

Not that Morland would be able to do anything. Bressen had taken control of his mind again, and he stood placidly in his borrowed body as if he were waiting for a play or sporting match to start.

Across from him, Jasper was anything but placid. He looked as though he was about to jump out of his skin, and beside him, Maziren stood so coiled with tension I was sure she'd snap any second now and kill us all.

I flinched when Samhail's voice cut the silence.

"Cyra? Are you alright?"

I looked up at him and tried to work a smile onto my face. He could clearly see I'd been crying. "I'm fine. Let's get started."

I stepped forward and placed the bone we'd retrieved on the ground in front of Morland.

In a few minutes we'd either be rid of Morland for good, or Aidan would be lost to us forever.

Tandem Read: Go to *Clash of Stone and Steel* (Bk 3), Chapters 44-47

Chapter 37

Bressen

Morland was finally dead. And this time I was certain of it.

Mostly, almost fully certain.

Part of me would always wonder if he'd managed to escape yet again, and I was sure Talyn and Samhail felt the same. Cyra had assured me that, according to whatever power she now had through the Nemesis, Morland was well and truly gone, but it would take me a while to believe it. I'd spent the rest of the day checking the minds of every servant and guard in the Citadel, just to be sure, but I found no trace of my old enemy.

Jasper and Aidan – the newly restored Aidan – spent the rest of the day in their own wing, and I imagined they had a lot to talk about, so I didn't disturb them.

Talyn came to see me in the afternoon and asked if she could leave or if I planned to send her to Revenmyer. I was surprised by her question, given the obvious connection between her and Samhail, but I told her she was free to go if she wanted. Part of me balked at the idea of letting a woman as dangerous as her just walk out the door, for multiple reasons, but I decided she'd earned her freedom. Her methods had perhaps left something to be desired, but she was ultimately the reason we'd gotten Aidan back as quickly as we had, so I was grateful enough to overlook some of her more questionable decisions.

I tried once more to get her to accept my offer of employment, but she refused, saying only that she couldn't stay.

Something urged me to tell Samhail of her plans to leave, since I was almost certain she hadn't mentioned them to him, but I was caught up in Citadel business all day, and it slipped my mind until later.

When Talyn appeared at dinner, I wondered if she'd changed her mind about leaving, so I resolved to stay out of it and let her and Samhail figure things out themselves.

Talyn was at breakfast the next morning as well, and — while she and Samhail were reserved around each other — I dared to hope that maybe he'd talked her into staying.

I'd seen little of Cyra the previous day after she'd pulled Morland out of Aidan, and she was already asleep by the time I dragged myself to bed that night, so I'd settled for curling myself around her before passing out.

I took her the next morning as soon as we woke, though. I settled myself in the cradle of her thighs and fucked her fast, both of us just needing a quick release before I was once again called away by my duties as lord. I promised her before I left to meet with Aidan that I'd make it up to her tonight, though. I had something…special in mind.

Bressen

Unlike the other pleasure houses in Solandis that sat on side streets or had hidden entrances that allowed their clientele to come and go discretely, The Sword and Sheath sat on the main thoroughfare with a large sign announcing its presence to passersby. The name and location were strategic. Many a soldier or mercenary had entered the building over the years intending to buy weaponry or have theirs repaired, only to be presented with a different kind of merchandise and service.

I already had my obfuscation glamour up when Cyra portaled us into a back room of the building that evening. The pleasure house was a place I'd come occasionally — no pun intended — before I met Cyra. I was usually with Samhail when the two of us didn't want to bother with the dance of finding partners for the night we didn't need to pay.

While Samhail and I were both attractive, or so plenty of women had told us, finding willing companions to warm our beds hadn't always been easy. At almost seven feet tall, Samhail towered over most women, and his powerful body could be intimidating.

And that was before women saw what was in his pants.

I'd had a different problem. My reputation as the Nemesis Incarnate often frightened women who were wary I'd melt their brains or hold their minds captive while I did depraved things to them. This was more of a problem in Callanus where political machinations and the rumor mill churned together outlandish tales of my supposed atrocities. It was less of an issue in Solandis where my people saw me more as a stern but fair ruler, and certainly not a cruel one.

It had been years since Samhail and I last visited The Sword and Sheath, and things had changed a bit. The furniture in the large parlor had been replaced by newer couches and chaises that were upholstered in rich colors of velvet or heavy brocade. Sheer curtains hung at intervals around the room and could be pulled closed to grant a degree of privacy as patrons sampled the house's offerings before making a final decision on who to take into a private room. Perfume hung heavy in the air, likely mixed with the essence of barba root to increase desire.

In general, the place felt more refined than before. It had always been one of the more upscale pleasure houses in Solandis, but the owner had taken it a step further since my last visit.

I took Cyra's hand and led her through the parlor toward an empty couch in the corner of the room. Her hand felt so small and soft, and I savored the feel of her fingers closed around mine. I didn't always believe it was real that she belonged to me, and it was simple things like this that helped make it real. I feared I'd wake up one day and discover it was all a dream, that she was only a figment of my imagination implanted by a mind wraith more powerful than me, a fear that was more salient since Praya had managed to alter my memories.

I'd always been careful not to abuse my mind abilities. I had the power to alter people's reality, and I was cognizant of the responsibility that came with such power. It was one of the things, I hoped, that set me apart from Morland, who'd had no problem playing with people's realities when he'd been a mind wraith.

I used my mind power now to keep anyone from bumping into us as people suddenly got the urge to step out of our way as we passed. Seconds later, I sunk onto a couch in the corner and pulled Cyra down so she was tucked up against my side. I draped my arm around her shoulders and kissed the top of her head as we settled in to watch what was going on.

Cyra nestled into me, and I willed my cock to relax for the moment. The barba root was already arousing me. Or perhaps it was just the feel of Cyra's soft body against mine, which – truth be told – was plenty to stir my lust.

As before, I didn't want to rush things tonight. The last few weeks had been difficult, and I was looking forward to spending some time with my wife, just holding her, appreciating her. We both needed this.

We were also celebrating our small victory over Morland.

I tried not to take delight in the idea of someone's demise, but I couldn't help it with Morland. I was too grateful to finally have him gone.

"Have you ever been to a pleasure house before?" I asked Cyra.

"No. The town over from Fernweh had a small brothel, but I never went inside," she said. "I suspect Brix could tell you about it, though."

I chuckled. I wouldn't be at all surprised if Cyra's younger brother had made a few trips to the place. I couldn't picture her older brother Jaylan going, but Brix was far less straightlaced than the eldest Fernweh sibling.

"How are your brothers anyway?" I asked. Jaylan and Brix had returned to Fernweh a little while ago, and I hoped the fact I hadn't heard anything since then was a good sign.

She shrugged. "Settling back in. So far no one has bothered them."

Cyra was still upset they'd left, and I sensed it wasn't something she wanted to talk about, so I let it drop.

"What do you think of the place so far?" I asked as I trailed my finger lightly up her arm. I smiled to feel the gooseflesh rise at the touch.

"Somehow it's both something I never could've imagined while also being exactly what I thought it would be."

I raised my brows. "Is that good?"

"It's fascinating."

"Fascinating? Not…arousing?"

"That too," she said. She rested a hand lightly on my leg, and I went rock hard.

So much for keeping myself under control. I shifted on the couch to ease the pressure in my pants as Cyra stroked her thumb against my thigh.

"Who are you watching?" I asked, curious as to which couples or groups had drawn her attention. I wanted to know as much as I could about what aroused her.

She was quiet a moment.

"Cyra?"

"I…I'm watching the two men across from us," she admitted.

I looked where she indicated and saw one man sitting on a couch while another knelt before him. The kneeling man's head bobbed up and down over the groin of the man on the couch as his head lolled back in pleasure. The man on the couch threaded his fingers through the other's hair and began to gently thrust up into the man's mouth.

"What do you like about that?" I asked her, curious.

She shifted against me.

"I'm not sure," she said. "As you've noticed, I like the male body. I supposed that extends to seeing two men together, enjoying each other."

I nodded.

"Did you and Samhail ever…" She trailed off.

I smiled. "No. Samhail and I don't mind being together with women, but I don't think either of us ever had a desire to touch the other. At least I didn't. I can appreciate Samhail's body to a degree – I'll even admit I'm impressed by it – but I was never attracted to him, and I think he feels much the same."

"So you'd never…"

I huffed a small laugh. "I don't think so. Sorry to disappoint you."

She smiled. "That *is* disappointing, but we're all aroused by different things." She looked up at me. "So who are *you* watching?"

Truthfully, I'd been focused on her, but I looked around now. An older man had two women on his lap, one perched on each knee. Two other men sat in armchairs watching as three women touched and kissed each other. Both men had erections bulging between their legs, and one stroked his through his pants. Nearby, a middle-aged woman stood between two younger men. She ran her hand over the chest of one while her other hand dipped down the pants of the second to stroke his cock.

I looked past them into another corner of the room and found what I was looking for. I sent the image into Cyra's mind, and she looked where I indicated.

A man sat on a settee in a dark corner while a woman straddled his lap. His hand grazed up and down her bare back, and he suckled her nipple as she rocked on him. Both were still mostly clothed, but there was nevertheless an intimacy between them that made my cock throb.

"Why them?" Cyra asked. "Do you want me to do that to you?"

I brushed my lips along her temple, and she trembled.

"I do want you to do that," I said huskily, "but I'm not drawn to them because of what they're doing. I want to watch them."

"Why?" The question was interested, not judgmental.

I thought a moment before answering. "There's something different about them compared to the other couples. I won't read their minds, but if I did, I'd be willing to bet that man comes here regularly to see that woman in particular. She's more to him than just a courtesan, or at least he wishes she was more. See the way they sit in the shadows where it's more private? He can get more time with her if he stays out here, but he'll bring her into the back soon." I paused. "I feel as though when I watch them, I'm seeing something secret. Something…forbidden."

"You like to watch," she said. "I didn't really believe you that time you watched me with Samhail, but you do like it, don't you."

I nodded. "Yes, but not just any sex. I like to watch sex where there's a kind of…intensity."

She considered this. "When you watched Samhail and I together…"

"It was both the best and the worst thing I'd ever watched."

She shifted so she was facing me, and there was concern on her face.

"It was hard for you to watch us," she said. It wasn't a question.

I nodded.

"Then why did you do it? Why did you let us be together?" she asked.

"Because you needed to be together once more. Both of you did," I said. "Watching you with Samhail that time was one of the hardest things I've ever done, but watching him fuck you also aroused the three hells out of me. I was so hard I could barely stand it."

"And…do you want to see another man have me again tonight?"

I exhaled deeply. "No. If you want someone else to take you, I…you can do that. I'm just not sure I can watch it." I paused, dreading the answer to my next question. "Do you want another man to fuck you, Cyra?"

She shook her head and nestled into me more. "No. I only want you."

I looked down at her and wished I had her truth seeing power since I desperately wanted that to be true. Her mind was open to me, and I sensed it was the truth, but I didn't dare believe it.

"Do you want to watch me with another woman instead?" she asked. "Is that why we came here tonight?"

My mind emptied of every other thought as an image of Cyra with another woman filled my head.

"No…I mean, yes. That is, I wouldn't mind watching you with another woman," I said quickly, "but I didn't have any particular plan in mind for coming here. I just wanted to get out of the Citadel for a while and spend some time with you, learn more about what you like."

"So we can do whatever I want to do?" she asked tentatively.

I hesitated. "Yes," I said, although something in her tone made me wonder if I'd regret agreeing to that.

She relaxed against me, and I reached my free hand up to trail it over her collarbone, the scars made by bear claws still faintly visible there. I slipped my hand inside the bodice of her dress and flicked her nipple with my thumb. She moaned softly and arched into my touch.

"Tell me if you see anyone you'd like to bring into a private room," I whispered against her ear. I slipped my hand out of her bodice. "I'm going to take the obfuscation glamour off us now as well as the compulsion that's kept anyone from coming over here."

She nodded. "Alright."

The fog of the glamour lifted, and I took the mind control off the people in the room, but it was still almost a minute before the owner, a man named Federlin, spotted us and hurried over, looking mortified.

"Lord Bressen! I didn't see you come in. I'm so sorry. No one notified me you were-"

"It's fine, Federlin," I interrupted him. "We snuck in so we'd have some time to take in your new furnishings."

The man smiled proudly. "Do you like them? Competition has become fierce among the brothels and pleasure houses, so one must keep up. We preferred to add more class, unlike certain *other* houses that went for more tawdry changes."

I cocked my head in question. "Such as?"

Federlin rolled his eyes. "The Bucking Harlot is now offering reins and riding crops to their patrons."

I blinked. Well, that was different. I shook the image away before it gave me too many ideas.

"But never mind all that," Federlin said, waving his hand. "What can I do for you and…"

He trailed off as he took in Cyra, and something twinged inside me at the way his eyes lingered on her.

"Is…is this Lady Cyra?" he asked.

"It is," I said. "Cyra, meet Federlin, the owner of The Sword and Sheath. Federlin, this is my wife, Lady Cyra of Hiraeth."

Federlin immediately went to one knee before Cyra and bowed his head. I felt her surprise at the gesture, but the man rose a moment later.

"If you're looking for a girl to take into a private room," Federlin said,

"I think I have just the one."

He signaled to one of his guards. "Find Helaina and bring her here," he told the man, who hurried off.

"There's no rush," I said. "When Cyra finds someone she likes, we'll be sure to let you know."

Federlin held up a hand. "Understood, my lord. But let me introduce you to Helaina anyway. She's an empath, so she'd be a good complement to you and your lovely lady."

I nodded my agreement. Empaths could sense a person's emotions. They couldn't read thoughts like mind wraiths did, but the result was often the same. A person's emotions could tell a good empath quite a bit about what that person was thinking. Empaths also had one advantage over mind wraiths in that a mind shield generally couldn't block an empath's read of a person's emotions. My own powers included empathic abilities, so I could usually sense emotions, and Cyra could as well.

I explained empaths to Cyra in her mind, and she gave a small nod.

The guard Federlin had sent off returned with a woman in tow, and I jolted to see how much she looked like Cyra. She had long dark brown hair, and there was a similarity in their facial structure that would've convinced me they were related if someone told me as much.

The woman had several distinct differences, though. Her eyes were dark brown as opposed to Cyra's silver ones, and her skin was more golden compared to Cyra's pale complexion. The woman's body was also a little fuller, her hips wider, and her breasts plumper.

"My lord, my lady, this is Helaina," Federlin said. "She's yours for the night if you so wish."

"Thank you, we'll let-," I started to say, but Cyra laid a hand on mine.

"Hello, Helaina," she said. "It's nice to meet you."

"You as well, my lady," the woman said, bobbing a curtsy.

"Would you like to join Lord Bressen and I tonight?" Cyra asked.

The courtesan paused a moment before answering. "It would be an honor to serve you," she said with another curtsy.

Cyra sighed at the slightly evasive answer. "I see you speak the truth," she said. "Can you feel my sincerity when I say you don't need to fear us?"

Helaina hesitated before nodding. "I can, my lady, and I'd like to try to please you if you'll allow me."

Cyra rose from the couch and turned to Federlin as I stood as well. "Helaina will join us," she told him.

"Wonderful," Federlin said. He put a hand on the small of Helaina's back and urged her forward. "Our best room is ready for you."

"Will you follow me?" Helaina said.

Are you sure? I asked into Cyra's mind.

Do you object to her? she returned.

No, but we don't have to accept her if you don't want to.

If you don't object, I want her, she said.

I nodded at Helaina to lead the way, then took Cyra's hand to follow the courtesan toward the back rooms.

I knew the room we entered well. It was the one Federlin usually gave me and Samhail, or just me if I was alone, but like the rest of the place, it too had been redone in a more lavish style. The new four-poster bed was larger than the previous one, and it was hung with both sheer and velvet curtains. I also noticed soft ropes attached to the feet, which were tucked under the bed until such time as someone needed to be tied to it.

An ornate couch of dark blue brocade sat against the left wall, and two large armchairs of the same upholstery stood on either side of it. The wallpaper was textured with an intricate design, and Federlin had invested in some fine new risqué art that hung around the room.

Helaina closed the door and turned to face us. "How may I please you both tonight?"

I looked at Cyra. "I think my wife wants to do some experimenting?"

Cyra blushed as Helaina looked at her. The courtesan cocked her head in interest, then furrowed her brows.

"If you'll forgive me, my lord," Helaina said carefully, "I don't believe that's what she wants. She's…afraid to tell you what she wants."

My gaze snapped to Cyra, and I saw the truth in her face. I read her mind, and my eyes widened. Cyra lowered her head, but I hooked a finger under her chin and lifted it. There was apology in her eyes.

"I don't understand," I said.

"I want to know what you felt when you watched me and Samhail together," she said.

It was on the tip of my tongue to tell her that's the last thing she wanted, but I held the thought back. I wouldn't deny her if this is what she really desired, but I had some of my own limits.

"I won't fuck her," I told Cyra. "I promised myself I'd never take another woman but you, and that's a promise I intend to keep. But I'll let her…prepare me for you if that's what you really want."

It was a few seconds before Cyra nodded.

"Are you certain?" I asked.

"Yes," she assured me.

I exhaled deeply again and nodded. "I have another stipulation," I told her. "If I do this, I want you to sit here and touch yourself for me."

Her eyes went wide. "What?"

"You heard me," I said. "Helaina, please help Lady Cyra take her clothes off."

The courtesan stepped forward, and Cyra turned to give her access to the fastenings at the back of her dress.

Now that Cyra no longer had a lady's maid, it was my job to do and undo those fastenings in the mornings and evenings on the days she chose to wear something that required assistance. On the mornings I wasn't in a hurry, I took my time helping her dress, letting my fingers graze her bare skin. I'd tease her until we were both ready to explode, and more than once this resulted in us fucking on the floor of the closet, Cyra's undergarment discarded, and my pants yanked down to my thighs.

Helaina took the same kind of care now with Cyra's dress as her fingers brushed sensually over my wife's skin. When it was loose enough, she slipped it down Cyra's hips, then looped her fingers over the waist of

Cyra's undergarment and pulled it slowly down her legs.

"My lady, will you help me with this?" Helaina asked Cyra as she turned to present the ties to the corset she wore.

"Uh…yes, of course," Cyra said as she stepped forward.

I smiled at the hint of fluster in her voice, but my mouth went dry as the courtesan lifted her hair, and Cyra pulled at the ties of her garment.

Fuck me. I'd watched women undress each other before, but watching my wife do it was a whole new level of eroticism, and all the blood in my body rushed straight to my cock. I'd thought it was bad when Cyra had shown me Talyn touching her in the bathtub weeks ago, but seeing it in the flesh rather than in my mind was far worse.

And by worse, I meant it was one of the best things I'd ever witnessed.

I swallowed as Cyra helped the woman pull the corset off to free her breasts, then looped her fingers over the woman's skirt and pulled it down her legs. My knees almost buckled as the two of them turned to me, naked.

"Will you help me with your lord, my lady?" Helaina said to Cyra.

Cyra obeyed, and the two women began to undress me. Their hands lingered on my body as they pressed themselves against me, and I stood as still as possible, wondering what in the three hells had made me think this was a good idea. The graze of their fingers over my skin as they peeled away my clothes was sweet torture, and for the briefest moment I let myself imagine what it might be like to throw them on the bed and fuck them both. Decades ago, it wasn't unusual for me to take two women to my bed, but I wasn't sure I could do it now that I had Cyra.

I groaned as Cyra undid the fastenings of my pants and both women pulled them down my legs. My cock sprung free, and I looked down to see the women on their knees, mouths hovering close to it.

I looked up again, trying to keep control. Gods above, I was going to spend myself before they even fucking touched me.

I jerked as I felt two separate tongues lick up the length of my shaft, but I didn't look down. Instead, I started thinking about Lord Marcus's speech on the ruling houses of Polaris just to keep from exploding.

Mercifully, Helaina stood and went to the couch to lay a blanket on top of it before motioning for me to sit. I did so as Helaina led Cyra to one of the chairs and seated her there.

The courtesan returned and dropped to her knees before me. She looked up at me, and I felt a stab of panic as she held my gaze, more assuredly than most people ever dared. She could feel my terror.

"It's alright for you to let yourself enjoy this, my lord," she said.

A nervous laugh jumped off my lips, and I realized just what a difficult position we'd put this woman in, trying to please two powerful people who wanted different things. I let myself dip into her mind and felt her own kernel of fear. I let out a deep breath to calm myself. If this is what Cyra wanted, this is what we'd do.

"I have no doubt you'll please both me and Cyra," I told her.

She seemed to relax as she bent over me once more.

I was semi-hard now, Marcus's speech and my doubts about doing this having cooled some of my ardor, but I grunted loudly as Helaina slipped her mouth over my cock and began to run her lips and tongue over me. I felt a jolt of something from Cyra as well, but I didn't have the mental capacity right now to interpret it as blood came rushing back to the fickle appendage between my legs. From my angle, the dark head bobbing up and down over my groin could almost be Cyra's, and I held onto that idea as I dragged my eyes up to find the real Cyra's face.

She bit her lip as she sat in the chair watching, and at least for now I read only curiosity in her mind.

"Touch yourself, Cyra," I gritted out as I fought the sensation building in my cock. I didn't want to think anyone besides Cyra could make me climax. I wouldn't let anyone else. Cyra had been the center of my world since I'd met her, and I wanted to believe my body responded to her and her alone. But of course, I was only human, and my gods damned cock couldn't tell it wasn't Cyra's mouth wrapped around me.

Cyra had started at my voice, but she lifted one hand to run it over her breast now while her other hand dipped between her legs to circle a finger around her clit.

My cock jumped at the sight, and I latched onto the notion that it was still Cyra driving my desire, even if it wasn't her touching me.

"Fuck!" I cried out as Helaina pushed me deeper into her throat and swallowed so the muscles contracted around my cock.

My eyes darted back to Cyra's, desperate to maintain a connection with her. She was still biting her lip, and she slipped forward in the chair so she could open her legs wider. She let out a soft moan as she dipped a finger inside herself, and I fought with everything I had not to come in the courtesan's mouth.

Nemesis take me. I wasn't going to last much longer.

I had the urge to thread my fingers into Helaina's hair as her mouth worked me, but I resisted the pull to touch her. Instead, I reached out on either side of me and gripped the back of the couch as I struggled to keep my hips from thrusting up.

My eyes found Cyra's again. *Are you enjoying this?* I asked into her mind. I needed to know she wasn't upset, or I'd stop this right now.

I think I understand what you felt, she said softly. *It's erotic to watch, while at the same time…*

She searched for the right words as my body strained against the pressure in my groin.

Keep touching yourself, I urged her.

Cyra pushed a second finger between her perfect pink folds and undulated her hips as she rode her hand. I saw the slickness coating her fingers as she moved them in and out of herself, and I wanted to taste it.

I groaned involuntarily as the courtesan's tongue swirled around my head, and I registered the spike of jealousy in Cyra's mind a second later.

Helaina must have sensed it too because she immediately pulled her mouth off me with a soft pop and stood up.

"My lady, it's time for you to take over," she said. She pulled Cyra up from the chair and helped her straddle my lap.

A surge of elation washed through me as Cyra lined herself up with my cock and eased down so her sweet warmth closed around me. It was like being admitted to the highest of the three heavens.

"I'm sorry," she whispered as she settled on top of me.

"You have nothing to be sorry for," I said as I wrapped my arms around her. "Now ride me before I fucking die."

She let out a small laugh and began to move her hips, pushing up and down, then grinding herself into me. I lowered my head and sucked her breast into my mouth, which made her gasp and rock faster.

This is what *I* wanted. Helaina's mouth had felt good, but nothing compared to the way Cyra felt when our bodies connected. It had been that way since the beginning. She'd been an itch I could never fully scratch, a thirst I could never quench, a hunger that was never satiated. With other women, I felt the pleasure of sex in my cock, but with Cyra, my entire body came alive.

Maybe I'd only tricked myself into thinking the crescent moon marks she and I shared meant something, that they tied us together in a way I could never be tied to another, but it was a delusion I'd happily maintain.

I pulled Cyra against me as the urgency of her movements intensified. One of my arms crossed her back and gripped her opposite shoulder while my other hand cupped her ass to help her ride me. We were both covered in a sheen of sweat, and I willed my body to hold off a little while longer.

"I need you to come first," I told her, even as my balls tightened.

"I'm almost there!" she gasped as she thrust herself onto me. "I'm-"

Cyra cried out as she climaxed, and her muscles clamped around me, sending me over the edge as well. I thrust my hips up as I released deep inside her, my seed pumping into her with each pulse of my cock.

Like Cyra, I wasn't ready for children yet, especially not with war on the horizon, but there was something about the idea of planting my seed within her and that distant possibility of getting her pregnant that drove me mad. Someday she'd have my child growing inside her, and the thought brought on another aftershock of pleasure. I grunted as my cock pumped a couple final spurts of my hot seed into her, and I savored the idea that even now I might have claimed her body in that way, that if the contraception we both took somehow failed, her belly would swell with the life I'd planted inside her. The notion was both thrilling and terrifying.

Cyra clung to me as we sat panting wildly. I surveyed the room quickly, half expecting Helaina to have quietly slipped out, but she stood near the door, eyes down, as she waited to see if she was still needed. I wondered if she'd watched us furtively, and the thought made my groin ache again.

I was more voyeur than exhibitionist, but a part of me was exhilarated to think she'd watched me fuck Cyra. I'd even found it exciting the day Axenus had caught us in the great room, although I wished he'd seen something a little less violent.

I stood up from the couch, taking Cyra with me. She wrapped her legs around me instinctively as I walked her to the bed. She uncurled from around me as I laid her on the mattress and turned to the courtesan.

"Helaina."

"Yes, my lord?" The woman came alive, as if she were a marionette and someone had just yanked her strings.

"I need a few minutes to recover, but I want you to bring Lady Cyra to climax again. Can you do that?"

"Of course, my lord," the courtesan said as she hurried to the bed.

"Bressen, what-" Cyra started to ask, but I held up a hand to stop her.

"It's my turn to watch, my love," I told her with a grin.

Cyra's attention jumped back to Helaina as the courtesan put her hands gently on Cyra's knees and pushed her legs open. Helaina waited for me to bring the chair over to the bed and sit down before she lowered her head between Cyra's thighs.

Then I sat back and let out a sigh of contentment as the beautiful sound of my wife's pleasure filled the room.

Tandem Read: Go to *Clash of Stone and Steel* (Bk 3), Chapters 48-49

Chapter 38

Cyra

Bressen and I returned from the pleasure house just before sunrise. We'd spent the whole night with Helaina experimenting and exploring my desires – as Bressen had once called it - and we were both exhausted but satiated.

Bressen had continued to refuse to take Helaina, but he was more than happy to watch *her* fuck *me*. The courtesan left the room at one point and returned with a box filled with tools of pleasure, 'toys' she called them, and she'd pulled out a large flexible cock that could be strapped to her hips. The cock was made from the resin of a tree that only grew in a specific valley in the country of Vidall, and it was fashioned into something that looked and felt like a real cock.

Bressen's delight had been nearly palpable as Helaina strapped the cock to her hips, put me on my knees in front of her, and fucked me with the thing until I'd moaned my pleasure into the bedding. Then Bressen had made me straddle Helaina while she lay on the bed with the toy inside me, and he'd taken me in my other entrance the way we'd once done with Samhail so many months ago. I hadn't thought myself capable of coming again by that time, but as it turned out, I liked being filled in both places, and I'd climaxed so intensely my legs shook by the end.

I'd barely had enough energy to open a portal back to our rooms at the Citadel, and then Bressen and I had fallen into bed to sleep just as the first rays of dawn lit the sky.

We were woken by a pounding at our door close to ten o'clock, and Bressen dragged himself out of bed to answer it. It was Samhail, who confessed he'd done something 'inadvisable' last night, and he needed us to get up.

It turned out Talyn had told Samhail she was leaving, and in an impulsive attempt to keep her from going, he'd claimed the Right of Primacy over her.

Bressen looked blankly at Samhail at this news, but I let out a surprised, "Oh!" as I remembered what Samhail had told me about this gargoyle custom at the reception for my own wedding.

Bressen's eyes gradually went wider and wider as Samhail explained that the Right of Primacy was the gargoyle equivalent of a proposal and marriage ceremony in one, but that Talyn wanted to reject his claim and had chosen the right to fight it through combat.

"Just so I'm clear," Bressen said to Samhail, "You claimed the most dangerous assassin on the continent as your wife against her will, and now you need to defeat her in combat in order to validate the claim. Does that about sum it up?"

"You forgot the part where she doesn't actually have to kill me to win, but she probably will anyway," Samhail added.

"That was a given," Bressen shot back dryly.

"Honestly," I added, "from what I know of Talyn, you're better off if she tries to kill you outright rather than more painful alternatives."

Samhail cocked his head to concede the point, then left so Bressen and I could get dressed.

The fight took place after lunch with Surgeon and Serise acting as judges to the legitimacy of the outcome.

And what a fight it had been.

I'd never seen Samhail fight as hard as he did then, and I was shocked to learn Talyn was good enough to match him fairly well. I was barely able to keep up with the action as my eyes tried to follow the blur of movement in the training yard as the two elite warriors fought.

I screamed when Samhail and Talyn stabbed each other at the same time and fell to the ground, and I rushed to Samhail, every fiber of my being roaring at me to help him, but he'd refused to let me work on him. He made me heal Talyn first, and I'd worked on the assassin as quickly as

I could before one of my best friends bled out on the ground. I healed her just enough to get her out of danger before going back to Samhail.

Still Samhail had resisted my attempts to heal him. He made Talyn accept her victory before he allowed me to work on him, and the assassin accepted it just in time, as I'd felt Samhail fading fast.

Then, in a move that surprised everyone but me, Talyn turned around and claimed Samhail by Right of Primacy instead. A full human had never claimed a gargoyle before, but Surgeon and Serise weren't aware of any prohibition against it. Thus, after a very brief gargoyle-style divorce, Talyn and Samhail were remarried as I worked furiously to keep him from dying.

To say I was exhausted by the end was an understatement, and Bressen carried me back up to our room to put me to bed for a nap. I wanted him to lie down with me, but there was again a knock at our door. This time it was Talyn, who asked to speak to Bressen, and the two headed off to his study.

I was asleep for maybe an hour when Bressen's voice in my head coaxed me awake.

Sorry to wake you so soon, my love, he said into my mind as my eyes fluttered open, *but Phaedrus is here with news about that piece of text he was translating for you.*

My eyes popped open. It had been a while since I'd heard from Phaedrus, longer than anticipated, and I was eager to see what he'd found.

I hadn't undressed for my nap, so I just threw myself out of bed and hurried through our suite to Bressen's study. Phaedrus was already seated at the large table with the tome opened to the page we'd found earlier.

"I expected to hear from you sooner than this, Phaedrus," I said as I went to the table to sit down. I stopped short as I got a good look at the priest, though, and I frowned.

The same symbol with interlocking triangles and radiant lines I'd seen on the foreheads of Bressen and the gargoyles flashed on Phaedrus's head, but that wasn't all.

"My lady? Is something wrong?" Phaedrus asked.

"You're…glowing," I said.

Phaedrus looked at me in shock. "What?"

"I noticed something like it when I first saw you in the Priory," I said. "I thought it was a trick of the light, but this can't be a trick."

Indeed, Phaedrus's entire body seemed to emit a faint white light. It wasn't the same type of glow I saw when someone lied. That was more just a rosy hue on their skin, much like a sunburn. This was an actual light that cast an aura all around the priest, as if he might light the room if we turned off the lamps.

"Cyra, what are you talking about?" Bressen asked, his brows furrowed in concern.

"You don't see it?" I asked.

"See what?" he asked as he looked Phaedrus over.

I looked back to Phaedrus, but he still wore a mask of confusion.

"You're surprised I can see the glow," I said to him. "Why?"

"It…It's not possible," Phaedrus said. "No one should be able to see what you're seeing."

"And what is she seeing?" Bressen asked. His voice had taken on a hard edge, and I saw the brief flash of red in his eyes. He moved quickly to put himself between me and Phaedrus, but the priest threw up his hands in a gesture of surrender as he stood.

"I mean her no harm, my lord," he hurried to assure Bressen.

"Then answer my question," Bressen said coldly.

"Bressen." I put a hand on his arm. "You can't think-"

"I think he's obviously been hiding something from me," Bressen said as he tried to push me behind him again, "and he better tell me very quickly what that is."

Phaedrus's gaze darted uncertainly between me and Bressen before he nodded. "My lord, I'm an awen," he said finally.

I frowned, but when I looked over Bressen's shoulder, his face bore a look of understanding.

"How did I not know this about you?" Bressen asked.

Phaedrus shrugged. "It's not something I think about much. It's something I just am, just as you're a man or an angelus."

"What's an awen?" I asked.

"Awen were made by the Creator," Phaedrus explained. "We're beings of inspiration and creative motivation. We're mentioned in the same part of the sacred texts as angelus and gargoyles."

"So you serve the Creator?" I asked. "The way gargoyles serve the Protector?"

"In a way," Phaedrus said, "According to several of the sacred texts of the Trinity, when the Creator made the universe, it granted its fellow gods each a gift. It allowed them to choose a type of being that would represent them, something that would help carry out their work in the world. The Protector chose gargoyles, huge, nearly invincible beasts with skin like stone who could protect all those who served the Trinity. So the Creator created gargoyles to guard the temples and the priests and priestesses who inhabited them."

"And the Hands of the Gods," I added.

Phaedrus considered this, then nodded. "Yes, that would make sense. I assume this is something you learned recently?"

"Let's just say it explained some things for me and Samhail," I said.

"Ah, I see," Phaedrus said.

"Go on," I urged him.

"As you may have guessed, the Nemesis chose angelus as its gift from the Creator," Phaedrus went on. "Angelus were made to help the Nemesis keep balance in the world, to ensure an equilibrium between light and dark and to mete out reward and punishment when warranted. They were given wings so they could see the world from above and remain ever watchful. With so few angelus left nowadays, these roles have largely fallen by the wayside, but you yourself still fulfill some of these duties in your overseeing of Revenmyer, Lord Bressen."

Bressen had relaxed now, enough for me to move out from behind him so I could see Phaedrus better.

Phaedrus nodded. "For its own purposes, the Creator made awen, beings that could spread creativity, inspiration, and motivation among humanity so they might thrive. We're supposed to operate largely unseen, but like gargoyles and angelus, we have another form, and that form is like light made flesh. Few people have ever seen awen in their true forms because we'd be nearly blinding to them. Of the three beings, though — angelus, gargoyles, and awen — only awen still exist to any great degree, and we're generally close by wherever there is lots of creativity. Music, dance, theater, writing, poetry, even the recording of history, which is my specialty."

"And why can Cyra see your light now?" Bressen asked.

"I'm not sure," Phaedrus said. "I assume it has something to do with her being a Hand of the Gods, but I'm not sure why she would only now be noticing it."

"Praya told me that as I became more attuned with the Nemesis I'd be able to-" I started to explain, then cut myself off with a gasp as I realized my slip.

But it was too late.

Bressen's expression turned to one of apprehension, while Phaedrus looked at me in confusion.

"Praya?" the priest asked. "Did you just say Praya told you something? As in the syphon Praya?"

Bressen's head snapped to Phaedrus, and the priest's entire body went rigid as Bressen seized his mind.

"Bressen, no!" I said, throwing myself between him and Phaedrus. I grabbed his arms and tried to push him back, but he didn't budge. "Please don't hurt him. It's not his fault I slipped up. You know Phaedrus. You know he won't say anything."

Bressen's eyes were still on Phaedrus over my shoulder, and I turned to see the priest's face was paralyzed in fear.

"Bressen, please," I begged him. "Please let him go."

"Phaedrus, nod if you can hear and understand me," Bressen said calmly, and the priest gave a single slow nod.

"Good," Bressen went on. "I want you to listen very carefully. Praya of Gonderil, Hand of the Creator, is alive. She didn't go down with her ship four hundred years ago as believed. She was living on an island far out into the Aspan Ocean, but we brought her back to the continent, and she's currently in Solandis. Do you understand so far?"

Phaedrus nodded again.

"I want you to answer yes or no to my next questions," Bressen said. "First, can I trust you not to tell another living soul what I just divulged?"

"Yes," Phaedrus answered.

I waited half a second to look for a rosy hue on Phaedrus's skin under the soft white glow wafting off him, but there was none.

"It's the truth!" I said. "He won't tell."

"Swear to it," Bressen said to Phaedrus.

"I swear," the priest answered.

"And do you understand that for the safety of Praya and her wife," Bressen went on, "I'll have to kill you if you break that promise?"

I gasped, but Phaedrus only nodded again. "Yes," he confirmed.

"And just to be absolutely certain," Bressen said, "are you going to give me a reason to kill you?"

"No," Phaedrus answered immediately.

Again I waited only a second before turning back to Bressen.

"He speaks the truth," I said. "Please, release him."

Bressen eyed the priest for another couple seconds before he relaxed, and I felt him break his hold on Phaedrus's mind.

Phaedrus inhaled sharply as he regained control of himself, and I swung back around to face him.

"I'm sorry!" I said, putting a hand on his arm. "I wasn't thinking. I didn't mean to let that slip and put you in danger. Are you alright?"

Phaedrus's jaw hung slack as he looked between me and Bressen.

"Please forgive me for that, Phaedrus," Bressen said to him. "As you can imagine, this is very sensitive information that we can't have getting around. I had to be sure we could trust you, especially since we just learned you've been keeping a fairly big secret."

The priest nodded absently. "Praya is…here?" he asked. "Can…can I meet her?"

"Not right now," Bressen said. "No one is supposed to know she's here but me, Cyra, Surgeon, Serise, and Axenus. I'll tell Samhail eventually, but I have to be sure we can trust his new wife first."

Phaedrus's brows shot down into a deep frown. "Samhail's wife? When did Samhail get married?"

Bressen smiled wryly. "This afternoon."

Phaedrus blinked, and I stepped back from him.

"It's a long story," I said, "and one I think we're too tired to tell right now. You said you had something for us?"

Phaedrus shook his head to clear it.

"I do have some news," he said. "My apologies for how long it took. There were two complications. To start, the song lyrics you provided me were fairly accurate. I was able to confirm they closely adhered to the text in the book with few deviations, except for one significant one. The last line of the song is completely different in the text."

I angled my head in interest. "How different?"

"You noted that you and your brother thought it was a convoluted love song, and the last line of your version supports this interpretation," Phaedrus said. He laid the paper with my version of the lyrics on the table, and Bressen picked it up to read it.

"But what's in the text suggests something else," Phaedrus finished.

"*Then will the separate once more unite, And live in peace again until our last.*" Bressen read the last two lines from the paper, then put it down and looked up. "What does the other version say?"

Phaedrus picked up another paper that held his notes and read. "*Then will the separate once more unite, And their triumvirate will be the last.*"

Bressen and I looked at each other in alarm.

"Whose triumvirate will be the last?" I asked Phaedrus. "What does that mean?"

Phaedrus shook his head. "I don't know, my lady. The song is too vague to draw any definitive conclusions."

"Do you have any idea why the last lines are different?" I asked.

Again Phaedrus shook his head. "I can't say for sure. I can only guess that perhaps when the song was passed around, people didn't understand the last line, so they changed it to something that made more sense, something that sounded more…optimistic."

Yes, the line I'd learned from my mother definitely had a more hopeful message than the rather ominous-sounding one from the text.

I swallowed, and Bressen slipped an arm around my waist.

"Don't worry just yet," he said. "That last line isn't inherently negative, and it could be talking about any number of triumvirates. We can't jump to conclusions."

Any number of triumvirates. Including the one he was a part of, which didn't ease my mind. Regardless of how you interpreted the line, there was a good chance either he or I were in danger.

"You said there were two complications," I noted, turning again to Phaedrus. "What was the second?"

Phaedrus pointed to a small marking that looked a bit like a butterfly. It appeared to have been drawn in the margin next to the second stanza. Bressen and I leaned over and looked into the book. The ink was slightly different here, so I guessed it was added later by someone else.

"I spent days trying to find a translation for this mark," Phaedrus said. "It's obviously not part of the original text or the song itself, but I have a feeling it's significant."

"Did you find what it means?" I asked. "It looks like a butterfly."

Phaedrus gave a small laugh. "It *is* a butterfly," he said.

My eyes met Phaedrus's bright blue ones. "I don't understand."

"It's not a word or a letter," Phaedrus said. "It finally occurred to me after about three days when I couldn't find a translation for it anywhere that someone had just drawn a butterfly in the margin of the book."

"Any idea why?" Bressen asked.

Phaedrus gave a shrug. "Your guess is as good as mine, but butterflies are often symbols of change or metamorphosis. Whoever drew it here might've been trying to suggest something about how to interpret the song, or they might simply have been bored and needed somewhere to doodle. Unfortunately, there's no way to know."

I nodded slowly as I reread the second stanza of the song.

"Though it sets each eve, closing out the day,
We trust its rise again upon the morn.
A sacrifice for love, a bargain's made
To grant a gift and help a bond reform."

I could possibly see a theme of change here, but how that change might come about or what it meant in the grand scheme eluded me.

"Go rest some more," Bressen said as he kissed my forehead. "You still look exhausted. I have a couple more things to discuss with Phaedrus, and then I'll be in to join you."

I gave Bressen an anxious look, but he held up a hand.

"Phaedrus will be perfectly safe," he said. "I promise."

I made a show of looking him over to see if his skin turned rosy, and he smiled. When it remained its normal lightly tanned hue, I nodded.

"Thank you for the work on this," I said to Phaedrus.

He bowed his head. "Of course, my lady. I'm happy to help."

"And rest assured, I'll check in to be sure he hasn't done anything to you," I told him, eyeing Bressen.

Bressen gave me a look that proclaimed his innocence.

Phaedrus only smiled. "I trust that Lord Bressen only acts in the interests of those who depend on him."

I rolled my eyes, but no rosy glow appeared on Phaedrus's skin. He truly believed what he said. It was a trust Bressen had earned from the priest, and I couldn't help but wonder what trusts and expectations – for better or worse – I was building with those who knew me.

Chapter 39

Cyra

Back in our room I made for the bed to lay down again, but I stopped halfway there and bent my head to sniff myself. The sharp odor of sweat, dirt, and sex assailed my nose, and I flushed to think Phaedrus might've been able to smell this. Gods above, I reeked.

Bressen and I hadn't bathed after our night at the pleasure house before we'd fallen into bed, and then we'd been called to witness the fight between Samhail and Talyn. Suddenly my skin felt tight with the salt of dried sweat, and I knew the remnants of Bressen's seed still crusted the insides of my thighs. Several coats of it, in fact. Then, over all that was a layer of dust from the training yard as well as some blood under my fingernails I hadn't quite gotten out when I'd washed my hands after healing Talyn and Samhail.

I veered away from the bed and headed toward the closet to get my nightgown and robe. It wasn't that late yet, but I planned to bathe, fall back into bed, and sleep for the next twelve hours at least.

I reached into my pocket and pulled out the small wallet that contained the paper butterfly that had been part of Aramis. Phaedrus had said butterflies were symbols of metamorphosis, and that was fitting for what I'd done to my father's body.

I now regretted transforming Clarice the same way. She hadn't deserved to be made into something beautiful as Aramis had. I should've turned her body to sand or dust motes or maybe a pile of shit.

I opened the wallet and took out the butterfly, and a pang of grief hit me. I thought about asking Praya again to reform Aramis, but I dismissed it almost immediately. As she'd said, it would only be his body. His spirit was already gone, and without that, the body would just be an empty shell.

If there was also a way to recall his soul, then that might…

I went still as pieces clicked into place in my head, and I held the paper butterfly in the palm of a trembling hand.

I *did* have access to Aramis's soul. I had spirit anchor power. What had Praya said? Spirit anchors could see and communicate with the dead when they were in close proximity to the person's body or an object that was important to them.

I had a piece of Aramis's body right here in my hand.

My heart thundered as the possibility of seeing Aramis again took hold. Not only could I use this butterfly to have Praya recreate his body, I could summon his spirit back and – maybe – put it back in that body.

I clutched the butterfly in my hand, trying not to crumple it too badly.

My father. I could bring back my father.

I didn't know how I'd called those spirits before on the battlefield, but I'd figure it out now. I held the hand with the butterfly against my heart and concentrated as hard as I could on thoughts of Aramis.

"Aramis," I whispered. "Please. I need to see you."

I opened my eyes and looked desperately around the room, but there was nothing. I must be doing it wrong.

Gods damn it. Why hadn't I asked Praya how this power worked?

I closed my eyes and tried again as I let my power reach out to…to wherever Aramis might be. I hoped he was in one of the three heavens, but there was no way to know for sure.

"Cyra?"

I stopped breathing at the sound of the voice. I tried to open my eyes, but fear kept them locked shut, fear that I wasn't actually going to see what – or who – I so desperately wanted to see when I opened them.

I forced myself to open my eyes at the same moment I inhaled sharply, and a rush of adrenaline hit me that nearly buckled my knees.

Aramis stood several feet from me, looking confused. His body was barely transparent, so I could see parts of the room behind him if I looked carefully. I hadn't noticed that about the spirits back on the battlefield, but I'd been too shocked by their appearance to take in the details.

"Aramis?" My voice was a croak as I managed to get the words past the massive knot in my throat. "Is…that really you?"

Aramis stood still for a moment before he smiled sadly. "It's me," he said. "Or at least a remnant of me."

I let out a sob and willed my legs to hold me. I wanted to rush to him, to embrace him, but I knew I wouldn't be able to touch him.

I opened my mouth to speak, but suddenly, I didn't know what to say. For weeks I'd imagined what I might say to my father if I ever got the chance to see him again, but now my mind was blank.

Then a knife twisted in my gut as I remembered.

"I'm sorry," I whispered. "I'm so sorry. I…killed you. I thought Magdalene had done it, but she said it was my lightning. I was so stupid. If I'd just had better control of myself…" Another sob ripped up my throat. "You'd still be alive. We'd still be together."

Aramis looked at me sadly. If I'd been hoping he'd contradict Magdalene, insist she was lying, I was sorely disappointed, and the knife in my gut twisted even more.

"I understand," he said after five of the longest seconds of my life. "I understand how you felt. I wanted to burn the world down when your mother died. You thought you'd lost Bressen."

Tears rolled down my cheeks, and I didn't try to stop them. "Instead, I lost you," I said. "I'll never forgive myself."

"Yes, you will," Aramis said. "You'll forgive yourself because I'm asking you to. You'll forgive yourself because *I* forgive you."

I let out a wail and fell to my knees as tears blurred my eyes so badly I couldn't see. Far from being comforting, Aramis's forgiveness was yet another twist of the knife.

No, it was a broadsword in my gut ringed by arrows.

"Cyra," Aramis said, and I sobbed all the harder.

Across the bedroom, the door slammed open as Bressen rushed in with a sword in his hand. He didn't normally wear one around the house, so I could only assume he'd had it stashed in his study somewhere.

He looked around the room wildly, searching for a threat. "Cyra, what's wrong?" he asked when he didn't find one. He rushed to me and dropped to one knee to gather me against him. His other arm still held the sword ready.

"Aramis," I whispered. "He's here."

Bressen's body tensed. "What?"

I pointed to where the spectral form of Aramis stood. Bressen looked, but his eyes darted around as his gaze found nothing solid to land on.

"Cyra, I don't-"

"I summoned him with my spirit anchor power," I said through hiccupping sobs. I held up the butterfly in a trembling hand.

"Oh, Cyra," Bressen said as his arm tightened around my shoulders. He sighed. "Up now." He rose, pulling me with him and holding me up. My feet touched the floor, but to say I was standing would be an overstatement. I wrapped a hand over his shoulder to help steady myself.

I looked back at Aramis, afraid he might be gone, but he stood there patiently.

"I can bring you back," I told Aramis. "I have someone who can recreate your body from this piece of you." I held out the butterfly. "Then you can just...go back in."

"Cyra, no!" Bressen had been trying to focus where I was looking, but his attention snapped back to me. "You can't do that."

"Praya can do it," I told him. "I can convince her. I can-"

"Cyra, I'm not coming back," Aramis said quietly.

I looked at him, not sure I'd heard right.

"What's he saying?" Bressen asked.

I ignored him. "But we didn't get a chance to be a family," I argued. "I know that's my fault, but we have a second chance now. We have-"

"I don't belong here anymore," Aramis interrupted again. His expression told me his heart was breaking as much as mine was right now.

Bressen's mind pressed at mine, a request to let him hear what I was hearing, and I granted it.

"I wish we'd had more time as well," Aramis said. "I wish I could've been more of a father to you. Fate was cruel to you and I in this world, but this isn't goodbye. We'll be reunited again. I promise."

My tears flowed in a torrent. "Please," I sobbed. "Please don't go." I wiped at my nose as mucus joined the tears running down my face.

"You shouldn't call me again," Aramis said. "As much as I love seeing you, this…this is too hard for both of us."

His own voice broke, and that only made me sob harder as I gripped Bressen's jacket so severely my nails would likely tear the fabric.

I jolted as Bressen's sword hit the floor, and he wrapped his other arm around me. He laid his head on top of mine.

"Cyra," he whispered soothingly. "It will be okay."

Aramis smiled sadly. "I always knew I was leaving you in good hands. Tell Lord Bressen I'm grateful you have him to take care of you."

Bressen lifted his head. "Thank you for trusting me with your daughter," he said, proof he could hear Aramis through me. "I hope we meet again in the next world, my friend."

"I don't doubt we will," Aramis said with a smile. He looked at me again. "There's one thing I should tell you before I go."

My breath hitched in ragged gasps, and I tried to get myself under control long enough to listen to Aramis. "What is it?"

"I didn't choose your parents by accident," he said. "The winemaker and his wife. I was drawn to that vineyard when I was looking for someone to take you."

I lifted my head off Bressen's shoulder. Aramis had my full attention.

"As a healer, I can sense other perimortals," he said. "I sensed a half perimortal there. The first one I'd encountered for dozens of miles."

"What?" I asked, my eyes wide now. "Who?"

Aramis had Bressen's full attention as well.

"I couldn't tell for sure if it was your mother or your father without doing an actual examination," Aramis said. "All I know is at least one of your grandparents from that family was perimortal."

My mouth hung slack as my mind struggled to take in this news.

"Could you tell what power it was?" Bressen asked.

"No, and I didn't ask," Aramis answered.

Bressen nodded his understanding.

Aramis looked back to me. "I need to go now, but I'm glad we at least got to say goodbye this time. For now."

I shook my head. "Can't you stay a little longer. Please."

"I can't," he said. "Just know that I love you more than anything, and I'm grateful for the brief time we had together."

Another sob tried to work its way up my throat, but I swallowed it down. There was one thing I had to say before I lost Aramis again.

"I love you," I said to him. The words came out in a rush of air, as if they'd been under pressure, as if I'd finally turned a release valve. I'd held them back so long there was no keeping them in anymore. "I love you so much, and I should've told you long before now. Back when I could've…when I could've hugged you too."

Tears filled my eyes again and ran down my cheeks. It wasn't fair.

My father smiled, and this time it lit his face. "I know," he said. "You didn't need to say it for me to know it. I knew. And I love you too."

More sobs burst free, and I buried my face in Bressen's chest.

"Goodbye, my beautiful little girl," I heard Aramis say, and I pulled my head away from Bressen in time to see Aramis dissolve into nothing.

"No!" I screamed and tried to lunge toward where he'd been, but Bressen held me fast.

"Goodbye, Father," I whispered before I burst into desolate, anguished tears.

Tandem Read: Go to *Clash of Stone and Steel* (Bk 3), Chapter 50-Epilogue

Chapter 40

Cyra slept late into the morning the next day, although I doubted she'd gotten much actual rest.

I'd tried to put her right to bed after Aramis left, but she'd stopped me, and through her tears I was able to make out she wanted a bath first. It was a good idea, since I'd realized as we talked to Phaedrus just how ripe we must smell. Thank the gods the priest was too polite to so much as wrinkle his nose in our presence, and it made me feel all the worse for seizing his mind and threatening to kill him. Cyra was right. Of all the people we could trust, Phaedrus was at the top of that list.

I undressed Cyra and got her into a bath, but she'd been nearly catatonic the whole time. I dressed her and put her to bed before taking my own bath, but I came out of the bathing chamber to find her tossing fitfully in the bed. When she hadn't settled down after thirty minutes, I used my power to quiet her mind and put her into a deep sleep.

I took the sleep compulsion off her in the morning, but she slept another two hours after that. When she finally woke, her eyes still bore the evidence of the crying she'd done last night, but at least she was more responsive than she'd been when I put her to bed.

When she emerged from the closet after dressing, though, I was shocked by the 'accessory' she wore at her neck.

The little demoni she now called Blink sat on her shoulder, its clawed hand resting across her collarbone, and my blood went cold at the sight of the thing. One swipe, and it could open her neck. Indeed, I couldn't help seeing the way it rested its hand there as a threat, and I glared at it, letting my eyes burn with the fire of my anger.

The creature only cocked its head and blinked at me in that alternating way that made me want to shake it.

"Bressen?" Cyra asked when she saw my eyes. "What's wrong?"

"What is that thing doing here again?" I asked.

"It…It just wanted to comfort me, I think," she said.

I blinked at her. Synchronously, unlike the demoni.

"Comfort you?" I asked incredulously. "Demoni don't do comfort."

She shrugged the shoulder not carrying the demoni. "Apparently this one does."

"Go back to Revenmyer," I ordered the thing, but it only wrapped its hand around a lock of Cyra's hair in silent defiance.

"Let it stay," Cyra said. "It's not doing any harm."

That was true enough, but I'd given the creature a direct order, and it hadn't obeyed, which was extremely concerning. Either I was losing control of the demoni, or Cyra's will was starting to supersede my own where they were concerned. Or at least where this one was.

Cyra ate very little at breakfast. She often lost her appetite when she was upset, but I wouldn't worry about it unless it persisted for a few days.

We all returned to Tide's End after breakfast, including Talyn, who'd moved into Samhail's quarters. The assassin had agreed to become my spymaster, although the requirements of the job hadn't sat well with Samhail. He'd laid into me so hard about taking his new wife away from him that I was worried I might have to break into his mind to keep him from beating the shit out of me. Thankfully it hadn't gone that far, but I expected that I might need some extra healing after he and I sparred next.

The first thing Cyra and I did when we got back to the manor was go down to the beach with Morland's body. We hadn't had a chance to deal with it yet, and it was time.

Much to my chagrin, the demoni, which had vanished while we were at breakfast, reappeared on Cyra's shoulder as we headed for the sand.

Praya and Ariel had asked to come with us as well, and they now followed us down to the water under an obfuscation glamour.

I laid Morland's body at the water's edge, and Cyra stepped forward.

She held a hand over him, and the body turned to a pile of sand. We stepped back as the surf swelled, and it only took a few waves before the pile that had once been Morland was leveled like a child's sandcastle under the rising tide. When it was gone, we turned to trudge back up the beach.

"Thank you for your help," Cyra said to Praya as we approached the couple standing up by the dunes.

"I helped fix a flaw in the natural order," Praya said.

I slipped an arm around Cyra's waist and pulled her close to kiss her temple. I often needed to touch her when I was around her, but the urge was particularly strong lately. Likewise, Cyra seemed to crave my touch more now as well. Our separation – though brief – hadn't been good for either of us.

I tried to ignore the demoni on her other shoulder. As long as it didn't hurt her or try to keep me from her, I'd tolerate it for now.

"Now that Morland is dealt with," I said, "we need to figure out what to do about Magdalene. If what Talyn told us is true, Sandrian is just a pawn in this game she's playing."

Ariel took a step closer to Praya, and I had the distinct feeling it was a gesture of protection. I didn't blame her, given that Magdalene had once sent three of the most deadly fighters on the continent after her wife.

"I feel the gods stirring," Praya, said. "Something is changing with the Trinity, and it's because of Magdalene."

"She wants to restore the continental Triumvirate," Cyra said.

Praya shook her head. "Not exactly. She wants to return to a time when syphons ruled the continent, but I don't think she intends to share that power with us, no matter what she told you."

"She wants to take your power for herself," I observed.

"We've been taught to view the Trinity almost as one entity in three beings, but they're more fractured than one might think," Praya said. "The gods don't get along perfectly, and there are times when one will grow more powerful until the others do something to restore the balance."

"The Protector must be working through Magdalene to gather

power," I said. Cyra nodded, but Praya seemed to purse her lips.

"I think there's something you should see," Cyra told Praya. "I know you don't want anyone to know you're here, but you should meet one of our priests. He's been integral in helping us learn about syphons and their role as Hands of the Gods." She paused. "Although clearly you knew most of this already. In any case, he recently translated a section of a very ancient text that contains an old prophesy in verse form. My seeker magic told me it's important."

Praya looked wary. "Can we see the text without meeting the priest?"

"I suppose," I said. "But I can vouch for Phaedrus. He won't tell a soul he's seen you." I decided to leave out that Phaedrus already knew Praya was alive.

"Let me consider it," Praya said.

The four of us began to walk back toward the manor, but we hadn't gotten far when a message leaf appeared in front of Cyra, and she plucked it out of the air.

The note was short and looked hastily scribbled.

Cyra's face lost all color when she read it, and I felt her spike of terror.

"What is it?" I asked urgently.

"It's from Jaylan," she said, her panic rising. "They're being attacked."

Cyra

My first portal was to the vineyard. I was certain the townspeople must be there trying to finish what they started, but there wasn't a soul to be found when we arrived.

I called my brothers' names until I was hoarse while Samhail and the twins took to the sky to look for them among the vines, but no one answered. Talyn went to check the ruins of the barns, but Bressen said he couldn't sense anyone around.

That only meant that there was no one *alive* on the grounds.

A thorough search of the house yielded nothing, but that was more of a relief given Bressen's news. I'd just stepped outside again when Surgeon landed in front of me.

"The village looks deserted as well," he reported, "except for one person. I saw someone from the air, but I didn't go down close enough to see who it was."

One person. The news was a double-edged sword. My heart lurched with premature relief that it might be one of my brothers, even as the stab in my stomach reminded me it could only be *one* of my brothers.

I drew a new portal into the center of town and dashed through it, Jaylan and Brix's names already past my lips before I fully emerged. I looked around frantically, but Surgeon was right. The entire place was empty of men, women, and children alike.

Jaylan had said they were being attacked, and I'd assumed the townspeople had been the aggressors, but it looked as though the whole town had been targeted…

Rage replaced fear as I strained my powers to find anyone still alive. As if summoned by that rage, Blink settled on my shoulder.

The Nemesis knew there were certain people in Fernweh I wouldn't shed a tear over, but there had also been people here I'd been friendly with, if not friends. Rodrick and Maeve at the very least. Pella the baker had always been kind to me as well, and her little boy was only three. If Magdalene had killed them, I'd make her pay.

I spotted the figure Surgeon had mentioned sitting on the stairs of the general store at the same time Bressen did. Was it…?

I broke into a run just as Bressen grabbed for my arm.

"Cyra! Wait!" he called after me, but every step I took closer to the figure made me all the more certain I knew who it was.

"Brix!" I called. Thank the gods! Brix was alive.

I was nearly to my brother when a steely arm wrapped around my waist and yanked me backward.

"Cyra, no!" Bressen hissed in my ear as he dragged me back.

"Let go! It's Brix!" I said as I tugged at his arm.

In the back of my mind, I felt like I was forgetting something, but I was too anxious to get to Brix to think of what it was. On my shoulder, Blink hissed at Bressen, but Bressen swiped at the creature, and it dissolved into smoke. It reappeared on my other shoulder, but he swiped it away again, and it stayed gone this time.

"Bressen, it's Brix!" I said again as I tried to free myself. "Let me go!"

"Cyra, I can't sense his mind!" Bressen yelled as he held me fast.

I went still in his arms as all the blood seemed to empty from my body. His hold tightened on me as my legs went numb, and I sagged in his arms. I wanted to deny the words, but I felt in my own mind the void where Brix's consciousness should be.

Brix hadn't yet risen from where he sat. He didn't come to greet me, to hug me, to explain what happened.

"No." The word escaped my throat as a croak.

"I'm sorry, Cyra," Bressen breathed against my ear as he held me against him. "I'm so sorry."

I was only distantly aware Samhail, Talyn, and the twins had come up behind us as Brix finally lifted his eyes to meet mine.

"Brix," I said, his name a sob.

"Cyra," Brix said, and his voice was sad.

"Brix, what happened? Where's Jaylan?" I asked.

Bressen still held me, and I was grateful now because my legs wouldn't hold me.

"Jaylan's gone," he said. Then he clarified, "They took him. They took everyone in the village. The woman, Magdalene, I think she said her name was? She left me here and told me to tell you what happened."

I let out another sob and lurched against Bressen's hold, but he pulled me back. My hands shook violently where I gripped his forearms as he held me around the waist.

"W-what did happen?" I managed to ask, but I already knew. If anger and rage strengthened my powers, then abject terror and grief must numb them, because I felt nothing inside.

"Jaylan and I came into town to get supplies," Brix explained. "We were only here a few minutes when they attacked. At least a hundred of those…those things you told us about. The sym…sym…"

"Symbionts," I whispered. "Brix, did they…are you…?"

I couldn't bring myself to ask the question as my insides twisted violently. Bile rose up my throat, but I swallowed it back down.

Cyra, we'll figure something out. We'll find a way to help them, Bressen said into my mind.

The unease in his voice rang as clearly as if he'd spoken aloud. Not unease at what Magdalene had done, but unease – fear – over my reaction to this latest blow. He was afraid of what I might do. Afraid of what *he* might have to do.

"They took everyone, including Jaylan," Brix went on, still sitting on the steps, his elbows on his knees. "I tried to stop them, Cyra. I swear I tried, but I couldn't do anything."

I shook my head. "It's not your fault," I whispered. "There was nothing you could do." My eyes filled with tears, and I pulled at Bressen's hold, but he held me fast.

"Brix," Bressen said softly. "Did…they turn you?"

We both knew they had. We couldn't sense Brix's mind, but Bressen wanted to be sure.

Brix's gaze landed on Bressen for the first time, and the fear in his eyes nearly broke me.

"I feel it inside me," Brix said, his voice shaking. "I feel it trying to control me. I can't stop it." The words were desperate now.

Brix stood finally and turned to us. He had something in his hand that had been facing away from us, and I looked down to see what it was.

"Dagger!" Serise shouted, recognizing the object just as I did.

I sensed movement behind me as the assassin and the three gargoyles all reacted to the weapon.

"No!" I yelled. "Don't hurt him!"

Brix raised his eyes to meet mine, and there was apology in them.

"Magdalene," he said. "She told me there was no way to kill the symbiont, this thing inside me, without killing its host. She said...she said you'd have to kill me." He raised the dagger to look at it. "Or she said I could do it myself so you wouldn't have to."

My entire body trembled as the agonizing choice Magdalene had given Brix settled over me like a shroud.

Magdalene wanted to break me. Everything she'd done since I'd met her was designed to gut me, to rip away at my humanity until I became the agent of destruction she'd seen. The monster that would kill thousands for her.

She might've finally found the thing to push me over as I stood faced with the idea of having to either kill my brother or watch him kill himself.

Brix raised the dagger. "I'm...I'm sorry, Cyra."

"No!" I screamed. I fought Bressen's hold with everything I had then. I felt him in my mind doing...something. Trying to calm me? I didn't know, and it didn't matter. The only thing that mattered now was getting to Brix before he stabbed himself.

"Someone get the dagger away from him!" Bressen yelled as he struggled to hold me.

Talyn ported a few feet in front of Brix, but when she tried to move forward, something pushed her back.

"There's a forcefield or some kind of warding!" she yelled as she turned to face us. "I can't get through."

Samhail surged forward, one of his swords in hand. He tried to slash the blade in front of Brix, but it glanced off something invisible. He tried punching forward, but he grunted in pain as his hand stopped dead a couple feet from Brix.

"I can't get through either," he said urgently.

Brix had looked momentarily hopeful, but resignation overtook him at the confirmation no one could get to him.

No, not no one. Instinctively, I knew I was the only one who'd be able to get through whatever warding Magdalene had put up around Brix.

I tried to push toward him again, but Bressen still held me fast.

"Let me go!" I yelled. "I can get to him. The warding will let me through. I know it!"

Bressen moved one arm higher so he held me across my shoulders. "I know it will let you through," he said, pulling me back so his lips were close to my ear. "It's what Magdalene wants, but you know he'll turn as soon as you get close, and once you're inside the warding, we won't be able to get to you."

"I don't care! I can help him! Let me go!"

"No," Bressen said. "I can't."

Brix's entire body seized then, and his eyes widened in terror. I watched, my own terror burning through me like wildfire, as the dark blue symbiont shell began to creep over his skin.

I'd seen the shells overtake their victims before, but the change was usually fast, often starting from the head or the back as the symbiont seeped quickly over the body.

Not so with Brix. The symbiont took its time now. It started at his feet and crawled slowly up his body as if savoring the look of horror on my face and the dread on Brix's. As if it wanted to prolong our agony. As if it had been instructed to make this as appalling as possible.

Brix looked at the dagger in his hand and then at me. I saw the intent in his eyes.

"No!" I screamed as I fought fruitlessly against Bressen's hold. "Brix, don't you dare! We'll find a way to save you! Please!"

Tears streamed down my face as I tried desperately to get to my brother. The shell had reached his waist, and, ironically, I willed it to go faster, to cover him over so he wouldn't be able to hurt himself. We'd figure out how to get the thing out of him later.

Samhail, Talyn, and the twins were all trying now to get through Magdalene's warding, but a pulse of power sent them flying backward onto the ground.

The symbiotic shell was at the base of Brix's neck now, and the dagger he held inched toward his throat.

"No!" I screamed as Brix tried to raise his chin above the rising skin, like a drowning man struggling to keep his head above the waves. "Brix, don't! Please!" I begged him with everything I had. I could see he didn't want to stab himself, but I didn't trust that he wouldn't.

I needed to break Bressen's hold! I needed to…to port.

My anger flared as I realized Bressen wasn't trying to calm me. He'd been trying to make me forget I could port, that I could get away.

"Cyra, no!" Bressen shouted as I ported out of his arms and through Magdalene's warding. "Cyra! Get out of there!"

I was directly in front of Brix as my eyes met my brother's. I grabbed his wrist with both hands as the blue shell crept up his chin, and I tried with all my might to hold it back. I no longer had Maziren's strength, but I had Samhail's forcefields, and I sent a concentrated field to push his hand away. To my relief, the dagger came loose from his grasp, but it was a small victory. The shell was up to Brix's lips now, and there was nothing I could do to stop it.

"Cyra, I love you," Brix said before the skin closed over his mouth, leaving nothing but smooth blue shell there.

I watched helplessly as the shell finished its lazy crawl up Brix's body to cover his terrified eyes, leaving those glowing yellow pits all the symbionts had. I heard Bressen behind me trying to get through the warding, but he sounded distant, as if my ears were stuffed with cotton.

Then Brix was gone, and I was standing in front of a creature that was no longer my brother. No longer even human.

I couldn't catch my breath as the symbiont and I stared at each other. For several heart-stopping seconds, I dared to think that nothing had changed, that Brix was still there beneath that blue skin, fighting the creature's control.

Then the creature let out an ear-piercing screech, and I felt white-hot pain across my shoulder as it slashed me with its claws. I screamed and grabbed the wound as I stumbled backward. I looked down at the tattered shreds of my dress. Months ago, a bear had slashed my shoulder open, and I now had a matching set of claw marks on the opposite side.

"Cyra! Get out of there!" Bressen screamed at me from outside the warding, but he still sounded muffled.

I lifted my hand. It was covered in blood, and it shook violently as I held it in front of me.

I'd once seen a villager in Fernweh snap the tendon in the back of his ankle. His foot had gone limp, and his calf muscle pulled up his lower leg as neither part had that critical piece holding them together anymore. Something in me snapped like that now, as if the last thread holding me together had just let go.

A primal scream erupted from deep within me. The world went red, and my power exploded, sending everyone around me – Bressen, the gargoyles, Talyn, and Brix – all flying backward to sprawl on the ground. I felt Blink materialize on my shoulder again as his sharp little claws dug into my flesh, and I welcomed the bite of them on my skin.

A heavy weight settled on my back then as voluminous shapes stretched behind me, and it suddenly felt as if someone had turned all my senses up. My ears rang with the din of every little scrape of a boot or heavy breath as the others rose. My blood thrummed through my veins, and I squinted as everything seemed brighter. I felt every fine hair on my arm as the air brushed against them.

The sensitivity lasted a few seconds before everything returned to normal. Everything but the weight tugging at my back.

On my shoulder, Blink made a soft clicking noise, and I wondered if it was the creature's version of a purr.

"Cyra…" Bressen's voice was full of awe as he picked himself up from the ground. His eyes were wide with shock.

I looked to either side of me to see what had drawn his attention.

Huge wings of deep crimson feathers extended out from behind my shoulders, sleek and beautiful like Bressen's black ones. Their color seemed to shift in the light from the bright ruby of newly spilled blood, to the deep burgundy of red wine, to the black of endless nothingness.

"Cyra, you're…you're an angelus," Bressen said with the same mix of awe and dread as before.

But he was wrong.

"No," I said. "I'm not an angelus. I'm…"

I flexed the wings behind me. They felt foreign, and the muscles in my back and shoulders protested the added weight. I let the wings beat once, my body instinctively knowing how to make them work.

"I'm not an angelus," I said again.

I paused to be sure the words felt right before I spoke.

"I'm the Nemesis Incarnate."

Epilogue I

Aidan drummed his fingers on the table, watching each one fall in succession. He savored the feel of control as he first let them drop slowly, deliberately, then drummed them faster so they tapped out a dull staccato on the polished surface. It was only days ago that something as simple as drumming his own fingers hadn't been possible. They'd been part of his body, but they'd been Morland's to command.

"Lord Aidan?"

Aidan's head snapped up, and his eyes met his steward's. Loreleigh eyed him warily, as if she expected him to snap at her. It was a perfectly reasonable reaction considering how he'd treated her recently. No…how Morland had treated her.

Aidan had quite a few women in positions of authority on his staff, including Loreleigh and Maziren, and it had quickly become apparent over the last several weeks that Morland had little respect for women in general, and even less for women of high rank. Aidan had been forced to watch Morland dismiss, demean, and degrade – or worse – several of the women in his household without being able to do anything.

The man who'd held his body and mind hostage was now dead – Nemesis damn him to the tortures of the lowest hell – but Aidan was still dealing with the fallout from Morland's behavior, and likely would be for some time.

"I'm sorry, what did you say?" Aidan asked. "My head is still a bit foggy from my illness."

The steward looked a bit taken aback at his apology, and Aidan knew she didn't know what to make of the radical changes in his demeanor lately. He'd gone from a level-headed lord who considered advice from anyone, to a mean-spirited and even cruel ruler who snapped at those around him, and then back again.

When he'd been imprisoned in the dungeons at the Citadel after Bressen had finally discovered Morland, the staff at the palace had been told he'd taken ill from something the healers couldn't help with. They'd only seen 'him' briefly the couple times the assassin had come to Seatherny and walked the grounds in his form simply to stave off rumors something had happened. He didn't know much about the woman, Talyn, but he was grateful to her for that at least.

Now came the work of rebuilding the relationships with his people that Morland had destroyed. Especially the relationship with his husband.

Pain stabbed through Aidan as he thought of what Jasper had endured while Morland had been in charge of his body, and he shuddered. He couldn't dwell on that now, though.

"You were saying something about the training camps?" Aidan asked.

"Yes, my lord," Loreleigh said. "They'll be set up and ready for troops in a week or so. Samhail will be here tomorrow to speak with you and the generals about how Hiraeth's camps are running."

Aidan nodded and glanced to the side where Maziren stood sentinel, ever-ready to defend him. She'd always stayed close to him before, but she seemed to be a couple feet closer now. He knew she felt like she'd failed by letting Morland get to him, but there was nothing she could've done. Not that he could make her see that.

Not that he could fully convince himself of that either. Until recently, his faith that Maziren could fight any threat had been unwavering, but she'd been powerless to fight Morland. An irrational part of him couldn't help blaming her, if only to keep from taking on all the blame himself.

Ever in tune with him, Maziren tipped her head toward Aidan as he looked at her, and their eyes met. He saw the question in them. Did he need something from her?

Not unless she could somehow erase the last few weeks from his memory and from those around him.

He suppressed a grim smile. Bressen could probably do just that if he asked the lord. Make him forget. Make them all forget. But that somehow seemed wrong. It was also the easy way out, and Aidan was determined to earn his way back into his people's good graces.

"That sounds good," Aidan told Loreleigh, turning back to her. "Is that all?"

The steward hesitated, and he knew it wasn't. Jasper and Maziren had managed to keep the city and the territory running well enough while he'd been gone, but there were things only the Lord of Derridan could handle, and those things had piled up.

"Nothing that can't wait until tomorrow, my lord," Loreleigh said.

It was a lie, but he was grateful for it. He wasn't in a state of mind to deal with any of this right now.

"Tomorrow then," Aidan said as he stood.

"Just one more thing," the steward added, standing with him. "Lord Bressen asked to meet with you at nine to discuss the succession in Polaris. He has a proposal that needs your approval."

"Very well," Aidan said. "Send him a confirmation please."

Loreleigh bowed her head. "Yes, my lord."

Aidan turned and strode out the door. He sensed Maziren behind him, and he wasn't sure if he found her presence comforting or grating.

She'd been in his service for nearly thirty-five years now, well before he'd become a Lord of the Triumvirate. Most of the time he noticed her about as much as he noticed his own shadow, which wasn't to say he took her for granted. He just always trusted her to be there without having to confirm she was.

Strictly speaking, Maziren had been in his father's service first. She'd been hired to protect Aidan from his father's enemies, although less out of love than out of a need to keep rivals from having leverage over his father. His father's business dealings had been incredibly lucrative for the family, making them powerful among Derridan's nobility, but those dealings hadn't always been especially legal.

Aidan had kept Maziren on as his personal guard even after his father had died and Aidan had dismantled the more unsavory side of his family's business empire. She was usually laconic, her tongue sharp when she did use it, yet somehow Aidan had grown close to the woman who fought ruthlessly whenever he was threatened. As luck would have it, he'd eventually been able to offer her a position more befitting her talents, that of Captain of the Guard and bodyguard to a Lord of the Triumvirate.

Aidan headed straight for his bedroom, Maziren's light footfalls drowned out by his own heavier ones.

He spent an inordinate amount of time in bed lately. Not sleeping. Just in bed. At times he was afraid of sleep because when he dreamt, he found himself shoved back down into the dark recesses of his own mind, forced to watch Morland do awful things to those he cared for, to those he'd sworn to protect.

He still remembered waking that first time in the temple. He'd known immediately something was wrong, but it had taken him a moment to realize he no longer had control of his own body. Then it had suddenly felt like someone pushed his head underwater, and he fought back with everything he had against whatever was trying to kill him.

It was only later he'd learned it was Morland in his head, that the man had tried – but failed – to kill his consciousness. Instead, Morland had at least succeeded in pushing Aidan down into a deep pit in his own mind, one from which he'd been unable to claw his way up.

Aidan was lost in thought again as he rounded a corner, but he pulled up short as he almost ran into someone. The servant gasped and went paler than he'd ever seen a person go. He reached a hand out instinctively to steady her, but she flinched back violently and dropped her head.

Aidan pulled his hand back and clenched it into a fist at his side, not in anger at her, but at himself.

Evory was the girl's name. He knew the names of all the servants who worked in the palace, and he knew why the sight of him sent terror through her. She was the one he…the one Morland had cornered in the library. Jasper had caught him – Morland – pinning the girl against the shelves as he shoved his hand up her skirt.

Evory had actually been lucky. Jasper had arrived before anything had happened. The girl Morland had stalked, raped, and killed later that night hadn't been as fortunate.

Aidan shuddered as he remembered his body doing things to the girl he couldn't stop, things that now woke him in the middle of the night in a cold sweat. He looked down at his hands, hands that had wrapped around that second girl's throat and choked her to death before he'd hidden her body in a crate in one of the nearby warehouses. He still remembered the feel of her pulse jumping wildly beneath his fingers, like a small animal struggling to nose its way free of his hold, while she herself fought frantically against him in a losing battle.

He looked back at Evory, who stood trembling before him. He was surprised she still worked here, that she hadn't resigned, but he supposed she must not have a choice.

"Evory," he said, his mouth dry. "I…I need to apologize for what I did the other day."

Evory's head snapped up, her eyes wide with fear. Far from being relieved, she looked even more terrified.

"I was sick," Aidan tried to explain. "It made me do things I shouldn't have done. I'm sorry if I hurt you."

The girl's breath stuttered, and she nodded, but he could tell his words did nothing to help.

Aidan sighed, knowing she just wanted to be out of his presence. "Go on now," he said, and Evory scurried around him to rush down the hall before he could change his mind. Part of him had hoped the apology might ease her fear, but he wasn't at all surprised it didn't.

Aidan looked back at Maziren, and, as usual, an understanding passed between them. She gave him a sympathetic look but didn't say anything.

She'd gone back with him recently to the warehouse where Morland had stashed the other girl's body. He hadn't expected the body to still be there, but it was, rotting and nearly unrecognizable now in its box.

He'd debated leaving the body somewhere to be found in the hopes someone might recognize the girl and let her family know what happened, but the body had been in a bad state, decomposed and feasted on by rats. Instead, he'd used his transfiguration power to transform the girl into several yards of beautiful silk, adorned with an intricate design, that he'd then buried in the cemetery and marked with a large rock.

It was all he could think to do, to give the girl a proper burial at least. Maziren had helped him dig the grave. It wasn't the first body she'd helped him bury, but he hoped it might be the last. Either way, he knew she'd take the secret to her own grave.

Maziren was the only one he'd told about the girl. He hadn't even told Jasper. He couldn't bear to see the look on Jasper's face if he admitted what he'd done…what his body and hands had done. He could tell it was hard enough for his husband to reconcile the incident with Evory, let alone what he'd…what Morland had done to the girl.

No, he would never, ever tell Jasper about the girl.

Aidan walked on. His bedroom wasn't much farther, and he was desperate to get there, to be able to lock himself in the solitude of his room. Finally, they reached it, and Maziren stepped in front of him to open the door and look inside.

"My lord, the lord consort is here," she said softly.

Aidan's chest tightened, partially in joy and partially with anxiety. He was glad Jasper was there, but Morland had damaged that relationship as well, and – despite his and Jasper's best efforts – rebuilding had been slow.

"Take your leave," he said to Maziren as he moved past her into the room. She'd stand outside the door all night if he didn't make her go. He wasn't sure what he'd done to deserve such fierce loyalty from her, but he'd long ago resolved to deserve it.

"My lord-"

"I'll call if I need you," he assured her.

She hesitated, then nodded and strode back down the hall.

Aidan steeled himself and went into his bedchamber to face Jasper. Interactions with his husband had been hit-or-miss lately. Aidan knew Jasper was trying his best to get their relationship back to where it had been before Morland, but Jasper occasionally had bad days where he could barely stand to look at Aidan, and Aidan didn't blame him. He was at least grateful Jasper remained in their quarters, that they still slept in the same bed together, even if Jasper slept as far on the other side as he could.

"Jasper?" Aidan said as he walked carefully to where his consort sat in a window alcove staring out over the city.

Jasper jumped but forced a small smile as he saw Aidan.

"Done with Loreleigh so soon?" Jasper asked, rising from the seat and coming to stand in front of Aidan. "I didn't expect you for another hour."

Aidan tried not to read into that, tried not to decide if there was disappointment in Jasper's voice that he was back so soon.

"We made it through some of the more important business," he said, "but Loreleigh had pity on me and let me go early. I have a full schedule of important meetings tomorrow with Bressen and Samhail, so I think she was giving me time to rest up and prepare."

Part of Aidan wished he could just tell people what had happened, that it hadn't really been him terrorizing them the last few weeks, but Bressen had advised against that, and Aidan understood why. Letting news get out that one of the Lords of the Triumvirate had been compromised by their enemies – his body literally taken over – would send panic through the country and would call into question everything Aidan had done in the past and would do in the future. Unfortunately, their best option was to stick with the story that Aidan had contracted some kind of rare illness that had warped his mind for a few weeks.

"What are you doing in here?" Aidan asked. Jasper had a host of projects and causes he was involved in throughout Seatherny, so it was rare to find him in their room in the middle of the day.

The smile Jasper tried to pull onto his face failed after two attempts. "I just needed some peace and quiet for a little while," he said.

Aidan reached out instinctively, perhaps to take Jasper's hand or touch his face, but he froze as the lord consort flinched back from him. Pain stabbed through Aidan, even as Jasper's eyes widened in horror.

"Aidan, I'm sorry," Jasper assured him quickly. "I'd didn't mean-"

Aidan held up his hands to stop his husband's apology, then swore inwardly as Jasper's eyes flew straight to them. He pulled them back but didn't lower them as he too looked at them. An image flashed in his mind of his hand on the back of Jasper's neck as he pushed Jasper's face hard into a pillow while he – while Morland – fucked him.

Bile rose in Aidan's throat, and it was all he could do to swallow it back down as he turned and hurried toward the bathing chamber, praying he didn't vomit before he got to the toilet.

"Aidan!" Jasper's panicked voice followed him across the room.

Aidan made it to the doorway of the bathing chamber but stopped, leaning in the frame.

"Aidan, are you alright?" Jasper asked, genuine concern in his voice.

Undeserved concern, something cruel in him insisted. He should've been able to stop Morland. He should've been able to push the man out, to protect those that depended on him.

His nausea had subsided for the moment, and Aidan looked at his hand that gripped the doorframe, his knuckles nearly white from the strength of his hold. He hadn't had control of his hands for weeks, and these hands had wrought so much pain and suffering in that short time.

Before he could stop himself, Aidan grabbed the handle of the door and slammed it closed as hard as he could on his hand in the frame. He screamed as sharp, stabbing pain shot through his palm and all the way up his arm. He felt something crunch in the hand, but whether he'd broken bones or not, he wasn't sure.

"Aidan!" Jasper's cry of shock was lost under Aidan's own wail of agony as he pulled the hand back from the door jam and sunk to his knees.

"Aidan, what in the three hells are you doing?" Jasper asked.

Aidan flinched as Jasper's strong arms came around him. Jasper pulled him close, but the throbbing pain in Aidan's hand kept him from savoring the feel of his husband's touch, the first real touch in days. Aidan wanted to melt into Jasper's warmth, to enjoy the press of their bodies against each other, but the ache in his hand and the mental sting of unworthiness only made his skin feel raw against Jasper's embrace. He resisted the urge to pull away and instead leaned in further despite the discomfort.

"I…I," Aidan tried to explain, but words eluded him. How could he explain that he'd wanted to punish his hands for what they'd done? As if they weren't a part of him. As if they'd somehow been acting of their own accord these last few weeks.

"I'll call a healer," Jasper said, starting to rise from his crouch.

Aidan grabbed his forearm, and he was so relieved Jasper didn't recoil away that he almost forgot the pain in his hand. "Wait, not yet," he said.

"Aidan, don't be ridiculous," Jasper insisted. "We need to get a healer in here in case you broke something."

"Not yet," Aidan whispered as he fell back to sit on the floor. He cradled the injured hand against his chest as he flexed the other one. Could he ever forgive these hands for what they'd done? Could Jasper?

Aidan jumped again as Jasper's own hand appeared before him, and his husband threaded his fingers through those of Aidan's uninjured hand.

"I know what you were trying to do," Jasper whispered, "but that's not the way you fix this."

Aidan looked up at him. "How do I fix it then?" he asked.

"You don't," Jasper said. "*We* do. We do it together, the way we've always done. It will take some time, but we'll get there."

Aidan let his head fall back against Jasper's shoulder. "I have nightmares," he said.

"I know," Jasper said. "I've woken a couple times when you had them. I stroke your hair when you do, and it usually calms you down."

Aidan furrowed his brow. He'd jolted awake a few times from the nightmares, but Jasper had always remained asleep on the other side of the bed. Yet there'd been other times when the nightmares had simply faded and given way to oblivion. Had those times been Jasper's doing?

Aidan looked down at his hand where Jasper clasped it in his. "I'm sorry. I'm so sorry," he whispered.

Jasper shushed him gently. "It wasn't you. I know that. It's just going to take my body a while to get the message. Please be patient with me."

Aidan nodded against Jasper's chest. There were several other people who would need the same leeway, not the least of which was Bressen's new assassin, although Bressen assured Aidan he wasn't employing Talyn in that capacity. Still, he remembered Morland, in his body, telling the woman in great detail what he'd done to her sister. He wouldn't be at all shocked to find her standing over him one of these nights, dagger poised to slit his throat.

"Do you promise to forgive me one of these days?" Aidan asked.

"There's nothing to forgive," Jasper said firmly. "Now let me call a healer for that hand."

Aidan nodded again, and Jasper slowly pulled away from him, untwining their fingers so he could go find a message leaf.

Aidan sat on the floor looking at his hands. One already had the makings of a large bruise, and it was bleeding from a cut across the palm. The pain had dulled to a pulsing ache, but the fingers didn't move easily when he tried to flex them. The other hand, just as guilty as the first, was unblemished and felt fine, although Aidan could still feel the ghost of Jasper's touch on it.

The healer would be here soon, and when she was done, the first hand would be good as new, with no scar or pain to mark what had happened.

Would that his soul were so lucky.

Epilogue II

Raina

Raina stepped through the portal at Tide's End and smiled at Cyra. Her friend stood waiting for her, and Raina was relieved to see Cyra's eyes were back to their usual silver, not red like they'd been a couple days ago.

True to her word, Cyra had arranged to meet with Raina earlier in the week to keep her abreast of important events. Unfortunately, the news hadn't been good, and Raina was horrified to learn Cyra's brothers had been turned into symbionts, the creatures they'd fought at the gambling den. Brix was currently locked in a holding cell under Tide's End where Cyra visited him daily, but Jaylan had been taken by Magdalene.

Raina shivered to recall what Cyra had looked like when she'd seen her last. Cyra's eyes had kept a steady red glow, and her expression was harder than Raina had ever seen it. She'd been distant, cold.

Cyra apparently also had wings now, which she'd shown Raina. They were giant feathered red ones that stretched out from her back, although those were gone for the moment now too.

Raina stepped forward and threw her arms around Cyra. Her friend hugged her back, but the embrace was reluctant, not as warm as they usually shared.

"I'm glad you reached out," Raina said. "I've been worried."

"Thank you, but I'm fine," Cyra said, her smile forced.

"And how is Brix?" Raina asked.

Cyra's smile fell. "No better. I visit him early in the morning when he's still asleep because once he wakes, I only have about a minute to talk to him before the symbiont takes over. Apparently caronium has no effect on the creatures."

Raina gave her a sympathetic look. "Well, I'm here now if you need to talk or need something to take your mind off-”

“Actually, I asked you to come because there are some important things we need to discuss with you,” Cyra interrupted.

Raina frowned. *We?*

It was only then she noticed they weren’t in the great room or Cyra’s bedroom where they usually met. They were in Bressen’s study.

Raina finally saw the lord sitting patiently behind his desk with one leg crossed over the other.

Raina’s head snapped back to Cyra. “What’s going on?”

Cyra gave her a tight smile. “Bressen and I have some things we need to discuss with you,” she repeated.

Raina recalled the message Cyra had sent her. *“Can you come to Tide’s End today?”* She’d assumed it was a social invitation, but apparently not.

“What is it?” Raina asked.

“Why don’t you take a seat,” Bressen suggested, gesturing to one of the two chairs across the desk from him.

“I’ll stand,” Raina said.

“Raina, please,” Cyra said as she sat down in the other chair.

Raina clenched her jaw but dropped into a chair.

Cyra and Bressen exchanged a quick glance, and Raina growled. “Just tell me!” she said. “Come out with whatever it is you need to say.”

Cyra’s face turned to resolve. “We’re hoping the first part of our news will be good,” she said.

Raina raised a brow. “But you’re not sure if it is?”

“That will depend entirely on how you take the conditions,” she said.

Raina opened her mouth to ask what she meant, but Bressen cut in.

“I’ve been negotiating with the High Council for a few weeks now for a way to officially make you part of the Triumvirate,” he said.

Raina’s mouth fell open.

“The council’s been dragging their feet long enough in selecting a new ruler of Polaris,” he went on, “and with war imminent, we need the Triumvirate at full strength. I convinced the council, with Aidan’s support, that it was time for them to cede control."

"And…they agreed to cede it to me?" Raina ventured.

"Yes," he confirmed, "Although you weren't their first choice, nor probably their second."

Raina furrowed her brows. "Then why are they giving me power?"

"Because you were *my* first choice," Bressen said, "and I'm good at making people see things my way."

Raina's brows shot up. "You took over their minds?"

"Nothing that extreme," he said. "But I can be…persuasive."

Raina nodded absently. Bressen didn't make a habit of hurting people, but he was still extremely powerful, and together with Cyra, people tended to want to remain on their good sides.

Raina frowned as she remembered what Bressen had said.

"Why would I be your first choice?" she asked him. "Do you think you'll control me? That I'll just go along with whatever you say because I'll be grateful to you?" She crossed her arms and leaned back defiantly.

"Raina," Cyra started to admonish her, but Bressen cut in.

"Actually," he said, "you're my choice because I know you *won't* just go along with what I say. But I also think you won't go against me just because you can. You're smart, you're fearless, and I've seen enough to know that you have a good head for politics."

Raina blinked. She hadn't expected the compliment.

"Thank you, my lord," she said hesitantly, uncrossing her arms.

Bressen scoffed and waved a dismissive hand. "You haven't called me 'my lord' in months. Don't restart now, or I'll take back everything I said."

"Fine," Raina said, "but what about being only half perimortal and illegitimate?"

Bressen shrugged. "Ursan was a powerful perimortal, and he must've passed at least some of that on to you. Your powers are probably on par with those perimortals of average abilities, and your lifespan will likely be closer to that of a perimortal than a mortal."

Raina winced at the mention of her lifespan, but Bressen didn't notice.

"Ursan was also generally well-liked in Polaris," he went on, "so we're banking that people will accept you more willingly than someone they don't know. To be honest, the field of contenders is a bit sparse."

"Yet the High Council still would've chosen someone else over me?"

Bressen nodded. "They were hoping to maintain at least some power, but you've been gradually chipping away at their authority. They were looking for someone they could control." He smiled at her. "And as you've said, that's not you."

"So how did you manage to convince them to let me ascend?" Raina asked, still not quite believing this might happen. Then she remembered what Cyra had said. "There are conditions. What are the conditions?"

To her surprise, Bressen actually looked down, not meeting her eyes.

Raina turned to Cyra. "What are the conditions?"

"There's really just one condition," Cyra said, "and it's meant to strengthen your position as much as possible."

"What is it?" Raina asked, suddenly wary.

"You have to understand-," Cyra began, but Raina slammed her hand down on Bressen's desk.

"What is it?" she repeated.

Cyra exhaled. "You need to accept a betrothal to a Prince of Kern."

Raina's jaw went slack. "Say that again," she said after a few seconds. "I can't have heard you correctly."

Cyra threw an angry glance at Bressen. It was a rare show of tension between her and the lord, and Raina wondered about the reason for it.

"You heard me exactly right," Cyra said with a resigned sigh. "As a condition of making you a Triumvirate Lady and the ruler of Polaris, the High Council stipulated that you marry a Kernish prince."

Raina was silent as she struggled to wrap her mind around this. They were going to make her...get married?

She barked out a laugh as the ridiculousness of it all sunk in. "How many Kernish princes are there? Do I get my choice?"

Cyra looked to Bressen.

"There are three Princes of Kern," Bressen said, "but I'm afraid you don't get a choice. It's the third or nothing. The first prince, the eldest, will inherit the Kernish throne, so he isn't available. The second prince will inherit the throne if – gods forbid – something happens to the first. The heir and the spare, so to speak. The youngest prince was the one Kern was willing to part with. Since he has no claim to anything, being the consort to a Triumvirate Lady will actually be a step up for him, which is one of the reasons Kern agreed to this alliance."

And there it was.

"Alliance," Raina said. She nodded her head knowingly. "That's why you arranged this. Not because you really wanted me to ascend to the Triumvirate but because we need allies in this war you expect, and one of the best ways to make easy allies is through marriage."

To her irritation, Bressen smiled. "As I said, you're a smart woman."

"Bressen," Cyra reproached him, but she didn't offer any denial.

"So I have no choice in this," Raina said.

"Of course you have a choice," Bressen said, leaning forward. "You can accept both, or you can refuse both. You don't have to get married, but if you choose not to, then you give up the Triumvirate seat as well."

"And what happens to me if I refuse both? Do I go back to being a servant?" Raina asked. She turned to Cyra with a scornful look. "I hear you have an opening for a new lady's maid again."

Cyra's grin had a hard edge. "After you've been living in a palace with servants of your own? Not a chance. I'll end up helping you get dressed and bathed instead of the other way around."

"So then what? They kick me out and I fend for myself?" Raina asked.

She hated to give up the luxury and comfort she'd grown accustomed to, but she could go back to working if she had to. She'd been taking care of herself for a while now. She could do it again.

"You'd have to leave the palace," Bressen said, "but you're still Ursan's daughter. The High Council would set you up somewhere comfortable, and you'd still have the inheritance Ursan left you. You don't have to work if you don't want to. You just wouldn't be a ruler."

"And they'd be fine with me living in peace? The person who eventually ascends the seat won't see me as a threat and send assassins after me?" Raina crossed her arms again. "Talyn would tell me if anyone approached her with a job, right?"

It didn't ease her mind that Bressen took a couple seconds to answer.

"If you don't accept the appointment, I can't guarantee anything," he said finally, "but you know Cyra and I will do everything in our power to make sure you're safe. As for Talyn, she works for me now, so rest assured you're safe on that count."

"But it would make your life easier if I just accept this arrangement," Raina said to him.

"It will make everyone's life easier, including yours," Cyra said seriously. "Glenora's child may also have a claim to the Triumvirate seat, but if you marry this Kernish prince, that will quash any notion of trying to ascend the child over you. Any attempt to overthrow you would also be an attack on a Prince of Kern, and Kern would react accordingly."

"So you think I should accept," Raina concluded.

Cyra's hand twitched, as if she meant to reach out, but she didn't, and Raina felt a twinge of hurt. This new version of Cyra was colder, more emotionless than the friend she'd known.

"I know this isn't ideal," Cyra went on, "and I'm sure your desire for independence is screaming at you to turn this down, but *if* you want to be the Triumvirate Lady of Polaris, this is the option that makes your claim the most secure. Yes, it will definitely help us in the war to have Kern as an ally, but having Kern at your back helps you as well. It's your decision, though. Bressen and I will support you either way."

Raina was silent as she considered this. "You don't think Kern will use this prince's position as my consort to try to take over Polaris and eventually Thasia?" she asked finally.

Bressen smiled. "You continue to prove my faith in you. There's always a remote chance Kern might use this alliance as a way to gain territory, but if you agree to this match, we'll do some investigating to be sure Kern has no hostile intentions."

"You plan to read their minds," Raina said, surprised. Cyra had told her that she and Bressen tried not to invade people's minds unless they needed to, but apparently this counted as a 'need to' situation.

"Among other things, yes," Bressen confirmed.

"We're not just going to hand you over to this prince without making absolutely sure he means no harm to you or Polaris," Cyra said. "We won't let anything bad happen to you, I promise."

There was a hint of compassion back in Cyra's voice that eased Raina's mind, and she was quiet as she tried to wrap her head around the offer.

"Can I have some time to consider?" Raina asked. "How soon do you need to know?"

"Soon," Bressen said, cutting off whatever Cyra had been about to say. "You need to be wedded and bedded before Glenora has her baby to be sure your position is secure."

Both Raina and Cyra glared at his bluntness.

"Sorry," he said, "but I'm giving you the unpolished truth. Considering what's at stake, Kern won't consider the alliance to be final until you've consummated the marriage. They may even expect you to stop taking a contraceptive to ensure an heir as quickly as possible."

"What?" both Raina and Cyra said together.

Bressen sighed deeply. "You can still say no to this union," he reminded her, "but if you say yes, you need to understand everything it entails. Kern will expect this to be a real marriage with everything that goes along with it, including heirs."

Raina had been leaning toward saying yes to the arrangement, but the prospect of becoming pregnant almost immediately brought that to a screeching halt. She didn't want to ascend to the Triumvirate only to have a child so soon after. She wasn't ready for that.

Luckily, she'd inherited all of the benefits of her perimortal half, including the highly irregular menstrual cycle. Maybe, it would be years, even decades before she conceived…

On the other hand, her luck hadn't been that great lately.

Then something occurred to her. "Has anyone seen this prince?" she asked. "How old is he? What does he look like? I'm not marrying anyone who looks like the ass end of a horse, and I'm certainly not fucking anyone like that."

Bressen's brows rose, but he shrugged. "If you let him take you from behind in the dark, it shouldn't matter," he suggested.

"Bressen!" Cyra snapped at her husband incredulously. He only grinned and gave her a quick wink.

She returned it with a scathing look before she turned back to Raina.

"Neither Bressen nor I have seen the prince, but Axenus has. We're told he's handsome," Cyra said. "I believe he's almost fifty, but he's perimortal, so he looks to be in his mid-twenties by mortal standards."

"We can make it a condition you won't accept the betrothal until you and the prince have met to be sure you're…compatible," Bressen said.

Raina stood up. "Well, you've certainly given me a lot to think about."

She turned to Cyra, but her heart sank at Cyra's uneasy look.

"There's more?" Raina asked.

"Not about the betrothal," Cyra said, "but there's something else you should know."

Raina crossed her arms. "What else?"

"Bressen and I went to see Glenora in Revenmyer a little while ago," Cyra said carefully. "As we were leaving…she mentioned your mother."

Raina uncrossed her arms slowly. "What about my mother?"

"It was nothing specific," Cyra said, "but we took it as a threat."

"Have you heard from your mother at all lately?" Bressen asked.

Raina shook her head. It had been almost two years since she'd seen or spoken to her mother after they'd fought about her coming to Callanus to meet Ursan. She still loved her mother, though. If Glenora had done something to her…

Bile rose in Raina's throat, but she swallowed it back down.

"What did she do to my mother?" Raina asked softly.

"Nothing so far as we know," Cyra said, "but Bressen and I have been trying to locate her, and we haven't been able to find her yet."

Raina's knees gave out, and she thumped back down into her chair.

"We're doing everything in our power to find her," Cyra said, "but we figured it was time to bring you in."

"Why didn't you tell me sooner?" Raina asked, her stomach in knots.

"At first we thought Glenora was just trying to get under our skin, and we didn't want to worry you needlessly," Cyra said.

"We looked into your mother's whereabouts to assure ourselves she was fine," Bressen said. "She no longer lives where she did when you came to Callanus, so we cast a wider net, but we've come up empty so far. We finally had to consider that Glenora's threat wasn't idle."

Raina blinked away tears. It had been so long since she'd seen or spoken with her mother. She'd thought hundreds of times about reaching out to mend their relationship, especially now that Ursan was dead, but stubbornness always got in the way. Would she have known her mother was missing sooner if she'd stopped being childish and reached out?

The thought sent a wave of nausea through her.

Her first thought after considering the betrothal to the Kernish prince had been that she needed to make amends so her mother could attend the wedding. Three hells, she'd already been imagining how to tell her mother she was going to be Lady of Polaris.

None of that mattered now as the possibility that Glenora had done something to her mother sunk in.

No, it wasn't Glenora's style to simply have her mother killed. She'd want to twist the knife first. Raina's mother was still alive but likely in grave danger, and Raina would do everything in her power to find her.

Did you like this book?
Indie authors very much appreciate your help spreading the word about
their books. Please consider rating or reviewing the book on Amazon,
Goodreads, or the platform of your choice. You can also share the book
on social media or recommend it to others.

Thank you so much for reading!

Acknowledgements

As always, many, many thanks to my alpha reader Karen Pasquale. I really made her work for this book and the previous one, since the tandem read was a slog to map out. She's excellent at helping me fill in the story gaps, and she doesn't let me off the hook when I try to gloss over parts of the story that need to be told.

Thanks to my husband Pat for his absolute and unwavering support of my writing and his continued acceptance of my dalliances with Bressen and Samhail. Sorry, Honey. Still no dragons, though.

Thanks to my beta readers – Joshua Hamel, Liza Boritz, Mindy Petruck, Emily Rice, Heather Lee, Erin Estabrook, Lana Zadrosny, and Denise Philbrick – for their keen eyes and great feedback. Everyone notices something different, and these books are so much better for each of you and your unique perspectives. I love hearing your thoughts on the books, and I thank you from the bottom of my heart.

Thanks to my cover designer Mick Estabrook for his endless patience and understanding, even when he disagrees with me about the design. And yes, you were right about the placement of the eyes. But I was right about the butterfly being upside down. 😊

A huge thanks to all my friends and family for reading the books and then yelling at me to get my ass in gear and write the next one so they can read it. Other writers complain that the people they know say they'll read their books, then never do, but I'm extremely fortunate to have people around me who have actually read and genuinely enjoyed the books. Your support means the world to me.